Sting of the Scorpion

By:

Col. Lee Martin

The McGowan Collection Series, Book 8

Edited and Produced by:
I.E.R. Media
Printed in the United States of America

ISBN: 979-8-9897104-7-8 (pbk)
       979-8-9897104-8-5 (ebk)

Acknowledgements

In writing this book, I was able to pull considerable information together from a goodly number of references and sources in order to be as historically accurate about events, time frames, government involvement and indigenous groups as possible. However, there are always the more technical aspects of a story where an author must go to those in the know to secure expert advice.

Thanks to two very bright experts in their fields: LTC Bill McShane, Ph.D, a fellow soldier in the Georgia State Defense Force and chemical engineer now retired from the CDC, and Dan Pennington, LCDR, mechanical engineer and System Engineering Manager in the Plutonium Production Facility recently retired from Los Alamos, both of whom allowed me to act like I knew something about the components of nuclear and chemical weapons and at what government sites they are deconstructed.

To my new friends at A New Chapter book store and The French Goat restaurant in Lewisburg, West Virginia. As Lewisburg and Greenbrier County are at least partial settings for the McGowan series, I am always grateful for the warm hospitality I never fail to receive each time I revisit that beautiful land of my youth.

To Sam McCowan and Shirley Romagnoli, avid Bruce McGowan fans. Thanks for allowing me to borrow your names.

The harsh winds of the desert will never be as stinging as dealing with me. Those who earn my ire will never see me coming.

McGowan

Table of Contents

PART ONE

Sting of the Scorpion

CHAPTER 1

In my retirement I no longer "seize the day"; I generally just poke at it with a stick. I Carpe Diem with my mug of black coffee and morning newspaper. And my coffee is blacker than ten thousand mile used-up motor oil. It's my version of Red Bull. As for newspapers, I despise them, especially the national and big city rags like the New York Times and Washington Post which contain all those opinionated editorials written by politically-ignorant buffoons that think there's anybody out there who really cares what they write. I do however read hometown papers such as the Mountain Messenger that lets me know where the weekend garage sales are and when the campfire girls troop is having a bake sale.

No, I have not turned into a sluggard and I don't lay around going with the flow.
Only dead fish go with the flow. If you think I do, you don't know me. I run the
Greenbrier trails nearly every morning and am still married to the vivacious Adriana McGowan who not only keeps me young, but physically, sexually and mentally active. You see, I like who I've become in my retirement…house husband, gardener, maintenance guy,

good neighbor, Rotary Club member and golfing buddy to three other hacks at the cow pasture they call the country club. But even though I thought I was having all the fun I could muster during my FBI and State Department careers putting bullets into bad guys and terrorists, I'm actually enjoying my new life more. It's been six years now and I'm having no regrets about hanging up my spurs.

But, every once in a while, just to reminisce, I pull from my old Army trunk photographs and memorabilia from not only my childhood and my wild adolescence, but those explosive, exhilarating years serving the government. Who I was doesn't matter anymore. At least I keep telling myself that. There are even times when I think I was actually someone else. Who was that dashing young action hero in the photo with the dark hair and wry grin? And that other of me when I was a Green Beret in Vietnam receiving the Silver Star from Creighton Abrams. And then how about that official FBI photo of me sitting at my desk at the J. Edgar Hoover Building? That one I hated. It made out like I was nothing but a desk jockey, which was far from the truth. Ah, and there is my wedding photo in the Gazette where I married the lovely Adriana here at Wolf Laurel. It was just after she came home from the hospital having been shot in the back at our first wedding ceremony by the domestic terrorist from my past turned mad man who sought revenge against me for kicking his gonads up into his intestines and tossing his sorry ass into jail.

But what was not in the old trunk was any history or evidence of my clandestine service as a counterterrorist operative for the State Department. No medals, no attaboys, no appreciation certificates, no letters, no nothing. However, there was the news clipping of the murder of one Lionel Byrd, my boss when I was with Team Zulu. The obit said nothing about him being the director of our organization…only that he was a State Department employee. Nobody but the President and the National Security Advisor knew our terrorist hunter organization even existed. Call us what you will…spies, assassins, government mercenaries, whatever. There was nothing on paper that proved we existed. I'm not even sure it still does. The last I remember was that my fellow team member, Keith Lambreau, assumed the director role and that was more than six years ago. I was wondering if the replacement President even continued the operation. I understood from Lambreau it was an agency the President thought went against his personal rectitude, not to mention the nation's moral consciousness. I still missed Lionel, the Birdman, and always would. If America ever had a James Bond, it would have been him.

Life is grand here at Wolf Laurel. We actually shut down our B&B business last year and although we somewhat miss the income, the country inn is long paid for. After a bit of remodeling, we decided to close off our upstairs and dwell principally on the seventeen hundred square foot main floor. We converted the larger guest room into our bedroom, a place where magical moments occur frequently. We live very comfortably off my government pensions and my social security, which I ended up taking early, as well as income from Adriana's part-time job at the antique store downtown. My guns are locked away, except my Glock 92 which rides on my hip every time I leave the house. It only lives in my car when I'm in the church house or out whacking the little white ball in the cow pasture.

And oh, guess who our cool town's mayor is as of five years ago this fall…my very popular, business-minded wife.

* * * * *

It's funny how we remember and associate things. I recall it was just after Adriana's election back in 2014 that my brother Joey, who is the funeral home director at McGowan and Sons, asked me yet again when I was going to work with him, me being one of the sons. "Like I told you a dozen times, it'll never happen," I replied.

"Not even a couple days a week? Even working part-time would certainly complement that retirement income," he said.

"I don't need the money, Joey. I'm doing just fine. You know I don't like being around dead people. I told you that a hundred times." Yeah, I made quite a few of them that way, but for the most part, I just hit and ran. Watching their blood pool around them, their clouded-over eyeballs staring at me and their bodies turning to rigor always freaked me out.

But Joey continued pressing. "It wouldn't take you long to get used to it and you might even find it intriguing."

"I can't imagine how."

"As an example, sometimes I talk to them…you know, like Ducky on NCIS."

"Yeah. Creepy, Joey."

"Well, even though my customers don't talk back to me, they can silently tell me a lot about how they lived and died. You might even find a bit of irony in how they died." "How so?" I asked.

"Like a couple of days ago when old Mort Habersham died from choking on a Life Saver."

"Oh yeah, that's funny all right."

"Not a joke…it's true, Brucie. That's really the way he went. I had some fun with that one."

"Yeah, as I recall, you go to great lengths to put the fun in funerals. I remember when you wanted to do a show-and-tell at Casey's third grade class at her career day. Not cool, Joey…and definitely not funny."

"I wasn't serious about that, you know. Just having a little levity with her."

"But Casey wasn't convinced you were joking and was afraid you'd actually show up with a corpse. She cried all morning that day, as I remember."

"And I was sorry about that. But, hey, we somehow got off course here. You could do a lot to help me that wouldn't involve embalming or otherwise handling of dead bodies, you being so squeamish about that."

"I'm not squeamish, Joey. I just don't like the atmosphere around here. You're constantly around relatives who are bawling, the place smells of mums and irises, which has turned me off of even going into a flower shop, and you have to walk around with a serious, mortician face talking like Lurch from the Adams Family that scares the hell out of little children. They're traumatized enough having to look at their dear old grandpas lying dead in coffins."

"Well, aren't you just Sylvester Sunshine today. The answer is still no, eh?"

"Not no, but hell no."

And so, on that day, the conversation about me participating in the mortuary business ended the way it always had.

A couple days later back at the ranch with the very much alive Adriana sitting across from me, I was at the dinner table enjoying my second helping of her killer lasagna when when the doorbell rang.

"I'll get it," she said. When the clacking of her flats down the wooden hallway ended at the front door, I heard a man's voice. You never know about people in today's world, whether they might present a threat; so in thinking only a couple seconds about it, I jumped up and headed for the front door myself. The young man on the other side of the screen appeared harmless and as I looked past him into the driveway, I saw a van with the words International Telegraph on its side. Adriana was already signing for the envelope and as I stepped in behind her, I greeted the lad.

"Hey, I thought telegrams went out more than ten years ago. Is that what you're delivering?"

"Yes, sir," he replied. "The telegraph service is still very much alive. More than ten million a year are delivered. Are you Bruce McGowan?"

"In the flesh," I said. "Is the telegram for me?"

"Yes."

"From whom?"

"I don't know, sir, but the sender is from Scotland."

I took it from Adriana's hand. "Scotland. I don't know anyone in Scotland."

"Well, apparently someone knows you," he said. He then put his fingers to the bill of his ball cap and turned to step off the porch.

"Hey, wait a second," I said. "Here's a five spot for a tip."

The kid, looking to be about twenty, smiled, took the five and said, "Thanks. You two have a good evening."

I sat back down at the table, shoved what was left of the lasagna aside and began slicing open the envelope flap with my butter knife. It was what I remember a telegram looked like, complete with the word stop after every sentence.

"What does it say?" Adriana asked. "Has anyone died?"

"Actually, yes. Appears I have…or had…a cousin named Angus McGowan in a place called Thornloch who passed away leaving me along with other relatives a sum of money."

"How much money?"

"It doesn't say, but the reading of the will is scheduled for the 18th, which is about two weeks from now."

"Do you have to be present?"

"I don't know. Nothing about that. It's to be at the Castle Braemoor, wherever that is."

"So, what are you going to do?" she asked.

I sat back in my chair and laid the message on the table. "We've been wanting to get away somewhere for a few days and I've never been to Scotland; what do you say?"

"Did you say the 18th? Remember I have an important town council meeting on Wednesday the 19th. If you go, you'll have to do so by yourself. We can one day do the entire British Isles."

"Not sure about this," I said. "I have no idea how this Angus McGowan is even related or why I'm in his will."

"I knew you had Scot ancestors, but never thought about you actually having living relatives somewhere across the waters."

"I'll have to think about this a day or so. First, I'd like to first do a little research, both on my family ancestry and on this village called Thornloch."

"How can you research your family? Your folks have long passed and you don't have any aunts or uncles still living."

"I remember Joey did one of those genealogy searches a while back. He was going to show me what it revealed, but I guess I never acted interested. Maybe I'll start with him and what he unearthed."

"Wouldn't he have gotten the same notification you did? I can't imagine this cousin, or whatever he was, leaving you some money and not Joey as well."

"I'll go talk with him in the morning, but for now will see what I can find out about the McGowans of Thornloch on the internet."

I sat at the computer table for almost two hours that evening, first checking out both Thornloch and Castle Braemoor. There wasn't much about either. The village was situated about forty miles west of Edinburgh. I did see the name Angus McGowan who was listed as the owner of Braemoor, but there was nothing else on line about him. I took it he wasn't any kind of lord or duke, but nonetheless, the castle had been in the McGowan family for at least three hundred years. There was a photo of Braemoor and its grounds, but other than being a massive structure comprised of slabs of ancient, moss-covered grey stone and a couple of turrets, it was unremarkable. There was also not much about the McGowans. Maybe Joey had something to help me connect the dots.

I woke the next morning eager to go talk with him as to what he had discovered about us McGowans. He would be at work within the hour. But, first things first. After my two mile run along the forest trail, taking in the beauty of the early fall foliage and the pungent smell of someone burning leaves somewhere, I returned to the ranch for a light breakfast. I then took a quick shower, checked my email and gave the Mrs. a lingering kiss on her way out the door to the beauty parlor. It was just before ten when I pulled into the driveway at McGowan and Sons Funeral Home. He was dressing ninety-six year old Drake Hawkins who finally gave up the ghost. "Mornin,' Bro," he greeted. "Didn't expect you this morning. Come to help?"

"No."

"You say you don't like hanging out here, yet how come you stop by two or three times a week?"

"Not for the ambiance, that's for sure."

"Whatever. Anyway, good to see you today."

"Better to be seen than viewed, little brother. But hey, I got to ask you something. Remember a couple years ago when you paid all that money to check out our family genealogy?"

"Yeah, what about it? You weren't interested back then, why so now?"

"I'll tell you why in a few minutes. But what did you find out about the family tree?"

"That most of our ancestors were hung from it?"

"Come on, be serious."

"Well, we weren't exactly royalty. The lineage goes back to the 1200s to a prominent landowner named Fergus McGowan. He had a large family, I think five boys and two girls. I got all this written down. He had fought at Bannockburn and…"

"Uh, just give me the Readers' Digest version, especially anything about who has recently lived around there."

"Why are you wanting all this, Bruce?"

I handed him the telegram. "Appears one of our patriarch cousins has died. Is someone named Angus McGowan on your list?"

Joey read the telegram and cocked his head to one side. "You're inheriting some money?"

"Did you get a telegram or attempted delivery?"

"No." He then chuckled. "Well, you always were the favored son. Seems you're the favorite in our cousins' eyes as well. Are you going to this reading of the will?"

"I'm not so sure this isn't some kind of scam. I don't want to take a trip like that without knowing if it's legit. Again, is there or was there an Angus McGowan living in Thornloch, Scotland?"

"Yeah, he's very much on the list and has two adult children that also occupy our old homestead."

"It's not our homestead, little brother. Hell, we don't even know these people. Even if they are related, they're strangers to us."

"So, how are you going to find out if this thing is legit? The telegram doesn't say who sent it and you probably have no way of contacting them."

"I'll touch base with the village police department. They will either know of them or will find out. If they tell me Angus passed away and there is a scheduled will event, I'll go. And half of anything that is willed to me you get."

"I'm not the espoused brother, remember."

I gave him a fist bump on the arm and said, "I know that, Joey."

I did finally get through to a Thornloch police officer after more than a half hour trying. There indeed was an Angus McGowan, a seventy-eight year old widower, the master of Braemoor and father to two adult children who lived with him. Neither the son, James, nor daughter, Fiona, ever married. However, Fiona, a thirty-three year old, did give birth to a girl child about nine years before out of wedlock. They looked after their father, attending to his physical and medical needs especially the last seven years of his life until he passed from a coronary occlusion. However, as I had the impression that Angus had most recently died, according to Chief Inspector Ryan Hildebrand, he had been dead nearly a year.

Hildebrand knew nothing about a will reading, but said the family was a bit reclusive if not strange. I told him that sounds like a McGowan family, especially the strange part. As far as the inspector knew, the family had been cattle farmers ever since he could remember. Angus at one time had served in the British government, but he didn't know in what capacity. As to the will, however, it didn't surprise him it took this long to be read. There might have been some discord between the siblings after their father died.

Although I didn't know why I was a beneficiary, given the fact I didn't know them and they didn't know me, I was intrigued. Before I went to bed that night, Adriana finally ended up convincing me I should attend the reading and at the same time get acquainted with my cousins. However, I hated to be going without her.

* * * * *

I opened my eyes the following morning around six-thirty to the aroma of two wonderful smells——the cup of Keurig-brewed coffee awaiting me on the night stand and the sweet aroma of the mayor's perfume. As I watched 'her honor' move around the room in her skimpy underwear trying to decide on the outfit to wear to the city council meeting, I was less interested in the cup of java she had laid out for me and more interested in the possibility of laying her out. I have yens like that some mornings…well, actually most mornings, but I knew this morning was not going to happen. She was running late and the very moment I gave her the Groucho Marx eyebrow treatment, she shook her head.

The mayor left around seven and I went to piddle in the flower garden. Weeds seemed to have sprung up overnight. Around eight when the fog had fully lifted, I went for a run along the Greenbrier Trail. The air was sweet and the sun was still an hour or so away from warming the landscape. I usually go about two miles, but that day, feeling more macho than usual, I stretched it to three.

After returning home, I showered, put on a Greg Norman golf shirt and a jacket and went out to the country club for a sandwich and some ice tea. Cute little Joyce Meadows, the eighteen year old with the voice of Minnie Mouse and body of Charlize Theron, flirted with me as usual, again telling me if I ever got tired of "that woman you live with," she would be all over me. She said, "So what if there's twenty years between our ages, I like older men, especially handsome ones that still have all their hair." Twenty years? Right. Try forty, Joyce.

I go there a lot for lunch and for the flirting whether I'm playing golf or not.

As I was leaving the next day for Scotland, I busied myself the rest of that day getting things in order, such as making sure I wasn't any less than six months away from renewing my passport (okay there), packing my BVDs, several shirts, a couple pairs of trousers and jeans and a light jacket. After selecting the clothes, I charged my electric razor and assured I had what I needed in my toiletry bag. I then went back on the internet to check out some of the attractions that would be near Thornloch or perhaps Edinburgh that may be interesting, if I had the time. I thought Linthithgow Palace and St. Andrews might be interesting. If the latter, I could brag to my golf buds that I played the Old Course where the gentlemen's game actually began.

Adriana was back from her lunch meeting with her friends and since it was the last afternoon I'd be home for three or four days, we took to the front porch with some hot tea and lemon cookies. It was our favorite place to relax and talk, especially in the early fall. With the sun, on the opposite side of the house and the ceiling fans going, we found it rather comfortable.

"So, what's new in the mayor's office?" I asked her.

"Me."

I smiled. "Does everyone stand and salute when you walk in?"

"No, but feel free to do so anytime I come in the house."

"Funny. I'm the wise ass in the family, remember?"

She then became serious. "I'm going to miss you the next few days. Wish I could go."

"Can't you blow off your meeting? You just had one today."

"This one is a special town council meeting where the public is invited. It's a discussion about building a new park and whether the city can afford it."

"Will it have swings and teeter-totters?"
"It's not that kind of park, silly. This park will have benches, walking trails and lots of flowers and trees."

"How does it feel to be in charge of an entire town…the police department, fire department, garbage trucks, dog pound…?"

"Let's just say it makes me feel good to be looking after the welfare of the town's citizens and meeting their needs."

"Everybody's needs?"

"Of course."

"How about mine? I have this need I'd like to get satisfied. Being married to somebody important is a big turn on. It would give me a sense of power to bed down the mayor of our town. So, how about it, your majesty?"

"You can't wait until tonight?"

"Well, I could, but I like to be able to see the things I get into."

She gave me a long, lingering look and smiled. "Can I finish my tea first?"

"Can you gulp it down instead of sipping it like you usually do?"

And she did. She then placed her hand on mine and pulled me up from my rocker. "I don't ever want it to be said I don't take care of my constituents. Come on. Just remember to vote for me again next year."

At just after six we left the house for dinner. As I had just enjoyed the 'prime rib', I thought maybe I'd like to get a burger at one of the more popular restaurants in town. Adriana looked bootylicious in her white sleeveless blouse, tight black skirt that accentuated her shapely legs and post-coitus glow. Yeah, I caused that last thing. She smiled a lot that evening, a satiated smile. Any of her constituents who saw her there that evening might have mistakenly thought the smile was for them.

CHAPTER 2

It was that next day, the evening of the 16th, when I kissed the lovely Adriana goodbye and boarded a puddle jumper at the Greenbrier Airport which subsequently landed at JFK at 9:18. I had to hoof it to Terminal 7 to catch my 10:10 British Airways flight. Eight hours later, given the time difference, I then touched down in Edinburgh at 11:22 the morning of the 17th.

I took a cab to the train station where I promptly hit the loo, which is what Brits and Scots refer to as the toilet. I was pleasantly surprised to find it nearly spotless and having a rather agreeable smell what with the aromatic wafers in the urinals and lavender soap on the sinks. A far cry from the gas station crappers in our country that makes one feel like he should have donned a hazmat suit before entering. I had to chuckle at the sign on the door though which read, "All you mates with short bats please step closer to the plate."

At the station's snack bar, I had a ham on rye and a Scottish ale called a Kilt Lifter. As I was enjoying my meal in the fresh air at an outside table, a bagpiper decked out in traditional garb walked back and forth while playing a lengthy version of Loch Lomond. It did much to get me to thinking about my ancestors…what kind of people they were and how far back the clan went. The music of the bagpipes was chilling and for some reason its wail made the hairs on my neck stand at attention. The early October day was a little cool, but the radiance of the noonday sun warmed my skin to a point where I ended up shedding my light jacket. While sitting there taking account of the countryside, I was awestruck as to how the Scottish landscape looked so much like the Greenbrier pastureland back in the good ol' Dubya Vee. It all kind of felt like home…welcoming, comfortable, tranquilizing home. A feeling that was almost deja vu in a **down memory lane** kind of way, like I had once existed there in centuries past. But then suddenly, my moment of sweet serenity was interrupted by a distant rumble and the blaring of a horn. My train to Thornloch was approaching.

The bearded man in the well-worn tartan tam sitting in the seat across from me had been dozing off and on. I had taken the West Highland Line from Edinburgh into the countryside around 4:00 in the afternoon which to this point had carried me through rich green pastureland punctuated by dark hedgerows and grey rock walls that had been carefully laid centuries ago. I don't think I had seen so many cows and sheep in any one place.

Occasionally, I caught glimpses of castle ruins along the horizon, some I imagined dating back as far as Robert the Bruce in the early 14th Century and the Battle of Bannockburn. It was what I had expected Scotland to be like. So far I had not been disappointed.

The train ride along the 40 mile trek took about an hour. We had stopped twice in villages similar to my intended destination which had slowed us down a bit. Each time we stopped, the man across from me who never spoke, raised his head, glanced out the window of our coach, then settled back in his seat and closed his eyes. He wore a suit jacket and a pair of dungarees. The bulge in his left coat pocket I thought resembled a flask and in taking a closer look, I did see what might have been the head of a silver cap. Filled with Drambuie I imagined. I had said hello to him when I first sat down in Edinburgh and he only nodded. His muteness was fine with me. I'm not very comfortable engaging in conversations with people I don't know anyway.

Ten minutes later, the train slowed a third time and coming into my view was a station house bearing the sign Thornloch. From under my seat I grabbed my suitcaseon-wheels and began pulling it down the aisle between rows of seats toward the exit door. It was my silent seat-mate's stop as well and he followed me off the train.

The telegram said a taxi would be waiting for me at 5:15 at the station parking lot, so I pulled my case across the wooden platform until the wheels touched down onto concrete. I did see a half dozen cars in the lot, but nothing resembling a taxi. In checking my watch, I found it was 5:05, so I figured I'd have a few minutes to wait. I could see along the road that paralleled the tracks a few buildings that appeared to lead into town. Not far from the station was a sandstone house with a thatched roof, looking very 1600s. The area, quaint and mostly rural, had a certain Robert Burns charm to it such as he might describe in one of his works. Again, not disappointed.

In looking back at the station, I saw the man again, the man who had shared the coach's seat with me that is, leaning against the building smoking a cigarette. He appeared to be waiting for someone. Maybe the same taxi coming for me would be carting him as well. Hell, maybe he was one of my distant cousins going to the same place I was heading. Five-thirty came and went and no taxi. The thing was, I didn't know the name of the taxi company unless there was only one in the small burg of Thornloch. But, I figured I could get a ride with someone to take me to my destination. After all, how many castles called Braemoor could there be in that whistle stop.

Momentarily, a black Audi flagship pulled up to the station and smoking man got in. Apparently, he wasn't one of my cousins. But then the car drove toward me and stopped within a few yards of my feet. Not only did the Scotsman get out, but the driver and passenger did as well.

The passenger, a large Arab-looking man about fifty in a suit and tie, approached me. Smoking man stepped in behind me, a move which always makes me uneasy. "Are you McGowan?" the Arab asked.

"Yes. Are you my ride to Braemoor?"

"Get in," he said abruptly.

I didn't like his tone or his threatening eyes. "I'm supposed to be picked up by a taxi. This doesn't look like a taxi, friend," I said.

The man behind me then spoke in a deep, Scottish brogue. "You were told to get in the car, mate."

The Arab man suddenly brandished a revolver and stuck it into my ribs. Not the welcome mat I was expecting. I was now feeling frighteningly naked without my

Glock. "One more time, McGowan, get in." This time I noticed his Mideast accent.

It was the nose of the revolver that ushered me into the back seat of the Audi. The smoking Scotsman slid in beside me. The flask in his pocket then turned into a silverplated automatic. The other passenger opened the door on my side and shoved a hood over my head. "What the hell!" I exclaimed.

"Be quiet!" he said. Before the daylight had gone away, I saw he was also an Arab and wearing a taqiyah, which is a rounded skull cap. "Do not ask questions…do not speak at all."

And so, here I was in another predicament, this time an unexpected one. My captors were a local who sounded a bit Gaelic and two not so local goons who sounded like terrorists.

It was not feeling like home anymore.

I couldn't tell what direction we were heading, but remembered from my Ranger training years ago that should I ever be taken prisoner and blindfolded, to call on my other senses: listen, feel every bump, assess the smells, listen again, count the seconds, count the left and right turns on the roadway. One thing not to do was to panic or lose touch with my senses. Also, understand they're likely not going to kill me or they wouldn't have shoved a hood over my head. They'd probably end up releasing me, eventually. They just didn't want me to find my way back to them when they did. On the other hand, I did see their faces, so…

We had stayed mostly on concrete and asphalt. I knew it was asphalt because at one point I heard the machinery of the road crew and smelled the tar. Four minutes into the ride, we also crossed a bridge that took less than ten seconds. After about twelve minutes, we turned off the hard road and traveled for two minutes along a straight dirt road. Loose rocks kicked up against the car's rocker panel as we encountered a good number of potholes. The car finally slowed to a stop. Wherever it was we landed, it was a fifteen minute ride.

We sat for nearly three more minutes while the two not-so-locals conversed in their Middle Eastern language. I recognized a couple of Arabic words, madaa and hadka, which are 'when' and 'soon', respectively. But then nobody spoke for what seemed like minutes on end. It had suddenly become eerie. Who the hell were they and what did they want? They knew my name and were set up to retrieve me. It had to have something to do with the telegram and the Angus McGowan clan. But, I was supposed to be riding in a taxi, which had been laid on for me and taking me to the Braemoor Castle. Obviously we had not gone there because anybody and everybody knew where it was and there would have been no reason to throw a hood over my head. I didn't think I was being held for ransom. My wife and my brother were not wealthy, so if big money was what they wanted, somebody would be finding my bones in some pasture strewn among the cow pies and sheep shit.

And then if by some silent signal, the three men quickly emerged from the sedan, dragging me out with them. It was the Scot who led me along a path and then told me to step up three times where we leveled out onto a wooden porch. He then whispered to me so the others wouldn't hear, "Look, mate, just do what they say and listen. Cause no trouble and ye will be fine."

Was this guy trying to befriend me or something? And what plight was it that lay ahead of me with the others? I suddenly felt like I was heading into the Twilight Zone.

We entered a door and almost immediately the hood came off my head. They then led me down a hallway and into a kind of sitting room. From what I could see, we were in a small, unremarkable house in a room with a wooden chair that had a broken side arm into which I was shoved. "You sit and don't move," said the larger Arab. All three then left the room and closed the door behind them.

In looking around from the chair, I first peered out the single window, seeing through the glass only wide-open pasture land and no other houses. We were indeed out in the boonies. The room was mostly barren and I doubted the house was inhabited except when someone wanted to kidnap a guy and hide him out. A well-worn sofa chair sat across from me beside a mangy couch and to my right was a fireplace which appeared to not have been in use for years. The walls were stuccoed, dirty and scuffed, with cracks and holes here and there. An end table was to my left on which sat a lamp. A naked bulb hanging on a wire from the eight foot ceiling directly over my head was the only other light in the room. I assumed that was where the third degree would be conducted.

I was allowed to sit there for nearly an hour before I got a case of the red-ass and went to the door to see if it was locked. It was. Maybe this was some kind of test to see if I would become so nerve-racked that I would be easy to break…that is if that's what they were trying to do. I did however go to the window to get a more panoramic view of the outdoors. From a 180 perspective there was still nothing but farmland and a few trees in sight. The window itself was sealed tightly and appeared not to have been opened for years. When I tried to raise it, it wouldn't budge. I could break the glass, climb out onto the ground and set sail, but my captors would hear the crash and I'd be dead meat. They were the ones with all the guns.

I then returned to my seat to do a little more thinking. Nothing came to mind…except Adriana. If she didn't hear from me by the evening, she'd be worried. If not by tomorrow, she'd be calling Scotland Yard. If she knew I'd been snatched off the street and didn't get to my objective, she'd be in a state of panic and might just get on the earliest plane to Edinburgh. She had lived through quite a number of my scapes, my having gunplay with terrorists and other bad guys. She had learned both first and second hand about all my pursuits when I was working for the State department and had often been both angry and relieved when I returned home. She had sometimes even seen me return wounded. She herself had been in danger, kidnapped and shot that one time. She had a right to be worried. However, I didn't know what this was about and this time my predicament was not of my own making. She might feel guilty, however, since she was the one who encouraged me to make the trip.

A half hour later the door to the room opened. At first I saw the larger Middle Eastern man. He appeared satisfied that I had followed his orders and was still in the chair. But then he stepped aside and another man, a skinhead about sixty-five or so with a small mustache, walked into the room behind him. The man's eyes, steel blue and unwavering, were glued to my face. He had a slight build, but I could see immense strength in his forearms and hands. As he strode across the wood floor, he did so with a sense of presence and dignity. If I didn't know already that he was going to be a villainous prick, I might have mistaken him for a professor or maybe a distinguished statesman. The Arab man remained in the room and now stood by the door clutching a carbine.

Upon sitting down, still not taking his eyes off mine, the skinhead finally spoke. "Obviously, you are wondering what all this is about, Mr. McGowan." He was British as best I could tell. There was a degree of both culture and self-importance in the way he had formed just those few words.

"You have me at a disadvantage," I replied calmly. "You know my name, but I don't know yours."

"Alistair Chalmers, Mr. McGowan. I would shake your hand, but that would be a bit tacky given our circumstances, don't you think?"

I nodded. I had somewhere heard the name but couldn't place it. His face I didn't recognize. "Okay, Mr. Chalmers, you seem to be a man of elevation and good manners, why have you detained me?" I could sound just as polished as him.

"I see you wish to get to the point of all this quickly. I have a very important mission for you. One of life and death."

"Life and death? Whose life and whose death?"

"So far you're asking the right questions; yours and the lives of two of your distant cousins, namely Fiona and Mary McGowan."

"Neither of whom I have met. Why should I be concerned?" I asked him.

"You may not know them, but they are your flesh and blood, one of whom is merely nine years old."

"And how are their lives involved?"
He smiled. Not a pleasant smile…more demonic than anything. "Their lives will end in two weeks if you do not accomplish the tasks I will lay out for you."

"I think it's time you told me more about yourself than your name and why you have kidnapped me."

He laughed. "I already like you, McGowan. You are very much to the point just as Lionel said you were."

I think I felt my jaw hit my chest. "Lionel?"

"Yes, the late Lionel Byrd."

I pushed myself from the chair, standing with balled fists. The big Arab make a move toward me, but Chalmers threw up his hand to stop him. "Please sit back down, Mr. McGowan. I will explain."

"You're damn right you will."

"You also just displayed the temper Lionel said you had." He laughed again.

"How did you know Lionel Byrd?"

Chalmers shoved a cigarette into a plastic filter and lit it. The way he chomped down on the stem while holding it into his mouth resembled photos I had seen of FDR. "Let me tell you a story, Mr. McGowan. I believe you were working for Lionel as late as 2003, were you not?"

"You say the name **Lionel** as though you were friends or collaborators."

"I wouldn't go so far to say we were friends, but we did collaborate."

"On what?"

"I was MI-6, Mr. McGowan. During that year we had many a conversation about Iraq. Your President Bush claimed Saddam had weapons of mass destruction which in turn was investigated by the U.N. After the inspectors were sent to Iraq to locate the WMDs, it was ascertained there **were** none. His Secretary Powell still continued to make the case against Iraq, but his words fell on deaf ears. Of course the world knows that your President then invaded Iraq mainly on the premise there were WMDs regardless whether they were found or not."

I bore down on him with my own steely blues. "I'm not going to debate that decision with you except to say there was evidence that within the lengthy time it took to get the inspectors in country, Saddam could have moved the weapons. And there should be no debate about the fact that he gassed his own people. So, what's all this got to do with anything?"

Chalmers took a drag from the cigarette and spewed a plume of smoke into the air. "First of all, Mr. McGowan, I knew about your CTT that Lionel created. He…"

"He would not have shared anything with you about what he did, so I say that you're only guessing…or lying." "He didn't have to tell me, Mr. McGowan. MI-6 is the equivalent to your CIA and we knew things that your government never realized we knew. We had our ways just like you had yours."

"And if you know so much about us, what did I do for the organization?"

"You were of course a counterterrorist operative on Team Zulu, Scorpion."

He must have seen my face turn beet red which caused him to laugh. "You seem surprised and even flustered that I know so much about you."

How the hell did he know so much about the CTT operation much less find out my code name? Again, only three or four people were supposed to know, besides all our team members of course. Did one of us betray the group? Was it Chuck Robinson, the team member I trusted the most, the Judas who assassinated Lionel and the rest of the team? Whatever Chalmers knew, I wasn't going to discuss it with him.

"Alright, Chalmers, let's get off of what you **think** you know about Mr. Byrd's operation and discuss what it is you want me to do. But first, I have a question for **you.** Was it you who sent the telegram about the McGowan will?"

He nodded. "Angus McGowan died more than eleven months ago and the estate has long since been settled. Yes, you were summoned here under false pretenses. You're not in any will, by the way. Angus was also MI-6…MI-5 before that which only addresses criminal and terrorist matters within the confines of Great Britain. The bogus will was a way to get you here."

"How did you know I'd come?"

"**Greed,** Mr. McGowan. How can one pass up the opportunity of receiving monies from an inheritance? Of course you'd come."

 "I almost didn't. I thought it might be some kind of scam."

"You were very perceptive to think so and although it wasn't necessarily a scam, you were still duped, you know."

"So what is it you are coercing me to do with the threat of taking the lives of two innocent people."

"Remember, Scorpion, I know a lot about you. I know you can be ruthless, but you are also a compassionate man. You would not allow the deaths of a young woman and her precious daughter."

"And how do I know you would carry out such a heinous act?"

Chalmers crushed his cigarette into the floor and placed the plastic filter into his vest pocket. "Come with me, Mr. McGowan; I have people for you to meet."

I followed Chalmers through the door down a short hallway to another room. The large Middle Eastern man, whose name I discovered was Hassan, was on my tail with his machine gun pointed at my back. When Chalmers opened the door, my heart took a leap when I saw them. A woman with dark red hair appearing in her thirties sat chained to a metal bed. Beside her was a very frightened looking young girl also cuffed to both the bed and the woman. Of course they were Fiona McGowan and her daughter, Mary. Who else could they be?

"Bruce McGowan, meet your cousins."

Fiona's upward arched eyebrows and sad, turned-down mouth screamed silently for help. Little Mary was sobbing.

"How long have they been here?" I asked Chalmers.

"Two weeks. They have been treated well, fed, allowed to sleep and watch TV. As you can see there are no marks on them. They have been waiting for you, Bruce. They know I will be sending you on the mission that will save their lives. You'll be on a kind of scavenger hunt and if you bring to me what I want, they will be released."

I turned away and passed back through the doorway into the hall. I motioned with my head for him to follow. In a low voice I said, "They've seen you and I've seen you. I know who you are and can identify you to the police. I'd be extremely naive to think you'd not kill us."
"If you complete your mission satisfactorily, you have my solemn word that not only will the three of you be

released, but no one will see hide nor hair of me again. I have my disappearance all arranged."

"Where is Fiona's brother James?"

"I will take you to another room. Follow."

We took a few more steps down the rickety hallway and Chalmers stopped at a door on the left. "Go ahead, open it," he ordered.

I stepped around him and did as instructed. It was the kitchen. There was a table, four chairs a sink, a refrigerator and a small freezer, but no James.

"Is this a joke? There's no one in here," I said.

That's when he walked across to the opposite wall and opened the lid of the freezer. "Come," he said.

I knew then what I'd see and it sickened me. Peering inside, I found a man's severed head wrapped in a plastic freezer bag.

"Say hello to James, McGowan. Now do you realize that I am not playing games?"

CHAPTER 3

I have to admit I was a bit traumatized at seeing the head of James McGowan, if in fact that was him. We returned to the previous room where big man Hassan shoved me back into the wooden chair. Chalmers again took the cushy one and lit up another cigarette.

"And so, Mr. McGowan, your observation?"

"My observation? I think you're an evil son-of-a-bitch."

He laughed loudly. "Now that you've got that off your chest, you haven't asked what you are to retrieve for me."

"Before I do, I will ask you this. How did you find out the Braemoor McGowans are related to me?"

He leaned back in his chair and began stroking his chin. "I do my homework, McGowan, and very well. I probably did more research on your lineage than you've ever done on your family. I found you in West Virginia and considering I have a parttime home here in Scotland, was pleasantly surprised to find that you had distant relations with a family almost in my very backyard."

"Why me? Why would you concoct this scheme to bring me here versus getting someone else to do your dirty work?"

"It's all about my association with Lionel Byrd. And oh yes, he was involved in what I have planned, so I fetched his best operative."

"**Former** operative, Chalmers, and you'd better start explaining how Mr. Byrd fit into your equation."

"Lionel didn't deserve ending up like he did. I admired him. He was well respected by friends and adversaries throughout the world when he was the CIA director. We at MI-6 then learned he was appointed to some clandestine position fielded by your former President. That's when our collaboration began. Oh, he was bloody tightlipped about his organization, but we at MI-6 were some smart and tenacious operatives ourselves. It didn't take us long to figure out he was putting his teams into major city locations to weed out the terrorist infrastructure imbedded throughout the U.S. And yes, we collaborated especially when your President refused to accept the findings of the Iraq Survey Group and the Verification and Inspection Commission. We all knew Iraq breached its obligations under the UN Resolution Pact by continuing to produce and use chemical weapons as well as other "weapons of mass murder," as described by Mr. Bush. We knew the inspectors missed it and that Saddam was given ample time to move these weapons out of country on board ships bound for Yemen."

"Okay, so you're a former MI-6 prick with knowledge about something arguable and unproven occurring over a dozen years ago."

"I wouldn't say merely arguable, Bruce. We know Saddam shipped out the WMDs. Lionel especially had a team working on finding the weapons and he was able to pinpoint where they went back in 2007 almost four years after the U.S. and its allies invaded Iraq. Unfortunately, Lionel didn't live to see it through and somewhere along the way, the plan to physically locate them died along with him."

"So, what the hell am I sitting here for, Chalmers. What is it you want me to do?"

"You get to the point quickly. I like that."

"I don't give a rat's ass what you like or don't like. Just tell me what you want with me."

"I want you to use your keen nose and resources to locate this major cache of WMDs in Yemen."

It was my turn to laugh. "Really? I thought you were not about playing games."

"I will again remind you this is no game. I am dead serious."

"And you had to snatch three people from their home to force me into pulling this off, then somewhere along the way decapitating one of them to show that you meant business. You couldn't have carried out your plan by using your own resources?"

"I have been retired since 2010, Mr. McGowan, and no longer have resources. Once we are separated from MI-6, we no longer have access to Intel or former documents."

"And you think I do on my end."

"Quite. I think you are a very resourceful person and considering what Lionel told me about you, you use unorthodox methods to make things happen. I see a fire in your eyes that I don't see often in others. I know these weapons exist and I know you will find them."

"So, you're giving me two weeks to find these fabled weapons in Yemen that nobody else has been able to find all these years."

He took a long drag from the cigarette, then leaned forward in his chair, placing his cold eyes on mine. "Only one weapon among the lot, Mr. McGowan. A weapon that Saddam obtained from a terrorist organization in Pakistan, a nuclear device that is somewhere in storage with the other WMDs in Yemen. We were provided information about the nuclear bomb by a double agent in the Pakistan Intelligence Community."

"And what do you intend to do with that device, Chalmers?"

"Sell it, Mr. McGowan. I have people waiting for it."

"Who?"

"That I won't tell you."

"Let me guess…Iran."

For a seasoned spy trained to maintain his guise, I saw the slightest of reactions. His eyes stiffened. It **was** Iran.

"You dealing directly with Rouhani…or is it General Soleimani?"

"Enough, McGowan. All you need to do is carry out my instructions. The lives of the two people in the back room depend on you. You don't deliver for me, there will be a most unsavory discovery in the back room of this house."

"And where am I to begin this search? How am I to get it back to you?"

"You are an intelligent and inventive person. It's up to you to figure out all the logistics."

"So, what happens from here?"

"Hassan and Shadid, the men who brought you here, will be with you every step of the way. They are both skilled in several languages and will be an asset."

"And the Scotsman out there?"

"He will remain here with me to attend to the ladies' needs. You and my Islamic friends will leave here in the early morning."

I turned my head away and drew in a deep breath. "You're a contemptible bastard, Chalmers. How does an MI-6 agent end up in bed with international terrorists, organizations that you had pursued in the past along with my boss, he being the most honorable operative I ever knew?"

"At this stage of our lives, we seize opportunities where we find them. I have no remorse about doing so. But, enough of this dribble. I will give you only enough time this evening to prepare your blueprint; then you will be off in the morning." He then tamped out his cigarette and left the room, locking the door behind him.

I leaned over in the chair and with elbows on my knees, placed my head in my hands. A hundred thoughts and questions ran through my brain…beginning with just how I would accomplish Chalmers's mission. And then I wondered if he had actually retired from MI-6, or being the deviant he was, if in fact he had been removed for some less than honorable reason. Maybe MI-6 had washed its hands completely of this guy; therefore, he neither had friends nor contacts left.

But then I started thinking about the task itself. Where would I begin? And of course there's such a thing as a visa. If I did happen onto any of the WMDs, specifically the nuclear device, how could it be transported back? And then there's no way I would just hand it over to Chalmers anyway. Any misstep on my part in the operation would be the death knell for Fiona and Mary McGowan. Even if I were able to break away and report their kidnapping to the Scottish authorities, I had no idea where the house was located. And when the police did finally locate them, they'd be found dead. I had been convinced of that.

I then began massaging my forehead, as though in doing so I would erase this nightmare. Just how the hell did I find myself in this mess? For the rest of my life was I going to be faced with one crappy dilemma after another? I'd been involved in too many already and some of them had been experienced after I fully retired. Maybe I'd get a break when I became a nonagenarian. Who wants to send someone in his 90s out on any kind of mission?

At just after eight that evening, Chalmers returned to the room with Hassan. "You will remain here for the night, McGowan. You can sleep on the couch. Here is a sub sandwich and a container of water. Hassan will remain here in the room as well. There will be no opportunity for escape, so don't even consider it. When you need to use the loo, you will be escorted down the hall. Tomorrow, you and your traveling companions, Hassan and Shadid, will leave at first light. Make yourself comfortable. I'm sorry there is no television for tonight's entertainment. Get to sleep early as you will have a long day tomorrow."

Chalmers quickly left the room and shut the door behind him. Hassan first placed a bedroll on the floor behind the sofa and then followed him out. Tomorrow may be long, I thought, but the night would be as well. I wasn't sure if I'd be able to do anything but lay and think…mainly think of how I could escape from the bastards. However, I'd also be contemplating what the hell was in store for me the next few days; and just how was I going to locate these weapons that probably didn't exist in the first place? Even if they did, no one had been able to find them in over a dozen years. I began the massage again. I was thinking myself into a headache.

I ate about half of the sandwich and then tossed the rest in a trash can. It was now dark and I laid down on the sofa, I also thought about Fiona and Mary in the back room. They had been tied to the bed and placed under guard for two weeks. I knew it was difficult for Fiona, but had to be doubly so for Mary. I felt for them. They would be the reason I needed to drop my thoughts of escaping. If I somehow managed to do so, no doubt they would be joining James in death.

I did fall asleep sometime after ten. I'm not sure exactly when. At some point in the early morning hours, I had the same recurring dream that had haunted me for years…the nightmare about the mother and daughter I killed in Vietnam. It was a dream that I thought had gone away for good a few years ago. However, it seemed the dreams were usually triggered by some disquieting event where death could be imminent. This particular circumstance also involved a mother and daughter; and in a very huge way, I would be responsible for their death if I refused to cooperate.

But suddenly I was awakened by the rude brightness of the room's overhead naked bulb. When I opened my eyes, the first thing I saw was Chalmers, flanked by the two Muslim men. I then heard Chalmers say, "Time, McGowan. Stand up. If you need to hit the loo, do so now." I nodded without word and Shadid followed me into the hallway. When he continued on through the bathroom door, I turned and said, "I can do this myself, unless there's something you want to hold." He then turned and walked back to the hall. I then completed my task and returned to the sitting room.

Chalmers then said, "From this point on, you belong to my friends here. Get used to them as you'll be spending quite a lot of time with them. They will get you to where you need to go. You'll be taking only changes of underwear and socks and a toothbrush with you in this knapsack. You'll be needing that jacket for the cool nights. The golf shirt you're wearing will be sufficient during the hot days. I expect you will be in some fairly rugged areas to locate the weapon I want. You cannot be dragging suitcases. While I gave you your thinking time, I hope you came up with a plan. And remember, you have two weeks to deliver. Tick…tock." He then turned to his guards. "Go ahead, get him out of here."

Hassan immediately shoved the hood back over my head and tightened it at the neck. After walking me out the front door, I was again placed in the rear seat of the Audi with Hassan sliding in beside me. Shadid would drive. For a long while we rode on what appeared was a four lane interstate type highway. I couldn't see, of course, but I could hear the traffic and feel the speed. Not a word was spoken over what was probably an hour and a half. Shadid was not a talker, anyway. I don't think I heard him say more than a handful of words since the train depot.

I then felt the vehicle slowing and after Hassan removed my hood, I could see we were at a rest stop. That's when he, keeping me at bay with what appeared to be an HS2000 Croatian pistol, grabbed me by my jacket with his other hand. "We will now use the rest room. You will behave when we leave the car, McGowan. Do not try anything. Talk to no one. Do not make me kill you. If that happens, the females will die back at the house. As you use the toilet, one of us will accompany you."

"So you're a couple of perverts, eh? I knew it."

"You will shut your smart mouth. You will now go piss. We will be right behind you."

In glancing at the map on the restroom wall near the door, I saw the 'you are here' star and that we were now in Northern England. From there, I didn't know what they had planned. We were near Nottingham and seemed to be on a path to London.

Back on the road again, I was now without the hood. As the beautiful Northern England countryside flicked by, I began feeling a bit of jet lag from my earlier flight. Not having slept on the plane, I was starting to fade. I took off my jacket, rolled it up into a ball and placed it against the side glass, forming a pillow. I was out in a flash.

I awoke an hour later rubbing my sore neck and saw that Hassan was still watching me like a hawk. He didn't have to, but obviously he hadn't figured that out. A fairly tall and sinewy man sporting a full beard and a baseball cap,

Hassan looked to be strong. However, one on one without the gun, I figured I could take him. A shot to the Adam's apple and follow-up punch to the nose, breaking the cartilage and shoving it into the forebrain would do the trick. I envisioned how quickly I'd make that happen. I think he must have sensed I had something like that on my mind, because he began gripping his gun a little tighter.

"Where are we going, Hassan?" I asked him.

"We will reach our location soon."

"Which is where?"

"You will find out."

Perhaps ten minutes later, I did. Shadid pulled off the motorway, as they call it, into a small village, turned down an alley and stopped at the rear of a business of some sort.

"What are we doing here?" I asked.

"Again you will see." He then pulled from his coat a cellphone and after reaching his contact, began speaking in Arabic. He tapped Shadid on the shoulder and told him,"It is okay to go in."

Shadid stepped out of the car first and looked up and down the street to see if anyone was watching, then signaled to Hassan and I to get out. Hassan half pushed me out of my side of the car and said to "quickly, go to that door."

Well, it didn't take a genius to realize this was some kind of illegal operation and that became a reality when we were greeted at the door by another Middle Eastern man brandishing an Uzi. As he gave me the once over, Hassan said, "He is okay and not armed."

"Why are we here?" I again asked.

"The man sitting at the desk will provide your visa into Yemen."

The man was older and Caucasian, likely a Brit who provided counterfeit documents to anybody and everybody. I immediately observed that he could also manufacture passports. A camera was to his right and a printer to his left.

"And just how will that be done?"

"He has the official document and will attach it to your passport. Give the passport to him. He is very good at this."

The process took about twenty minutes after which he took Hassan's and Shadid's passports to insert visas into them likewise.

"What if a set of sharp eyes detect these are counterfeit visas?"

"You are not to worry about that."

"I might start to worry if I'm thrown into a Yemeni jail."

Hassan looked irritated at the comment, but said nothing in return.

The visa did look authentic and it was apparent the Brit was a master at his craft. Hassan paid him in pounds, the denominations which I couldn't decipher. But the man was satisfied. The only words I heard him speak were, "Come again."

I had been wondering whether we were going through other countries to get to Yemen, if Yemen was in fact our destination. We would have to either be flying directly or cruising both the Mediterranean and Red Sea to get there.

Less than forty-five minutes later we were on the outskirts of London. Shadid then turned off the road and onto another street that took us to a small airport. The sign on the entrance read Biggin Hill. Chalmers had arranged a flight for us. He had gone to great lengths to plan things out while engaging any number of people and resources along the way. I wondered if he had also arranged tickets for us on a commercial airliner or had he chartered a private plane? It didn't take me long to find out. Shadid drove directly to a gate on which there was a sign that read Charter Services. A security guard held up his hand for us to stop. He was English and asked for our passports. Shadid handed all three of the documents to the guard who one by one checked them against our faces. Appearing satisfied the mugs matched the photos, he directed us to Building A to check in.

"Again, McGowan. Do not cause trouble. I will be watching you to see if you signal anyone."

I didn't reply. I allowed only the contempt in my eyes to respond.

Shadid brought the car to a stop in the Building A parking lot. Both men then took off their guns and holsters and placed them under the floor mats. Shadid gave Hassan and I back our passports. After we exited the car and entered the building, we immediately encountered a metal detector. Shadid had laid his keys in the tray and both he and Hassan had taken off their belts prior to passing through. The alarm didn't sound on them, but did with me. Hassan gave me an angry look. Maybe he thought I didn't ditch any metal I had on me on purpose. A very attractive female agent asked me to step off to the side and then began wanding me. My watch was the culprit. I took it off and placed it into the basket she was holding. I was sent through again and set off the alarm once more. A re-wanding ensued and this time she ran it over my crotch. "Careful, there might be a steel rod in there, sweetheart," I quipped. I think I caught a slight smile on her face, but moving the wand toward my pocket, she found the challenge coin given to me sometime back by a fellow Ranger. I've carried it with me for years for luck. It appeared I was going to need a hell of a lot of it.

"Okay, you're good," she finally said.

"Very good, my dear," I replied, winking. "I assure you."

Another smile.

As we passed on through, a second agent checked our passports and motioned us to continue on.

Hassan then led us directly toward a door where we were met by another Middle Eastern-looking man who had apparently been waiting for us. I took it he was our pilot. He said something to Hassan in Arabic and then passed back through the door.

Hassan gave me a bit of a shove and the three of us followed the pilot to the tarmac. I'd have thought we'd check in at one of the counter desks before leaving out, but apparently their procedure with chartered planes was a little different from ours back in the USA.

The plane we were about to board was a turboprop King Air 200. Not first class by any means. It looked like something I might have seen in some movie puddlejumping through the Amazon picking up dope and getting shot at on the way out. Before boarding, I looked it over good, mostly checking for bullet holes around the engines and on the wings. I figured the range of the craft was 1500 to 2000 nautical miles, so we'd have to land at least once for fuel before making Yemen. I was not at all happy with Chalmers for failing to charter us at least a

Lear or an Embraer Legacy. But, considering he was engaging terrorist types to do his dirty work, you get what you get. I hoped our pilot wasn't one of Mohammed Atta's relatives.

Once on board, the pilot handed both Hassan and Shadid semi-automatic pistols. The FAA wouldn't be happy about that. Of course, we weren't in the U.S. I think, however, there's an IACO or something that is the equivalent of the FAA.

The excessive black smoke from the port side engine when started alarmed me and suddenly made me remember I hadn't been given an opportunity to call Adriana. Not hearing from me like I promised, she would soon be getting worried. And if the piece of crap I'd be flying in fell out of the sky over some desert or into the Mediterranean, she would never find out what happened to me. She'd have to wait seven years to proclaim me dead before remarrying. But that was the least of my concerns. Unfortunately, Chalmers had taken my cellphone and in all of the excitement of my kidnapping and being shown my cousin's frozen head, I forgot to get the phone back. Of course, I wouldn't have gotten it back anyway.

We were already on the plane when I said, "Hey, Hassan. I need to go back inside and call my wife before we leave. How about it?" I know it sounded stupid and both Hassan and Shadid glared at me with their black eyes.

"You will sit there and shut up, McGowan," Hassan replied. "That is a stupid request."

See? I told you it was.

CHAPTER 4

There were other times and circumstances in my life as an action guy that I had faced danger by being taken prisoner, beat up, shot at and even plugged, but this time for some reason I didn't actually feel the danger, even though I was being thrown down the rabbit hole. I could have refused to take part in this coercive scheme, but had I refused to help Chalmers get his device, not only would an innocent mother and daughter perish, but Hassan would have been ordered to put a bullet in my head. Of course, should I now change my mind, I could find opportunities to take each one of these bastards down and forget the McGowan girls. But I knew Chalmers **would** kill them. I didn't want to have that on my conscience. But then I thought, he might just kill them anyway. Maybe, even if I delivered, he'd send someone after me and have me killed as well. That last thing I was not worried about. But again, one thing I knew for sure: even if I did locate the nuclear device, I sure as hell wasn't going to put it in his hands.

I didn't know if we were actually on our way to Yemen, but I could see we were flying south. It should be about four hours until the plane had to be refueled and that would take us somewhere near Italy, maybe Naples or Polenza. I had been wondering all along if the pilot had filed a flight plan and would our landings be legal? Would we land in some hostile field like drug smuggler Barry Seal did?

At this point, however, I was more concerned about the condition and worthiness of the aircraft. One of the engines had sputtered a few times and when we encountered some turbulence over the English Channel, the plane creaked and squeaked like pieces of it would come off at any time. I was wishing for a parachute. I remember back when I **was** a paratrooper, people would ask me in jest why I would ever jump from a perfectly good aircraft. Well, this was no perfectly good aircraft.

Although there was no sleeping on the old bird, when the ride became smoother, I did force myself to relax and settle back in my seat. Hassan was sitting next to me, gun still cradled in his hand as though I were actually going to go somewhere, while Shadid lay across the seat in front of us sound asleep.

"Alright, Hassan," I began. "Not having any knowledge of exactly where we'll be going or who to contact or where the WMDs are, you're going to have to become more communicative. What is in store for us when we get to where we're going?"

I thought he might again just tell me I will find out or to shut the hell up. However, he surprised me by saying, "We will land outside of Sana'a where we will meet a friend. He will guide us into the city of al-Hudaydah on the coast. From there you must use your resources to locate what we are looking for."

"Why there? Is that where Iraq supposedly dropped the WMDs?"

"It is only one of the ports in Yemen that will accommodate a vessel large enough to have as many weapons as Mr. Chalmers believes were on board."

"But you must understand, I **have** no resources. I was never involved with any covert operations regarding these weapons. My job was to hunt down terrorists bent on attacking the United States. The man Chalmers talked about, my former boss, died at an assassin's hand a decade ago and any plan to find the weapons he may have been working on died along with him. I have no contacts with that organization any longer. I see no way I can just drop into Yemen and locate what Chalmers wants."

"Then why didn't you just tell him there was no way you could do this and that would be the end of it?"

"As though I had a choice in the matter. I don't want to see the woman and her daughter killed. And was it you who severed the head of James McGowan?"

He nodded. "It was necessary for you to see that we were capable of taking what you call 'drastic measures' to get what Mr. Chalmers wants."

"Which is how ISIS does business. And that tells me you are not only just working for Chalmers, but are a terrorist bastard as well."

He sneered. "You are like the rest of your people. You throw that word 'terrorist' around and do not know that we are far from it. We are the Soldiers of Allah who must punish those who are not only against the Islamic State, but do not subscribe to our beliefs. We are jihadists and our mission involves peace."

"Jihadists? Really? I'm sure if you weren't here, you would be out there laying roadside bombs or in your machine gun-mounted Toyota pickups trying to pick off our troops in Afghanistan. Or maybe you'd be in your terrorist hideouts doing shit like raping your own women for exposing an ankle or a girl child for learning to read."

He glared at me with his cold, black eyes. "You are trying to anger me, McGowan."

"The truth hurts, doesn't it, prick."

That's when he backhanded me across the mouth. In reflex, I gave him a chest shot with my fist that caused him to drop the pistol and momentarily lose his breath. It was the kind of death punch that stops a man's heart and it **could** have if I had hit him hard enough. He then stood up and grabbed me by the throat. In defense I clasped my hands and thrust my arms up under his to break his hold. That accomplished, I slammed both of my palms into his ears causing him to cry out in pain. When he sank back into his seat, I reached down for the pistol. However, as our ten second scuffle had rudely awakened Shadid, I turned to find the muzzle of his .45 six inches from my skull. I then raised my hands and sat back down.

Hassan, having finally gotten his breath, sat holding his ears which had gone through a hell of a shock. While Shadid held his gun on me, Hassan then picked his up from the floor and placed the muzzle between my eyes. "I should shoot you now for your insolence and then inform Mr. Chalmers that you tried to run."

I wiped the blood from my mouth and replied, "You won't do that, Hassan. Number one, he would have you killed for failing to control me; and number two, I know you want a piece of the action when that nuclear device is sold to Iran."

"The money I receive for completing this mission will be used to purchase weapons for my brothers to kill infidels like you. Perhaps we will be allowed to keep some of the chemical and biological weapons to kill even more of you."

"Right. And that's your Muslim maggots' perception of peace. Hassan, you're living in dream world. There's no way we're ever going to find these weapons and I'm not sure they even existed in the first place."

"You spoke highly of your friend Lionel Byrd, but according to Mr. Chalmers, Byrd knew the weapons existed at the time they were shipped out of Iraq. Are you now saying your friend was wrong or lying? If not and you believe that he had a plan to go after the weapons, then you will find a way to complete his plan. Did or did you not believe in him?"

Yeah, I believed in Lionel Byrd, but I didn't trust Chalmers. He may have just been using Lionel's name to get to me. I don't doubt he learned about me if he **was** collaborating with the Birdman on the weapons. Sometimes high level collaborators do talk about their people, but then again I'm not sure Lionel would have done that. He was proud of his operatives and I can't imagine he would have given out any information on us, considering the top secret nature of our organization. He touted me more than once how I was the brightest and most cunning of his operatives. If he wanted it done and done efficiently, he laid the mission in my lap. So, did Chalmers find out about me on his own or through Byrd? I didn't know what to believe.

"Alright, Hassan. If I am to try this, I'll need a phone. I still have a couple of contacts in my former group." At least I had a couple of numbers. "I'll need to call them. You have your contacts in Yemen. Between the two of us, maybe it's possible…but a long shot."

"Remember, if you cannot do this by the the 4th of next month, you know what will happen. And you will die along with them."

"Are you set up with your phone service for international calls?"
"Yes. I pay ten pounds a month extra to call and text."

"I suspect we'll have no service on the plane since we're flying Podunk Airlines. So, when we land for fuel, I'll need some time on your phone."

He nodded. "What do you mean by Podunk Airlines? I have not heard of it. I do not think this plane is part of them."

I almost smiled at the ignorant bastard.

Hassan and I had apparently gotten the anger and hostilities out of our systems with our little tete-a-tete. I think we needed that scuffle to clear the air between us. No, we weren't friends now and never would be, the terrorist prick that he was; but at least we could be civil to one another. We had a common purpose for different reasons. His was money; mine was to save lives. Was it an impossible task? A team of inspectors, experts in their fields had been unable to find any WMDs. But, Lionel was convinced the weapons had been moved. Saddam had warning of the coming inspections; he had time to move them; and he had the resources to do so. I'm sure Lionel would have informed the President of his discovery. He also probably knew to where they had been moved. Unfortunately, he lost his life before he could tell the President and to follow through with his plan. It's the only thing I believed about what Chalmers told me. Lionel knew. Apparently, he never told Chalmers or Chalmers would know where to find the weapons. And I believe he didn't tell him because he didn't trust him.

The rickety King Air 200 had more miles in it than I thought it did. By nightfall we had made Preveza Airport in Greece. I didn't know if the airport was on the pilot's flight plan, but we landed there without any problem. Hassan said we could not disembark as we had no visas for Greece. We would also be sent through security and customs and that could be trouble. Greek law enforcement had a very suspicious nature about them and might find reason to detain us. We would spend the night inside the plane. On the plane was a small refrigerator that contained bottled water, cheese, bread and fruit. It didn't quite make a meal, but it was enough to quell my hunger pangs. There was also a compact toilet room that smelled to high heaven; however, it was either stand over the filthy pot for the ninety seconds it took to relieve myself or open the cabin door and whiz onto the tarmac.

Just after nine-thirty. Hassan handed me his phone to make my calls. I told him I would first be calling my wife, then follow-up with my former colleagues in Washington, that is if the numbers I had were still good.

"You will make the wife call quickly, McGowan."

I nodded and dialed the number. She answered on the second ring. "Hello."

"It's me, sweetheart. How are things there at the ranch?"
"Did you make it in okay? I thought you'd call before now."

"I made it fine. It's been a long day, though."

"Did you find your cousins yet?"

"Yes." I didn't elaborate.

"What number are you calling from? I see the number and it's not your cell."

"I lost my cell and am using someone else's."

"Well, how am I to get hold of you at any given time?"

"I'll just have to call you."

"Are you okay? You sound different."
"Just tired is all. Also, I expect the distance we have between us makes our connection a little garbled. I hate

to make this so short. I don't want to use up all this guy's minutes."

"Well, you know I love and miss you. Come home as soon as the will reading is over. When will that be?"

"I haven't been told. Maybe a few days."

"Oh. Well, I hope your cousin left you a gob of money."

"We'll see. But gotta go, now. I love you, babe."

"Have a good time and take some pictures. One day maybe we'll both go there."

"Bye bye, my dear." I then pressed the END button on the phone.

Hassan nodded, signaling that he was satisfied with the call. I then took from my wallet a well-worn slip of paper that contained a handful of phone numbers. Beside the numbers were the first names of friends and former cohorts. The one I dialed belonged to Keith Lambreau. It was his cell.

There was good news and some not so good news with the call. It was still Keith's number, but I got his voice mail. He was traveling out of country and may be in an inaccessible zone until the weekend or for two more days. I left Hassan's number and told him when he called, don't be alarmed if someone else answered. Just ask for me.

I felt better that I was able to reach Adriana and that she would not be worried. I'd be able to sleep better. The Arab men and I then stretched out the best we could in our seats and waited for sleep to take over.

My sleep would not come all that soon. I was tired, but my brain wouldn't shut off. Amid all the snoring, I tried to imagine how the coming days would unfold. Although it appeared we were indeed heading for Yemen, I didn't have a clue as to where we'd land, who would be waiting and how to begin the search. I had never before felt so handicapped. Authentic missions in my combat role and in my counterterrorist capacity had solid plans, target locations and mapped out courses of action. But this deal had too many unknowns. I had no idea where to even start. It appeared I'd be making crap up as I slugged along.

It might be days until Keith Lambreau called me back and even when he did, would he be privy to anything Lionel Byrd was working on before he was killed? Would he even know that Lionel had knowledge of actual

WMDs and where they might have been stashed? Did he come across any Top Secret paperwork upon taking over the director position? And if he had anything at all, would he share what he knew with a former operative who had officially been retired for as many years as I had? For all he knew, I could have gone to the dark side like MI-6 operative, Alistair Chalmers.

After having a breakfast bar and a Coke from the small fridge, I saw that a truck was pumping fuel into our tanks. As soon as we were full up, we'd be on our way. Hassan said we should be touching down in Yemen in about four and a half hours.

"We need to talk about today, Hassan," I said. "Where exactly are we landing, do you have people waiting and what's going to happen when we get there?"
"I have people waiting to guide us to what you might call a base camp. There will be people there who might know others who have knowledge of where the weapons were brought in, but that is not for sure. But it is you who were to have a plan once we were in the country. Mr. Chalmers said you were intelligent and resourceful. So, it is all on you. I know nothing of the weapons myself and can only be your interpreter to people who know something. Maybe the contact you tried to call will provide the information you need."

"And are these people your ISIS brothers? I don't deal with terrorists and certainly don't trust them."

"Do not again refer to us as terrorists, McGowan. You have been warned. If you intend to be hostile with these men, they will kill you and the mission will be lost. You must show respect or they will give us nothing. They must believe you are a supporter of their ideals and sympathetic to their cause. Do not disrespect our Islam belief or make jokes about Allah and Muhammed as you infidels do. Your head will immediately fall to your feet."

"And you schmucks would certainly know all about that."

He didn't reply. I took it that beheading people was a hobby for him and people like him. I wasn't going to forget what he did to James McGowan.

"Okay, Hassan. Once we get there, maybe we can end up talking to the right people. If the weapons are somewhere in Yemen, somebody's got to know it."
 "If it were that easy, we would not need you. Mr. Chalmers and those that he has hired like me could as you have said 'waltz' in and take them."

"I suspect whoever has them or are guarding them wouldn't be giving them up that easily. Chalmers would have to pay through the nose to get them. He thinks I'll be finding a way to steal the device he's looking for."

Hassan smiled. "See? You figured that out already. You are very perceptive."

Much of the way across the Mediterranean there was no further dialogue between us. The engines sputtered a few more times which compelled me to again think about where a parachute might be located in the plane…and a raft. In the interim, I was trying to recall what I had learned sometime back about Yemen. I remember watching on the news about all the civil strife the country had gone through, the battles between the Shi'ites and the Sunnis, the splitting of the country into North and South Yemen and the ongoing political crises that have existed for decades. Although since I retired from the State Department I've only gotten my knowledge of happenings in the Middle East through the media like most everyone else, I understand the Yemeni government was now in the hands of the Houthi rebels. Not so long ago, the Saudis invaded in an attempt to restore the former president's government and over 50,000 people had since lost their lives mainly due to strife in the streets, skirmishes and bombings. That contributed to a famine which occurred primarily as a result of food and water contamination. Adding to Yemen's health woes, there were over a million cases of cholera from which 3,000 people had died. I was so looking forward to landing there.

Chapter 5

When we were halfway over the Red Sea off the coast of Saudi Arabia, Shadid who had not said a handful of words the entire flight looked out the port side of the plane, then turned toward Hassan and me with an excited look on his face. His eyes were as big as steely shooters and grin, wide as Joe E. Brown's. I thought maybe he had seen a UFO; however, he proclaimed he had just spotted "Mecca! Mecca!"

"Well, whoop-tee-doo," I replied.

Hassan frowned. "I do not know what this whoop-tee-doo means, but I think from your tone of voice you are mocking our faith. Mecca is to us like Jerusalem is to you infidels. Mocking our religion gives us license to kill you."

Well, I didn't want to get into another scuffle, which of course he'd lose. As much as I hated admitting it, I needed him for navigation and translation purposes.

"I apologize for that, Hassan...and Shadid. For some reason, I haven't been myself the last couple of days."

"I accept," replied Hassan. Shadid continued smiling and nodded.

I was hoping there wouldn't be any **salat** praying and wailing going on. Thank God there wasn't.

Some twenty minutes later, our terrorist aviator was banking the plane toward land which I assumed was the shoreline of Yemen. We were surely in Yemeni airspace and I wondered if we were expected…or would the Air Force be scrambling its jets? After dropping the bird dramatically to a level I assumed would be under Yemeni Air Force radar, minutes later I saw we were flying nap of earth just over mountainous treetops.

We had not been over land more than two minutes when the left engine began sputtering again. Then suddenly, thick black smoke billowed and the engine quit entirely. Although we still had the right engine, it began smoking as well. Slowly we began a descent which I surmised was unintentional. The aircraft then began shuddering and dipping to the left. Out my left side window I was alarmed to see nothing but mountains, rocky and jagged, with a smattering of trees, all of which were coming up to meet us. Hassan yelled to the pilot something in Arabic and the man shouted back at him, his voice full of panic. Hassan and I were seat-belted, but Shadid jumped up and grabbed the pilot's seat back and screamed something which I assumed was a plea to get us down safely. Then suddenly to our horror the right engine began coming apart. That's all it took to send us like an errant missile into the treetops. Remembering all the flight attendant instructions about crash protocol, I grabbed my head and dropped my chin into my knees. The plane suddenly spun helplessly, clipping the tops of at least three trees and then crashed onto the rocky face of the mountainside.

My entire body, having experienced such a grievous shock from the impact, felt as though every bone in it had been broken. That's the last thing I remember.

When I awoke, my head was jammed into the back of the seat in front of me. My neck was not broken, but severely sprained and my low back felt as it an elephant had sat on it. Carefully I unseat-belted myself and rubbing my hands over my chest and legs, felt for fractures. None apparent. I then wriggled myself around in my seat to see if everything worked. Had I actually survived a plane crash without a serious injury? I would find out for sure when I tried to stand.

In the seat next to me, I saw that Hassan was bleeding from a cut on his head. I couldn't readily see other injuries, but if he was still alive, he could have had fractures. I checked his pulse at the carotid and it was strong. I then looked forward in the cabin and saw that Shadid, who had been standing and shouting at the pilot, had been thrust through the windshield of the plane and impaled by a large tree branch, looking like a punctured hefty bag from which a gallon of tomato soup had spilled. The pilot had likewise been killed on impact. His face was horribly mangled from striking the instrument panel.

I was able to stand and was elated to find the legs actually worked. I then stood with my hands on the seat back, bowed my head and said a few words to the good Lord that He had delivered me. Very carefully, I unsnapped Hassan's seat belt and laid him down on the floor. I knew I had to get both of us out of the plane as the right engine which had exploded was smoldering. The plane could go up in flames at any time.

I then walked to the small fridge and took out a bottle of cold water, popped off the cap and poured the liquid into my palm. After applying the water to Hassan's face, he started coming around. "Hassan," I said. "Can you move?"

I could see he was in shock, but he still managed to nod.

"I've got to get you to your feet and out of the plane. It's on fire. If you can't move or walk, I have to carry you out of here. Try moving around." But then I was afraid he may have internal injuries such as a ruptured spleen or fractures and any movement could mean his death.

He finally spoke. "I will try to get up if you will help me."

Grasping his palm, I let him move on his own. He was able to get to his knees, but not without groaning in pain. "My back…it is not good." However, slowly he was able to get to his feet. He then steadied himself by grasping onto the seat and looked around the cabin. "We are alive. Allah be praised."

"Let's get out of here," I said.

"Shadid?" he asked.

"Alas, poor Shadid. While we make our way down the mountain, he's going to be sticking it out here."

"What do you mean?"

"Take a look, Hassan." I then pointed toward the shattered windshield.

Upon seeing Shadid's body, he turned his head and winced. "He was a good friend."

Hassan then moved gingerly toward the door, which had broken off, and stepped out onto the rocks. I pulled the remainder of the water, fruit and bread from the refrigerator, shoved it in the canvas bag Chalmers had given me and after reaching out the pilot's window to search Shadid's clothing for his weapon, found in his belt the .45 pistol. I then saw that the entire instrument panel was crushed as was the plane's radio. I checked it anyway, but found it in pieces. Before exiting the plane, from the wall near the door I ripped off the first aid kit.

Once outside of the aircraft, I took account of the plane's damage. The right engine was still ablaze, but I was surprised to see a half dozen bullet holes in what remained of the left engine. The left wing had also been peppered. What I had thought was mere mechanical failure of a thirty-some year old rattle trap, proved to be the result of automatic weapons fire.

I found Hassan sitting on a large rock about twenty feet from the plane holding his head. After opening the first aid kit, I began wiping Hassan's forehead with an alcohol swab and then placed a large bandage on his wound. Standing beside him on the rock, I then took account of where we were. It was rugged country all right. We were about halfway up on a slope that appeared to be more than three thousand feet high. Below us lay a vast, sweeping valley with no sign of civilization in sight. It seemed we could see for ten miles, reminding me of places I had been in the western United States, maybe Colorado or Utah. Remembering where we had crossed the coastline, I thought we may be fifteen or more miles from the sea.

I told Hassan "The plane just didn't fall out of the sky due to blown engines; we were shot down."

"Someone shot us down? Who might do that?"

"Maybe the rebels, maybe the Yemeni government, maybe your al-Qaeda friends?"

"Understand that I am not al-Qaeda, McGowan."

"Oh, I forgot…ISIS. You and al-Qaeda are not the best of friends."

He glared at me again. He had done that a lot this long day.

"Do you still have your phone?" I asked him.

 "Yes." He then pulled it off his belt.

I knew we were not in any cell tower range, so we wouldn't be able to call for help.
Still, I turned it on to see if it still worked. It did, but gave me the message, No Signal.

"Why did you do it?" Hassan asked me.

I thought he meant I had something to do with the crash. "Do what?"

"Pull me from the plane."

"As you can see, it's now on fire. Why wouldn't I?"

"You would be free to walk out of here and find some help. Then you could return to your home."

"I don't want to see **anybody** go up in flames, Hassan, even if it's a terrorist prick."

He smiled at that. "I cannot figure you, McGowan. You know if things were different and I had you on my sights as an enemy, I would pull the trigger."

"And I **have** had people like you in my sights and **did** pull the trigger."

He nodded. "Well, I wish to thank you for my life."

"Sorry you missed out on the 72 virgins today. Maybe soon, huh?"

And to that he laughed which caused him to wince in pain.

"Have you been in Yemen before?"

"Yes. I trained for my cause here."

"What are these mountains called?"

"They are the Sarawat Mountains. I believe this range is called Jabel an-Nabi Shu'ayb."

"A long name. What does it mean?"

"Nabi means prophet. Shu'ayb was a holy messenger."

"How far is it to the next town?"

"I do not know…maybe ten or more miles. This is tribal land. The tribe called alAkhdam is in these mountains. Also the Zaidi, maybe 400 or more tribes."

"You said 400?"

"Yes, many."

"If we walk out of here will we soon find somebody?"

"Perhaps. I don't know if I can walk. My back pain goes to both of my legs."

"If I go and leave you here, I may either get lost or killed by one of the tribesmen. You'd be stuck here to die. You'll have to try."

"I think you are right. Maybe I will. I see you have a pistol now."

"It's Shadid's. Does that bother you?"

"I think you had the chance to use it on me."

"You were at a disadvantage. There's no fun in that." I then took the clip out of the automatic and as I saw the gun was a German H&K, it had a 13 round magazine. All rounds were present and accounted for. Good boy, Shadid. Sorry you didn't make it.

I then picked up a thick tree branch, broke it in half over my knee and tested it for strength. It was strong enough for Hassan to use as a cane or crutch. I passed it to him. "We need to go down the mountain. I see a trail at the bottom. Come on."

It was slippery in places and both of us slid and fell a couple of times on loose rocks. To cover the distance, it took almost an hour. Hassan was having serious problems with his ambulation and we had to take our time. A lot of moaning and groaning every time he slipped. When we reached the trail, I decided we should go west toward the coast. Most villages are near water and the chances of encountering tribesmen were better. The sun was blazing which added to the soreness in our bodies, making both of us even more miserable. But Hassan was used to 110 degree heat and didn't need as much water as me. People such as him were like human camels. I ended up throwing the fruit away as it didn't take long to shrivel up and spoil. We did stop under a grove of dragon blood trees resembling canopies and which offered us shade. We each had a drink of our water, saving as much as we could, considering there were no rivers flowing that season in Yemen. We then gnawed a few bites of the bread which had pretty much turned to cement.

About a mile further to the west we saw them. A small caravan of Bedouin tribesmen sitting with their camels under more dragon blood umbrellas. When they saw us, two of them hopped on their camels and hustled out to intercept us. Would they be friends or foes?

We found out in a hurry as they quickly slid off their mounts, training their rifles on us. After looking us over and seeing that only one of us had a similar complexion to them, they shouted at me, "Ealaa al'ard!"

I looked at Hassan. "What are they saying?"

"To get down on the ground."

So I did.

Hassan then began communicating with them in Arabic. They exchanged words for more than a minute, the Bedouins apparently still shouting demands.

While lying with my face in the dirt, I finally asked "What are they saying to one another?"

"They want to know what a White man is doing in this part of their country and if they should kill you. I told them you are a friend. Our plane crashed up on the mountain and we had to walk down here. They said they saw the plane in the sky and it looked to be in trouble. Then they saw the smoke. They want to know why I am traveling with you. I told them we had business near Sana'a. I asked for more water and some food. They said to come with them. Their village is two miles from here. The tribesman said you can get up now."

So I did. "Maybe we can rest up there and get some transportation to where we were to meet your contact, wherever that is. Were you ever going to tell me where we were going?"

"I will tell you now. A small landing strip near al-Hudaydah. That city is on the sea. We passed over it."

"Why don't you Arabs come up with names that westerners can pronounce like Dallas or Miami?"

I caught a slight smile. "We will go now."

Well, since we had no rides, we had to follow the camel jockeys on foot. The sun was sizzling and I was slowly roasting. My body's check engine light was on, but I still drove on. When we finally got to their oasis, they gave us more water and some Saltah, which is a kind of vegetable stew that I found fairly tasty. Maybe it was because I was hungry as hell. However, I was pretty damn concerned about the cholera epidemic in the country. I was hoping the outbreak was only in the cities and urban areas and hadn't hit the tribes. After we had satisfied our stomachs, the Bedouins actually let us ride on two of their pack camels to their village.

It was what we might call in the U.S. a hole-in-the-road. The village of Yahini consisted of five buildings and a series of tents with a population of what looked like forty Shia Bedouins. Although Hassan was able to communicate with them in Arabic, most of the people spoke Soqotri. Their skin color and features reminded me of the Montagnard tribes I worked and lived with in Vietnam when I was there as a Special Forces advisor. However, I didn't find **these** people as friendly. I guess since I didn't look like them or speak their language, they automatically didn't trust me. Hassan was welcomed to spend the night, but several of the tribesmen wanted to turn me out into the desert. Hassan again interceded on my behalf.

I was given a bedroll and slept in a soft, sandy spot under the stars while Hassan enjoyed a tent. They offered him some kind of dessert called honey cake, but not me.

When everyone bedded down for the night, he came out to slip me a piece of it. I guessed he was still being grateful for saving his life back at the plane.

CHAPTER 6

When morning broke and we found ourselves well-rested, I bowed and thanked our hosts and then we set out to the west for al-Hudaydah. Hassan was still not ambulating well and our pace was going to be slow. We had about eight miles before reaching the outskirts of the city at the location Hassan thought he was to meet his contact. The thing was, the pilot, rest his soul, knew exactly where he was to land. Hassan wasn't sure. Those who know me also know I'm a jogger and in pretty damn good shape. I wouldn't have run those eight miles, but I would have covered the trail a whole lot quicker to avoid the noonday heat.

Fortunately, halfway to our objective we caught a ride with a family from alHudaydah in the back of their pickup.Their two children sat across from us not one second taking their eyes off our faces. Our smiles tried to convince them we were not child murderers. We got out at the city's outskirts where we started seeing businesses. I was surprised at how large the city was. Hassan said the population was well over two million.

When we saw the small park a block or so in toward the city, we sat down on a bench to check Hassan's phone for service. He had two missed calls. The first was from his contact who wanted to know where he was and why the plane had not landed. Hassan called him back, taking about three minutes to fill him in on the details of our plight. When he ended the call, he told me we would meet the contact at seven at a hookah bar in the city on Rasulid Street near the al-Hudaydah seaport.

The other missed call was from the number I had dialed which belonged to Keith Lambreau. I listened. "Bruce, good to hear from you. Sorry I missed your call. Yes, we to catch up. I'm accessible now, so give me a call when you can."

I knew it was just after seven in the morning back in Washington and I didn't want to make the call when he was probably on his way to work on the Washington Beltway. Maybe in an hour or so.

We then took a cab to the hookah joint which also served American burgers. They did not serve alcohol as its consumption was illegal in most Middle Eastern hookah locations. Inside the bar dressed both in modern, westernized suits and traditional thobes and futa skirts, men, women and teens alike sat with their water pipes drawing fruit and honey flavored tobacco, cannabis and opium into their lungs. Those who were not doing the hookah shit were content with their khat, which were green leaves of a plant that grew in southern Arabia that eighty percent of the population chewed. A stimulant containing both cathine and cathinone was like taking in alcohol in chewing tobacco form, making the users dinky dau as I remember hearing the people say in Vietnam.

Before we ordered our dinners, Hassan looked around the room for his contact. Maybe we were a little early as he didn't see him. But after we sat down at a table, a man in his forties dressed in a skull cap came up behind Hassan and placed his hand on his shoulder. If you posted a photo of an ISIS or al-Qaeda terrorist on the mostwanted bulletin board in the Hoover Building, it would look like this guy.

Hassan stood up and they planted kisses on each others' cheeks. The man then took a chair at our table after which Hassan introduced him. "This is my friend, Abdel Aziz who lives in the Yemen capital, Sana'a. He will speak English so that we can all understand one another. Abdel, this is Bruce McGowan who at one time worked for the American government."

"Is he the man Mr. Chalmers said would be coming?" Aziz asked.

"Yes. He will also talk with his contact in Washington who we hope can locate information about the cargo we discussed. Mr. McGowan's former boss along with Mr. Chalmers had information in a file about the cargo more than ten years ago, but it has never been found since. McGowan's boss was killed before he could investigate his suspicions further."

I jumped in, "Mr. Aziz, if I may ask, what is your role in this? Do you have any information as to whether the discussed cargo actually came into port here and was stored somewhere in Yemen?"

"I and three others who have allied in the past with Hassan on, let's say certain
'projects', were hired by Mr. Chalmers to transport the cargo, if found, to his location. We do not know how large the item is, but we have means and resources to get it to him."

"The second part of my question pertained to any actual knowledge you had that this cargo was moved here back in 2003."

"We had heard rumors that a ship bearing the cargo we mentioned had entered one of the entrances to the port, but heard nothing more. That was in the fall of 2002 before the inspectors went into Iraq. Also, about the same time, a young Akhdam boy named Sameer from one of the tribes supposedly came upon four large trucks stopped on the road to Ta'izz. One of the trucks had smoke coming from under the hood. The trucks were similar to the military two and a half ton trucks with canvas covers on them. He watched as one man came from the back of the broken down truck to join the driver and a passenger who were looking under the hood."

"Where was the boy when he saw them?"

"Very close to the road behind some large rocks. The three men in the second truck got out with rifles in hand and stood off to the side well away from the trucks to smoke cigarettes. When they turned their backs to watch a caravan of Akhdam tribesmen in the distance, the boy then climbed up into the bed of their truck. He was only inside it a few seconds, but what he described to his father and childhood friends were large crates with the international nuclear symbol on them. He also described what was thought to be large projectile rounds."

"Did no one back then follow up on his story and question him?"

"He did not tell his story until years later when he was a teenager. By that time, no one seemed to care and the inspections had long been completed. Saddam Hussein had also been captured and hanged. The story had little value."

"Let me ask another question: who are the Akhdam people?"

"They are a social minority with darker skin who are looked upon the way you White people in America have treated your Black people for centuries. They are on the bottom rung of our society and live separate from all other groups. They hold the dirtiest of jobs if they are allowed to work at all. They live mostly in slums and tent villages. That is another reason the boy was not taken seriously."

"Does Chalmers know about him and if so, why didn't he dispatch people like you to go find the boy? Chalmers concocted an elaborate plan to get me to come to him. Yet, I haven't been in his kind of business for years and am out of touch with everything and everybody."

"I do not know the answer to your question. Maybe he needs the information you will get from your contact to complete the puzzle. He is a very thorough man as we have done work for him before."

"Maybe the Iraqis who transported the WMDs went back later to retrieve them when things simmered down. Seems by the end of President Bush's second term, we didn't hear anything more about the weapons. Nobody was interested any longer."

"I said the same words with Mr. Chalmers. He said the transport people were members of the Special Republican Guard in Baghdad. When bombings of military targets began and the American troops invaded, the Republican Guard soldiers were either killed or deserted. By the end of 2003, there were none to be found. Saddam went into hiding and had no control over any of the special forces. There was no one left to go after the weapons."

We sat in silence for a lengthy time until I decided I had to get something off my chest. I felt like I was sitting there collaborating with the enemy…the same kind of terrorists that I had for more than five years hunted down and terminated on both American and international soil. So, I had to think long and hard before finding the right words. I said to them, "I don't like what we're doing here. I am actually sitting here making plans with people who hate Americans. I know that both you and your friends have been involved in radical jihadist activities where innocents have been shot, blown up by roadside bombs and decapitated. My former boss and Chalmers had hunted down and destroyed people like you in the name of counterterrorism. Yet, now you're doing his dirty work. How do you feel about that?"

Hassan and Aziz exchanged glances and I took it that one was waiting for the other to answer. Finally, Hassan said, "Yes, we are doing this job by his direction, but we do not like him. Still, we are hoping we can find this weapon he wants. We will be paid much money that will go to our brothers-in-arms to…"

"To continue waging war on Americans and others that you refer to as infidels who don't follow your faith and your law," I said.

Hassan glared at me. If circumstances had been different, I figured he would have killed me for saying what I did. Or **tried** to at any rate. Instead, he surprised me by responding rather philosophically. "This is a harsh world, McGowan. There will always be strife between people who have different faiths and ideologies." For a lowlife terrorist prick, not only did he sound educated, but he had a good command of the English language. His accent was still thick, however.

"I've been meaning to ask you, Hassan, where were you educated?"

"I studied International Law at the American University of Beirut."

"And you waste that education on terrorist…excuse me…jihadist activities."

"I do not consider carrying out my purpose and my objectives a waste."

"You know you'll have to pay for James McGowan's murder. You didn't have to kill him to convince me of Chalmers's resolve. And you know I'm only doing this to save my cousins' lives."

"I wish to get off that subject and concentrate on what we are here to accomplish."

"Fine. So, how far is it from here to the seaport, Aziz?"

Aziz replied, "About four miles further into the city."

"Do you have a car?"

"Yes."

"Will you take us there after we have dinner?"

"There is nothing to see there and no one to talk to."
"That's okay. I'd like to see where that ship would have come in. It helps me with the overall picture."

Hassan jumped in, "You said Chalmers was a thorough man; I think you are as well."

We ordered our dinners. I had a cheeseburger and home fries while both Hassan and Aziz had ogda which is a mixture of lamb and chicken with potatoes, carrots and onions. It looked good, but I didn't like the way it smelled. We had eaten potatoes and eggs for our breakfast at the Bedouin camp, but had nothing since. I pretty much inhaled my burger while the two men at the table were taking more time with theirs. After I finished, I took Hassan's phone off to a quiet corner of the bar and made a call to Lambreau. Hassan wanted to sit in on my call, but as I had convinced him along the way I was going to play ball until we located the WMDs, he yielded.

I found a spot as far away from the chatter and laughter of the smokers as I could and dialed the number. It was a 50/50 chance he would answer, but as he had previously called the number, he should recognize it when my call rang in.He answered on the third ring.

CHAPTER 7

"Hello, my lethal friend. How the hell are you?"

"Still having all the fun I can stand."

"And Adriana?"

"Still beautiful and adoring me."

He laughed. "I don't hear from you for three years and then suddenly out of the blue I do. Are you looking for your old job back?"

"Never, old pal. But I do need something from you."

"Sure, how much…ten bucks, twenty?"

"Funny. What I'm going to ask you, I'm not in an immediate position to elaborate on."

"Sounds serious. Is it something we need to discuss in person? You said you're on someone else's cell."

"We have to talk about this now. It's about Lionel."

"Now you've got me intrigued. What about him?"

"I can't tell you why I'm asking this, but did he leave documents pertaining to any work on locating the WMDs Saddam was supposed to have? In other words, did he actually have a covert fact-finding team dispatched and were they successful in determining the actual existence of the weapons? Specifically, I'm looking for any findings he may have come up with between 2003 and 2007"

Lambreau let out a low whistle. "Whoa, my friend. I gotta know where you found this out."

"By your reply, are you telling me he **was** engaged in hunting down the WMDs?"

"This is so out of the blue, Bruce. It's a subject I can't talk about over a cell phone.
Can you come to Washington for a sit-down?"

"No, Keith. I'm in a dire situation that involves the location of these weapons and just need some quick answers."

"What have you gotten yourself into, man? You've got me concerned."

"Just answer me this: when you took over as director, did you inherit any plans and documents that Lionel was working on pertaining to this matter? Yes or no."

"I can't tell you yes **or** no. We really have to talk privately about this. Come on, what's going on with you, Bruce? You sound like you're in trouble."

"Yeah, something like that. Do you have anything on paper that involves one Alistair Chalmers, retired MI-6?"

"I know about Chalmers. Are you mixed up in something with him?"

I let out a deep sigh. I didn't have the time or the cellphone minutes to explain all what was happening with me. He wasn't going to tell me anything about Lionel Byrd's work on the WMDs. And if he even had a clue where the weapons were taken and hidden, he wouldn't tell me on the phone. And I didn't blame him.

"You didn't answer me, Bruce. All I can tell you is that Chalmers was involved in some pretty nasty shit where he was collaborating with al-Qaeda. He was arrested and placed under house arrest. He escaped and disappeared more than five years ago. It's no secret as it was all over the news back then. If you've somehow run into him, know that he's on Britain's most wanted list. Tell me how you know about him."

In the essence of time, I gave him a shortened, two minute synopsis of what had happened to me to which he replied, "Good God, man, you **are** in a predicament. Do I need to send a team after you?"

"No. You do that and my two female cousins die. Let me work this out on my own.
Now that I've told you everything, can you answer any of my questions?"

"Lionel and Chalmers at MI-6 did in fact acquire tangible information on the existence of the WMDs. But when Lionel found out about Chalmers' treasonous activities, their collaboration on the matter of course came to an end. Yes, I do have Lionel's file on the WMDs; however, the whereabouts of the weapons were never determined. But there is one other thing you should know, Bruce."

"What's that?"

"It's about the presidential candidate Jack Randall who was involved in Lionel's and the team's murders. We think Chalmers also had a hand in those murders."

"How so?"

"In overturning Randall's entire office and email train, the FBI found messages between Randall and Chalmers. And as your teammate Chuck Robinson, who killed Lionel, was mixed up with Randall and would have provided him information on Lionel's plan to take Randall down, we think Chalmers and Randall together planned

Lionel's assassination. Now what you're telling me makes more sense. When Chalmers got canned and subsequently arrested for espionage, only Lionel had the **official** knowledge of the existence of the WMDs. As Chalmers then went on the lam, his covert work on officially tracking the WMDs had ended. Apparently, Chalmers had plans all along to go after the weapons with the intent to sell them to Iran. You have just provided the missing piece of the puzzle to the WMD conspiracy. Lionel's file has lain inactive for all these years. Maybe it's time for me to reopen it and discuss the matter with our current President."

"But is there anything tangible in the file that indicates where the WMD loaded vessel came into port?"

"I'll have to open it back up and see. Admittedly, I only gave it cursory attention when I took over as director. I'll have to relook at it. It seems to me though that the satellite image showed the ship docking at a deepwater inlet and not the actual port. Can you once more be in service to your country and your old team?"

"I'm here, so I might as well."

"We can also either send a team into Scotland to hunt Chalmers down or engage the agency to do it for us."

"I'd rather you not do that, Keith. Even if they do find out where his hideaway is, he will see them coming for a country mile. He'll then kill the ladies without batting an eye."

"Alright then. I want you to find a way to destroy that cellphone you're talking on."

"How will I get back with you if I find anything?"

"Kill the bastards and make your way to the embassy in Sana'a."

"I can't do that, Keith. I just told you why not. And realize that I have just over a dozen days to deliver for Chalmers."

"Do the best you can, Bruce, as I know you will. I will have a team ready do business when the timing is right. Unfortunately, the females back in that house may end up as collateral damage anyway."

"Yeah. Well, gotta go, Keith."

"Good luck, pal."

My call had taken about ten minutes and I saw that Hassan's phone was down to one bar. I wasn't sure if he had a charger with him, but I was sure he could pick one up in some al-Hudaydah mobile store. It didn't matter. I was going to find a way to get it lost or destroyed. There wasn't any way I knew of extracting my conversation from the phone; but as I was no techie, I couldn't be sure.

I returned to the dinner table finding Hassan and Aziz engaged in an Arabic dialogue and was sure my future had been the topic of conversation…how long that future would be. I had no doubt if I was somehow successful in locating these weapons, my life and those of my cousins wouldn't be worth a plugged nickel anyway.

"You were able to make your call to the contact?" Hassan asked.

"Yes."

"And what was the result?"

"He knew nothing of any existing file on the weapons, whether they existed or if they did, where they were shipped it. When my boss was murdered, even though my contact took over the position, he was not given any information on the weapons. Any investigation Chalmers said was going on, died with him."

"That is too bad. Then we will have to rely on what we can find out here."

I guessed that he believed me or at least he let on that he did. There was no change in his expression nor exchange of glances between the two men.

"I see that you're done with your meals. Can we pay and go now?"

Hassan summoned the server and rubbed his thumb and fingers together which I understood was the way to request the bill. The server then removed it from his apron and handed it to Hassan. Hassan in turn laid onto the table several pieces of currency called rial and then we moved toward the door. I saw the pain in Hassan's face when he stood up and wondered if he had cracked a vertebrae in his back when we crashed the day before.

Aziz took us to his car which he had parked on the side of the street a block down. I got in the back and Hassan took shotgun. Aziz said, "I still do not know what value there is in going to the port. There is nothing there that would pertain to what may have occurred those many years ago."

"Just humor me, Aziz."

CHAPTER 8

As Aziz was pulling away deeper into the commercial part of the city, I began seeing the evidence of the continued hostility between the Houthis rebels that had been controlling the city and western part of Yemen for the past four years. It was only the week before that the official government with the backing of both Saudi Arabia and the UAE launched an assault on al-Hudaydah to regain control of the seaport. Although the downtown buildings were already in a state of disrepair, I saw where the Saudi artillery had made huge holes in them, causing in some cases total collapse. However, street vendors were still out selling their fruits, vegetables, linens and trinkets and even at eight o'clock both the vehicle and pedestrian traffic were causing jams on nearly every byway. We were caught in one of them.

The city's infrastructure had not only fallen victim to the warring government and rebel strife, but Aziz said al-Qaeda had set off two bombs the week before that killed over two dozen citizens. Passing by one of the government buildings, he pointed out the bomb's devastating destruction. Besides the seaport, the Saudis had taken control of the airport and that was one reason we were to land in a field on the outskirts of alHudaydah.

I wondered which faction it was that had pumped rounds into our King Air 200.

Anyway, Aziz told us that the Saudi-backed coalition had recently conducted air raids on select targets near both the airfield and port, so don't be surprised if we see jets screaming overhead. However, people continued to scurry about talking, smoking and doing business on the streets as though nothing further could occur to put them in any additional danger.

No sooner was I taking note of that, we saw, heard and felt a loud explosion only two blocks ahead of us. The fireball lasted several seconds after which a five story building crumbled to the ground, reminding me of an old hospital I had seen intentionally demolished a few years ago outside of Chicago. Aziz jammed on his breaks to avoid fleeing people. It appeared the battle for Yemen and this important port city was going to continue indefinitely. And then suddenly several men in bandana masks tore into the street we were on and began spraying both pedestrians and vehicles with automatic weapons fire. Ours caught several rounds, mainly the grille and right-side fender. A couple went into the windshield. The problem was, we were stuck in bumper-to-bumper travel and vehicle occupants were jumping out to run.

When the shooters moved closer toward us, still spitting bullets, to go on the offensive I jumped out and fired several rounds from Shadid's .45, striking one of them in the head. When the other two realized someone was returning their fire, they trained their guns solely on our vehicle. Unfortunately, one of the bullets tore through the windshield, catching Aziz in the throat. I then put two rounds in that shooter's chest while from his open window glass, Hassan unloaded on the third terrorist.

Suddenly, within a scant millisecond, it seemed our entire block erupted, the apparent bomb sending brick, glass and other debris flying into adjacent businesses and passersby. The fiery shock wave blew me back inside the open rear door of the car at the same time turning it over on its side. The blast which caused my brain to feel like it had imploded took away nearly all of my hearing. Lying twisted up against the passenger side door of the car, it took me a few moments to regain my faculties, if not my very sanity. All of the noise around me…the screaming, the sirens and crumbling of structures on the left side of the car…was muffled and garbled. I opened my mouth widely several times to see if my hearing would return, but to no avail.

Hassan was clawing around in the front seat attempting to climb over the dead Aziz and out of the driver's side door. The cut he received on his forehead from the plane crash had opened back up. Otherwise, he appeared fine. Me? I was bleeding from cuts on the left side of my face and my left arm and a large shard of glass was sticking out of my left thigh. After yanking it out, I began climbing upward across the back seat and out through the door.

There was nothing but mass chaos. Scores of people lay dead on the sidewalks and roadway. Just as many of the badly injured were lying in pools of their blood, dismembered and crying out for help. Mothers knelt over their dead children, hands in the air and wailing. Both Hassan and I went to those who were still alive, pressing on wounds to try stopping the bleeding. A woman whose burka had been half burnt off was gasping for breath, but then stopped breathing altogether. I dropped to my knees and began CPR on her, applying regular chest compressions with my palms and then breathing twice into her mouth before the next compressions began. She suddenly coughed and after a few moments began breathing again, but erratically. In a few minutes city police and medical techs were on the scene and took over. I didn't think there would be another bomb or IED in that very spot and although I figured we were safer to stay there, I told Hassan we still needed to hustle out of the metro area and head for the suburbs. Forget the seaport.

It took me a few minutes, but I found the pistol that had been blown out of my hand by the blast. Hassan hated to be leaving the dead Aziz, but there was nothing we could do about it. It would have been ironic if the masked gunmen were from the same terrorist group as Aziz, maybe al-Qaeda or ISIL. But I thought they were more likely Houthis rebels who had been carrying out terrorist attacks for months, keeping the populace on edge. It was always the citizen who was caught in between the Yemeni government and the rebels. In the three year battle for control of the port system, over 6,000 innocents had been killed by either air strikes, artillery or random terror attacks. And when adding to all that strife their economic woes and the pervasive cholera epidemic, Yemen had become one of the poorest and most dangerous countries in the world.

We were hoofing it again and by nightfall, we had made it to the edge of the city. Hassan had no idea how to meet up with Aziz's other cohorts. They would be the ones with the resources to transport the nuclear device from where it would be found to Chalmers in Scotland or to a location elsewhere that he had designated for temporary storage. But, considering what we had encountered these two days, our mission had been sidetracked. We seemed to be starting again from scratch.

As we were walking, I snatched from a street vendor's table a linen sash of sorts and ducked into an alley to wrap and compress the wound on my thigh. However, my bleeding had stopped on its own more than an hour before from crusting over. A hot shower later would do wonders to help clean it, that is if we could find a place to bed down.

As both of us were tired, beat up and bloodied, we began an active search for a hotel. Hassan said he had several million Yemeni rials on him and could pay for a room for each of us. When he told me that, my eyes widened, until he explained that one American dollar equaled about 40,000 rials. There was no way we'd split a room, however, he being a terrorist prick, and me a filthy infidel.

Ultimately, we found a fairly decent-looking hotel on Garesh Street near where the lights of civilization ended. Hassan paid for our rooms at which time I discovered we were on different floors. When I stepped into my room, the stench of curry hit my nostrils which nearly makes me gag every time I take a breath. But I was too tired to care. As the night progressed, I'd be getting used to the smell. I think they call that nose-blindness.

I took a shower which provided all the pleasantries except hot water, soap and a clean towel. Well, there **was** soap in the bathroom, but it was only a sliver, having had been used a few times. A thick black hair was stuck to it. In the commode was a good size turd that no one thought to flush. I then found out there was a reason it was still there. The toilet wouldn't flush at all. I was thinking that if I didn't fall victim to cholera, I'd probably still end up with typhus or hepatitis from the hotel's unsanitary conditions. As I needed to redress my wound, I did find a tube of Neosporin and a large bandage in the first aid kit I had shoved in the knapsack. The bandage was the last one. I hoped infection would not be setting in.

I placed my dirty undershorts and socks in the sink, allowing them to soak for a few minutes after which I laid them out to dry on a chair. Considering there was no air conditioning, I was fairly sure they'd dry in an hour. From the canvas bag, I pulled out fresh pairs. I also found a small tube of toothpaste in my knapsack with a new toothbrush. I must have brushed for five minutes to get the two day old bad taste out of my mouth.

The bed sheets looked as though they had not been changed in weeks. I wondered how many stinking bodies had laid between them. I was afraid to check to see if there were yellow stains. After a while, I just said what the hell and plopped down on the bed atop the spread. My head was still aching and ears ringing. Thank God sleep came over me within minutes.

It was the sunlight through the window that woke me. Just as it was still daylight at nine-thirty in the summer evenings, mornings came early in Yemen. My watch said it was 6:35. I wondered if it was 6:35 from last evening since it had gone through the same shock as my body when the bomb was detonated. I then checked it again in about five minutes seeing that it was now 6:41. I was glad I had chosen to wear my thirty dollar Timex on the trip to Scotland. My high dollar Citizen that Adriana had bought me would probably not have survived. But just like my body, the Timex obviously had taken a licking and kept on ticking. John Cameron Swayze would be impressed.

My headache was a little better and I think I had 80% of my hearing back. The cuts on my face from the flying debris were superficial and would heal in a couple of days. The wound on my thigh I was not so sure about.

Grabbing up the canvas bag, I went to the hotel lobby where I found some bottled water for sale. I didn't know what they cost, but since the tap water in Yemen was probably cholera producing, the cost had to be at a premium. As I didn't see Hassan, who could shell out some rials for a bottle or two, I waited until someone else began checking out at the desk. When the clerk who had previously had his eyes on the White dude eyeing the water diverted his attention to the other guest, I swiped three bottles, shoved them in my knapsack and hustled my ass out the front door.

I found Hassan outside sitting on some rocks in the hotel's version of a botanical garden that contained three cacti, some spurges and a lovely growth of weeds. He had somewhere found a clean bandage for his forehead and appeared much refreshed.

"I didn't know if you would be sleeping all day," he jested with a chuckle. "Did you find your room satisfactory?"

I didn't want to begin the day bitching and moaning, so I merely replied, "I slept. How about you?"

"Fine, but my room I found very dirty as well as my sheets. I also found many bugs. The toilet did not work either."

I stifled a smile. "Mine was much the same, but I was out cold in a matter of minutes."

"And so, McGowan, what do we do from here? You were to be the 'man with the plan' as you Americans say."

"I haven't had much opportunity to think about it. I'm still smarting from that terrorist attack. You've been up for a while; did you hear anyone talking about it?" "I watched the television in the lobby this morning for a few minutes. It was not ISIS or al-Qaeda as you suggested last night. The dissidents loyal to Abdul-Malik al-Houthi and the rebels took credit for the bombings and the dispatched gunmen that shot many people all over the city. These outbreaks are common, the news said. It is amazing that they can happen so frequently and within a day, the people move about the streets as though nothing will happen again."

"Well, in answer to your question, Hassan, I think we should get some transportation to Ta'izz and look up this so-called Al-Akhdam tribe in the outlying areas of the city. Aziz told the story of the boy named Sameer. If his experience occurred in late 2002, he would be a young man now. Unfortunately, as Aziz was killed last night, we only have what he told us to go on. Have you been contacted by his other friends, the would-be transporters? Maybe they know more."

"I have not received any calls and have no way to get to them."

"Then we'll have to do the leg work on our own. Have you checked us out of the hotel?"

"It has been done. I also purchased some bottled water and honeycomb rolls for our breakfast." He took from a plastic sack one of the rolls and handed it to me.

"Thanks." I was about to add 'you're a good man' but I knew he wasn't. He might have had a good heart in some ways, but he was still a terrorist prick.

I swallowed several gulps of the water to hydrate before we set out, then tried to read the label on the bottle. It was in Arabic. "What does this say on the label?" I gave the bottle to Hassan.

"It says Spring Water."

"What else?"

"From the municipal water facility of Sana'a."

"Oh, hell," I said.

"I do not believe we will get sick from it."

"Keep on thinking that, Hassan. Hopefully, we won't end up in some Yemeni medical facility."

"I think we can get a bus from here to Ta'izz. It should only be a few rials for the both of us."

"As we were walking here last night, I saw a bus stop, maybe four or five blocks away."

"Then we will go."

We finished our buns and I took the last swig of the water he gave me, hoping that dysentery didn't overtake me halfway to Ta'izz. We then walked about a quarter mile back toward the city and waited for the bus. In reading the schedule on the sign, Hassan told me the bus to Ta'izz would stop there in the next 45 minutes. The sun was by this time beating down on us and the air temperature seemed to already be in the 90s. From what I had read, the temp that time of year could reach the 110s. But as I was told one time by a friend who lived in Phoenix, "it's dry heat, Bruce," I reminded him so was oven heat. It's still heat!

I was just getting ready to break out another bottle, one of my stolen ones, when the bus came. Hassan handed the rials to the driver and we found the last two seats on the bus. He took the seat beside the Arabian princess with the pretty eyes in the colorful head scarf. I was compelled to sit beside an old man with a sun-baked face full of wrinkles and no teeth. His breath laced with curry and cigarettes could melt the chrome off a trailer hitch and he otherwise smelled to high heaven of B.O. And oh, did I mention he was holding in his lap a crate containing three chickens. The hour long bus ride to Ta'izz might have just been the longest year of my life.

CHAPTER 9

The ride did give me an opportunity to recall the conversation I had the day before with Keith Lambreau. Gnawing at my brain was the bomb he dropped on me of Chalmers's email communication with Congressman Jack Randall who had ordered my former teammate Chuck Robinson to murder Lionel Byrd and others on Team Zulu. In both Randall's and Robinson's heads, by the way, I had happily placed bullets. Now in thinking back, believing all along the team murders were at Randall's direction, could it be it was Chalmers who had ordered the hits? If he was scheming to somehow intercept the WMDs and remove from the cache of mass murder weapons the nuclear device, and Lionel found out about it, maybe that was the motive for my friend's slaying. And that was a matter that I would soon on my own be investigating. If I found it true, Chalmers was going to die a horrible death.

I also sat pondering what fate my cousins back in Scotland were facing. Would Chalmers kill them anyway? I was pretty damn sure he would. For the time being, however, they were pawns. In the remote possibility we were able to uncover the location of the alleged WMDs and arrange to place them in Chalmers's hands, he would then have no reason to kill them. It didn't matter they had seen his face. He said he would disappear. But, I had seen his face as well. And I am very good at finding people. Of course at any time, whether the WMDs were found or not, I could go down with a bullet in the back of my head at the hands of Hassan or any of his cohorts. In the end, I figured it was in Chalmers's plan that we'd all die.

But the lives of my cousins were not the only reasons I wanted to locate the weapons. The idea alone of finding them intrigued me. The weapons had been the subject of years of controversy. Did they exist or didn't they? If I was able to prove they did, I, Bruce McGowan, would be providing the world with the answer. I'd be contributing to history. The only thing was, the world might never find out Saddam had them in the first place if I and my cousins were dead and buried. But, by God, I was not going to allow that to happen. And neither was Chalmers ever going to get his hands on the WMDs. I'd sure as hell see to that.

We exited the bus at the first stop just north of Ta'izz. After walking a block to where we spotted a diner, we went inside for something cold to drink. I had a bottled Coke, which I thought was a safe drink, depending of course **where** it was bottled, and Hassan a lemonade. As it was 10:45 and too early to eat, we were satisfied with only the drinks. The server seemed annoyed we were taking up restaurant space without ordering food. But then Hassan dropped on the man 50,000 yers of rial equivalent to a couple of U.S. dollars and the server lightened up. However, Hassan held on to the yers until the man gave him some information in exchange. Communicating in Arabic, Hassan said he asked the man how to get to where the Al-Akhdam camps were. During their dialogue, I could see the server was becoming a little agitated and I thought that might be because Hassan still had hold of the money. And so did the man receiving it. Finally, Hassan let go. The server then laughed and walked away.

"What was that about?"

"He asked why I would trouble myself going to talk with such a people as Akhdams. They were dirty and disgusting. As most are ditch diggers and latrine cleaners they are not allowed in this establishment when they do come to Ta'izz. He said we should be prepared to pick up some kind of disease if we go to one of their villages."

"Lovely," I said. "But we have to find this young man. It's going to be our only prospect of locating these weapons, although I don't have much hope about it."

"The waiter told me there is a taxi service not far from here that is operated by a Khadem (meaning a singular Akhdam person) that goes into the villages. He said to go and enjoy ourselves and then he laughed."

We finished our drinks and walked the hundred meters to the where several taxi owners were awaiting customers at the curb in front of a hotel. Hassan asked one of the drivers if there was an Akhdam taxi that would take us to one of the encampments. The man pointed to a white Corolla, vintage 1980s. I took it that the Akhdam driver only transported his own people to and from Ta'izz and we may have been his only fare the entire day.

Sporting a nearly toothless grin, the driver dressed in a turban and light-colored clothing opened both rear doors for us. Before we left, Hassan negotiated the fare with the man and agreed on a sum that was comfortable for both. The cab smelled of alcohol which I figured was some kind of village moonshine, and although the consumption of alcohol is forbidden in Yemen as well as most other Muslim countries, the authorities couldn't care less about what the Akhdam's drank, they being at the very bottom of the Yemeni social strata. Moreover, the police probably didn't want them stinking up their jails.

And so we were on our way into the roasting, mountainous desert to visit the people
Yemeni society refers to as 'the untouchables.'

The beat-up old Toyota coughed and farted much as our plane did, but this time we were in no danger of falling out of the sky. However, as we drove over some treacherous dirt roads chocked full of pot holes and uneven terrain, the jarring of my already traumatized brain from the previous day's blast was making me feel like I was suffering from a concussion. The taxi as I expected had no air conditioning and the interior of the car felt like an oven. I know…bitch, bitch, bitch. I was a man having had numerous hardship tours behind me, so what's a little misery in the desert land of a sweltering, war-torn, disease-ridden country where I could be decapitated and served up to savages on a rotating spit over a fire. Wait a minute. Maybe with that last thing I was thinking about the Congo. Either I had seen too many Humphrey Bogart movies or my wounded brain was apparently still not operating on all cylinders.

Hassan had told our cabbie, whose name was Farhan, we wanted to go to the first Akhdam village we came to. As Aziz had told us the village was on the road to Ta'izz, it seemed more probable that it would be where the boy had lived. But things change in a dozen years. The boy was now a young man and likely no longer lived in the same village. He may have relocated to one of Yemen's cities or could even have been accepted at Yale and was in New Haven, Connecticut.

Our trek took about fifty minutes. Had we been traveling on a real highway, it would have taken twenty. The village called Mazut consisted of about twenty huts made of flimsy wood, cloth and thatch. Again, I was reminded of Montagnard villages in the mountains of Southeast Asia where I lived for a year many moons ago. One might also equate them to the American Indians and the way they lived in the Nineteenth Century western U.S. When we pulled in, dark-skinned children came running up to the taxi and our driver glad-handed them through the door's open window. Maybe they were thinking he had candy for them or seeing us in the back seat, we were wealthy strangers bearing trinkets. Yet again, he could be their daddy as it appeared the fertility rate was off the charts. I saw several women standing outside their hooches with four or five children, a couple of the women pregnant again.

 Farhan then got out and began talking with one of the village elders who nodded and went into a larger hooch I thought might be the community center. The cabbie then grinned and told Hassan something. Hassan in turn relayed that the man went to get the Khadem named Sameer. A minute later the old man walked from the building with another man that I told Hassan immediately was not the person we were looking for. When the man got closer, he agreed. This Sameer was between fifty and sixty years old. I knew people tended to age rapidly in the blistering desert sun, but this was no early twenties man.

Hassan took the liberty of conversing with the man anyway, just in case the information we had was wrong. Maybe Sameer was not a boy after all when he took a peek inside the broken down truck hauling the sensitive cargo. After they talked a while, Hassan shook the man's hand and came back to the car. "I was not able to fully understand him as some of these Akhdams who still speak Arabic have different dialects. It varies from village to village. A few who came from the Zaidi Imamate regime even speak different languages. But, I was able to determine that as we suspected, this is not our Sameer. This man knew nothing about trucks carrying weapons years ago. This Sameer migrated to this village only three years ago anyway. Yes, he is not the man we are seeking."

"Okay, just tell Farhan to go to the next village. We'll check there."

As we pulled away from Mazut, the children who had greeted us ran alongside the car again, smiling and waving us off. I felt sorry for the lot of them. Hassan said some of them would not live to their teenage years as they would die of cholera, malaria and dyspnoea, the latter, which I remember from my Anatomy 101, is a breathing disorder much like asthma or poor oxygen circulation. I was suddenly feeling less conscious of my own woes.

Only two miles away, this time further into the more mountainous region, we came upon the smaller village of Khomen, so named after one of their tribal chieftains, our driver told Hassan.

"How many more of these villages are ahead of us in this region?" I asked.

Hassan in turn asked the cabbie. Farhan held up four fingers. I guess math is the same all over the world and in any language where it comes to fingers. So, there were four more. Each of these villages apparently had a common meeting house where the men sat down to smoke and tell stories of ancient lore, pretty much the same as our old men meeting for breakfast at Hardees for a biscuit and coffee, telling lies of their war experiences or about the eight pound bass caught last Saturday which he threw back in. The aforementioned Montagnards had such a place they called their Happy House.

When we pulled up to Khomen, there were no children greeting us. Farhan told Hassan that sometimes the children age 5 and up went to the fields to work with their fathers and that's where they could be today. This was a village where there were more sheep and goat herders than vegetable farmers working the fields, as opposed to Mazut where the soil was much richer. However, Farhan said it was not a very friendly village and it was possible the people went inside when they saw the vehicle approaching. The people were not good with strangers.

As we saw no one moving about the village, Hassan decided he should go inside to find someone. As soon as he put his foot on the steps to the central meeting house, a man in a thick, black beard wearing a long tunic thobe over his pants appeared at the door. I couldn't hear their conversation, but the man was quite animated. Hassan held out his hands while talking indicating he was appealing to the man for information. But then the man shoved Hassan and began pointing his finger in his face.

Knowing this did not set well with Hassan, I almost expected him to pull out his pistol. However, when I reached over our driver's shoulder and beeped the horn three times, Hassan turned and began walking back toward the car.

When Hassan slid into the back seat with a huff, he said, "I should have killed the man. No one pushes me and insults me." He then told the same thing to our driver in Arabic. I took it that the villager felt not only denigrated but abashed when an educated Middle Eastern man who would normally not give him the time of day appeared at the door asking for information.

"I assumed you asked him if there was a young man named Sameer in the village."

"Yes, I did, but he did not tell me that right away. But then the last thing he said was
"there is no Sameer here" and then he cursed me for being on village property."

"He must not have had his prune juice today," I quipped.

"We have to get out of here or I will go back there and make that goat humper wish he had never been born."

He then touched Farhan on the shoulder and gestured for him to go.

I had to laugh at Hassan's retort although it was obvious from his glare at me he didn't appreciate it. I was seeing the worst of his temper and convinced that if I weren't around and we were not on this quest, he probably would have gone back to shoot the man.

He was still fuming as we moved away from the village. "I may come back for him tonight and burn down his house."

And so I saw his vindictive side as well.

Via Hassan's translation, I asked Farhan if he lived in any of these villages in the mountains. He said he actually lived in Ta'izz in a one room apartment so that he could more easily operate his taxi business. He was not married, but he'd like to be one day. He lamented that he was not treated well by the people in Ta'izz. They had spit on him and threatened to run him out of the city. The couple who was renting him the apartment, however, were the only people who had befriended him. He only made enough from his business to pay his rent, buy a few groceries and put gas in his car. Few people want a Khadem for a taxi driver.

CHAPTER 10

We moved on to the third village which sent us through a pass and back down into the wide valley. We were quickly running out of villages and both of us out of patience. If we were not successful in locating the WMDs in now just over ten days, I wondered if Hassan had his orders to go ahead and kill me. Whether or not that was the case, I would be vigilant. We had actually gotten to the point where we were talking civilly to one another and I suppose that was my inherent weakness. Maybe I was being too nice. However, I was not going to forget that he had separated my cousin's head from his body and had committed other atrocities as well. He was a freaking terrorist for God's sake.

The village in the valley was called Jatoi. The swarming children were back. A different group, that is. Some of them looking malnourished and sickly with swollen bellies. As they ran along the side of the car touching the fenders and doors, both Hassan and I reached out our hands to them. I wasn't afraid of touching their hands; I just had to remember later not to stick my fingers in my mouth.

Two men inside the village who stood talking turned their heads toward us when they heard the engine of the approaching car. Farhan came to a stop and I thought I saw Hassan stall just a moment, maybe wondering when he ventured into the village, was he going to get pushed around again. But, Farhan had apparently told him it was a village of good people, because Hassan quickly exited and began making his way toward the tribesmen. He shook hands with them and began what appeared to be a friendly dialogue. A couple minutes later, he signaled for me to join them.

When I got within a few feet, they bowed. I bowed back and then shook their hands. I turned to Hassan and asked, "What's going on? Have you learned anything?"

"They said there is a young man here in the village named Sameer. He has lived here all his life."

It was the first real glint of hope we had felt since we left Scotland. "Ask him if he is here," I said.

Hassan did and the man shook his head. He told Hassan that Sameer had gone to Ta'izz to get a part for the tribal chieftain's truck. "He says he is a very good mechanic. Sameer is supposed to return in maybe two hours. We are welcome to join him and others in what they call 'the Big

House.' That is the building there." He pointed to a wooden structure with a thatched roof. "He says it was built by Sameer and his friends two years ago."

"Sameer sounds like he's much appreciated here in the village," I commented.

"It would seem so. We will go inside now. I think both of us will need a break."

"How about Farhan?"

"He is welcome, too. I will give him a few more rials to stay."

As we strolled along toward the Big House, a small dog trailed along beside us barking. One of the children then ran to where we were and snatched him up. He grinned and said something which of course I didn't understand. Hassan told me he was apologizing for the dog. I smiled back at the boy and nodded. The dog reminded me of a mutt I had when I was about thirteen. I had to get rid of it because his favorite bone was in my leg.

The inside of the Big House was one large open space with a score of wooden chairs placed in town hall fashion where I imagined their community meetings were conducted. However, much of the floor was left bare-bones where salat was conducted. I saw several prayer rugs rolled up and stacked in one corner of the building.

One of the village elders set down a bucket of water containing a ladle and offered for us to share the water with them. Hassan and I glanced at one another quickly after which he told the man we had water with us and didn't want to take theirs. Water was a precious commodity to the Khadems as well as to the entire country of Yemen. Unfortunately, it was also the primary source of the cholera epidemic. "Thank you anyway," Hassan said with a head gesture and smile. The man smiled and nodded in return. It brought to mind the quote by Mother Teresa that "Peace begins with a smile." I felt as welcome there as I have at any place I'd visited. To the Khadems, it didn't matter if I was White, an American rich man and an infidel. Both Hassan and I took water bottles from our sacks, popped off the caps and began sipping it at the same time the two elders passed the ladle back and forth between them.

In casual conversation, the elders told Hassan that their village had more recently suffered its share of illness. There was at least one sick child in every house. Several had died, most of whom had not lived to the age of five. One out of two newborns did not last but hours and days.

Physicians would not come to the Khadem villages as they themselves did not want to risk getting some contagious disease especially from people of the lower caste. It was just something the people had to live with…and die with. As I sat listening to Hassan interpret what they were telling him, I had again one of those deja vu moments thinking about the Montagnards who had their share of health issues. I chose not to drink the rice wine they passed around in their Happy Houses since every other person sitting on their haunches had either tuberculosis or diphtheria. It was all very sad to me that in this modern, advanced world, there was still such rampant poverty and disease.

We were offered food as well…some legumes, roasted meat and flatbread, but Hassan lied that we had just eaten, thanking them just the same. In reality, we hadn't put a thing in our mouths, except our bottled water, since the breakfast buns. I hated to refuse their kindness, but I was pretty fond of this body of mine and didn't want it to end up ravaged with some kind of disease. However, the elders didn't appear to be offended. The very fact that we had come into their village center at all to spend some time pleased them.

At just after four, more people including women and children began coming into the building and grabbing up prayer rugs. Hassan told me "it is the time for the al-'asr salat" and he would like to join them. I was also offered by the chieftain to participate, but Hassan told him I had a different religion. Before the prayer time began, I left the building and returned to the taxi which sat baking in the afternoon sun. In hearing the prayer leader's voice, it brought to mind another very long day when I laid on a damp Virginia hillside watching and listening to all five salats prayed by a terrorist faction which was planning another 9-11 type attack on America. It was that same night that I set the charge in their munitions bunker that blew them and their camp to Kingdom Come. Those were the bad Muslims…these were the good.

At the moment salat was over and the villagers began leaving the building, another vehicle entered the village. The chieftain told Hassan it was Sameer, the young man for whom we had been looking.

He was a nice-looking kid in his mid-twenties with big, bold, black eyes, clean-cut and dressed in western casual wear. In his hands he toted what looked like a water pump which he handed off to his leader. The chieftain placed his hand on Sameer's shoulder in thanks and both walked in the direction of a well used-up Nissan truck, one of only four vehicles in the entire village. When the two of them had a bit of dialogue about the truck, Sameer came back to where we were standing.

I was surprised that he actually spoke some broken English. "Hello," he said. "I am Sameer. I know you have look for me."

"That's correct, Sameer," I said. "If you're more comfortable with Mr. Hassan here speaking with you in Arabic, I'm okay with that."

"No, it is fine. I need practice to talk English. Please to sit down." There was a bench outside the Big House and he slid onto one side. Hassan and I took the other.

"Sameer, it is a pleasure to meet you and we thank you for talking with us." I would try to keep my dialogue with him simple and understandable. Hassan would jump in to explain some things Sameer didn't understand in Arabic.

"I have not meet you before and I ask what I can do with you…excuse please, for you."

"We had talked with a man who heard about you. The story is that when you were a small boy, you saw a truck broken down on a road that was with three other trucks.

When the people in those trucks were not looking, you climbed up inside one of them and saw large crates with this symbol or picture on it." I then drew a picture of the nuclear symbol in the sand with a stick. "You may have seen other things like bombs and very large bullets." I showed him an image of some missile rounds. "Was that boy you?"

Sameer shuffled his body on the seat and looked at both of us with his large black eyes. "Am I in trouble?"

"No, no. Nothing like that. We just wanted to know if it was you who was there."

"I will not be put in jail?"

"Again, no. We are looking for what was inside those trucks."

"Yes. I was that boy. I was ten years then."

I looked at Hassan. He nodded and smiled.

"Now, Sameer. We would like your help. Did you see where the trucks went?"

"The men fix the truck. Added water to the radiator. I was hiding with the rocks when they left. They went into mountains…those mountains there. They are called the Jabal Kanin mountains and are maybe 15 miles from Sana'a."

"How far from here?"

"Maybe 10 miles."

"How did you know they went to those mountains?"

"I follow them. I had bike."

"Why did you follow them?" Hassan asked.

"I am…I do not know the word. I **want** to."

"You were curious?" I suggested.

"What is curious?"

"It means interested."

"I know that word. Yes, curious."

"Did you see where they stopped?" Hassan asked.

 "Yes. They took the trucks to a big cave. They met other men."

I clinched my fist and shook it. "Yes!" I said in a whisper. Hassan looked at me and nodded.

"Do you think you could find that cave again?" I asked.

"It was very long time ago. Maybe I could. It is not far from Nu'en, a village at the end of our road."

"Good. Maybe when you see the area again, you'll remember."

"I think yes I will."

"You speak English better than you said you could, Sameer. Where did you learn it?"

"There was an English man in Ta'izz who own garage. He teach me English when he teach me to work on cars. I work for him for four years. I learn much. He help me fix up the truck you see and then I buy from him for small amount.""

"Good for you. Not every young man like you may get such an opportunity."

He nodded and smiled.

As it was getting late in the day, I said, "Could you take us to look for the cave tomorrow? We may need to take your car and will pay you well."

Hassan added, "I will pay you many rials." He wrote a number down on a piece of paper.

Sameer's eyes enlarged. "I will do that. It is more than I can earn in one year."

"How much is that?" I asked. "With all of the digits it looks like twenty million bucks."

"It is about $500 American dollars."

I was glad he would be given the financial opportunity whether we found the WMDs or not. He seemed like a nice young man and good for the village.

Sameer said, "If we leave for the mountains tomorrow, are you good to staying here with us tonight? You can sleep in the Big House. We give you pads to sleep on."

"I'm good with it," I said. "How about you, Hassan."

In almost a whisper so that Sameer and the chieftain couldn't hear, he replied,"Yes, but I am wondering about our food. We should not eat their food for reasons we discussed."

I nodded in agreement. I'd been pretty nervous about eating the food and drinking the water even in the larger cities. Now that we were in a Khadem village where the health conditions were even worse, I was not anxious to eat anything they might send my stomach into convulsions…or put me in the grave. Everything is edible; some things are edible only once.

I grinned. "Got any more of those cinnamon buns?"

"They will not sustain us for the time we are in the mountains and we may be there several days."

He was right of course. It was something that had been on my mind ever since we left the hotel. Was I going to have to break down and eat their chow? All I had in my canvas bag were three of the protein bars that I took from the fridge on the plane.

But it was Sameer who answered Hassan's concerns…and mine. "I will see that you are eating. Some food we make here I want you not eat. The pork is not so good and we make soup over fire that you are not to liking. I try to stay with good health and when I go into Ta'izz, I get cans of the Dinty Moore. It is from your country and very good. I also buy fruit and the good bread in the city. I will have much for you to take. In my house is good water in bottles. We have many people who get sick on food that is made here and the water from river which is almost dry. It is with much mud and the animals make shit in it. The food sometimes is rotting. I try to keep our people to not be sick when I bring good food from the city. The people pay me to get the good food with money they make from jobs in Ta'izz. Many of our people work there doing cleaning."

"Thank you, Sameer," I said. "I'm sure you'll be the village leader here one day."

He laughed. "I think my wife will not like that. We have talk that we sometime move to Sana'a and I will get good job there. Maybe work on cars."

Yeah, Sameer had a good head on his shoulders and I hoped would have a good life ahead of him.

CHAPTER 11

Just after eight, as Sameer and the two of us sat talking about what would occur the next day, Hassan's phone rang. I would have thought there was no cell coverage in the village, but apparently as we were halfway between Ta'izz and Sana'a, a cell tower must have been erected somewhere close by.

When he answered the call, I heard Hassan say the name Sanush. If my memory served me correctly, Aziz had told us his friend Sanush and two others were to meet us in al-Hudaydah last evening; however, as bombs had been detonated and an immense number of people ended up dead in the Houthi rebel attack, the rendezvous hadn't come off. They talked for about three minutes and then Hassan's phone was out of juice. Hassan told me that before the phone died, he had made arrangements to meet his terrorists buddies in the town of Nu'en. Sameer said we'd be going through there on the way to the Jabal Kanin caves. They would be waiting in a GMC white cargo van for as long as it took us to get to the town. Hassan told him we would be in a silver four-door Nissan truck and a young Khadem male would be driving.

And so it was all set. We'd leave at first light. Sameer said it would take us an hour over the rough terrain to get to Nu'en.

At six-thirty that next morning we heard Sameer's truck start up and a couple of minutes later he was outside of the Big House. Hassan and I rolled up the prayer blankets we had been sleeping on and I stepped outside to tap the kidneys. I asked Sameer to give me a couple more minutes while I brushed my teeth. Using a small amount of water from the bottle I drank from the night before, I got the job done. Thank God I had answered the call of nature at an outdoor latrine in the village before I sacked out for the night, so I didn't have to go that morning. I hadn't eaten enough the past couple of days for it to be a major job, anyway. The one thing I did miss was my hand sanitizer, but having found the small bottle of peroxide in the first aid kit, my hands were now sterile. I'm really not OCD or a sanitary freak; I just don't want to die from typhus or some other medieval infectious disease.

Sameer had loaded into the bed of his truck a case of the Dinty Moore along with some canned fruit, two loaves of appetizing-looking bread and a wheel of cheddar from one of the Ta'izz markets. And then we found that he had killed a chicken in the early morning hours, plucked it, roasted it and placed it in a covered plastic bowl. Since he himself had done this, I knew it was safe to eat. I also saw he had placed in the truck's bed a case of the all important bottled water. It looked to be enough food and drink for the three of us for three to four days. He had taken care of us. We were on our way. Now, what would we find?

On the trip along the pitted and jagged roadway, there were certainly enough bumps to jar my eye teeth. And my kidneys felt like they were taking shots from Mike Tyson. Hassan rode shotgun alongside Sameer as I jostled around in the back seat. At the point the road smoothed out a little, Sameer began posing questions.

"What was it I see in the back of that truck many years ago?"

"They would have been the kind of weapons that will do much damage, Sameer," I replied. "They were what is called chemical and even nuclear weapons. Are you familiar with those words?"

"Yes. They are very bad weapons. When they explode, many people die. With the chemical, people have sores and lose their stomachs. Then they die later."

"Exactly. With the nuclear, not only does the bomb cover miles and miles, but there is something called radiation that causes those who were not immediately killed by the blast to die later within days."

"I cannot think of such a thing, Mr. McGowan. Why would people make other people die like that?"

"It's called man's inhumanity to man, Sameer."

"I do not know the word 'inhumanity.'"

"It means someone does horrible things to have power over others, sometimes without reason at all. Hate is everywhere. You know that as well as anyone, Sameer. The people in Ta'izz and Sana'a might treat you badly because you don't look like them or you live in poverty. Sometimes people even hate people because they don't have the same religion." Hassan turned and looked at me. His eyes were icy. The statement wasn't necessarily meant for him. Well, maybe it was. He then dropped his eyes and turned back around.

"What will you do with the weapons if you find them?"

Hassan said "We will take them away and dispose of them."

"Dispose?"

"Destroy them," he replied.

That was a good enough answer, I thought, although a lie. The question I was asking myself was, could I do anything to stop Chalmers from getting his hands on the nuclear weapon? I had to find a way to make that happen, yet at the same time keep him from killing the McGowan ladies. Standing in the way, however, would be Hassan and his friends. It was a dilemma that would unfold as things happened. That being the case, I would play the stall game as long as I could. But hell, we probably wouldn't even **find** the WMDs…if in fact they existed.

Nu'en was another Khadem village, only its houses and buildings made of block and hardwood were more permanent in stature. There was also an open air market or souq that sold mostly fruits and vegetables. Men wearing ancient faces sat in chairs and on the ground hocking worthless trinkets, sun-bleached cloths and what they might call exotic soaps and lotions. In reality they were the small bottles that some entrepreneur-minded person had collected from motel bathrooms throughout the country. But, as nobody in the country used soap, I wondered how many would be sold.

We spotted the white cargo van with the extended body almost immediately parked off to the side of the souq. Hassan told Sameer to pull up beside it. At the same time Hassan exited our vehicle, three men in the van did the same. Dressed in common pull-over shirts and trousers, two of them wore skull caps while the third had on what was called a fly whisk turban. All had dark beards and piercing black eyes. If they didn't look like ISIS or al-Qaeda terrorists, I'll eat my shorts. Hassan talked with them for about five minutes and then returned to the truck. Each of the men looked in my direction, giving me a glowering stare for a few seconds, then stepped back into the van. I was not anxious to meet them once we stopped at our objective.

Sameer said it would be several more miles before we entered the Jabal Kanin range. The road on our climb was supposed to be even more treacherous than we had negotiated on our way to Nu'en. I couldn't wait and neither could my kidneys. The narrow trail going up had an incline of something over 12% and I was set to wonder how the four deuce-and-a-halves had made it. I was also sure that the boy child Sameer had to have walked his bike up the steep terrain. Looking out the rear window of our truck, I saw that the van was keeping up. It was short of amazing since the piece of junk was not a four wheel drive.

 Finally, the road leveled off somewhat and we began encountering less ruts. Before us loomed the Jabal Kanin. Sameer said the top of the mountain was over 5,000 feet, but we wouldn't be going to the top. After we had covered another half mile or so, he stopped and looked over the landscape.

"Is this it, Sameer?" I asked him.

"I am thinking. It has been a long time since I am here." He then got out and began walking off to our right. Hassan and I stepped out as well and followed him. The men in the cargo van stayed put. Sameer walked over to a large flat rock that overlooked the valley below. Then he turned his face back toward higher ground and pointed. "There. The cave is back there." He was pointing at a recessed series of rocks where we saw only a piece of the cave's opening.

Hassan waved to his cohorts and motioned for them to come. As they made their way to where we were, Sameer then led us further along the trail until the cavernous hole came into full view. "Yes. I am sure this is it."

I said, "They had to have had a guide to get them here; otherwise, who would have known the cave was here?"

"That is a good point, McGowan," Hassan said. "The men who transported the cargo here were Iraqis. I am also wondering how they turned the trucks around to get them back down the hillside."

I then looked around to see if I could answer his question. Something caught my eye off to my left about two hundred feet down the slope. "Only three trucks made it back down, Hassan. Look." Both Hassan and Sameer peered over the edge and saw the mangled truck at the bottom. It had come to rest against a tree after sliding off.

"Did you see this happen, Sameer?" I asked.

"I only saw them enter the cave. I did not see them carry what was in the trucks into the cave. One man see me and yelled out. I ran back down with my bike as fast as I could."

When Hassan's friends had finally reached us, he showed them the wrecked truck. As they spoke no English, they communicated in their native Arabic. He then dispatched one of them, named Bakhar, to shinny down the slope and look inside it. We waited patiently while he searched the cargo bay. A few minutes later he came back up and told Hassan the truck was empty, except for one thing…the bones of the driver who was killed when the truck tumbled down.

I'm not sure why, but for a few minutes we all stood at the mouth of the cave waiting to go in. What came to mind was a small child staring at his present at Christmas, holding off opening it to imagine what could be inside. But then Sameer led us in, allowing the beam of his flashlight to illuminate our pathway. The kid was resourceful, having remembered to put his 12 inch Maglite in the truck. Knowing we would be looking inside a cave for the WMDs, I hadn't even thought about it.

While we stood there, Hassan talked strategy with Sanush, Bakhar and the third man named Nadeem. But then he asked where were his manners and introduced them to me. "They are also from Sana'a and were friends of Aziz. They are all sad today."

I didn't react one way or another, instead saying, "Well, we're burning daylight. Let's do this."

We then entered the cave's opening. It was like stepping out of an oven into a cool cellar. There was very little headroom in the cave and we all had to stoop as we walked, watching out for low-hanging jagged rocks as we went. Unfortunately, we had only gone about 200 feet when we encountered a mass of rocks belonging to a cave-in. Our approach was completely blocked. The collapse was also not recent. "What do we do?" Sameer asked.

"We start pulling away rocks, piece by piece," I said.

"That will be dangerous and may take much time," rebutted Hassan.

"Do you want to leave it and go home?"

He shook his head. "No. You are right. We will try to remove them."

"This happened to my brother and me," I said. "Only we were inside an abandoned coal mine when it collapsed. It took us almost an entire day to dig until we made a hole to crawl through. Of course, a mine is a different kind of cave. I think we can safely remove these rocks if we do it carefully."

"Then let us begin. Since you are the expert, you direct us."

I thought about it for a few moments. I certainly was no expert, but knew we had to accomplish the feat using common sense. "Alright, we'll set up what we call a bucket brigade."

"What is that?" Hassan asked.

"Instead of all of us attacking this mess and taking away rocks, it'll be safer for us to form a chain of men. I take away a rock, hand it to you and you pass it on. There are six of us and after each hands off a rock, the last man lays it down and waits for the next."

"Some of the rocks are very large and may take more than one to handle," Hassan said.

"We'll get the smaller rocks out first and then tackle the larger ones. If we can't pick them up, I saw a rope in the bed of your truck, Sameer. We'll place the rope around it and carefully drag it away."

Sameer set his flashlight on the wide beam and placed it to where we could see the entire mass. I couldn't tell the width and depth of the cave-in, but if it was as deep as I suspected, it would take us at least the rest of the day.

And so we began.

I started as close to the top as I could. Even the smallest rock was the size of a basketball with the exception of a few crumbles here and there. Occasionally, in moving a rock, two more would tumble causing others to move as well. That's why I didn't want all six of us pulling rocks away at the same time. It was tedious work and after an hour, I couldn't much see that we had made an impact. I was hoping the batteries were good in the flashlight or that Sameer had more in his truck. The good thing was, we weren't performing manual labor in the heat of the sun.

We stopped just after one o'clock to eat something as we needed to sustain our strength. Sanush and his compadres had brought with them meals packaged in plastic bags similar to MREs which were sold in larger city markets. They had also brought water in containers that resembled the American thermos. Sameer and I shared a large can of beef stew with a ring on top that peeled back the lid. He even brought plastic spoons. I had a banana which provided potassium and a bottle of the water. Hassan also ate a banana and some of the chicken Sameer had roasted.

Our lunch having taken less than half an hour, we were back to work. We continued pulling off rocks well into the mid afternoon. The last man in the chain, Bakhar, had placed the rocks we had collected on both sides of cave in a line that stretched toward the opening more than 50 feet. By five o'clock, I had whittled the pile down to where there was a three foot opening from the top of the rocks to the ceiling of the cave, allowing me to see further inside. The depth of the pile was a dozen feet, less than I thought it would be. Another hour's worth of work and we should be able to crawl over the rocks and on into the cave.

We rested for about fifteen minutes around five forty-five and took in some water. I had a protein bar to replenish my strength and the others consumed the remainder of the fruit and some almonds. Sameer's Maglite was fading, so he went back to his truck for replacement batteries.

"Okay, I think we are at a point where we can get through. When you crawl over the remaining rocks, do so carefully or some might come loose and trap your legs or a foot."

I then took Sameer's light and began working my way over the rocks. When I was halfway over them, I felt something plop onto my neck. Whatever it was, it either bit or stung me. Quickly brushing it off, I shined the light onto a six inch long scorpion. I then picked up one of the smaller stones and smashed it. Maybe it was some kind of omen, considering the critter was my code name when I was with Team Zulu.

As I continued crawling, with Hassan directly behind me, I shined the light further back into the cave until the beam fell on something that caused me to shiver.

CHAPTER 12

I stopped before touching down on the other side of the rocks.

Hassan said, "McGowan, why did you stop? What do you see?"

I dropped to the floor of the cave and stood with the beam of light focused on the bones of several humans.

Hassan joined me and said, "Ibn al Kalb!! May Allah protect us!"

I counted at least ten sets of skeletons enshrouded by shirts, pants and thobes, their skulls still bedecked in caps and turbans.

The others following then stepped over the rocks and stood looking at the grisly scene in horror. Sameer quickly turned his face away and I thought he might be sick.

"What do you think, McGowan? Could these be the Iraqis who transported the weapons and they could not get out because of the cave-in?"

"If they are, what happened to the trucks?"

"Perhaps the Khadem people who live in these mountains took them."

Sameer said, "Maybe two years ago, I saw a truck that look like the ones I follow here. It was on the road to Ta'izz.

I began going through the skeletons' pants pockets to see if there was any identification. There was nothing. Just like I or any other covert operative would do, if I were on some type of clandestine mission, I wouldn't have any form of identification on me. And so, this was the reason the transporters didn't return to retrieve the WMDs; they never got out of the cave.

I then shined the light further back into the cave where it opened up wider and higher until it fell onto several crates stacked all the way to the cave's ceiling. Hassan then grabbed me by the shoulder. "As you Americans say…Bingo!"

The six of us walked further in toward the crates. I counted twenty-two. The first crate was as large as a Volkswagen and had Arabic scribbling on it. Hassan told me it said 'munitions.' I didn't have anything to break open the box, but Sameer stepped up with a knife that had an eight inch blade. I took it from him. After prying the lid in several places, I lifted it off. Warheads. Eight of them. On the warheads was the symbol for chemical weapons. Probably sulphur mustard and soman, nerve agents that inhibit a body's acetylcholinesterase. I didn't even want to get close to them. Fortunately, they had been stored in a cool place, but could any of them have been compromised? If anything was leaking, we might be dead in a matter of hours. I didn't even want to think about it.

In shining the light around the cave, I saw that all the crates had the same writing. All contained chemical warheads. But then behind those crates was another differentlooking crate, a long narrow wooden box with no lid. Hassan took the light and bent down to look at it. He said the symbol on the crate was of the Pakistan flag. But on each end was another symbol. The nuclear symbol. We had found it. The Silver Chalice. The Ark of the Covenant. Whatever you wanted to call it. It was the crate that contained the nuclear bomb. I had never seen one, only photos of one.

I then took the flashlight back from Hassan to inspect it myself. It looked like any number of devices I had seen in graphic documents and documentaries when I was in counterterrorism. About 10 feet in length with a nose and a tail fin, it would easily have filled up the cargo area of a deuce-and-a-half. Again, I didn't know much about nuclear weapons, but it would either have been a uranium-enriched or plutoniumbased device. Its delivery system was probably air-to-ground, fitted to either the French Dassault Mirage III or one of the F-16s which Pakistan had purchased a couple years back. More than likely an 8 to 10 kiloton weapon, it could also be set up on its own to detonate in some U.S. city by some terrorist organization. One very unfunny feature on the bomb was an arrow near the nose at the end of which was an American flag.

As I continued to inspect the device, Hassan and the three transporters began a conversation. At first it was a simple and orderly conversation, but as they continued their discussion, they became animated and the volume of their dialogue escalated. In a few moments an argument ensured.

Hassan then looked at me and shook his head. "McGowan, I must speak with Sanush and his men outside the cave. We will return soon."

"What's going on, Hassan?"

"It is about the movement of this bomb. We cannot agree."

The four of them then climbed back over the mass of rocks and headed toward the exit. Even though I didn't understand their conversation, I didn't have a good feeling about it. Thirty seconds after they had cleared the cave, I said to Sameer, "I don't like this. Come on with me."

After the two of us had negotiated the rocks and came within a few feet of the cave's opening to the outside, I placed my index finger over my lips and whispered to Sameer, "I want you to listen to what they are saying." He nodded.

The argument between Hassan and Sanush continued and then I saw Hassan put his finger into Sanush's chest. But to my horror, Sanush pulled from under his shirt a revolver and fired a single round into Hassan's stomach. In reflex and without hesitation, I bounded out of the cave with the .45 in hand and shot Sanush in the head. When the other two men began digging into their pants for their weapons, I placed two rounds each into their chests. I then heard Sameer scream out and watched him disappear back inside the cave. He probably thought he'd be next.

I hustled over to Hassan who lay bleeding and gasping for breath. "Hassan, what happened here? What was this about?"

"They…they said they would not…" He then winced in pain. "…agree to deliver the device to…Chalmers. They had…a contact in Iran and would sell it to …the Irani regime."

"Bastards," I said. I laid my pistol on the ground and checked his wound. I then ripped off his shirt and used it to compress the wound."I have to be honest, Hassan. It doesn't look good."
He smiled weakly. "And so I will die here." He coughed up blood. "You may think this is funny, McGowan, but I…I liked you. Chalmers is planning…to kill you anyway. He gave me an order to…to do it. But, I would not have…"

"Don't speak, Hassan. Save your strength. I have to get you off this mountain to a hospital somewhere."

"I will never make it. You know that. I want one last favor, McGowan."

"What, Hassan?"

"I do not know how long…until I die. Take your gun and end my life now."

I shook my head. "No. I won't do that."

"I am in much pain."

"I know, but it's not in me to do that."

"You must have mercy."

I took the pressure off his abdomen and blood gushed profusely. He would bleed to death in a matter of minutes, anyway. While I was watching the fountain of blood leaving his body, I hadn't seen him pick up the pistol I had laid beside him. Before I could grab it from his hand, he placed the muzzle against his temple and fired. The gun then fell from his hand and his breathing stopped. His open eyes stared at me in death. I closed them.

Four men now lay dead at the mouth of the cave. I returned inside and called for Sameer. I knew he was in a state of shock. And although I knew he had likely seen other human beings die from diseases, he had never seen violent deaths.

He answered me weakly. "Please do not kill me too, Mr. McGowan. I have a wife and…"

"I'm not going to kill you, Sameer. Those were very bad men who shot Hassan. I had to end their lives or they would kill you **and** me."

Cautiously he came out from the shadows looking like a scared puppy. I placed the .45 in my belt and put my arm around his shoulder. "I know this was hard for you to see and am sorry you did."

"What do we do now?" he asked.

And that, I didn't have a clue.

I pulled the four bodies off to the side of the cave and down the hill a piece into the shade so that Sameer wouldn't have to look at them. We then sat on a large rock drinking our water for several minutes. I had a lot of thinking to do. However, suddenly I began feeling faint and felt like throwing up. I also noticed some slight tremors in my right hand. I was thinking the worst. Radiation sickness from the nuclear device or exposure from the leaking of one or more of the chemical weapons.

"Sameer, do you feel alright?"

"I feel fine, yes. I am over it…over seeing the people die, I think."

"You don't feel a little sick in your stomach?"

"No, I did when I saw the bodies, but I am okay now."

I was also feeling like I had a fever. Then I thought about the cholera epidemic. Does one get sick with it in two or three days? Whatever was going on was almost putting me in a state of panic. Maybe there'd be another body for Sameer to get down the mountain.

However, I decided to bear with it and think of what needed to happen next. For one thing, we had to get the bodies and Sanush's cargo van out of the area. If some nomad or a Bedouin tribe found them, they might go into the cave and find the WMDs. If they tinkered around with either the nuclear device or one of the chemical weapons, not realizing what they were, the entire mountain could go up. At the very least, one of the chemical weapons could detonate, causing the deaths of the entire tribe. "Sameer, what we will do is place the bodies of the dead in the van and take them down in the direction of Nu'en. Somewhere in the desert, we will bury them. As you know under Islamic law, a person must be buried within one day after the death. We need to do this before dark. It is now six-twenty."

"I am ready to leave this place now, so I am good with going," he replied.

I was compelled to load each body into the van by myself, because Sameer said he didn't want to handle someone dead. Well hell, neither did I. However, he would help dig the graves at the place where we chose to bury them. Here I was handling dead bodies when only days before, I was telling my brother I didn't like being around them. I'm sure if Joey knew what I was doing, he'd be laughing his ass off.

With some effort, I got the van turned around and started back down the mountain road. Sameer followed in his pickup. After we had reached bottom, I saw a spot where the soil was sandier and the rocks few. I checked around us to assure there were no Khadems or roving Bedouin caravans and told Sameer that was where we would dig four graves. Unfortunately, we couldn't dig them at the same time because Sameer only had one shovel in his bed. I dug the first, he dug the second and so on. We probably only dug down about five feet deep versus seven since both of us were physically exhausted. I hoped a coyote or a grey wolf wouldn't come sniffing around and dig them up. Sameer only had one blanket to wrap one body, so I told him it would be Hassan's.

I then said a few Christian words over the graves, words that Sameer had never heard. Nonetheless, he thought the words were beautiful. He followed with a chant from the Quran. Although we had combined to give the dead a proper sendoff, both of us had different ideas as to where their souls would be going. He told me on the way back to his village, however, with a wink and a smile, he didn't think any one of them deserved to have the 72 virgins awaiting their arrival.

CHAPTER 13

I returned to Sameer's village for the night and he put me back up in the Big House. Before I turned in, he brought his wife for me to meet. Her name was Alishba, which in their language meant beautiful. And she was. She had cooked a stew and I knew that if it was from her, it would be fine to eat. She did not speak English, but she told me a lot with her beautiful eyes. Before they left to go home, I gave him the money Hassan had promised him, money that I took from Hassan's wallet. I had buried the wallet with him. I kept his cell phone and what was left of his dough after paying Sameer his $500, something over 21 million rials. I'd have the equivalent of about $450 American dollars to get a hotel, some new clothes and real food.

"I will be leaving early tomorrow in the van," I told him. "If I don't see you, I want you to know that you are one of the finest young men I have ever met. And I wish you all the blessings of life."

"Thank you. Mr. McGowan. Where will you go?"

"To Sana'a where the American Embassy is. They will help me get out of Yemen."

Both he and his wife then smiled and nodded. We shook hands and they walked away.

I was still feeling nauseous and dizzy at times. The labor of digging two graves had caused me to feel even worse. But when I put Alishba's stew in my belly and drank a bottle of water, I began to feel a little better. The good thing was, I no longer had the hand tremor nor was my stomach now balling up in cramps.

I didn't go to sleep right away. I thought about Hassan and how we had slowly begun to tolerate one another, even though he was a terrorist prick and I was a freaking infidel. And then it came to me that I didn't even know his full name or what country he was from. Did he have a family…a wife, kids? Someone had to be waiting for him to come home. The sad part was, they would never know what happened to him. Unfortunately, his body would soon be feeding the desert worms.

When dawn came, I was off. Sameer told me the night before that when I reached Nu'en again, I would take the N1 road and follow it all the way into the city. "It is very beautiful driving," he said.

Well, here I was in a vehicle that should I be stopped by the police, I couldn't prove where I got it or who owned it. If it was registered like we register our vehicles, they would find it belonged to a Sana'a resident named Sanush. And I really couldn't tell them how I got it, that I had killed Sanush the day before, then stole his van. My biggest concern was that if I did get stopped, there was a mess of human blood on the cargo floor. But at least they'd not find a nuclear bomb.

I guess it was about halfway to Sana'a, when suddenly I began laughing. Laughing at myself. I didn't have chemical or radiation poisoning. I hadn't contracted cholera either. I had been stung by a freaking scorpion. Remembering the residual effects of a sting, I had all the symptoms. If I had the radiation or the cholera, my symptoms would have worsened overnight and I'd be flat on my backside. A scorpion. Son of a bitch.

Sanush's van was a clunker, pretty much like every other vehicle in Yemen. But it was getting me there. The gas gauge didn't work, but neither did all the other gauges on the dash, so I didn't know how much fuel I had left in the tank. My plan was to drive to a hotel, get a room, go back out to a department store or men's shop, if there was such a thing, and buy a shirt, pants, socks and a couple pairs of underwear. Then I'd go back to the hotel, shower, pitch my rotten clothes and go have a nice lunch. I would then drive to the embassy where I'd park and leave the van with the keys in it for somebody to steal. I'd be off the hook.

Upon entering Sana'a, I was not only surprised at how large it was, but its wonderful mix of modern infrastructure and ancient culture. The first structure I encountered was the ornate walled gate to the city, its sign reading Bab al-Yemen. But like most other large cities of the world, the traffic was nearly impossible to negotiate. It seemed almost every vehicle was either a small Japanese pickup, a minivan or motorcycle taxi and they flooded the streets. However, the city's slow pace allowed me to take account of upscale restaurants and hotels on Hadda Street where I also saw a KFC. But, hallelujah, I came upon the Sheraton Sana'a, a clean-looking but aging building that looked as though it could comfortably keep my body for a couple of days. I then pulled off the street and into the parking lot. After exiting the heap, I checked in at the hotel desk. When the bell captain saw I had no bags, he gave me the look…the look that said I was only going to need the room for an hour and to expect a young lady.

I found the room satisfactory and the commode actually flushed. After washing my face and hands, I pulled from the bathroom rack a for real terry-cloth towel. I then sat in the sofa chair for probably more than ten minutes taking in the cool air of the room's air conditioner, an exhilaration such as I hadn't felt in days. I went back down to the desk in the lobby and began asking the concierge, a dark-skinned, Arab Brit who spoke both languages, all the important questions. He then directed me two blocks down the street to a massive souq where I found a good number of shops. It didn't take me long to find the clothing that would carry me through the rest of my adventure. I remembered to bargain with the sales clerk and got a few rials off the inflated price. Upon my return to the hotel, I took a long, hot shower after which I shaved my two day growth and donned my new clothes. It was also the first time I was able to see the red mark on the side of my neck where the scorpion got me. I'd live.

I then went out to a restaurant called the Khaleej which served the traditional Yemeni food as well as burgers, pizza and the like. I had a slice of pizza and asked for a bottle of Perrier which I knew was safe to drink. There was actually a sign on the wall in both Arabic and English warning me to "avoid tap water at all costs." The 'costs' could prove fatal. Satisfied and clean, I grabbed a newspaper from the hotel lobby and went back to my room. Although I couldn't read the paper, there was photographic coverage of the attack in al-Hudaydah. And to my surprise the continuing photos on the second and third pages included a close-up of yours truly and Hassan giving first aid to the wounded. I then took the paper to the lobby, again seeking out the concierge for him to read to me what it said. Over the picture of me were bold words and hieroglyphics. "It says Foreigner Gives Aid to Wounded, Do

You Recognize This Man?" He then looked at me and back at the picture. "It's you. Yes. I believe the bloke is you."

"He does resemble me, doesn't he? But this was taken two days ago in al-Hudaydah. Couldn't be me. I'm here."

"Then he is your twin."

"All us Yankees look alike." I then chuckled at my own quip. "But say, can you tell me where the American Embassy is?"

"Yes. Down two blocks and over one. Rather close, it is."

"Thank you, mate," I said in my best British brogue. The photo of me was taken by an AP Photographer. That meant it had hit the press everywhere. If it made the Gazette, I wondered if Adriana had seen it?

Thinking of her reminded me I had to get a replacement charger for Hassan's phone. I went back down to the marketplace and walked around until I saw a battery store that also sold cell phone chargers. They had one for the Motorola. Things were finally going my way.

After going to my room, I put the phone on charge and then stretched out on the bed…a real bed and with clean sheets. In a matter of minutes, I was asleep.

It was three fifteen when I woke from the nap. I splashed my face with some cold water and ran my new comb through my hair. Grabbing up the cell phone and my passport, I set out for the embassy. The embassy, like war-torn Sana'a, had had its share of embattlement. Just ten years ago I remember seeing the TV coverage of an attack on the compound where a group of terrorists dressed as police fired rocket grenades and poured automatic weapons rounds onto defenders of the outer gate. They then set a bomb and tried to blow a hole in the wall. All the terrorists were killed along with an equal number of security and innocent civilians waiting at the gate to get in. Al-Qaeda claimed responsibility. Other attacks had occurred in 2009 and 2012. When sitting in my easy chair back then watching the news reports, I gave it little thought, never imagining that one day I'd be standing at the gate where it all happened.

Almost daily, like in seaside al-Hudaydah, there had been attacks by either the Houthi rebels or both ISIS and al-Qaeda terrorists.

I showed my passport to the security guards at the gate while an American Marine stood close by. I waited more than twenty minutes while the message was relayed by the guard to embassy staff that a displaced American needed assistance. Finally, another Marine came from inside the compound to the gate, searched me for a weapon and told me to follow him. I had astutely left the .45 in the safe in my hotel room.

Upon entering the building, I first had to go through the metal detector accoutrement and was then led down a hallway to an office where my passport was examined, assuring that I was an American citizen and not an expatriate having some kind of political dissidence. They fingerprinted me and then pulled up my prints, ultimately finding my photo and revealing me to be a retired State Department employee. A staffer then asked me what function I had with the State Department. He raised his eyebrows when I said I worked in counterterrorism. The entire process took an hour until I was sent to another room to speak to a lovely young woman higher up the food chain named Shirley Compagno who began asking me for my story.

I told her the big lie that I was a contractor conducting government business for the State Department and was abducted off the street by people that were either terrorists or because I was a wealthy looking White American and could be a ransom candidate. I then, being a former Green Beret and Ranger, used my skills to escape them. I left out the part about the WMDs and that I had killed people in al-Hudaydah and outside a cave in Khadem country. I thought that would bring on a shitload of more questions. She wanted to know more, but I was all out of lies and my nose was growing longer. I in turn asked her if I could use an embassy phone to call my director at the State Department in Washington who was waiting to hear back from me.

She replied, "In the essence of time and to circumvent all our red tape, of which I'm sure you are much aware, I think you need to tell your story directly to Ambassador Simmons who will want to know more about these people who abducted you. You can make your call from his office."

She made her call upstairs to tell somebody we were on the way and then led me down the hallway to the elevator. While **in** the elevator, I performed a closer assessment of Ms. Compagno…thirty-eight to forty, an expensive-looking gal dressed to the nines in a tight blue dress, wearing both an elegant perfume and a smile, intelligent, beautiful Italian eyes and a shape that belonged to Jennifer Aniston. However, I didn't take all that good a look. But then the image of the lovely Adriana

McGowan, the prime rib I had left back home, suddenly began forming in my brain and Shirley Compagno quickly became chopped liver. It reminded me I had another call to make.

Shirley left me with another lady, a plump, short-haired blonde with glasses who I found out was the ambassador's assistant. "Mr. McGowan, Mr. Simmons will see you now."

I thanked her and she opened the door for me to his office. Simmons was younger than I expected, maybe forty-five, medium build and well-groomed features. He was in a dark suit with a light blue tie, kind of what an ambassador should look like. On his desk was a photo of him with his lovely wife and two girls. Even though my tan shirt and forest green trousers were new, I still looked in comparison like Mr. Gun and Garden next to Mr. GQ.

"I'm Jack Simmons. You must be Mr. McGowan," he greeted, reaching across his desk to shake my hand. As spiffy as he was, there appeared to be nothing haughty or pretentious about him.

"Yes, sir."

"I understand you were abducted by some bad guys. Did you go to the local police?"

"No, I came here instead. Now, please allow me to tell you the **real** story."

I told him everything, beginning with the telegram I received at home all the way up until the present. It took more than twenty minutes to go through all of the details. He sat mostly with mouth slightly agape and eyes wide like a kid hearing The Night Before Christmas for the first time.

"Amazing story, Mr. McGowan."

"Please call me Bruce, sir."

"And you don't have to call me sir, either. I would normally think everything I heard was some wild, fabricated story manufactured by a schizophrenic. But I did see this." He then showed me yesterday's New York Times that featured on the front page the AP Photo of me bending down on the street helping a badly wounded citizen. "And there you are."

My eyes began rolling around as I suddenly imagined one of Adriana's friends coming by the house with a copy of the Charleston Gazette and my mug plastered all over the front page.

Simmons continued. "You're sure about these WMDs."

"Deadly sure."

He let out a low whistle. "You need to write a book when you get back home."

"I need to **get** back home. But first I have to go after Alistair Chalmers. My cousins are soon to die."

"I understand your predicament. Will your friend in Washington have some direction for you?"

"Actually, I need to call him. Do you mind if I do so now? I can go down the hall to make it."

"Why don't you make it here? This is a secure line as classified information is discussed on a daily basis. Before you make it, there is someone who is here in an office a few doors down I'd like you to meet. Can you bear with me while I go speak with him? There's bottled water in my cooler or something in my bottom drawer a bit more spirited. There have been a lot of troubling days in this country that have driven me to that drawer." He then chuckled.

"I'm fine with the water, Mr. Simmons."

I must have sat for thirty minutes waiting for his return. I didn't know who he was speaking with, but took it that he was retelling my story to someone either important or official. But then at just before five-thirty he entered the room with a man about my age with salt and pepper hair wearing a brown shirt tucked into khaki slacks——looking much like a safari hunter without the hat. Holstered on his hip was a Glock 19. A fed, I presumed.

"Bruce, meet Sam Galloway. Sam, I'll leave it to you to tell him who you are."

We shook hands and Simmons directed both of us to fabric sofa chairs on the window side of the room. As soon as we took seats, Galloway said, "Mr. McGowan, I'm with the Agency. While the ambassador was telling me your incredible story, I did some electronic research on you. Sounds like you've lived an exciting life: Airborne

Ranger, combat vet, twenty plus years with the FBI and some kind of position with the State Department…I believe you told Ms. Compagno you were in counterterrorism. Do I have all that correct?"

"Yes. But I'm no longer performing duties for the government. I've been retired for several years."

He nodded. "Sounds like you still are; you just don't know it. The electronic file on you says you're in your low sixties, but you look fifty. You obviously keep yourself in great shape."

"I try."

"And you're sure you're not here with the government, chasing these alleged
WMDs?"

I resented the implication that I had made up the story. "Look, Mr. Galloway, I'm not in any game with the government. What I told the ambassador is the gospel truth. All
I want to do at this point is go get my cousins safely out of the hands of this Alistair Chalmers and then fly back home."

"I understand. I believe you, Mr. McGowan. I'm very interested, however, in these

Iraqi WMDs you saw. You said you'd be calling your friend with the State Department to go over your findings with him. Would you mind putting us on a three-way call where I can talk with him about what to do with the WMDs?"

"I don't see a problem with that."

"Good deal. Ambassador, can you have your assistant set up the line and Mr.
McGowan, you can then make your call."

CHAPTER 14

As it was mid-morning in Washington, I hoped to catch Keith at the right time. I dialed his cell number and got his voice mail. "Keith, Bruce. Can you call me as soon as you can at this number, country code 967-1-324-769. I'm sure you can see it, but if you can't, I'm at the Yemeni American Embassy. Just ask to be patched through to the ambassador. I'm with him and will be waiting for your call. Thanks."

We sat talking for a while discussing some of the specific details of what had happened over the past 3 to 4 days. The spook, Galloway, wanted to know Hassan's nationality and whether he specifically admitted he was either ISIS or al-Qaeda.

"I wish I had explored his country of origin, but didn't. I suspect he might have been Iraqi and knowing Chalmers and his history of tracking al-Qaeda terrorist organizations along with my former boss, Lionel Byrd, he likely turned coat and became bosom buds with some of them."

"You said Lionel Byrd? I knew him. He was the CIA director when I came aboard. What an outstanding man.

So, he headed up the counterterrorist team you were part of. Sounds like that was a big time action group."

"I won't go into it, but we had some interesting missions."

"I have an idea how we can not only find Chalmers' location, but set a trap for him. I want to also engage Scotland Yard and MI-6."

"What do you have in mind?" I asked.

"First, his number should be on Hassan's phone. I'm sure he either contacted Chalmers or was supposed to contact him when you located the weapons. Call his number and I'll get my people to do some triangulation and locate that house in the Scottish countryside."

"Then what will you do…send in the cavalry? No, they rush in to take him and my damsels in distress die."

"I wasn't going to do that. You and Hassan were supposed to locate the WMDs and then the people that you blew away were to transport the nuclear weapon either to him or to a location previously designated. When you are able to get hold of him, explain that since you killed the guys that planned to double-cross him, you personally will arrange to get the nuke to him."

"I of course would just me telling him that and not actually arrange to have it delivered to him."

"Correct. We'll arrange to deliver **something** to him. The agency has a faux nuclear bomb that contains the exact components of a real bomb; however, the guts are nonfunctional. It would take an actual nuclear physicist or builder of a nuke to determine that it's not the real McCoy. Real bombs will have a fissile element such as uranium. The element we will put in there will be radioactive, but will instead be something similar to what makes up an x-ray. If radiologically tested, it will provide the results. It will have the same wiring, low intensity metal parts, tamper and pit cavity. Only the expert eye can tell the difference. We arrange a delivery to him and you go get your ladies."

I thought about the plan for a moment and didn't find any immediate holes in it. I myself had no alternative plan. I did like the idea of finding Chalmers's location through cell trace. If I knew where he was, I'd get the hell out of Dodge this very day and go after him. He wouldn't be expecting me and with my tactical skills and stealth, I would take him down in a flash. The thing was,

I didn't know how many more of his terrorist friends and local yokels like the Scotsman on the train were in his employ. He may have ordered that if anything happens to him, they would kill the hostages. So, for the time being, I'd have to play Galloway's game.

"Alright, Mr. Galloway. Sounds like a good plan. So you have a fake nuclear device. That's what I always liked about the CIA when I was with the Bureau; you guys have all the neat toys."

He laughed. We then talked for a few more minutes and Simmons's assistant buzzed him that a Mr. Lambreau was on the line. I picked the call up.

"Hello, Bruce," he greeted. "So, you got yourself in trouble and were turned over to the embassy."

"Not quite, Keith. I ran out of money and am here bumming a ticket back home."

Simmons smiled at that, but then nodded.

"What's your status? By the way, I saw your photo on the AP Wire. I thought you were staying low profile."

"I tried my best but fell into the middle of a terrorist attack."

"You're trying your best to get back in the game, aren't you, Scorpion?"

Galloway mouthed the word, "Scorpion?"

"Listen, Keith. I've got Ambassador Simmons and a gentleman from the Agency, Mr.
Galloway, on speaker here. They need to chat about what they have in mind with the
WMDs."

"You found them?!"

"Yes. They did exist after all and so does the Pakistani nuclear weapon. We found them in a mountain cave, thanks to a young Khadem man. When he was a boy he followed the trucks that picked up the weapons from the port in al-Hudaydah and watched them drive up a mountain to a cave. He took us there. Yeah, I know exactly where they are."

"What will you do now and how are you going to find Chalmers and your cousins?"

"I'm going to let you speak to Mr. Galloway. He'll explain his plan to you."

"Great, I take it we're both on secure lines."

"Yes," I replied.

Galloway took over the conversation and conveyed his plan to Lambreau. Keith thought it could actually work.

"What will happen to the WMDs, Mr. Galloway?"

"After we secure them, the nuclear weapon will be transported to DOE Pantex near Amarillo for deconstruction. I think the scientists there will first take a look at the research on the weapon and then dismantle it. The chemical weapons will be neutralized by federal mandate at PCAPP which is the Pueblo Chemical Agent Destruction Pilot Plant, depending on the weapon's composition."

Keith said, "Sounds like it's all planned out. Go for it. And by the way…this photo of you that hit the papers…"

"How far will that photo be circulated?

"All the major newspapers will run it for sure…and maybe some home town papers. You're an international hero, Bruce. You can always get a job with the Red Cross."

"Funny man, Keith. I gotta go now. Talk another time."

After our phone call, Galloway said, "Do you mind if I check out that phone you have? Maybe we can tell what number belongs to Chalmers. The IT guy here can determine Chalmers's location." But then I thought, what if he wasn't at the house when I called him?

I followed Galloway back to the office where his team was set up. I didn't realize the CIA and American embassies were such buds. However, it served to reason.

Knowing that Chalmers was from somewhere in Scotland, his cell phone was likely rooted in England. However, the prefix +44 was the same throughout the UK. The number +44 64782 9334521 we found twice on Hassan's phone. As there were no other +44 numbers, we both agreed the calls must have been either to or from Chalmers. There were also two missed calls from the number attempted last night. Galloway's assistant, Mike Daniels, whose official international code authorized the securing of information for government purposes, contacted several major cell service providers such as EE and Sky Mobile to see if they had an Alistair Chalmers. On the third attempt, we had a hit. There was a Chalmers, but it wasn't Alistair. I remembered Keith told me he was a fugitive. The number belonged to a Bernard Chalmers. Still, had to be the same guy. Carillon was his server.

The Agency apparently had the cell phone tracking system down pat. Of course, I'm sure the FBI and the other alphabet agencies did as well. Galloway told me the location of one's mobile phone can be determined by using the service provider's network infrastructure anywhere in the world. But first, one had to contact as many providers as necessary to find out if they had a particular customer. To pinpoint the phone, the searcher also had to determine the sector in which the phone was located, which in this case was the area close to the village of Thornloch, and then estimate the distance to the base station. While the hood was over my head, I had counted minutes and estimated traveling speeds on both the major motorway and secondary roads. I told Galloway it was between thirteen and fifteen miles. He said he could make the determination even more accurately by interpolating the signals between towers by using the trilateration timing method. Being technologically ignorant, I had no idea what the hell he had just explained to me.

Galloway said, "Considering that all of Chalmers's worker bees are dead, what will you tell him about how the bomb will be transported to him?"

"Where is your fake bomb located?" I replied.

"Our SOG or Special Operations Group has it stored at Fort Stewart, Georgia."

"What do you generally use it for?"

"For training our agents and other clandestine groups to recognize the components of a nuclear device should they encounter one on a mission. They would then be able to determine the difference between a conventional and nuclear bomb."

"And just how do we get this fake bomb to where he is or a designated rendezvous point?"

"That we will just have to work out. Maybe he has more of these Islamic radicals on his payroll that he could dispatch. You'll have to feel him out on that when you talk to him."

"Okay, I'm ready," I said. "Go for it, Mike?"

When Mike Daniels had Chalmers's server on the line, Galloway gave me the green light to make the call. I dialed the number. On the third ring, the person on the other end answered. "Hassan, you bloody sand flea, why haven't you picked up on my calls?"

"He's taking a dirt nap, asshole," I replied.

CHAPTER 15

"McGowan." He actually recognized my voice. "What do you mean by that and why do you have his phone?"

"He took a bullet…I took his phone."

"Are you saying he's dead?"

"Everybody's dead, Chalmers. Everybody except me."

"How? How did they die?"

"I'll start with Shadid. He died because he wouldn't buckle up before our plane was shot down. Yes, we were actually shot down. Your arranger here in Yemen, Aziz, was killed during the terrorist attack on al-Hudaydah. I'm sure you must have read about it. Hassan himself was murdered by one of your would-be transporters named Sanush and I killed him. His friends tried to pull out their pieces and I put bullets in them as well. Seemed like the right thing to do at the time."

There was only silence on the other end.

"You still there, Chalmers?"

"You are very smug about all that, McGowan. Why did Sanush kill Hassan?"

"They argued over the WMDs. Appears Sanush was going to betray you, take the nuclear device and sell it himself to the Iranians, cutting you out of the equation."

"That is if you had found the weapons."

"Oh, but we did."

"What? How? Where?"

"Which of those three questions do you want me to answer?"

"Don't toy with me, McGowan. Where did you find them?"

"Aziz told us the story of a young boy who saw…"

"Yes, yes. I know the story. Aziz told me about him over two years ago. And so you found him and he led you to where they were."

"Now you have the whole story."

"Not quite, McGowan. You haven't told me where they are."

"I hired some indigenous people to move the bomb from the mountains where we found it for safe keeping."

"And where would that be?"

"Not so fast, Chalmers. You won't get your hands on it until you release my cousins."

"You're in no position to bargain with me. I don't make deals with people. I don't compromise and I sure as bloody hell don't play games. I thought you understood that when I produced to you the head of James McGowan."

I looked at Galloway and he nodded. "Keep him talking," he mouthed silently.

"Yeah, you're a real prince, Chalmers. You're nothing but a damn terrorist yourself."

"Is this phone call all about insults and aspersions, McGowan?"

"No, it's about me getting rid of this bomb and you releasing your hostages. So, how do we go about doing that?"

"I have more people of the Arab persuasion at my beck and call. I can send them to retrieve it. Once it is in my hands, I will release the women."

"No. I don't like the deal. It has to happen at the same time. We meet somewhere in a neutral place. I drive to a designated place with the bomb. You drive to meet me with my cousins. You inspect the bomb, I check the ladies. If we are both satisfied, we go our separate ways."

"Let me think about that…how it could be arranged."

"You do that, Chalmers."

"I'll call you back on this phone."

"No. You think about it now. I'll wait."

Sam Galloway nodded. I took it he and Mike needed more time.

"Alright, McGowan. I will myself fly to the Sana'a airport. I will have two of my employees with me. You have the locals you hired to move the device to the airport as well. I'll also have a physicist with me to inspect the bomb. If it checks out, I'll call Quinn here at the house to release your people. Is that to your liking?"

"I'll agree to that." I was sure that the Scotsman didn't have it in him to kill Fiona and Mary. I had looked into his eyes. "I want you to understand something, Chalmers. If I return to Scotland and find them dead, that you didn't uphold your end of the deal, I will make it my lifelong crusade to come after you wherever you are and cut you till you bleed out every drop of your blood."

There was a long pause. Then he said, "And I think you would do that, McGowan."

"When do you want this to happen?"

"In two days…Wednesday. I'll touch base with you before then to arrange a time and place. Considering the flight time, it'll be the evening I expect. Don't disappoint me, McGowan." And that was his 'goodbye.'

Galloway gave me a thumbs up. "Good call. You handled that great."

"I hope I didn't commit to something you aren't able to deliver. Can you get your fake bomb here in two days?"

"Yes. I'll go ahead and order its transport today."

"Won't Yemeni airport security inspect your plane when you land it? They might be just a bit concerned about finding a warhead not knowing it's fake."

"Don't worry about it, Mr. McGowan. C-130s have been flying in arms for years in support of the Saudi-backed regime. None of our aircraft have been attacked or inspected for the past three years. My question for you is when Chalmers flies in with his people, how do you then envision the deal going down?"

"I haven't fully worked it out in my head, but how about this? Your 'device' lands here. We hire a couple of locals with their van to set up in a hangar. The device gets transferred into their vehicle. Chalmers and his inspector arrives and via cell phone, I tell him where I am with the bomb. He meets me at the hangar. His man checks out the bomb and then I tell Chalmers that before he leaves with it, he makes the call to his man in Scotland to release the hostages. I'm listening to the call. Once done, you and the FBI take him into custody. Does that sound doable? Can you get Bureau agents here for the arrest?"

"As you probably know, a team of agents is already based here in Yemen in a covert location. So, yes. But how can you be assured that Chalmers is actually calling his man back in Scotland? Or maybe he's prearranged that when he does make the call, it's actually the green light to go ahead to kill them. And then what if his physicist checks out our device and determines it's fake?"

I shook my head. "I don't know. These are very good questions. It's a chance I'll have to take."

"We have a couple of days to work out the details. In the meantime, have you arranged for a place to stay?"

"I'm at the Sheraton, but not sure I have enough rials on me for the extra days."

"Don't worry. The embassy will comp your bill."

"Thanks. Sorry to be dropping this kettle of fish in your lap."

He laughed. "Hey, not to worry, pal. We people in our business get our rocks off on shit like this. This will be a fun one."

It hadn't been much fun for **me**. I just wanted the nightmare to be over so that I could finally get back home to my cushy job as a house husband. Damn but I must be getting domesticated.

"By the way," he said. "Once you're in for the evening, don't go out on the streets. You're a White guy and you'll be a target. This is the most dangerous country and city in the Arabian world. Not only is this a war zone, but both ISIS and al-Qaeda terrorists are out there killing people, some for fun, some for money, all doing so in the name of Allah. The State Department has issued warning notices to travelers that say, and I quote, 'Travel to Sana'a is strongly discouraged because of civil unrest, general lawlessness, and the serious risk of kidnapping and execution.' So beware even when you're out in the daytime."

"Thank you for that, Mr. Sunshine."

He laughed again. "Just heed my advice, Bruce, okay? By the way, with all your adventures here in paradise, did you manage to pick up a piece?"

"The piece is in my room safe. It's an H&K .45."

"Good. If you have to go out, take it with you. Three quarters of the people you see on the street are armed. Don't leave home without it."

"Good advice. I intended to do so anyway."

The last bit of business was about the next day. Galloway had laid on a chopper for us to fly south into the Jabal Kanin range. He wanted to check out the WMDs first hand. I'd meet him at the embassy at nine. He gave me his cell number in case I encountered any trouble.

When I returned to my room at the Sheraton, I took a Coke from the small fridge, plopped down in the sofa chair and dialed Adriana's cell. She picked up after the first ring.

"Hello."

"It's me, sweetheart."

"Where are you, Skip? (my nickname) I thought you'd have your business done there and would be home by now."

I wasn't sure what to tell her. Once again, I had found myself in a situation where I had to lie to her. But I had no choice. I couldn't tell her anything that would make her worry.

"We're delayed again, Adriana. A tragic thing has occurred. One of the primary beneficiaries, Angus McGowan's son, has been killed."

"Oh, my God, how?"

"I wanted to spare you the gory details about that, but he was murdered."

"Who could have done that? And why?"

"Just pure meanness, I reckon."

"Sounds like you're in the middle of an Agatha Christie story. Maybe one of the beneficiaries is killing the others off. Aren't you afraid to stay around until the will is read?"

I laughed. "No. Apparently, this was just a freak occurrence. Anyhow, if you're okay with it, I'm going to stick around here for a few more days to see the end of this thing."

"I'm fine with it, Skip. Just relax and enjoy the country and the people there."

Right.

"Okay, then. I'll call you in a couple of days. Don't be worrying. Love you, babe."

"And I love you. Bye bye now." I then heard her place a couple of smooches onto her phone.

So, I really didn't end up lying to her. I just didn't tell her the real truth about where I was and what I was dealing with.

CHAPTER 16

It was drawing on 7:30 and the sun was still lighting up the evening sky. I was hungry and had no desire to order room service and just sit around watching state sponsored propaganda messages in between Yemen's lame TV programming. So, I decided to walk to one of the restaurants down the street from the hotel. As I intended to be back before dark, I didn't think I was defying Sam Galloway's warning. Grabbing the pistol from the safe, I shoved it into my belt up under my shirt and began my walk.

Three blocks away from the hotel I happened by what appeared to be an upscale restaurant, the Marib Raha. I figured I'd be less likely to end up with cholera from eating there, but I still wasn't drinking the water. Ornate on the outside, it was even more so on the inside with its ambient lighting, Arabian decor and large, vivid paintings on the walls of serene oases with stately palms, placid streams and colorful flowers native to the country. Another painting was of a sheik standing regally in one of his palace rooms with a harem of alluring, burka-clad women with beautiful eyes and facial features sitting devotedly in a circle around him.

I was readily escorted to a small table that would seat no more than two and handed a menu. I could see right away I was going to have trouble ordering something as it was in Arabic. No English. However, there **were** pictures of most of the dishes beside of the script that allowed me to guess what was on the plate. I felt like an illiterate child looking at a book that contained illustrations, using his imagination as to what the book was about.

But lo and behold, three tables from mine were a couple of familiar faces…Ambassador Simmons and Shirley Compagno, the smoking hot elevator chick. As they were looking very adoring at one another, occasionally touching hands, I wondered if I should wave and embarrass them. Although I decided to leave well enough alone, it was the babe who spotted **me**. **She's** the one who waved. I acknowledged her with a smile and nod, but that was only the extent of it. Simmons turned to see who she was signaling and when he saw me, he looked as though he had just swallowed a guppy. But he did throw up his hand and that was when I spotted his wedding ring. The photo of his wife and children on his desk immediately came back to me.

But, it was none of my bees wax and I merely kept on reading the pictures on my menu. I ended up ordering something that resembled spaghetti as it had noodles and a red sauce. In advance of my dinner, I ordered a Heineken which went down like golden ambrosia. I thought about ordering a glass of merlot as well and looked around to see what others were drinking. They weren't. Then I again remembered that Muslims are forbidden to consume alcohol. But to hell with them anyway; I was the ugly American infidel who would be flaunting his freedom to enjoy the beverages I knew they wanted but couldn't have. Nanny nanny boo boo.

The dinner was actually very tasty, but I couldn't finish all of it. I think given the fact that I had eaten very little the past four days, my stomach had shrunk. I again glanced over at the loving couple, noticing they were no longer touching hands. The embarrassed ambassador also never looked back my way. I paid my bill, trusting the server to take from my hand the correct amount of bills, and then departed the restaurant, leaving the couple to do all the touching they wanted.

Even though the daylight was waning, I decided to walk down a few more streets and tour some of the sights. Yeah okay, I was ignoring Sam Galloway's advice. But as I continued walking, I came upon a most impressive-looking mosque in that southern section of Sana'a at Al-Sabeen Square. Although it was now called the People's Mosque and under Houthi control, the sprawling structure, still called the Al-Saleh Mosque, had been erected by the former regime named after the dethroned president, Ali Abdullah Saleh. At least that's what I read on the walls. The inscription was in both English and Arabic. As it was late and now closed, I thought I might visit it sometime during the day tomorrow along with the nearby grand presidential palace…that is if I had a couple of hours. I really wasn't all that interested, but since I was on vacation in this touristy, exotic land, why not see some of the sights?

But, as I had ventured a little too far, about halfway back to the hotel, it began getting dark. A few streets over I heard gunfire; however, as it wasn't on my street, the people around me didn't seem all that apprehensive. After all, they were used to hearing it, and if bullets weren't flying their way, who cares. The pedestrian traffic then thinned out as I understood always happened at night and I suddenly found myself alone on the street…except for the two men wearing kufis behind me. As I quickened my pace a bit, so did they. My radar was definitely beeping and I didn't at all have a good feeling about the situation.

At the point where I had run out of streetlight, I heard them coming. That's when I pulled out the .45. And that's when they put on the brakes. But then out of the corner of my eye, I saw something shiny on my left. A third hood was waiting in ambush with a jambiyah, an eight inch curved knife. Swinging the muzzle of the .45 in his direction, one of the other two men took a swat at me with some kind of club. As I ducked, it still caught me on the shoulder, nearly causing me to lose my grip on the pistol.

After I kicked the bastard in the nuts, sending him to his knees, I moved aside just in time to avoid the blade the third man had thrust at my throat. It was time to throw bullets. I fired dead center at his chest, the impact first sending him against the wall and then face down onto the street. As the one man who had not engaged me took off, the assailant with the busted balls tried to get to his feet. However, before he managed to do so, I crushed his skull with the butt of the pistol. Whether it killed him or not, it should have.

Gun in hand, I quickly left the scene and broke into a trot the rest of the way to the hotel. With all of the strife that had gone on in the city for years, the two men's deaths would be too insignificant to make the news. Once back in the hotel, I stopped by the bar, got a shot of whisky and went directly to my room where I remained for the rest of the night.

It all caused me to wonder why the hell that shit kept happening to me. Something I might have read sometime ago suddenly came to mind. A man reaches a certain age where he doesn't want any drama. He doesn't want to fight anyone, but if forced to, he will not fight fair. He will not quit and there are no weapons he will not use. Just leave me alone with my coffee and bourbon. Don't threaten me and don't poke me— —I will hurt you. Or kill you.

* * * * *

Upon finishing my coffee and a sticky bun in the breakfast bar, I struck out for the embassy. At ten minutes till nine outside the gate, I called Sam Galloway. I told him I was preparing to come in, but as I had my .45 on me, could he come down to usher me through? He said "Sure."

When he had walked me through security, he took me immediately to the roof of the building where a vintage Huey sat waiting.

"Sheesh," I said. "Does this thing still fly?"

"She might smoke and belch a little, but hasn't failed us yet." he replied, laughing.

"I think the last time I was in one of these was at Fort Hood in the mid-70s. I thought the military had long since phased them out."

"They did. We got the salvage."

"Wonderful. Who's flying us?"

"Mike, who you met yesterday. A man with many talents."

As the two of them took their positions in the pilot/co-pilot seats, I took one of the three canvas seats in the rear. Both Sam and Mike looked like the spooks they were in their military aviator sunglasses, cargo pants and ball caps. Mike pointed to a headset hanging above my seat. Considering the noise the old bird made, if we were going to communicate in the air, I needed it.

Before we took off, Galloway said he had some favorable news. "I'll let Mike tell you."

Mike turned and handed me a slip of paper on which there was some writing. "The address of the place where yesterday's phone call originated. Seems it is a residence at 42 Downing Way in the County of Perthshire. As you recall, Chalmers made the statement, "…I'll call Quinn **here** at the house to release your people…" Note the word **here.**"

"Thanks, Mike. Good work to nail this down." I placed the paper in my wallet.

After we took off, I told Mike to fly south and follow the N1 highway. When we reached the town of Nu'en, I'd direct him toward the Jabal mountains and on to our objective.

I told Galloway, "The last time I flew in a CIA aircraft it was with Air America in Vietnam. Those were mostly fixed wing aircraft, although I did do a couple recons with them in Hueys."

"Yeah, I do a **lot** recons in this bird."

"Considering the Houthis, Hadi supporters and all the terrorist factions that seem to be shooting the entire country up, has anyone ever taken potshots at you guys?" I asked him.

"We've been sniped at a few times," Sam said, "but never shot down. Don't worry…we patched up the holes."
"I hope you're getting combat pay."

"Before this job, I was Army and received $200 extra a month in Iraq which was called 'imminent danger pay.' Hardly enough for what some of us went through."

"You guys were raking it in. Mine was only $50 'hazardous duty' pay."

I then saw where we were over Nu'en. "Okay, Mike, take us north along the trail there until you get to that peak. See it?"

He nodded.

"Now if you look closely, you'll see the opening of a cave just below that mass of large rocks."

"Got it," he replied.

"Any place you can find to set down, it's your decision."

Mike circled a couple of times and then decided on a spot that was flat and open well below the cave. After we touched down and exited the chopper, we began climbing the hillside. It would be about three hundred meters until we reached the cave's mouth. I then pointed out to Daniels and Galloway the wrecked deuce-and-a-half I had mentioned.

When we reached the cave, Galloway stood on the large rock near the mouth and looked out over the valley below. "This country has its own desolate beauty in places.

Too bad the cities are war zones." He then looked down at his feet at the dried blood. "So, four people died here, eh Bruce?"

"Yeah. One of them I hated to see."

"Let me ask you something. How does it make you feel to pull a trigger on someone?"

"Do I take it you never have?"

"I have. I just wonder about you. I don't generally ask people that, but when I do, I get a variety of responses. I'm interested in yours."

"When it's happening, I don't think about it. I just react. Mostly, I have killed in selfdefense and you can't go through any thinking process to do it. It's split-second reflex."

He replied, "I get it, but I also take it that you have had occasions to think about it when you put a bead on someone and have time to pull the trigger."

"Why are you asking me this right here at this time and place? Are you pursuing your doctorate and doing research for your dissertation?"

He laughed. "No. Nothing like that. It's just that people's answers to these questions tell me a lot about them." He scuffed his boot toe over the stains.

"Why don't you and I discuss this some time over a couple of beers later."

"You're right. Let's see what you found."

Mike was the one with the flashlight, but he handed it to me to lead them inside. We walked the couple hundred feet until we encountered the pile of rocks and then I began climbing over them. They followed. Once the three of us were on the other side, Galloway swept the beam of his flashlight over the skeletons. "Lovely," he said, and then set the light on the series of crates. He didn't say anything else until he got to the last long and narrow crate.

"So, there it is. There's the Pakistan flag and on the weapon itself, the American flag at the nose, just as you said."

"Can you duplicate the Pakistan flag and Arabic hieroglyphics on your fake missile and crate?" I asked.

"Yeah. We can get that done." He then took several pictures with his mini camera.

"And how will you get these weapons out of here?" I asked.

"We'll bring up as close as we can a couple of large military flatbeds. Once we get the crates down, we'll have the Marines escort them to the airport where they'll be flown out on 130s to Pantex and the Pueblo location for examination. From there, they'll all be destroyed or deconstructed."

Galloway took his time looking inside the crates, then said, "Gentlemen, do you kinda feel like Indiana Jones in here?"

I hadn't thought about it, but in response, nodded. Mike replied, "Yep."

"You're looking at history here. A war was fought on the premise that they existed and then everyone said they didn't. Men and women lost their lives fighting that war. And then suddenly, all these years later…eureka. They exist again." Galloway seemed almost melancholy for a few moments, then added, "Well, I guess we're done here. Shall we go?"

CHAPTER 17

Back at the embassy and on the way down the hall to Galloway's cubby-hole, I ran into Ambassador Simmons talking with someone in the hallway. When he saw me, he had this sheepish look on his face and tried his best to avoid speaking. I couldn't help but say "Good afternoon, Mr. Ambassador."

"Oh, hello, Mr. McGowan. Did you all get accomplished what you set out to do?"

"We did. Again, I appreciate the embassy's hospitality and your paying of my hotel bill. Thanks as well for the flight I'll be taking back to Scotland."

He nodded. He also had a kind of dumfounded look on his face when I mentioned my ticket back. I made that one up. Galloway had only committed to comping my lodging while I was there. And no, I wasn't attempting to blackmail the ambassador. He would come to the decision as to my airline ticket on his own.

That afternoon about six, I met Galloway and Daniels for a light dinner and a couple of beers at a diner near the Sheraton called Mateam Sana'a. It wasn't as swanky as the restaurant the evening before, but they served burgers and fries. As there was a McDonald's a block away, I assumed they were trying to give the Golden Arches a little competition.

When we were settled in at our table, Galloway began the conversation. "Alright, Bruce, tomorrow we make this happen. The C-130 with the fake bomb is supposed to land at 1000 hours. We hired two Khadem men from just outside the city to be at the airport at 1300. We'll also provide a cargo truck to load our device onto it and place the Khadems in it. That little charade should be convincing. I assume you haven't heard from Chalmers yet."

"No."

"If you do so this evening, give me a call, regardless of the time."

"Right."

"Anything else you can think of we need to consider?" he asked.

"Do you have the Bureau agents on board?"

"I arranged that as soon as you left the embassy this afternoon. Special Agents Tyler and Janssen will be there to meet with us when the C-130 arrives."

"I can't think of anything else then."

When our server finally materialized, the three of us defied Islamic protocol, being
American infidels, and ordered booze. I had a Sazerac and both of my table mates, Scotch. We'd nurse them a while and then get on with the dinner.

Galloway seemed eager to revisit something he had started earlier in the day. "And so, my friend, pursuant to this morning's conversation, let's say you are camouflaged and laying somewhere with your sniper rifle and a human being is in your crosshairs. You wait, wait and then fire. What is it you feel?"

"Recoil."

He smiled, but I could tell he didn't like my answer. Maybe he had heard the smartass quip too many times already. "I'm talking about emotions, Bruce. What was going through your mind as you anticipated pulling the trigger."

"I don't know. How about you, Mike? Has Sam ever asked you these questions?"

"Yeah, but I told him I never killed anyone. Hey, don't be alarmed. Sam asks every badass he meets these questions."

"I'll then ask **you** this question, Sam. Why do you bring up the subject? Is it because **you** have killed people and it's imbedded in your conscience?"

He was quiet for a moment, but then gulped down the last of his drink. "You're very perceptive, Bruce. I'll tell you two something I've never told anyone, except the Langley psychiatrist. Three years ago I was given the order to place a hit on an ISIS terrorist who had blown up an Air Force officer's club in Afghanistan where nine of the officers were killed and a shitload of others were wounded. The Intel we received on this character was that he was hiding in a small village south of Kabul. A mole we had in the village pinpointed his house. I sat in an abandoned building near the house waiting for him to appear for days, not moving except to relieve myself on the floor in a corner. And then I saw him pull up in a vehicle occupied by other insurgents. When he got out, I put a bead on the back of his head. When he opened the door, a small boy maybe five came out to greet him. I had the shot and I sat there wondering what kind of trauma the child would endure the rest of his life when he saw his father's head explode."

"So, did you take the shot?"

"I did."

"And?"

"Unfortunately, the father had picked up the child to hug him. As I was pulling the trigger, he spun his son around, so happy to see him. My bullet splattered the head of the boy instead."

"My God," I said.

That's all I had in me to say. I just stared at the man. Galloway was a seasoned and hardened CIA operative, but shit like that can happen to the best of us.

He continued. "And so, Bruce McGowan, every night when I close my eyes, I see the happy little face of a boy welcoming home his father, and a second later, his head exploding in the crosshairs of my scope. And you wonder why I'm asking this question?"

"Sam, I'm no psychiatrist, and I don't know whether you're looking for peace, forgiveness or just understanding. It's probably all the above. You wouldn't be the first person who was doing what was asked of him by his country to have killed some innocent person. Of course, this happened to **you**. I don't think questioning others on the subject will get you the answers you're seeking. People with similar experiences have their own feelings and deal with it the best they can. Some will have remorse while others it won't affect. You can't find your answers from the answers others give you. They're not you…you're not them."

He nodded. "So, whaddayuh think? Do I need a head doctor to help make all this go away?"

"I've only known you a couple of days. To me you come across as tough and calloused, even cagy as one might expect from a CIA operative. Yet you're shrouding something like this that's gnawing your insides. Now I know why you're pressing me so hard on the matter. You finally met a guy like me that has pulled the trigger on a lot of people. And I'm somebody who might finally give you your answers."

I then took the last sip of my Sazerac and settled back in my chair. "Let me share something with **you**. I had a similar experience in Vietnam that has haunted me to this day. I see in my dreams the face of the Vietnamese girl whose arm I blew off and whose mother I killed with a grenade launcher. But I've come to terms with it. It was unintentional. It was an accident. I know that now. I never liked the term 'collateral damage,' but unfortunately that's what it is. But you know what I think, Sam. You're going to be all right. You getting this out has been a catharsis. Did you hear what I said? You're going to be all right."

Galloway sat for a while stroking his forehead with his fingertips and then he nodded. "Yeah. You're right, Bruce. Hell, yeah. I'm going to be just fine." He then laughed. "You're in the wrong line of work, you know. You should have been a therapist."

"Hey, I'm not in **any** line of work, pal. In real life, I'm nothing but a house husband." I then paused a moment to pose another question I had to ask. "But I gotta know something more."

"What's that?"

"Did you end up killing the terrorist as well?"

He smiled. "I immediately threw in another round and blew his head off."

I returned the smile and shook his hand. "And therein, my friend, is your closure."

CHAPTER 18

Sam Galloway swung by the Sheraton at 1230 where I stood waiting for him to take me to the airport. I wasn't sure whether I should check out or not, but my bill had not yet been paid. The plan provided that after Chalmers was taken into custody, my flight back to Scotland would follow at 2035. Although I wanted to fly directly to JFK and then on to Charleston, I had to be sure after Chalmers arrived that the cousins were released and had not been harmed or worse.

"The mockup arrived on schedule at 1000, Bruce," he said. "Mike is there with it now. He has also picked up the two Khadem men and the cargo truck should be there at 1400 according to our embassy Marine who set it up."

"All we need now is to hear from Chalmers," I remarked. "I'm a bit concerned that he hasn't contacted me. By now, he should be in the air. We don't know how he's flying in or if he will have cell capability on the flight."

"Then we wait."

When we arrived at the Sana'a airport and were waved through by the guards, Galloway drove us to the hangar where we saw the truck. We then walked to the covered bed where the lift gate had been lowered. We both jumped up inside and took a look. The people preparing the transport at Fort Stewart had done a good job with the markings. On the crate was the international nuclear symbol. On the fake bomb itself was printed the Pakistani flag. With the exception of the American flag at the nose, the fake device was identical to the real one. I hoped the guts to the mockup would be as well.

1430 and 1500 came and went. We stood and paced and stood some more. I kept checking my watch which made the time pass slowly. Finally, at 1615 the phone rang. I put it on speaker for Galloway and Daniels to hear. The number was the same cell number we recorded when Chalmers called two days prior.

I answered. "Chalmers, have you arrived?"

"Change of plans, McGowan. You won't see me today."

"What?"

"Like I said, I've changed the plans."

"To what?" I replied sharply.

"You're going to bring the bomb to me."

"To Scotland?"

"No. A bit south of here…to England."

"Why are you jerking me around, Chalmers? You said this wasn't a game, yet you're playing one."

"I'm just keeping the upper hand is all, McGowan."

I looked at Galloway and he shook his head.

"I don't have a way of getting the bomb there, Chalmers. I can't just put it on a commercial flight. And then there are other impediments if I chartered a plane…security inspections at departure here and arrival in England, customs declarations…"

"Stop!" he barked. "You won't have any of that to worry about."

"What are you talking about?"

"I have already arranged for a charter out of there. Not from there in Sana'a, but from a field outside of Al-Bayda which is to the southeast. I'm sure there is GPS on Hassan's phone. I'll send you the coordinates. Find it. You'll fly to meet me in Britain with the bomb."

"And where do I land in merry old England?"

"Ah, but that's not for you to know. You'll have Scotland Yard meeting the plane and I can't have that." Then he laughed. "The charter pilot will know where it is. I will have your girls there in exchange for the device. So there you are, Bruce. All planned and you don't have to worry about British Airport Security."

"Two concerns, Chalmers. The last charter flight I was on was shot down. Had it not been, it would have crashed anyway, the piece of crap that it was. And then what do you think will happen in British airspace? Without a flight plan, it will be considered a hostile aircraft and the RAF will shoot it down."

"Contraire. It **will** have a flight plan, McGowan, to land at Cathcart. But for some reason, it won't make it. The plane will land in a field and be reported as lost off radar. By the time it's found, we'll have removed the bomb and gone. I think this is a much better plan, don't you?"

I clinched my fist and shook it at the phone.

"I think you're a first rate asshole, Chalmers."

"There you go with the insults again, Bruce. If we're to do business together, we must get along you know."

"You're also a snide bastard."

"Sticks and stones…"

"Alright, when do we do this?"

"I already have it planned for Saturday, three days from now. You will be at the coordinates at 2:00 in the afternoon, your time. The plane will be there with my employees. Have the weapon ready to load onto the plane at 1:30, if you don't mind."

"Just how many of these Islamofascist bastards do you have on your payroll?"

"More than you can ever realize. And be careful not to call them Islamofascist bastards to their faces, my friend. One of them may dump you into the English Channel."

"And I take offense in you calling me your friend."

"You have your marching orders, McGowan. Enjoy Yemen the next few days. Lovely, peaceful country, you know." He was then gone.

I felt like throwing the phone onto the tarmac and stomping it. But, I needed it.

"What a pompous ass," Galloway remarked.

"Yeah, you nailed it. Now I'm open for suggestions."

"I think we have to do what he says. We'll be putting my toy bomb on the plane in three days."

I turned around and began pacing, my hands clasped behind my back. It's the way I do my heavy thinking.

"No. Here's what I'm going to do. My plane for Scotland leaves this evening. I'll be on it. As I've now got the address of that house, I'm going after this guy."

"You can't do that, Bruce. You might put your relatives' lives in danger."

"Their lives are already in danger, Sam. I think this is my best course of action. If I can't find him to take him down in two days, I'll then get a flight back here to meet his plane."

"I don't know. Let me think about it. Let's go to the airport coffee shop and talk it over. Mike, you want to get our 'bomb' out of here?"

"Where do I take it?"

"The only place we can so that people won't think it's real and get excited…our storage unit in the embassy compound. Tell the Bureau boys false alarm and we'll do it again in a few days."

"Will do. On my way," he said.

We then walked back to Galloway's sedan, and after pulling it out of the hangar, he drove across the tarmac to the terminal parking lot.

"Are you really going to do this?" Galloway asked me.

"Damn right I am. It's time I took the offense. This prick has been in control of the game too long and I have to do the unexpected."

"If he sees you coming…"

"He won't."

"He might have lookouts all over that place."

"Doesn't matter."

"You can't take that .45 on a commercial flight, so are you going to do this without a weapon?"

"I'll figure it out, Sam. I'm pretty damn resourceful where it comes to individual tactics and taking people down. I just have to get this done and get back home."

"Suit yourself. What if you don't find him or your relatives? Maybe he moved them."

"I'll beat it back here in time for Chalmers's plane to land in Al-Bayda."

"That would be cutting it close. What happens it you get taken down in the process by one of his people?"

"Then it won't matter. The ladies will either already be dead or he'll eventually release them."

"But I won't know whether you're dead or alive."

"If I'm not back here or if I haven't called you with the details of his take-down, assume the worst. Then you don't have to worry about meeting his plane. And you get to keep your fake bomb."

He stirred the spoon in his coffee. "I guess it all depends on your success in Scotland. Good luck, old boy. Don't get yourself zapped."

CHAPTER 19

My flight to Edinburgh was on time and I was wheels up on the American 737 at 8:50. After we had leveled off at 36,000 feet, the flight attendant served a small, prepacked snack. With it I had a beer. I had been running hard the past couple of days and using brain cells that I had not used before. I was drained. As I hardly ever do anything but doze a few seconds on a plane, I actually fell asleep. I think I was at a point where it didn't matter whether I was awake or asleep if the plane crashed.

When the sky outside my window was still dark the next morning, I was awakened by the scurrying of flight attendants serving breakfast. The coffee, the black nectar of the gods, smelled delightful. We would be landing in less than an hour. I've never been good with calculating time differences, so I wasn't sure of the local time. I was pretty sure, however, it was Thursday morning.

All I had with me was the same canvas bag I had started out with which contained my single change of clothes and toothbrush. When I went through customs, there was nothing to declare. I had refrained from buying any souvenirs, bottles of booze and cigars while on vacation in Yemen. But, what I mostly felt naked about was not having a pistol on me. I was pretty sure a non-citizen couldn't purchase a gun, so I had to get creative to obtain one.

I still had my wallet. Nice guy Alistair Chalmers had allowed me to keep it along with my credit card and I still had a few sterling pounds on me, more than enough to purchase yet another train ticket to Thornloch.

When the train pulled into the station, it was eleven-fifteen. I had a lot of daylight hours to kill before stopping by Chalmers's location for some evening tea and scones. I had planned not to get there before around nine. You see, I always do my best work in the dark. Ask Mrs. McGowan about that.

In drifting about town, the only thing I was going to be wary about was bumping into the Scotsman on Chalmers's payroll, the man he referred to as Quinn. While visiting the quaint little shops, I was as hawk-eyed as I could be to look at every face, at the same time keeping my head down. On the shelf of one of the shops, I was well-taken with the majestic and noble-looking Clan McGowan coat-of-arms. I had seen one before, but this one was magnificent. On its shield, a medieval red griffon was perched beneath the head of a wild boar which was in turn flanked by two fleur-delis. I thought maybe I'd return the next day for it after I killed Alistair Chalmers. It would look fantastic in my den.

I did purchase a souvenir dirk, a kind of thrusting knife complete with a sheath and ornate handle that resembled the kind of weapon Sixteenth Century Scottish warriors carried. I learned a long time ago you always carry a knife with you in case there's cheesecake or you need to stab someone in the throat. I then decided to spend a few hours at the town's small library learning about my ancestors. I had not gained all that much from my brother Joey about our kin, him being the novice genealogist that he was.

Upon entering the library, I was greeted by the most lovely of redheads that I had seen maybe ever. She was in her early thirties and having the sensuous look about her of an Emma Stone or further back, a Rita Hayworth. Her voluptuous breasts clearly defied gravity. The way she moved around was like music; but what captivated me the most were her dancing green eyes. However, I reminded myself immediately that she was too young and I was too married. Still a man can look at the menu, can't he? He just doesn't have to order the dessert. And that she was.

Anyway, upon telling her I was visiting her fair village from America and wanting to spend some time in her history section researching my family lineage, she asked my family name. "McGowan," I said proudly.

"Oh, very common name hereabouts, much like Smith or Jones in the U.S."

"Some of my kin folk live at Braemoor. Do you know where that is?"

"Everybody knows Braemoor. I suppose you know that the patriarch there passed some time back. Are you here to visit them?"

"Yes. I haven't been there yet; I just got off the train. Where is it?"

"Not far. You take the road that runs by here, go perhaps three miles and then take the road numbered 265. You might miss the sign if you're not watchful." She had the most fanciful Scottish brogue. The full Scottish package.

"Do you know who lives there now?"

"Yes, James and his sister Fiona, but I don't know them well. Fiona has the most adorable daughter. I don't see them much except when the little girl is brought here by her mother to check out some children's books. The castle itself is a bit run down, but still has its old world charm. Goes back to the 14th Century, I think, and is considered one of our area's landmarks. Are you going there?"

"I may later this afternoon."

"I'm sure you'll love communing with them." She then turned her attention to one of the bookshelves. "You will find three books on the history of Thornloch and our county. You'll see in one of them…this one…some reference to the McGowans and Braemoor. On the computer, which you are free to use, I can direct you where to go to the McGowan family history."

"You're very kind, Miss…"

"It's Mrs."

Of course it was.

She continued, "Mrs. Rose Quinn."

Uh oh.

"Quinn," I repeated. "Is that also like a Smith or Jones name…lots of you around?"

"Throughout Scotland, yes. But it so happens there's only one Quinn family in Thornloch and that's us."

Not good, I thought. I knew the Quinn doing Chalmers's dirty work was in his fifties and could be her husband, but for some reason, he didn't seem to be in her class…or in her age group.

She added. "It's just me and my bonny daughter, Kathleen now. My husband left us two years ago and is somewhere in France I think. After our divorce, I took back me name."

"Good…I mean, I'm so sorry."

"Oh, and my father lives just off the town boundary."

Damn. Her father. I knew then I had let too much out. I could hear her now: "Oh, Dad, I just met the most delightful man from the colonies. He's related to the McGowans of Braemoor." I knew she probably left when the library closed at eight. If she met up with her father afterward, that is if the man **was** her father, I had to find my way to Chalmers within the first hour of darkness. But, maybe Quinn would still be there.

While Rose busied herself with a couple of other patrons, I sat thumbing through the pages of the book on Thornloch and Perthshire County. There was a picture of Braemoor from the 1950s which obviously was in its better days. It was the same photo I had seen on the internet back at Wolf Laurel. It mentioned Angus McGowan as being the current owner and that he was a descendent of Mad Richard McGowan who as part of the Scottish Peerage was the Lord of Roxbury. He fought in the Battle of Bannockburn with Robert the Bruce in Scotland's battle for independence and afterward settled down to raise his family. When I accessed the internet for more information, I learned that many of the McGowans through the years were blacksmiths. Those preceding Angus were Oliver, Aaron, Lewis, Callum and so on. All were owners of Braemoor. And then I found a Bruce McGowan from the 1830s who left Braemoor for London where he was one of the founders of Scotland Yard. So, I got it honest. Thanks, Cousin Brucie.

When I was done at the library, I bid the fair maiden, Rose, goodbye. It would have been nice to sit at a pub with her to enjoy a mug of ale with the playin' of the pipes in the background. I actually wanted to know more about the town and Scotland in general. However, I was correct in assuming she was not off till eight. If I finished my business tonight, maybe tomorrow.

Anyway, she gave me a hug and said, "Tha mi a 'guidhe gach toileachas dhut."

"What language is that and what did you say?" I asked her.

"It's English, Mr. McGowan, or an early form if it…Gaelic. I said I wish you every happiness."

"Thank you, Rose. And the same to you. Maybe I'll see you around before I leave."

CHAPTER 20

Rain had begun to fall, but I expected it would be gone in a matter of minutes. All afternoon it would drizzle for a brief time and then the sun would reappear. That was Scotland on most days, I understood. After leaving the library, I ducked next door into a coffee shop for about forty-five minutes to enjoy a ham sandwich and a Coke.

As it was now seven and still too light to set upon my mission, I summoned a taxi to take me to the Braemoor Castle. From the pictures I had seen of it, I already knew it was not a sprawling, majestic structure high on a mountain such as the Edinburgh and Stirling Castles, but it was impressive enough just the same. Sitting about threehundred meters down a much grown-over lane, it appeared as something gothic and mysterious, maybe even haunted by the souls of its former owners. As Rose had told me, however, it was indeed in need of repairs. A couple of its stones weathered over the past six plus centuries had fallen victim to the elements, cracking or even crumbling in places. The current occupants had allowed the ivy adorning its walls to grow out of control and three of the grey lady's windows were broken.

I did find that the large, wooden entrance door was locked, so at least Chalmers was thoughtful enough to secure it on his way out after taking away my relatives. I knew it wouldn't have done me any good to try the tarnished door knocker since no one should be there. But I did stare at it for a couple moments. For some odd reason, I thought about cockeyed Marty Feldman standing at a similar door in the movie Young Frankenstein making a joke about knockers. A smile broke out on my face. However, as I walked around the castle, I found that a door to what appeared to be a basement was unlocked. At least the thumb latch on the handle allowed me to think that. It didn't push open all that easily, so I had to use my shoulder to force it. The door obviously hadn't been used for quite some time. The mass of cobwebs covering the inside of the doorway corroborated that.

The basement was not exactly a dungeon, but it felt like one…dark, damp and cool. There were a couple of rooms, however, that might at one time served as a dungeon, but I couldn't imagine any reason one would have been held prisoner there. But who knows what went on back in those early centuries. Maybe one of my ancestors was some kind of sadist.

After climbing the long, stone stairway, I found myself on the main floor of the castle. Ceilings were high, maybe thirty feet tall, and the walls were covered with roughhewn wood. Much of the place had been modernized through the years, but still way behind the times where it came to current upgrades. It seemed the McGowans could have used the help of Chip and Joanna on HGTV. You might think I just sit and watch shows like that in my retirement, but…okay, maybe I **have** seen a couple of them.

There was a large dining room where sat a long table with a dozen large chairs, much as you might expect to see in a dwelling like that. Red and green tapestries hung from the walls as did paintings of savage-faced Scotsmen standing nobly with tartan sashes draped over their shoulders and fierce looking swords hanging from their belts.

Ambling further through the castle, I found the kitchen where on the countertops lay moldy wheels of cheese and rotting meat of some sort. It appeared the family might have been preparing a meal when it was suddenly interrupted by uninvited guests. An uncorked, half-empty bottle of wine sat beside a turned-over glass, further evidence of a hurried departure.

Upstairs I found the bedrooms. Although two of the doors were opened, another was not. When I went in, I saw that it likely had not been in use for months. It was larger than the others and more masculine-looking. Shirts, trousers and coats hung in the closet and on a writing desk lay a journal with the name Angus McGowan embossed on the cover. I opened it and the last entry was at 8:45 in the morning on January 6th, clearly eleven months ago. It read, "I am not feeling so well today and have the worst heartburn. I took a Bromide powder and trust it will work." I surmised it wasn't indigestion at all and he may have been suffering a coronary.

I then trekked down the hallway to the other rooms. The castle looked to be over 7,500 square feet, yet only one bathroom. I didn't see one downstairs as well. One of the three other bedrooms looked to belong to the second male, James, while it seemed both Fiona and her daughter slept in an adjacent room together. There was a canopy covering the double bed while further into the room against the wall I saw a single bed with a doll lying on the pillow. As all of the beds had been made up and I found the rooms neat, it didn't appear any of the three had been snatched from their sleep during the night. I spent a total of an hour and a half in the castle, not finding anything of significance. Of course, I actually didn't know what I was looking for, anyway. At eight-thirty I called another taxi. The dispatcher I could scarcely understand. In the entire village I don't think I could decipher what more than two people were saying, Rose being the most understandable. But they **were** speaking English, laced of course with a strong dose of Gaelic.

The cabbie took over twenty minutes to arrive, but that was okay. The last rays of daylight had given in to the dark.

"Where ye want ta go, mate?"

"This address, 42 Downing Way, but I'll tell you where to stop. Such a nice night now, I'd like to walk the rest of the way."

"I know the place," he said. "It belongs to me friend, Liam Quinn. Should I call and tell him I'm bringing ya?"

"No, no. Don't do that. I want to surprise him."

"You be a stranger, yet ye know him."

"Yeah, I spoke with his daughter in town today and she said he'd be happy to share a pint and swap tales."

"Ah, ye met the darlin' Rose. Yep, he likes havin' company, but I haven't seen the likes of his arse in weeks. Tell him I said don't be no stranger."

So, my speculation about Quinn being her father was right on. And the house where I had been taken belonged to him, not Chalmers.

"And your name?" I asked.

"T'is Stewart. Connor Stewart. And yours?"

"McKenzie, sir." That was just in case he called Mr. Quinn anyway.

"Good, lad. Have a bonny evenin.'"

Stewart let me off where I asked him to stop on the side of the hard road. He said the Quinn house was back off the road in a field about a quarter of a mile down. The moon was in its first stage and it was stone dark save for the brilliant stars that shone like diamonds on a blackboard sky. The night had cooled and I found it downright comfortable. The right kind of night for a man to die. I hoped it didn't have to be Mr. Quinn.

I was good at this. I could still sneak up on the best of 'em and cut their throats without the slightest snap of a twig. I got off the path that led to the house and began my approach from a small grove of pines. Keeping a low profile, I took a few steps at a time, then dropped down to listen and get a fresh view of the house. When I was within fifty feet of the house, I smelled cigarette smoke. My night vision now in full focus, I saw the smoker. He neither had the silhouette nor body movement I remembered Quinn having. Probably another one of Chalmers's Islamic insurgents. If so, where was he getting them? He obviously had a network of these jihadists to which who he was providing aid, support and promises.

And then I saw that I was correct. The man cradling an AK-47 had stepped out of the shadows and under the outside spotlight. I definitely could see he wasn't from around these parts. Wearing a skull cap and sporting a beard that carried down to his chest, he was every bit Middle Eastern. Standing now within 10 feet of him, I wondered…should I put my new blade against his throat and ease the rifle from his grip or grab him from behind and snap his neck. I figured either way, he might pop a round off. I chose instead to slice him from ear to ear. And so I did. When he stepped to the corner of the house, I was waiting around the side. That's when I slipped up behind him and threw my left hand over his mouth, at the same time sweeping the blade left to right. It cut deep into the flesh. He emitted only a choking sound as his voice box along with everything else in his neck was severed. Before he dropped the AK from his hand, I grabbed it. He crumbled to the dirt in a heap. I then pulled his body out from under the light into the shadows on the dark side of the house.

But were there others? Usually, they worked in pairs…one roving, one standing and watching. This guy wasn't doing a good job watching. I waited…waited maybe thirty seconds and then I heard someone on the other side of the house calling the dead man's name. Walking now in front of the house and not seeing his partner, he brought his AK up in a ready position. He called the man's name again and then stopped. Now he was getting agitated. I couldn't wait much longer. After taking one quick peek around the corner of the house to see exactly where he was standing, I prayed my next move would prove accurate. I wasn't at all familiar with the knife in my hand, but I had to try it. Cocking my arm, I threw it as hard as I had ever thrown a baseball. The blade struck the man squarely in the heart. He emitted no sound as he hit the turf, but his AK did clatter onto the rocky soil. I was going to like this knife.

After dragging the second man's body into the darkness, I waited to see if there was a third guard. Five minutes passed and I was then satisfied these were the only two outside men.

So, as this was Quinn's house Chalmers was using, I wondered if sweet little Rose had visited her father lately. It had been three weeks at least since Chalmers had kidnapped the McGowan cousins. One of those weeks I was in Yemen. Maybe she worked too hard to get away and her father had been making it a point to visit her. I didn't think she would have been in on the deal. Also, I had given her too much information about me and the McGowan family. If she were in on it, she would have called her father the very moment I began looking at the book she gave me.

It was then Liam Quinn himself who stepped outside the front door for a smoke. First he took in a deep breath of the cool, evening air and then lit the cigarette to fill the same lungs with tobacco smoke. As he didn't see the guards about, he began looking in all directions. And as the second man had done, he called out a name, "Akmel." And then the second man's name, "Daiyab." After a few moments, he called their names again. Silence.

When he started getting agitated, I stepped around the corner with one of the AKs in hand and placed the muzzle into his chest. "Don't say a word, Quinn," I said in a low voice. "And don't make me kill you."

He dropped his cigarette and raised his hands. "McGowan. How did you…?"

"Never mind that. Is Chalmers inside?"

He nodded.

"And the McGowan ladies?"

"Yes."

"Why are you in this? Why are you working for this bastard?"

"I'm not."

"What do you mean, you're not?"

"He threatened to kill my Rose…my daughter in the village. I arranged to get you here and I have been takin' care of Fiona and little Mary, seein' to their needs. I get paid nothing."

"Why should I believe you?"

"It's either ya do or ya don't, McGowan. But I'm tellin' ya the truth."

"Maybe I do. But if I find out you're lying, Mr. Quinn, you take my first bullet."

"I swear on my sainted mother's grave and my daughter's life, I'm not a lyin.' I want to see the man inside go down hard."

"Is anyone else in there with him?"

"No. No one."

"By the way, the two Arab guards are lying dead at the side of the house. Are there any more of these Muslim bastards that are soon to arrive tonight?"

"I don't believe so."

"Where is he inside?"

"I have three bedrooms. Fiona and Mary are in the room down the hall in the back…the same one you found them in when you were last here. I have the bedroom next to theirs. Chalmers has taken the first one and has used it both as a bedroom and a place to conduct his business. Before I stepped out here, that's where he was."

"Okay, Mr. Quinn. We're going inside. You lead the way and then you sit down in your living room. I'll be making a move on him. Stay put and be quiet."

When we walked in, I was counting on Chalmers not taking notice as to who was coming through the door. He would have known that Quinn went outside for a smoke and so it should have been him returning to the inside. Quinn sat down as instructed and with AK in hand, I walked cautiously toward the room where Chalmers was supposed to be sitting. The door was closed. With my left hand, I threw the door open wide and thrust the barrel of the rifle inside. To my surprise, the room was empty. I went to the small closet and pushed the sliding door to the right. Not there as well. So where the hell was he?

Stopping to look into Quinn's room, I saw it was also vacant.

"Don't tell me," I said to myself, fearing the worst.

When I threw open the door to where I had last seen Fiona, I saw only her, sitting on the bed. Her lip was quivering. She then glanced to her right and back to me. And standing with his arm draped over Mary was Chalmers with a pistol to her head.

"McGowan. Well, this is disconcerting. You disappoint me, yet amaze me at the same time. Makes a man wonder how you found me."

"And it makes me wonder how you knew I was out here."

"I'm not a complete fool, you know. I was a fool to trust that you would carry out your assignment. I usually don't make mistakes, but I underestimated you. How did I know something was not right out there? I heard Mr. Quinn's voice. My two Muslim friends don't speak a word of English; and I know he doesn't speak Arabic. Why then would I hear English-speaking voices? My guess is that you've disposed of my incompetent Arab buggers out there or they'd be in here putting bullets in you."

I didn't respond to him. The muzzle of the AK I was holding was aimed at his head. However, realizing that, he hunkered down a little more so that Mary's head would be in the line of fire.

He continued, "I'll thank you now to lay the weapon down, McGowan. This child is only seconds from dying."

"She dies, you know damn well **you** die."

"Bruce, Bruce. You came all the way back here to save your cousins' lives. Why then would you risk this girl's death?" Resembling a cur, he snarled his teeth and bellowed, "**Put the gun down…now!**"

Yeah, he was holding all the cards and he knew it. Without word, I laid the AK on the floor. But for a while, the gun he was holding remained fixed on Mary's skull. Suddenly, he pushed her aside and pointed the gun at me.

"And so you're back here and not doing me a bit of good in Yemen. I suppose you've turned the device over to the State Department or FBI."

"No. It's sitting there waiting for you to fly in to retrieve it. If me coming here to rescue my family didn't work out, I hired a couple of people to get the device to the coordinates you were to give me. You give them to me and I'll call my contact. Then you'll have your bomb."

"I'm of course supposed to believe that. Whatever the case, McGowan, I don't need you anymore. I will take the pleasure of sending you to hell." He then cocked the hammer on his revolver and aimed it at my head.

The report was deafening and I thought for sure it had burst my right eardrum. Mary commenced screaming as Chalmers stood with the revolver still aimed at my head for several seconds. He then fell backward onto the floor. I turned to find Quinn over my right shoulder at the door with a still smoking 9 mm in his hand.

"Is the bastard dead?" he asked me.

I went to where Chalmers lay and checked his pulse. Blood was now bubbling from the wound in his chest. "He's shaking hands with the devil now, Mr. Quinn. Good shot." The Scotsman had ended Chalmers's life with the same silver-plated gun I saw him carrying the week before.

"I'm surprised Chalmers allowed you to carry that. You were not exactly one of his trusted goons."

"He figured he could trust that I wouldn't try anything. He told the Arab pricks that if something ever happened to him they would kill my daughter. But, I always told me self if things were ever different, I'd use it on him. It became different tonight when you kilt them rats out there, leavin' just him."

"Thanks, Mr. Quinn. Guess I'd be a dead duck right now if not for you."

Mary then ran quickly to her mother and wrapped her arms around her neck. I went to the both of them and sat down beside them. Fiona was still tied to the bed frame, but apparently Chalmers had released her daughter to become his ace in the hole.

"It's okay, it's okay," I said softly. "My name's Bruce and I reckon I'm your kin."

Tears streamed down Fiona's cheeks and she began shaking. I cut loose her bindings with my dirk and then hugged her. We sat there for several minutes without word and then I unwrapped my arms.

"Mary," she said, "meet your cousin Bruce."

I smiled. "A distant, distant cousin."

Fiona smiled back at me, wiping her moist cheeks. "But a true McGowan, just the same."

I got to my feet and walked to where Quinn still stood, gun now down at his side. "We owe you, Mr. Quinn. We're grateful to you for our lives."

"The whole time I was tendin' the ladies and keepin' that dog from hurtin' 'em, I was thinkin' of me own daughter. I'm glad to be of service to ye, Mr. McGowan. We can all now have peace."

"That we can, Mr. Quinn."

I found my cell phone in the room Chalmers was using as an office, but the batteries had died. I still had Hassan's phone, so I called Keith Lambreau's number. He might be on his way home from work, I thought, given the hour in D.C. But he picked up on the second ring. "I recognized the number, Bruce. Just getting ready to leave the office. What's going on?"

"Good news, Keith. I came back to Scotland and went after Chalmers. He's dead."

"You sum bitch, you got him. Are your cousins okay?"

"They're fine. A very noble Scotsman ended up killing Chalmers. It's a long story, Keith, and I'm too tired to tell it. I've got to get the Scottish cops and the coroner out here to deal with Chalmers's body. I was going to call Sam Galloway, but it's in the wee morning hours there in Yemen. Will check in with him later. Then, first thing tomorrow, I'm getting the train back Edinburgh and flying home. I'm tired, my friend. I'll call you when I get back to West Virginia. Will give you the full details."

"Good. Rest easy, Bruce. You deserve it."

A police inspector from the locals arrived at nine forty-five along with the medical examiner. Both Quinn and I told them our stories of how Chalmers and the two Arabs met their demise. It took longer than anticipated to convey it as the officer seemed to have trouble grasping all the minute details. However, he was an old friend of Liam Quinn and trusted both him and his veracity, so it helped him more readily accept my wild tale.

Fiona was still distraught over her brother James' gruesome beheading. His body's location was most likely going to remain a mystery. I speculated that Chalmers had already had one of his guards bury it in a place it might never be found. Fiona said she would nevertheless see to it his head had a proper burial in the McGowan plot.

Quinn and I then took Fiona and Mary back home to Braemoor. She saw the place was as she had left it, except James sadly wouldn't be returning. Quinn and I went through the castle to assure the place was safe. I didn't tell anyone I had already been there earlier in the evening.

I had planned to find a hotel in Thornloch to bed down for the night, but Fiona begged me to stay with them. I could understand her apprehension about being alone during her first night back home. Quinn had offered me a bed as well, but I respectfully declined. Before he returned to his house, he went back out to his car for a bottle of drambuie to celebrate my cousins' liberation. And his as well.

As we sat and clinked glasses, Mr. Quinn broke into a song…an old Scottish folk song which I had heard somewhere before, maybe from my father when I was a child. As I remember, it was usually sung at wakes and when good friends parted. Its name…The Parting Glass:

Oh all the money that e'er I spent
I spent it in good company
And all the harm that e'er I've done Alas, it was to none but me
And all I've done for want of wit
To memory now I can't recall

So fill to me the parting glass
Good night and joy be with you all
Oh all the comrades that e'er I've had
Are sorry for my going away
And all the sweethearts that e'er I've had Would wish me
one more day to stay But since it falls unto my lot
That I should rise and you should not
I'll gently rise and I'll softly call
Good night and joy be with you all
Good night and joy be with you all

We clinked once more and turned our glasses up to savor the last drop. And then Mr. Quinn was gone.

Before I sat down to commune with my newly-found cousins, I made a quick call to Sam Galloway, telling him what had gone down. It was six-thirty his time. I said, "No plane will be landing in Al-Bayda, so looks like you have a Saturday off."

"That's all great news, Bruce. I'm impressed. No doubt in my mind you were a hell of an operative. You would have done Lionel Byrd proud."

"I can't say I had all that much fun on this trip, but glad we found the WMDs. I assume they'll now be transported for deconstruction."

"That's the plan."

"Well, I'd better get back to my relatives here. It's late and I think all of us want to turn in. Take care of yourself, Sam."

"Be well and good luck to you, Bruce. It was great knowing you."

CHAPTER 21

Although the three of us were tired, Fiona wanted to sit that evening in the parlor and talk…not about their being taken and not about James' horrible death…but about who I was. She first took Mary to her bed, then returned to the kitchen brew up some hot tea to go with our chat. Fiona herself was fair skinned, had fiery red hair, was well-spoken, a bit plump, and came across as a jolly, effervescent sort having a contagious laugh that I had not heard to that point. I asked about her family history, but she first wanted to hear about me, my family and where I was from in the States. In the smallest capsule I could, I told her about my daughter Caroline, my wife Adriana, my only close McGowan family member, my brother Joey, and other than having a long history working for our government, there was nothing at all that remarkable about me. I told her of my brother's ancestry search, having found that her father Angus McGowan was a second cousin to my father. Obviously, Chalmers had connected the dots as well and had fabricated the story that I was in Angus's will.

"Oh, Bruce," she began. "I am so sorry that you were not. My father died almost a year ago and although there was a will, it was read only a week after his death. Even had you been in the will, he left us very little…only Braemoor and the few pounds he had in the bank. There has been no wealth in our clan since before my father's time. My ancestors were smithies for the town of Thornloch and all they had to their name and fame was Braemoor. James worked all his life as a conductor for the railroad, gone most of the day on trips to and from Edinburgh. When I believed that Mary was old enough to stay at home during the summer months, last year I went to work as a waitress at the hotel restaurant in town. That will now be the only income for us. I hate that you were hoodwinked to come here for nothing."

"It wasn't for nothing, Fiona. Even though I came here under false pretenses, when I saw you and Mary were being held, I knew I couldn't desert you. For the past week, I've been working hard to do what Chalmers ordered me to do to keep you alive." "The entire time we were being held captive, I never learned what that was about, Bruce. What was it he was coercing you to do?"

"He knew I was a government operative in my former work life and I was resourceful enough to locate some weapons of mass destruction that we weren't sure even existed. He wanted to sell them to a terrorist nation."

"O mo creach!" she exclaimed, which I'm sure either meant "Oh my goodness!" or "You've got to be shittin' me!"

"But, that's behind us, now."

"The man half scared us to death. I wasn't sure if Mr. Quinn, who we've known for years, was in with the bugger, but glad to find he wasn't. He kept the man from harming us, I'm sure. And those dreadful Arabs that would come and go, I was afraid the Chalmers man would let them have their way with me or would hurt my Mary."

"Mr. Quinn was also coerced to do what he did. Chalmers threatened to kill his daughter."

"Rose? Well now I'm even doubly glad the man is dead and Mr. Quinn killed him."

"Sorry about James, Fiona."

The tears came suddenly. "He was a good man, Bruce…hard working, looked after his sis and my darling Mary. What kind of monster could kill a man like that? Although it was one of the Arab men who did it." She then gasped. "Mo Dhia, he must still be out there somewhere."

"No, he's dead as well."

"You're sure."

"I saw him die in Yemen. The other man who was with him is dead as well."

"Thank the Good Lord."

I tried to trap a yawn, but Fiona saw it. "I am sorry, cousin. I am not a good hostess, keeping you up like this. I want you to take James's bed for the night. We have only one bath and I will let you have it first. I will lay out fresh towels for you. Come with me and I will show you where everything is."

I slept well that night, more soundly than I had done in a week. But, before I was fully ready to open my eyes, the morning sun streamed through the window onto my face like warm honey. Still, I laid in the bed for probably another ten minutes thinking about my conversation with Fiona. She had not mentioned what her father's line of work was and I wondered if she knew he was both MI-5 and MI-6 as Chalmers said he was. Respectfully, I didn't explore that with her. Chalmers insinuated that day I was first taken prisoner that they had some kind of association, but he could have been feeding me a line. Chalmers deserved to die, not just because he had separated James McGowan's head from his body, but he was a collaborator with Jack Randall in the killing of Lionel Byrd and every member of Team Zulu.

However, as I didn't want to waste the morning thinking back over conversations or revisiting the events of the past week, I swung my legs over the side of the bed and jumped into my clothes.

Suddenly, I just remembered something. When Quinn was returning to the castle that morning to take me to the train station, he wanted us to first stop by Rose's house to enjoy one of her hearty breakfasts. He had already set that up with her before he had left Braemoor. My watch read six-twenty and he was to pick me up at seven.

I heard Fiona stirring in her room and thought it would be a good idea to get into the bathroom before her. After I performed all my functions, I stepped out into the hallway to find her waiting at the bathroom door.

"Oh, sorry, Fiona. I hope you didn't have that dire of a need to get in here."

"Not to worry, cousin; I was up before five and am already through with my ditties. I would have liked to prepare a good breakfast for you, but I know you and Mr. Quinn will be off soon. I have to take the jalopy out anyway to get groceries since I haven't been in the house in a month. I have no knowledge of what might be in the house anyway and some of my food I know is now spoiled."

When it was close to seven, I made my way downstairs to the parlor. Mary was also already up and sat reading a children's book on the sofa. Given the lateness of the hour the night before and realizing she was still crying when we arrived at Braemoor, I hadn't had an opportunity to talk with her. However, she was now all smiles and no doubt happy to be home, the trauma of what she had experienced now behind her.

Seeing me, she immediately burst into a conversation. "Are you really my cousin?"

"As true as true can be," I answered.

"Are you leaving us now?"

"Yes, Mary. I have to get back to my home in the United States."

"I would love to go to the United States someday."

"I'm sure you will. You can come to see me anytime." I then looked at Fiona. "Both of you have to come for a visit. My door is always open."

Mary then frowned. "If your door is always open, won't a burglar get in?"

I smiled. It was just like an innocent child to say something like that.

Fiona said, "Mary, what he meant is that we are always welcome at the McGowan castle in America."

And then I laughed. "Well, it's far from a castle, but it's home."

As I heard Quinn's car outside, I gave my cousins a hug and thanked them for the bed.

"I want you to come back some day for a long visit, Bruce," Fiona said. "And you must bring Mrs. McGowan with you."

"I will, Fiona. You can count on it."

I then left Braemoor wondering if I really **would** be back. But, I had promised, and I don't break my promises.

When we arrived in town, I took a moment before exiting Quinn's ancient Buick to call Adriana. She was delighted that I was at last coming home. I told her I'd be catching the afternoon train to Edinburgh and then booking a flight back. I wasn't sure when I'd be flying out or when the plane would land, but would damn sure be on the first flight having an open seat.

Rose's small, turf-roofed cottage, so very quaint, made of stone and wood, reminded me of a photo I had seen of Mr. Shakespeare's wife, Anne Hathaway. After entering the house, I was welcomed by the aroma of back bacon on the griddle, sausages, eggs, and bannock which I learned is a Scottish skillet bread baking in the oven. I didn't know whether she had made the breakfast just for me or was it something she did on a regular basis. But she also whipped up a bowl of baked beans, on which I passed. Even though it's a food every restaurant in Great Britain serves for breakfast, I prefer mine for dinner. And then what neither looked nor sounded good was her black pudding or pig's blood cooked inside of an intestine. Whether it sounded appetizing or not, I was sure it would have been a gastronomical disaster for me right about the time I was getting on the train.

I know I shouldn't have been, but I was well-taken with the lovely Rose…the beautifully-arched eyebrows over those fiery green eyes, her perfect teeth, which only one percent of people in Great Britain had, warm chestnut hair, full, sensuous lips and wearing a thin, batiste dress where every luscious curve of her hourglass shape was sublimely accentuated. Good God Almighty, I had to get home.

Why Rose had never been snatched up by any of the locals on her second go-round was beyond me. I actually asked her that and she said she did have a boyfriend who was a semi-pro golfer in the St. Andrews area. I wondered why the bloke didn't just chuck that sport and move down to Thornloch to take up a different, more pleasurable sport…romancing the gorgeous Ms. Quinn, the putz. I knew there was a conductor job opening up with the railroad.

After the stuffing of my innards, while the bonny Rose put away her dishes, I stood out on the porch for about a half hour talking with her father while he smoked a cigarette. He had not told his daughter what he did for Chalmers, even though he was compelled to do it to protect her. Maybe if the cops were not tight-lipped somewhere down the road, it might leak out, but I didn't think so.

Quinn apologized once more for aiding Chalmers in capturing me now over a week ago. I knew back then somehow he was a good man as he had warned me not to cause any trouble; just do what Chalmers said. I told him I would not think another thought about it. Both of us were alive and my cousins were released unharmed. All the bad guys had paid for their sins with their lives. He smiled and held out his hand. I shook it. "You're a good man, Mr. Quinn, and a good father. Take care of that lovely lass inside."

"Oh, don't ye worry about that, Mr. McGowan. I'll always be watchin' out for her…and for your kin."

I nodded. "Guess I need to get to the station. I can walk from here. First, I have to say goodbye to Rose."

When I returned inside, Rose had just finished cleaning up the kitchen and was preparing to leave for work. When she saw I was leaving, she smiled and gave me a hug, in the process pressing her magnificent ta tas against my chest. Okay, I wasn't cheating on my wife, even in my mind. I was merely appreciating God's heavenly handiwork.

She grabbed hold of my hands. Although I could feel the power in her grip, she still had a soft, gentle touch. "Fair thee well, Bruce McGowan."

"Ah, me lass, goodbye. 'But to see her was to love her'," I said.

Her smile broadened. "Robert Burns."

"Aye."

"Come back to see us, Bruce."

"Maybe someday. Take care of your father. He loves you more than you'll ever realize."

She nodded and I released her hands from mine. I had a train to catch.

CHAPTER 22

The Thornloch to Edinburgh line left at 11:20. Using Hassan's phone, which I would soon toss in the drink, I called British Airlines and managed to get a seat on a flight leaving at 7:30 that evening. I would land at Reagan National around midnight. I'd have a layover until 8:05 the next morning when my flight from there to Charleston, WV departed. If all went well, Adriana would pick me up at Yeager around 9:15 AM.

It didn't. Go well, that is. By the time my delayed flight left the ground in Edinburgh and I was delayed again in Washington, she waited all day for me to finally end my trip at the Kanawha Airport at 3:30 PM.

I think she knew right away there was something awry about me. My face and arms were tanned and even burnt in places; I was wearing strange and different clothing; my eyes were bloodshot and haggard looking; and having had only a half hour before viewed myself in the plane's restroom mirror, I had the general appearance of a sewer rat. When she spotted me at the jetway door, my first thought was she didn't recognize me. She had this stupefied look on her face. But then realizing it was actually me, she finally ran to me, wrapped her arms around my neck and kissed me. Then taking a step back to again look at me, she shook her head and said, "Okay, lover man, I just can't wait to hear the story."

It would be a two hour trip home. I drove. And as we sailed down the mountain toward the interstate, she wasted no time prodding me.

"So, did you take a side trip to Hawaii or something? You didn't get that tan in cool and rainy Scotland. You also look like you've been on a week-long drunk. And how did you manage to lose both your suitcase and cellphone? What happened to you, Skip?"

The third degree I didn't expect. She definitely wasn't the woman I had kissed goodbye a little over a week ago. And her machine gun style interrogation wasn't like her at all. But I think her seeing me in my condition may have shaken her a little, causing her to go inquisitorial on me. I got it.
"Yeah, sweetheart, you deserve an explanation. And do I have a story to tell you." I thought that was a good lead-in that might soften what I was about to tell her.

My story which began there in Charleston wasn't finished until we were crossing the Glad Creek Bridge the other side of Beckley. I know what ye might be thinking. I should have left a lot of stuff out, especially about the gunplay and the people I put in the ground, but I told her everything. I prefaced the story by saying "what I'm about to tell you of my trip, my dear, was not anything I planned or asked for. Understand that everything I experienced was thrust upon me."

She sat attentively and without interruption the entire hour it took for me to convey the details of my excellent adventure. When I was done with my spiel, she had a look of bafflement on her face. I don't think it was because she didn't believe me; I think she was just overwhelmed by everything I told her.

"And now aren't you glad you decided not to go with me?" I said.

She shook her head. "I just can't believe all this. It's like you can't go anywhere unless you end up in an atmosphere of danger. So, how many people did you kill this time?" she asked.

"Only those that needed it."

"And you're sure you weren't on the government payroll. You weren't taking part in some planned mission."

"Hey, you read the telegram. All this started out in Scotland. There was no government assignment. I would not lie to you. I hope you know that. I was a victim on this trip, the entire time, except for the few hours on the tail end where I spent time with my cousins."

"Well, I'm glad you're home and didn't come back with any bullet holes in you like usual. Just don't plan any more trips unless it's you and I at the beach somewhere. Of course, then you might find out the cabana boys are actually ISIS terrorists targeting American tourists."

I laughed. "You have a vivid imagination, my dear."

"Ha! You know I'm not that far off base."

Before we got to the house, we had a nice dinner at our new Italian restaurant in our little burg which has historically been called the Coolest Town in America. We finally arrived home at seven. It had been a long ass day. I was beat…almost too tired to romance the Mrs. But I'd have to be drugged, passed out or have one foot in the grave for that not to happen. From all that I had been through, for me it was something akin to angry, voracious, pent up sex. And my poor wife? She probably felt like she was more victim than love partner. Nonetheless, my lights were out before nine either from the jet lag or I had slipped into a coma from a condition which in Latin is called sexuous maximus.

For the first day in more than a week, I had some real, uninterrupted time to do nothing but rest and just think. Yeah, Chalmers was dead, my cousins safe and I had survived yet another harrowing adventure. The disappointment in all that was…the inheritance I was supposed to be getting was bogus. But then there was that good thing; I had gotten to the bottom of the WMD controversy over which a war was fought. The weapons did exist and I was part of the effort that located them. I knew our doing so would make the former president's day when he found out about it and all his critics and nay-sayers would be eating crow. The world would also be a safer place when they were destroyed.

Several days went by and I found myself contemplating my Yemeni experience less and less. I was now focusing on important matters like my golf game and where we would go for dinner on any given night. However, on a Friday morning in late October my cell phone rang. It was Keith Lambreau.

"I thought I was done with you," I said.

"I don't go away that easily, Scorpion. I couldn't find your phone number; then I remembered you called me from your new Arab friend's phone."

"But I see you found me anyway."

"Yeah. Hey, got a problem, Bruce."

"Sorry, pal, I'm all out of solutions. But okay, go ahead if you must. What's going on?"

"The WMDs…they're gone."

"Yeah. That was the plan. Galloway and the CIA were supposed to send them to
Pantex and Pueblo. They **should** be gone by now."

"They're gone all right, but so is Galloway. He's gone rogue, Bruce."

"Sam Galloway? All-American, red-white-and-blue Company man?"

"We believe he intends to put the weapons in terrorist hands. His assistant there at the embassy, Mike Daniels, said he heard him speaking Arabic and saw that he was on the phone with someone in Syria. The next day

Galloway was gone, desk cleaned out and classified documents missing. The Agency is looking for him. Daniels then flew to the mountain cave where you found the weapons and they too were gone."

"Holy H-bomb! They're **all** gone? Nuclear **and** chemical?"

"Correct."

"He had to have a hell of a lot of help getting them out. It was four trucks that transported them there in the first place."

"It would have been a logistical feat for sure."

"Do you believe they're still stockpiled somewhere in Yemen or did he somehow get them out of country?" I asked.

"The weapons obviously made it into the country relatively unnoticed all those years ago, but with the satellite imagery we now have, I don't think they were convoyed that far from where you found them. Any such unusual activity should be available on both federal and private imagery. The government is at this moment attempting to gain access to images that Google and

Microsoft may have. We are also viewing images that NASA and the National GeoSpatial Intelligence Agency may have captured over the past week."

"What if he moved them at night…or over several nights?" I asked him.

"Good question. There are satellites that use infrared capability to see at night, even through clouds, but mainly it captures lights and weather changes. The ability to detect movement during the hours of limited visibility is not there yet. If it was known that the weapons were being moved, we could have put up drones with IR capability, but that would have to have been real time."

"To get all of the weapons out of that cave and down the hill to an awaiting flatbed would've taken heavy equipment and several men. They also had to get the large weapons crates over the pile of large rocks and we barely got our bodies through the opening that we made."

"I of course wasn't there with you guys, Bruce, but I'm thinking that Mike Daniels may have the answers to your questions since he went back in there a couple days ago. He and the Agency have been feverishly looking for

Galloway, doing sweeps by air all over the Jabal Mountains."

"If they secured and transported those crates and got out of those mountains all in one night, there are plenty of places to hide."

"Yemen covers a lot of territory, like stretching from Southern Virginia to Massachusetts."

"And may I add it's a shit hole." I quipped. "So, do you and CTT have a dog in the hunt in this matter?"

"I think we eventually will, Bruce. For right now, it's the FBI's and CIA's baby. If at some point terrorist elements operating in Syria get their hands on some of these weapons, we'll be added to the list of alphabet agencies to go after the kingpins. Right now the Bureau is taking the lead in the investigation while the Agency is using its resources to find Galloway. Anyway, I just called to let you know about all this. It may be that some agent who's on the hunt will be calling you since you had partnered with Galloway on locating the weapons in the first place."

"Fine. Just know I ain't going back."

He laughed. "I thought you enjoyed yourself over there…lots of sunshine, nice warm temperatures, adventure at every turn, beautiful Arabian women…"

"Did I tell you it was a shit hole? You may not have heard me the first time."

"I don't know what goes from here, but because you started this thing, I'll keep you apprised…if you're okay with that."

"Yeah, I would like to know the outcome of all this. I thought we had put a cap on it."

"By the way, Bruce, the locating of the WMDs is still classified. I was reminded of that in my last conversation with my boss at the State Department."

"I'm sure the government especially doesn't want it to leak out that it found the WMDs and then lost them. Too bad; it would have been the news story of the year.

"For sure. Well, gotta go, Scorpion. Enjoy life down there in the great WV. Come see us if you get bored."

"Life's good. Chao, G Man."

CHAPTER 23

And so we had a **new** villain. Lambreau's news of Galloway's traitorous act had just ripped my shorts. He had deserted not only the Agency but his country as well. There went his pension. Too bad…I actually liked Sam. I guess he got the idea of selling the WMDs to a terrorist nation from the English prick who thankfully was now taking the eternal dirt nap. Bad idea, Galloway. You can't win this.

Adriana wanted to know who was on the phone. After telling her it was my friend Lambreau at the counterterrorist division, I quickly added "no, his call was not an invitation to go back to work there. He just wanted to bring me up on the status of the WMD retrieval." I did remind her that everything I told her about our locating the weapons was the government's secret. During my last couple of years with Team Zulu, we were newlyweds; being the insightful and perceptive wife that she was, she had managed to discover the particulars of a couple of my classified missions. So, maybe I was being redundant in my reminder. She already knew the drill.

It was good to get back out on the links with my weapons of self-destruction. I'm not the best of golfers, but I enjoy the camaraderie, the smell of green, green grass, the golden Greenbrier countryside and the intoxicating mountain air. One of my bobblehead friends, Billy "Buck" Rogers, jested that I hit like a woman. At first, I thought he was talking about my swing, which is not exactly as long-hitting as a Phil Mickelson or accurate as a Bubba Watson, both of whom, by the way, are property owners at the Greenbrier resort a few miles away. But then, to avoid a rabbit punch to the throat, he quickly retracted and clarified what he meant. It's that I don't King Kong the ball 275-300 yards like the rest of them. But, I hit it straight down the middle. So, while they're looking for their slices off in the woods, I'm waiting patiently for them in the center of the fairway at somewhere around 200 yards down range.

At the 19th hole, Buck, Tom Bianco, a new guy I hadn't met before, Johnny Ray Haynes, and I sat talking over a beer. "Where'd you go a couple weeks ago?" Bianco asked me. "Edna was talkin' to Adriana and she said you had to go to a will reading somewhere in Scotland. You come into some money?"

"A distant cousin passed away and I was supposed to be in that will. I went all that way and found out I wasn't."

"Must've pissed ya royally."

"Well, it was good to see family I didn't even know I had. No big deal."

"The wife was okay with you goin' by yourself, hangin' out in the pubs with all those big-breasted redheads?"

"Yep. She trusts me unconditionally and in reality has no reason not to. You see, I married an honest-to-God angel, Buck."

New guy Johnny Ray quipped, "You're lucky, McGowan. Mine's still alive," sparking a round of laughter.

But it was another of my friends at an adjacent table, David Baxter, who overheard our conversation. "Bruce, is there something else you want to share with us?"

"Like what, Dave?"

"Like what you were doing over there in Yemen."

"Come again?"

"Since I knew you'd be playing here today as usual, I brought something to show you." He unfolded the newspaper clipping and laid it on our table. "Now tell me that isn't you."

And there it was…that same up-close photo of me providing first aid to an alHudaydah victim."

The others passed it around and began nodding in agreement. "That's you alright, Bruce," Bianco said.

I glanced at each of them, at the same time trying to think of a response. "It's a good likeness of me, whoever the guy is."

"It's you, Bruce," Dave insisted. "That's your face and that's our club logo on your shirt, clear as day. Charlie Poindexter was over in Richmond a couple of weeks ago and picked up this copy of the Times-Dispatch. He spotted your mug immediately. You wanna tell us about this?"

I was stuck. I don't make it a practice of lying to people, especially to Adriana and my friends. But I couldn't come clean. The 'mission' which was forced upon me and its findings couldn't be let out.

"Fellas, I value our friendship. We've been golf chums now more than five years. And Buck, you and I go back all the way to grade school. You knew that I at one time was a government employee and sometimes still do contract work for it even though retired. So, would you all do me a kindness and not ask me about it?"

Buck smiled. "Just like we thought all these years…CIA."

"Not every government contractor is CIA, Bucky," I replied.

Dave, a historian and social studies teacher, and who was probably the most intelligent talking head of us all, said, "Here's the thing, Bruce…Yemen is considered the most dangerous country in the Arab world, engaged in civil strife and a hot-bed for both al-Qaeda and ISIS. What would you be doing in a place like that as a government contractor and right in the middle of a terrorist attack?"

"If he told you he'd have to kill you, Dave." I looked at Buck and shook my head. Come on, get original, pal.

"Hey, guys," I replied. "I gotta abandon this conversation. It's just something I'm not at liberty to talk about. Let it go."

As I was now feeling a bit uncomfortable, I think they sensed it. Thereafter, nothing more was said about the photo, nor did they spout out any additional wisecracks about me being CIA or some kind of mercenary. However, as I was the first of us to leave Club 19 that afternoon, I was sure I'd still be the topic of conversation. Their speculation about me would continue.

I like it when there is complete closure with my undertakings. But, Sam Galloway had screwed that up. It would have served my brain well for the WMDs to have been removed from the cave, turned over to the folks at DOE Pantex and Pueblo and everything wrapped up into a nice, neat package. But my efforts, whether driven by Chalmers or not, had ended in vain. I don't like failure. In school I may not have gotten the best grades, but I never had an incomplete. And I pride myself in not having failed at any of my courses. Although I can't say I personally failed at the Yemen undertaking, the end result was disappointing. A mad man initially wanted the nuclear device delivered to him to sell to the Iranians. Now, a traitor had possession of both the nuclear and chemical weapons to sell to the Syrians. So, where were the weapons now? And had he gotten them out of Yemen?

As these questions were nagging at me like a toothache, I made a phone call. Maybe I shouldn't have, since the matter was being addressed by the FBI and CIA. Could be that Keith Lambreau had a piece of the deal as well, I wasn't sure. I no longer did.

"Hello, this is Mike Daniels."

"Mike, Bruce McGowan."

"Hello, Mr. McGowan. I never thought I'd hear from you again."

"Like a bad penny, I turn up sometimes."

"I guess you heard about Galloway."

"Yeah."

"Are you on a secure line?"

"No…my cell."

"No matter. We can keep it generic. What can I do for you?"

"Maybe fill in the blanks for me?"

"What do you want to know?"

"Any idea where the cargo was taken?"

"It was removed and loaded on a flat bed at night."

"Just as I figured. But how do you know?"

"Satellite images."

"I thought satellites didn't see at night."

"They can pick up lights…in this case, flashlights. Six were counted going up and down hill over a period of seven hours. Considerable cargo, as you know."

"Were you able to track them beyond the retrieval point?"

"All we know is they went north."

"So, they didn't make the coast for loading aboard ship."

"No. We believe they were going in the direction of the northern border, maybe crossing over into the next country."

"Given their mode of transportation, that had to be difficult traveling through thick, thick sand. A lot of dunes and sabkhahs as I recall reading about."

"Would have been."

"And if they crossed the border, wouldn't the perps have been detected, even apprehended?"

"The border covers a hell of a lot of miles and is relatively undefined in places. The subject we're discussing would have known where the best place to cross was." "But once into the country, where would they have gone? Certainly, once inside, it's all well patrolled. Could mean certain death bringing such cargo in."

"The nation is friendly to the U.S. and we would have been apprised of such activity. The suspect and cargo would be returned to American soil. We've heard nothing from them or our consulate."

"It's a mess. Too bad he did what he did."

"I worked with him four years and apparently never knew him."

"Sometimes, Mike, it's the people that are close to us who we know the least. I know that first hand. I didn't know your co-worker well enough to either see something like this coming or be that surprised about it."

"Well, we're a pretty perceptive bunch in what we do and I didn't anticipate it. We did a lot of after-hours shit together."

"Do your higher speculate on his whereabouts?"

"They've been fairly tight-lipped about their investigation and much of it I don't know about. Other aspects of the case I can't divulge."

"Understood."

"I know you remain interested as you have some time and effort invested. I just don't have much for you."

"I appreciate you talking with me. Hope the subject is caught and the cargo found once again. I'd like to see a good ending to the matter."

"Yeah," he said. "He gave us a black eye and from a professional standpoint, we've been damaged. But, lots of stones to overturn."

"You'll find him. Keep the faith, Mike. Talk again one day."

"Adios, Bruce."

PART TWO

CHAPTER 24

I pulled up on my computer the map of the Arabian Peninsula to perform a SWAG (Sophisticated Wild-Ass Guess) on where Galloway could have gone. Although the conversation was about him and the cargo (weapons), we were non-specific in case the phone lines had ears. I doubted Galloway had set up a way for him to monitor any conversations that came through the Company line; that was Mike's specialty. If anyone were eavesdropping or lines tapped, one wouldn't have had to be a genius to figure out what we were discussing. The land to the north was of course Saudi Arabia. The desert was Rub 'al-Khali or Empty Quarter which covered the northern sector of Yemen well into Saudi land which constitutes the the largest area of continuous sand in the world. My question was——even if he could navigate in that area, considering the Rub 'al-Khail was virtually uninhabited and even unexplored, where would he find the populous support to wherever he was heading? Even the Bedouin tribes were sparsely settled in that region.

However, all these guesses and suppositions were now moot as far as I was concerned. Sure, I wanted closure, but Galloway and the weapons of mass destruction were the government's problem. I did wonder, however, where Galloway went. The Company takes betrayal by one of their operatives more personally than do the other alphabet agencies and I wouldn't have been surprised if and when they found him, he was made to disappear from the face of the earth. There are ways they can make that happen and no one will be the wiser. If you're not already crazy when you hire on with the CIA, you **will** be in short order. But as far as I was concerned, it was going to be a mystery until the day Christiane Amanpour announced the discovery of the infamous Iraqi WMDs somewhere in the Middle East. Hopefully, they wouldn't be found in the hands of terrorists or used by a rogue government against another nation.

* * * * *

Ironically, a month later, Adriana and I happened to be in Washington, D.C. for the

America's Small Town Mayor's Convention when my cell phone rang. It was Keith Lambreau.

"Hello, Bruce. Where are you these days?"

"In your back yard of all places."

"I beg your pardon?"

"In D.C. for a convention my wife is attending."

"Really. How long will you be here?"

"Two days. Adriana had an all day meeting today and half a day tomorrow. There's a dinner tonight."

"Are you all going back home when things break up tomorrow?"

"We were going to do a little touring around the mall area, specifically to see what's different at the Museum of American History," I said.

"Shouldn't be much different from the last time you saw it. History doesn't change; it just gets added on to. How about us having dinner tomorrow evening?"

"I think we can do that. It's been a while since the three of us got together. What was it…three or more years ago?"

"At least."

"If we do this——where?" I asked.

"The Capitol Club around six."

"I'll see if the Mrs. is okay with that. She may have arranged to meet one of the other mayors later."

"Other mayors? Adriana is a mayor?"

"And a good one."

"I'm impressed."

And as I remember, he was even more impressed the first time he saw **her.** His eyes stayed glued on her all evening. Just understand, Lambreau, she's mine. I saw her first.

"And so were you just calling to chat or was there something pressing?"

"Well, if we're going to have dinner tomorrow, let's begin our conversation then. Too much to get into."

"Obviously you want to talk more about my recent Yemeni adventure."

"Let's save it for tomorrow," he said.

"That is if the mayor has nothing else going. Is what you want to discuss with me for **her** ears as well?"

"Not particularly; we'll have to keep things generic. But, at some point we'll definitely need her stamp of approval."

"Who's **we**? Sounds like you're trying to pull me in on something. Whatever it is, she won't go for it."

"What are you doing right now?"

"Sitting in a coffee shop waiting for her to come out of today's meetings."

"Can you meet me for a couple hours? I can come there."

I checked my watch. "No can do. It's just after three and will soon be heading back to the hotel to get ready for our dinner."

"It would actually be better to sit and talk without Adriana, but if you can't, you can't."

"Understood. Looks like dinner tomorrow is our best opportunity to get together."

"Alright, but you probably realize what I want to discuss is classified. As you've already found yourself deep in this Yemen mess, the government wants to reactivate your TS/SCI clearance for a limited time."

"No, Keith. I'm done with this. I can't stress that enough. The government's wasting its time reactivating my clearance."

"Just listen to me is all I ask. But, again, there are some things we won't be able to talk about in Adriana's presence."

"But she **is** a mayor after all," I quipped.

"Be serious, Bruce. We'll have to have the **big** talk in private."

"Well again, Keith, if it's what I think you're suggesting, she'll put the squelch on it in a hurry."

"Let me just do what I can to prime her pump tomorrow evening."

"You could have chosen a different way to put that, pal."

That got a laugh out of him. "Capitol Club at six, Bruce. Have a good evening."

Even though only three small town mayors per state had been selected to attend the conference, the adding of spouses pushed our dinner numbers to over 300. Although a nice enough affair in the Magnolia Room at the swanky hotel, the dinner program still lasted way too long, given all the speeches that bored me to tears. I'm just never good listening to people on their little ego trips who love hearing the sound of their own voices. After more than two hours, all I hear is walla-walla-walla, an assembly line of unintelligible words drowning in a sea of apathy. You know that you're in Dullsville, USA when the best part of the evening is the New York Cheesecake with the three blueberries. But I was there to support my hometown mayor and determined not to doze off and fall out of my chair. Never a good impression for one to leave with all the other mayors.

Adriana was good with us having dinner with Keith the next evening. She said it would be great to see him again. "I remember him as rather nice looking…tall wavy blonde hair and so adept at priming pumps." No, she didn't say that last thing. "Did he ever get re-married?"

"I don't think so. At least in our brief conversations, he didn't mention anyone."

"Considering you and Keith will be talking manly stuff, it would have been nice for me to commune with another woman."

"I'm sure you'll be included in the conversation in some manner." And I knew what that would be. Lambreau and company were going to try pulling me back into the Yemeni matter, likely on a contract basis, and he wanted Madam Mayor's blessing. She wouldn't be privy to any discussion of the whats and whys beyond that.

Following Adriana's morning session the next day, we had lunch at Cafe Bonaparte in Georgetown and then trekked over to the Smithsonian for a dose of American history and culture. While Adriana was checking out Judy Garland's ruby slippers and Fonzie's leather jacket, I was looking over Richard Petty's # 43 race car that chocked up his 200th NASCAR win. But we did meet back up to walk through displays both of us wanted to see such as the Lincoln artifacts, the table and chairs from the McLean House in Appomattox where Lee and Grant signed the surrender papers, and of course the Star Spangled Flag from Ft. McHenry. Oh say, but we saw quite a bit that afternoon. It was actually the first time we had visited a national museum together.

We arrived at the Capitol Club at six fifteen, just a tad late. Friday evening traffic along Pennsylvania Avenue was at a standstill for more than ten minutes to allow the President and his motorcade to cross the intersection a few blocks away. I understood he was on his way back home after attending a special ceremony at Arlington.

I guessed the counterterrorist business had been a bit rough on Lambreau as that wavy, blonde hair he had the last time we saw him was now white and thinning. He also appeared gaunt and well-worn. I almost didn't recognize him. But I suppose neither of us was still wearing the spartan looks we had three years ago. Of course, Adriana still looked as ravishing as she did that first moment I saw her at Wolf Laurel more than thirteen years before. Lambreau thought so as well. When he greeted us at the table, he made a grab for her hand before he extended his to mine. Mine, Lambreau. But then a few moments later he finally saw that I was actually with her.

"Bruce, you're looking fit, my friend. This retirement thing is really working for you.

And you still have that gunslinger swagger that I remember."

"And you, Keith, look uh…different."

He laughed. "Your affectionate way of saying I look like shit."

"No, no. I guess it's the…"

"The white hair, right? I'm fifty, you're sixty-something and I look like your older brother."

"You look good, Keith."

He ordered a Scotch and water and told the server to bring us what we wanted. He would treat. Adriana wanted a white wine and I asked for whatever was on draft.

We had some small talk, catching up on who was doing what. At first he danced around what the organization had evolved into, trying to be as vanilla as he could, given that Adriana wasn't supposed to know anything I had done government-wise. She quickly set him straight. "Keith, you don't have to talk in code around me," she said. "I know just about everything there is to know in regards to my husband's former career…counterterrorist operative, code name Scorpion, member of Team Zulu who turned down the director job when Mr. Byrd was murdered, and deadly assassin who took out the terrorist known as The Viper."

Lambreau's widened eyes reflected his surprise. "You know all this? How would…"

"Keith, a woman can't be married to a guy like Bruce and not figure things out. I also know about the Yemen matter, mainly because he wouldn't have been able to keep it from me. A man goes to Scotland for the reading of a will, stays a week and comes back with not only empty pockets, but looking like he had been drug through the sand. Bruce may have been a super stud agent for the government, but Top Secret or not, I have seductive ways of finding things out."

Whoa. Who was this woman and what had she done with my wife?

"You know about Yemen?"

I interjected. "I've trusted this lady with sensitive information on a good number of occasions. You may have heard about that Christmas we were entertaining the former President and First Lady and our home was shot up by terrorists. Adriana was thrown right in the middle of it. She has not only unwittingly been involved in a couple other of my missions, but ended up being kidnapped and shot as well. Yeah, she has no government clearance of any sort, but being married to me, she's figured a hell of a lot of things out."

He nodded. "Well then, I guess I don't need to tip-toe around any conversation we'll be having this evening. We will need to keep our voices low, however. You also see I asked for a table far from the madding crowd."

"What's on your mind?" I asked him.

"A team is being formed we'd like you to be a part of."

"What kind of team and for what reason?"

"Well, you know the WMDs got lost again along with a government operative. The
Bureau is taking the lead on finding Galloway and fielding a team made up of a new Company man assigned to the embassy, the technician Daniels, an FBI Special Agent, an FBI Legat in Yemen, also based in the embassy, maybe myself and hopefully you. Everyone would have a reason to be part of the team."

"I would have no reason."

"I think you would. Daniels said you clicked with Galloway and actually got into his brain in regards to something you talked about. Also, it was you who initially found the weapons and with your keen nose you could be instrumental in sniffing them out again."

Adriana interjected this time. "How much danger is involved here? I have almost lost my husband on several occasions and fear every time the government calls, he might just use up the last of his nine lives."

Lambreau smiled at that. "This would just entail conducting a comprehensive search…no gunplay. Bruce is no longer an operative. He'll be doing contract work and will be paid for his services."

"How much?" I asked.

"50K plus per diem…and a nice Thank You letter from the President."

"I already have a letter from a president. Actually two. And I made a hell of a lot more than that nailing the number one terrorist in the world."

"Understood. But that was a far more dangerous mission. Is money what's holding you back?"

"Not necessarily. There would only be two things holding me back…apathy and the lady sitting on my right."

"What's the apathy all about?"

"I already spent a week there and the entire country is a smelly wasteland, a worse experience than trudging through rotting garbage in Bangladesh. And who knows how long I'd be there this time? It could take six months or an infinite amount of time to find Galloway and the weapons. For the amount of money offered, I could make more than that greeting down at the Walmart."

"Is this the same Bruce McGowan I once idolized?"

"It's a retired, leisurely Bruce McGowan, and my action days are behind me."

Adriana said, "Double the offer and maybe he'll consider it."

Uh, what? Okay, once again, just who the hell was this woman anyway?

"I'd have to clear it with the Department of Justice. They will be the agency putting the bill. So, how about it, Bruce? You started all this——inadvertently of course, so you should be in on it."

"I don't know. I did tell myself the other day I would liked to have had closure on the matter. I'll have to think about it and talk it over with my partner here…" I then gave her a look. "…who seems to also be my financial arranger. When would we leave country?"

"I'm not sure…maybe a week. With the exception of Daniels and the Legat in Yemen, the rest of us will meet in advance at a designated location and day to plan out the mission."

Our server finally came to take our order. For some reason, I discovered I was not as hungry as I was ten minutes before. Adriana ordered a salad…as usual. I had told her countless times, "If God wanted us to be vegetarians, He would have filled the ark with broccoli and lettuce." But, in a way, I **am** indirectly a vegetarian; cows eat grass…I eat cows. Anyway, I went ahead and ordered a steak; but, to appease Adriana, a small one. After doing so, I then envisioned me back in the boiling 110 degree desert having dinner in some Bedouin camp on goat kabobs, again risking cholera or TB, and me telling myself if I ever got out of the hell hole, I'd never set foot in Sandland again.

So, there I sat, trying to figure out what was wrong with that picture. Was I really going to do this? And was Adriana actually going to sanction it?

The remainder of the evening, Lambreau talked some about the operatives still left in the State Department's Counterterrorism Team. My Team Zulu did not get replaced, but Xray and Yankee Teams still existed. Lambreau of course was the overall director.

The new name for the CTT was Bureau of Counterterrorism and Countering Violent Extremism, but the last part of the cumbersome name was seldom used. Keith said my name sometimes comes up as I am used as an example of the model operative for new trainees. I told him I appreciated hearing that, but then wondered whether it was my proficient side or my ruthless side that was being emulated.

Lambreau said he would be in touch within a few days when a meeting was scheduled, but he and the Bureau would like to have my answer as soon as possible. Oh, and did I have a visa? As I knew the counterfeit one created by Chalmers's man would not fly, I told him no. He would expedite one through the system.

CHAPTER 25

We stayed in D.C. another night as planned, this time at the Cambria which offered us a swanky room for a decent price and a picturesque rooftop view of the city for a bonus. The night had cooled to a comfortable 59 degrees and as I stood with my arms wrapped around the lovely Adriana, I felt like I was twenty-five again. Her long, brown hair still smelled of her shampoo and as I nuzzled her neck, the scent of her Carolina Herrera began cranking up my juices. A woman who could be soft, elegant and sensuous as she was that night, could also be a spitfire when it suited her…especially in the bedroom. The every-woman. The kind of woman every man dreams of marrying. Small wonder Lambreau was so taken with her as were a half dozen of my other chums back in the dubya-vee. So, I asked myself Dirty Harry's question, "Do you feel lucky, punk? Well, do ya?" Damn right…every day. And the way both of us were allowing our bodies to writhe on one another while standing there in the dark looking out over the nation's capital, I knew in about ten minutes I **was** about to get lucky.

As I lay in a post-coital sweat trying to cool off, Adriana made little circles with her fingers over my chest hair.

The smile on her face? Yeah, I put it there. I was wearing one as well. But after both the big brain and little brain are satiated, that's when the world changes from surreal to rational. That's when conversations begin. It's certainly what a woman wants. It took me a while to realize that. I thought you were supposed to sleep after sex. However, this was a woman with whom I actually **liked** talking. Only this night I had a good idea of what it would be about.

"So, you're really thinking of going back there," she said.

"I wasn't, but apparently you are. You surprised me, you know. I thought at
Lambreau's mere mention of me joining the mini task force, you'd pitch a fit."

"Would it have done me any good to do so?"

"I don't ever like going against your wishes. I think you know that."

"The money will come in handy since we no longer have a business."

"We're doing okay," I said. "We're not exactly strapped for money, you know." That chunk of dough I got for killing The Viper had gone a long way. We fixed up the house and the place had long been paid for.

"Well, if you're going to talk yourself out of it, who am I to protest. I just don't want you going to the badlands and risking never coming back to me."

"From what I gather, the operation will be more of a 'search and find' mission. If there'd be any hostilities, the Bureau would handle it. The detachment of Marines in Sana'a would also be at the ready as needed. Per Keith, I would only be along because of my keen insights."

She cuddled her body up next to mine. "Well, I have seen over the past couple of years how antsy you've become…like you don't know what to do with yourself. You've always been a man of action. Lately, the only action you've been getting is your golf game."

I let out a chuckle. "And what would you call the thing that happened just a few minutes ago?"

She slapped me playfully on my abdomen. "Some pretty sweet action. You go away for a few weeks or however long it takes and you see what you'll be missing?"

"You don't play fair."

"No, I don't. And as you just found out, I play rough too."

* * * * *

Three days after we returned to Wolf Laurel, Lambreau called again. "Bruce, the deal we're putting together is going to happen sooner than I thought. Can you come back up here tomorrow?"

"Let's see…tomorrow's Tuesday. Yeah, I guess I can blow off the tournament. What time and where?"

"Let me give you the address. Got a pen?"

"Yeah…go."

"It's one of the Bureau's safe houses…1542 Barbarossa Street."

"Who'll be there?"

"You, me, a CIA field operative from New York who just flew in, named Jake Zant, FBI Senior Special Agent Lew Jarvis from the Counterintelligence Division, and an old friend of yours."

"Who's the old friend?"

"Will be a surprise."

"What time?"

"Eleven. Considering your travel time and the Beltway traffic, you still might have to get your lazy ass up at zero dark thirty to get here by then."

"Worry about your **own** lazy ass, Lambreau. I'll be there in plenty of time."

"Wow, you're testy today, old man."

"Sarcasm is just one more service I offer," I replied.

"Chao, then. Say hello to the lovely Mrs."

Keith's message was short and sweet. As his and two more of the alphabet agencies were involved, this was going to be classified as Top Secret, Sensitive Compartmented Information (SCI). What was surprising was that other G people would now know of the State Department's super clandestine counterterrorist unit. When I was on the team, only the President and the National Security Advisor knew our organization existed. We went after the most dangerous terrorists in the world and only we knew they were taken down. Mostly, we made them disappear without a trace. If they **were** found with their brains splattered in the dirt, no one knew where the bullet came from. Now-a-days nearly all the agencies have counterterrorist operations. I wasn't sure if our CTT division was all that surreptitious anymore. However, I understood from Lambreau that the remaining teams in my old organization only went after the highest caliber targets.

I was so used to Mrs. McGowan almost begging me not to accept any contracts offered by the government that I felt like I was lying or cheating on her when I left the next morning to meet with our Special Response Team. I just couldn't figure why she had now become so accommodating. Was she resigned to the fact that I was going to do what I set my mind to do anyway? How many times had I stretched the truth about the kind of mission I was on only to come home wearing new holes in my body. A couple can only argue about such things just so many times and then somebody's gotta concede. However, I wasn't going to debate myself over the matter any further.

The house on Barbarossa Street was an unremarkable two story unit in the middle of the block among a dozen other row houses. Ordinarily, the place was used as a defensive safe house to temporarily house individuals who fell under the witness protection program, most recently offering shelter to a young woman who testified in federal court against a mob kingpin. Neighbors might be set to wonder about men and women in black going in and out along with common-looking people of all genders, races and ethnic backgrounds, different boarders every week or month. However, when the house was not occupied, it was often used by the Bureau for meetings such as ours or a place out of which covert operations might be conducted.

As I was meeting with three, maybe four other professionals that day, I was going to be one of those men in black looking very much like the G man I used to be. Finding the front door locked, as expected, I rang the doorbell and waited for the approaching footsteps on the other side. Lambreau opened it.

"Morning, Bruce. Good trip up?"

"Got any coffee?" was my response.

"Yeah, come on back. The Bureau and Company got here earlier." He led me to a room that appeared to have been a parlor of sorts at one time which contained a table and chairs capable of seating no more than ten people. "Meet Jake Zant, CIA, and Special Agent Lew Jarvis.

Gentlemen, this is Bruce McGowan, retired counterterrorism operative." We all shook hands and nodded to one another and then I spied the coffee pot on a small table that also contained a variety of pastries.

"If you need to hit the head, it's the second door on the right down the hall."

"I forgot you were former Navy, Keith," I said.

"Whether on land, sea or in my apartment, the toilet room will always be the head."

Before jumping into the meeting, and to break the ice, we all began exchanging pleasantries. If we were going to spend days or even weeks in one another's company, we needed to find out if all of the egos would get along.

Jake Zant, 47, not a bad looking guy about six feet with a thick, dark mustache, was wearing a brown patterned sport coat over an open-collar white shirt, his shoulder holster quasi visible beneath it. He was a former Air Force Special Investigations Officer having served fourteen years active duty followed by a stint with the Portland Police Department doing undercover work. For the past six years as a field agent, he had seen duty in both Iraq and Afghanistan as a Paramilitary Officer. I guessed he was personable enough, but his gruff voice and crusty demeanor told me he wasn't going to be much of a party animal.

On the other hand, 35 year old Special Agent Lewis Jarvis looked to be the quintessential Joe Friday just-the-facts-ma'am Bureau dude straight out of the J. Edgar Hoover playbook. Wearing a black suit, a thin black tie and not a hair out of place, his low-quarter shoes looked as though he had taken the entire previous evening applying a glossy spit shine. A graduate of the Harvard Business School, Jarvis was recruited out of an accounting firm eight years before. Although he was reluctant to brag on himself, he did tell us he had catapulted to the position of lead agent quicker than anyone in the Bureau's history. No doubt a rising star, as he had never had anything but white collar assignments, I wondered how this young man would be able to perform in the harsh, war-torn desert environment we were soon to enter. And why was the likes of him selected for this assignment? Maybe somebody above him wanted him to finally get his feet wet...or in this case, covered in sand. And then I began thinking...if this was to be a Bureau-run operation, was this kid going to be our boss? Maybe I needed to re-think the deal.

I did need to hit the latrine…I was Army, remember…and upon my return to the room took a seat with the others at the table. Before Lambreau began, however, the doorbell rang again and he jumped up to let in the last attendee.

I was elated to see yet another time my old friend and former Bureau partner from yesteryear, Preston Johns. It had been just over two years since we put our heads together to nail one Zufar al-Massoud who was out for revenge on me for the assassination plot on his brother, The Viper. I had heard that Preston was still the National Security Advisor having survived from the previous administration into this new one.

"Bruce, my man. How the hell are you?"

"Better than I deserve to be."

"What's the matter with you? Can't you stay home for once and quit getting yourself mixed up in these international matters?"

"It wasn't my idea, Preston."

"Yeah, I heard how you got into trouble over in Scotland and wound up in

Sandland…and don't get me wrong, I understand how all that was thrust upon you. But you did manage to stumble onto the WMDs everybody said didn't exist."

"And then lost them."

"Well, **you** didn't lose them. But that's why we're here, isn't it?"

"Yes, Mr. Johns," Lambreau remarked. "And thank you for being here. Your advice and insights are going to be most valuable, I'm sure."

Brown-noser.

The others shook hands with Preston and we each took a seat.

"Well, officially good morning, gentlemen," Jarvis began. "I am only acting on instructions from Senior Special Agent Roy Tyler who is honchoing the mission. He mans the Legat on site in Sana'a."

I think everyone caught my sigh of relief.

The junior G man continued. "Each one at this table has a reason to be here. Agent

Zant, who is a CIA operative out of New York, will collaborate with the new Company agent in Sana'a, Tom Gerard. Mr. Zant is also an expert in the field of nuclear and chemical weapons. Mr. Lambreau heads up the counterterrorism team for the State Department and will be most interested in former operative Sam Galloway's partner-in-crime who I will discuss momentarily. Former agent McGowan actually located the WMDs and was able to get inside Galloway's head for a time while he was in Yemen."

And what was **your** reason to be on the team, Sonny? I thought to myself.

"As to the the logistics of this operation, we will leave country via Agency's plane from Andrews next Thursday the 25th at 1530 hours. We'll actually meet here and carpool directly to our gate, bypassing security. You'll have one carry-on, your passport, visas…we still have to get you yours, Mr. McGowan…and one-each semiautomatic of your choice plus five magazines of ammo. We will fly to the Caserma Del Din Base in Northern Italy, refuel and then on to Sana'a. Mr. Zant's Agency counterpart will meet us at Sana'a International. We have permission to land from the Yemeni Air Force. They will also guarantee our safety to land. We'll then travel by armored vehicle to the embassy. That's the short of it. I'll turn this over now to Agent Zant who will provide a sit-rep."

The boy did appear organized and articulate in his briefing. I'll give him that.

As Zant had brought with him a portable projector, before beginning his brief, he flashed a photo of a face onto a wall screen. I knew immediately who it was. "This is a recent photograph of rogue CIA operative Sam Galloway taken from his file. We have no clue as to where he is. This photo, however, is of his suspected accomplice in the WMD heist, Jarum Muhammad, who had at one time served as an interpreter for the embassy; however, we also found out from an Arab confidant, Muhammad is a high echelon leader in al-Qaeda. He and his people have launched continuous attacks this past year onto the American-backed government military. Muhammad reportedly sprang out of the Hashid tribe and has assembled more than thirty followers whose attacks occur nearly every day. We believe Galloway is either living in one of the northern tribal villages in the Empty Quarter desert area or is in Muhammad's camp. The Agency is newly aligned with another tribe, the Humaydah, which is of the Bariq people and who have been resisting al-Qaeda attempts to infiltrate and recruit new members."

I remarked, "Similar to my war an eon ago where the Viet Cong filtered into both Vietnamese and Montagnard villages to gain populace support of the North."

"Exactly. And both Agent Gerard and the legal attache, Special Agent Tyler, believe if you and Mr. Lambreau can locate this Muhammad, who is currently the number one terrorist in Yemen, he will lead us to Galloway and the weapons."

Johns said, "Wait a minute. Your team is made up of five or six people and if Muhammad is running with a force of thirty or more, isn't that a little unrealistic? If you locate him, don't you need a force of friendlies to do battle with them?"

"Yes, sir," replied Zant. "We've trained a good many of the Humaydahs in desert tactics, not that they weren't already skilled from decades of conflict. Plus we've issued them weapons and furnished them with vehicles…"

"I assume the small pickups like the Hilux," I said.

"A few, but also a couple of older Humvees. They'll be at our beck and call ready to engage as needed."

"Where is this tribe and is it located in proximity to where Galloway disappeared with the weapons?" Lambreau asked.

Zant stretched out onto the table a large map of Yemen. He pointed to an area where the Rub 'al-Khali began north of Sana'a. The tribe is largely in this area and the last that was seen of Galloway's hauler was here, maybe an area of around six klicks long and four klicks deep." "That area you're pointing to is nothing but sand and mountains," I said. "There are dunes as high as skyscrapers and as the sand is always blowing, the flatbed of weapons could be swallowed up and buried twenty feet deep in a matter of hours."

"Whether Galloway himself has remained with the weapons, we think he may have found another mountain cave to store them."

"Do we have drone activity in the area?" Johns asked.

"Constantly…day and night. All that we've been picking up are Bedouin nomads on the move, camels, goats, a few pickups and we know several of the sheiks have Land Rovers. Nothing in the way of a flatbed truck or large cargo vans. But our antennas are up and the few sources that we have remain active."

We continued speculating the better part of the noon hour and then broke for a quick lunch. Jarvis sent out for subs and soft drinks. We would reconvene at one-thirty.

CHAPTER 26

On our lunch break, I had some time to catch up with Preston Johns. Preston, a stellar African-American listed many times in the Who's Going Places annals, served as a special agent with me at the Bureau office in Atlanta years ago. If there was to be operational oversight on this mission, he would be it. However, he and the President would be directing nothing. That was up to the Justice Department and they were handing the whole platter off to the Legat in Yemen, Roy Tyler. I was anxious to meet the guy. I wasn't sure why I didn't when I landed at the embassy a few weeks before. He was one of two agents ready to nab Chalmers at the airport when he flew in.

Preston asked about Adriana as I did about his wife, Juliette. He had managed to hang on to his wife. I hadn't. Of course, I ended up with a much better deal the second time around. We recounted some missions we worked on together and he asked if I had heard from the guy I last partnered with on the two major terrorist takedowns, former hit man Atticus Steed. I told him the last time we talked, which was nearly a year ago, he was still enjoying life with his wife in Antigua.

Our meeting cranked back up promptly at one-thirty with Lambreau placing a photo of his own on the screen.

Here's a picture of a real humanitarian. His mug made international headlines a few weeks ago in Yemen when, as you can see here, he feverishly rendered first aid to a number of victims after a terrorist bomb went off in al-Hudaydah, a Red Sea port city. Looks like he has his hands full of goo here. The look on his face says it all, doesn't it?"

I shook my head. "Should I smack you now or wait till our company leaves?" That brought a collective laugh.

"Seriously, gentlemen, I don't have to tell you that this is the kind of image you may see more than once as Yemen is the most dangerous of the Arab nations." And I'm sure he added this for young Jarvis's benefit. "If you think this mission will be a cake walk and that you'll never be pulling your gun, I guarantee you will be mistaken. I hope you don't, but you may find yourself ankle deep in blood."

I was glad he didn't become so graphic about how the mission could go when Adriana and I were having dinner with him. My ass would be staying home.

"I have a question for you folks," began Johns. "You say you have contacts or sources out there in the Arab world; do they know anything specific about this relationship between Galloway and Muhammad?"

"I'll take that," replied Zant. "Our main source, whose name is Sa'ayd, knows Muhammad. They grew up together in Syria and ventured to Yemen at the same time about five years ago. As I said, Muhammad took the job as an interpreter or translator at the embassy as he spoke nearly perfect English. After a couple years, Sa'ayd, who worked as a photographer for the Sana'a Al-Shaura newspaper, also got on as an interpreter about a year before Muhammad went the way of al-Qaeda. However, even though they have differing political values, they've remained friends. Muhammad has tried his best the past couple of years to convince Sa'ayd to feed him Intel on American and Saudi government plans and activities, but Sa'ayd has not. At least we believe he hasn't. Just last week they met at a khat house and over a chew, Muhammad admitted he and a CIA operative have the weapons hidden somewhere north of Sana'a. As Muhammad still has contacts in Syria, he and the operative have entered into an agreement with the Syrian government to sell the nuclear device for a cool five million. The chemical and biological weapons, which you also discovered in the twenty-two crates, Mr. McGowan, are going for another three."

I shook my head. "My question, Mr. Zant, is how either of these people, being Syrians, got jobs in the embassy, especially as translators. There would have to be conversations of classified nature at times."

"They both attended the American University of Armenia, majored in Political Science and when Muhammad applied for the translator job, our government saw fit to give him a secret clearance. Sa'ayd was given one as well when he came on."

"What idiot gave these camel jockeys security clearances?" I exclaimed.

"Uh, that would have been the State Department in this case, Bruce," Johns replied. "Your former department. And I would have had the final sign-off where it came to foreign nationals."
Ouch.

Lambreau asked Zant, "Does the Yemen government know we are joining with the American embassy to conduct an investigation and what it's for?"

"All they know is that the embassy is missing one of its people. Of course, the missing man as we know is not in actuality an embassy employee, but they don't know that. We didn't tell them how he became missing nor do they know anything about the discovered WMDs. Everybody that knew about the weapons except this young tribal man is dead. Muhammad and al-Qaeda won't tell anyone. Neither will Sa'ayd.

"But besides al-Qaeda and the Houthi rebels, another group we have to watch out for is the Mukhabarat which is the Political Security Organization or PSO. They're all over and are a bunch of cutthroats. And then we may run into hostile tribes, although if they realize we're Americans, they'll probably leave us alone. Everybody responds to Yemeni rials, which is their money system. We come upon a PSO checkpoint, we might have to put a few million Rials on them."

"Million?" exclaimed Jarvis.

"One million Rials might equal $25.00. That's probably a week's pay to the PSO officer in charge."

"Sounds like the entire country is corrupt."

"That would be an understatement. And as I said, dangerous as well. Probably the most trusted people we encounter would be in the tribal areas. The chieftains, which are referred to as sheiks, are friends with the Saudis who funnel them money. As Saudi Arabia is our ally, in principle that makes us also friends with the tribes. But we have to be alert. As Saudi Arabia continues to bomb Houthi rebel positions, the rebels currently being in control of the government, you might find yourself in harm's way with friendlies as well. And there's no love lost between the tribes and the rebels, either which might get you caught in a crossfire."

"Seems you folks have a lot of challenges," Preston said. "And I appreciate your undertaking this operation. Mr. Zant, I know you want your man…and we want that nuclear weapon. No way we can allow Syria to get its hands on it."

"We'll make it happen, Mr. Johns," Lambreau said. "We have a good team assembled. And you and I both know what Bruce can bring to the mission."

"That I do. Thanks for stepping up, Bruce."

"Gives me something to do."

Lambreau added, "By the way, Bruce, I need to talk with you in private about your remuneration."

"I wish you would."
After getting a few more questions out of the way and doing a brief wrap-up, we left Jarvis to lock up.

Everybody went home to their wives except Lambreau and me. He didn't have one and mine was four hours away. As Adriana didn't expect me back that night, I got a room at a Holiday Inn Express in Falls Church. Keith and I met for dinner and drinks at a pub down the street from my motel at seven.

I was in the mood for a glass of Merlot, but I was also in the mood for fish and chips. As they didn't mesh, I ordered a Johnny Dortmunder on draft.

"Alright, let's talk money, Lambreau."

"Nothing to talk about. I thought we were already agreed."

"On what, your offer at dinner the other night?"

"You didn't like it?"

"My wife didn't like it."

"Your wife is not going on this vacation."

"But she laid it out for you. If I'm going, you have to pony up."

"I can see who wears the boxer shorts in your family."

"And she looks sexy in them."

"Well, I guess I've had enough fun with this. You get your hundred grand, Scorpion."

"Plus expenses, plus per diem."

"Yes, yes. All of it."

"And a case of cold Heineken on the flight over."

"You want all of us to arrive in Yemen drunk?"

"You've never been there, have you?"

"Nope."

"It's a giant cesspool, Keith. Being drunk will make what you find in Yemen a hell of a lot more palatable. And you won't find alcohol when you get there."

"Are we going to have to put up with your bullshit the entire time we're there?"

"You're gonna need a little levity after about the second day. You'll be on khat by the end of the first day."

"What is this khat you keep mentioning?"

"Miracle drug. Amphetamine. Better than marijuana. Eighty percent of the population chews it. Men **and** women. And children over five. Keeps everyone hyped up. Lots of manic people walking around with AK-47s. It's also an appetite suppressant, so there are no fat people in Yemen. Gotta try it. Blend in."

"Sounds to me like **you've** been chewing it. **You** seem a little manic."

"It's the Johnny Dortmunder. I think I'll have another." I got home just before noon the next day and gave Adriana the news. I'd be leaving Washington on the 25th. So, I had a week to get prepared…mentally. Yeah, I didn't want to go back in the worst way. But, it might be fun, hanging with a bunch of guys with guns, enjoying goat kabobs around the campfire in some Bedouin village, learning kumbaya in Arabic and chewing khat. Lots of khat.

CHAPTER 27

When Adriana packs for a trip, there are two suitcases, a
hanging bag, a make-up bag, a shoe bag, a purse that's
like another piece of luggage and half of her wardrobe.
There has to be a different outfit for each day and night,
colorful bras to match the panties, a hair dryer, a hot
comb, and even though the shoe bag is full, there are four
different kinds of sandals shoved down in the pockets of
the suitcases. She takes longer to decide on what to take
than it takes to get to her destination. And that
preparation and packing is when we travel to see her
parents for a week. When I go on the trip with her, I take
a duffle bag with a pair jeans, one pair of Bermudas, golf
shirts, socks and underwear crammed inside it along with
my shaving kit.

But I do take a good bit of time deciding on the choice of
weapon that goes with us…or should I say weapons. In
our SUV I'll have my Remington 700 sniper rifle with
night vision scope (you never know) locked in the rear
compartment, my Smith and Wesson 1911 series .45
under the front seat, my Springfield Armory XDM in the
glove compartment, my .44 Magnum in the center
console, my Glock 23 on my hip and my James Bond

issue Walther PPK strapped to my ankle. Oh, and I never go anywhere without my Ranger Ready Detachment knife with the 7.5 inch blade on my other hip. I'm not paranoid…I'm just always ready. So, in packing for Yemen, I probably took as much time as Adriana in preparing for her travel to select just the right manner of personal protection for me. It had to be the perfect gun…the right size and grip, easy to handle and fire, powerful and dependable. For me that was my Glock 23. But I would also take the Bond gun as my back-up. And of course my knife.

When it came down to crunch time that next week, I awoke the day I was leaving to the feel of her gentle hand stroking my abdomen. When I opened my eyes, I saw that her head was close to mine on the pillow and her lips brushing my cheek. "Did you sleep well?" she asked in almost a whisper.

"Like a baby."

"Are you really going to leave me today?"

I smiled. "Is this a trick question?"

"You can change your mind, you know."

"I know."

Was she having guilt pangs about encouraging me go out on the mission, something she had never done before? As she had allowed herself to mellow over time to get to this day, it now seemed she was having regrets.

"I won't tell you not to go."

Which meant, "Please don't go."

I took her in my arms and held her close into me. The bath oil on her skin smelled delightful and her firm breasts beneath the silken nightgown caused my loins to surge. I took my time with her that morning, caressing her, kissing her forehead and then her lips, tenderly removing her gown, then lightly sweeping my fingertips and lips over every part of her body, causing her to breathe rapidly and deeply. We were music together like riders on the storm, my heart pounding like thunder, my arteries feeling as though lightning was surging inside them. My labored breath became like the wind. Then suddenly, like a billowing tempest, our rhythmic crescendo peaked, spawning a simultaneous, mind-blowing climax, a perfect finale to our most splendid symphony.

When our love-making was complete, I laid across her, spent and perspiring, for several minutes until she suddenly threw me off, announcing, "Hey, I gotta pee!"

I took my shower and then went to the kitchen to prepare her breakfast…her usual, a bagel with cream cheese and a bowl of fruit, strawberries and blueberries. After her shower, she came to the kitchen to join me as I ate my oatmeal and toast. The smile was still there. Although her eyes said, "Don't go," her small voice whispered "I'm going to miss you."

I left the house just after ten, just after our long kiss goodbye. She said, "You come back to me, lover man. You get yourself killed and I'll never speak to you again."

I laughed and kissed her one more time. From my rear view mirror, I saw that she was still standing on the veranda leaning against the banister watching me until I went out of sight.

It was a long four hours to the safe house. I parked my car in the driveway in back of the house, pulled out my duffle bag and locked up. I had remembered to remove all the weapons from the SUV on this occasion as I had no idea how long my Suburban would be parked. I couldn't imagine we'd be lucky enough to find Sam Galloway and the WMDs the first few days after our arrival. It actually might take a matter of weeks. But if he was still there somewhere, we would find him.

The government was definitely spending some money on this operation. It not only wanted that nuclear bomb, but had to assure it did not fall into the hands of a nation that bred terrorist factions such as Syria and Iran. I assumed that the government entity that was paying the bill was the Justice Department since the FBI was supposedly driving the train. However, I could have been wrong about that.

The four of us were picked up at the safe house by a stretch limo and wheeled directly to our plane at Joint Base Andrews. This time I saw that I was flying in style on a Gulfstream GV. Although it was an aging jet, it looked to be a well-maintained government aircraft. The good thing about this plane, unlike the last one into Yemen, the Gulfstream's engines didn't smoke, hiccup and fart. The aviators were Agency contract employees wearing actual uniforms, but where was the sexy flight attendant. Did we have to get our own coffee and snacks? And where were the in-flight movies? Not even a magazine. It was going to be a long 4,500 miles to our refueling point in Italy.

Of the eight hours it took to cross the Atlantic, navigate over Europe's land area and enter Northern Italy's airspace, I slept an hour, drank a beer, had a CIA packaged sandwich and chatted with the other team members about everything from politics, on which we mostly agreed, to what everyone should expect when we arrived in Sandland. Only Zant and I had been there, so we shared with the other two a few important things such as how many diseases there are in Yemen and how easily one can contract something, how scorpions have over-run the country and crawl into everyone's sleeping bag, and the fact that everybody wearing a jambiyah is looking to put the head of an American on their trophy wall. But not to worry…as long as we refrain from eating or drinking anything and never going to sleep, we had a 50-50 chance of survival. I was pretty sure Lambreau knew we were jesting, but Jarvis was suddenly noticeably quiet.

We landed only briefly at Caserma to refuel and in less than an hour we were back in the air for another four hours. As no one was saying much the remainder of the flight, I took a long cat nap.

Upon entering Yemeni airspace, we were quickly shadowed by two Yemen Air Force MIG-21s. However, as one of our pilots spoke Arabic, after a few back-and-forth transmissions, the MIGs broke off and allowed us to land. Following our taxi to the same hangar where I had waited a few weeks ago for Chalmers to arrive, we grabbed up our bags and disembarked the plane. Waiting for us at the bottom of the steps was one of the embassy's Land Cruisers. Jarvis recognized from a photo the man standing beside the vehicle, his Legat attache counterpart, Special Agent Roy Tyler. The driver appeared to be an Arab guy. Gerard was not with them.

Tyler introduced himself and we told him who we were. He then introduced his driver as Sa'ayd Osmani, the man who also served as an interpreter for the American Embassy. The guy with the secret clearance and who in my book, bore watching.

As we drove deeper into Sana'a, passing the Old Walled City, Tyler pointed out several historic landmarks and attractions such as the Sira Castle, the Dar al-Hajar Palace, which was pretty impressive, the Al Saleh Mosque, which I had skirted around on my last visit, and a number of other mosques which were not at all on my list of interests. But, there was one place we passed that jostled my memory…the spot where the thugs following me a few weeks before had tried to whack me, likely for the small amount of rials I had on me. I saw that someone had thankfully removed the two guys' bodies from the alley where I left them. Considering all of the gun battles that go on in the city day and night, if anybody heard my gunshot, I doubted anyone would have paid much attention. A guy goes down on the street, who cares? Well, maybe his mother did. The moral of that story was…those who live by the sword get shot by those who don't.

Agent Tyler seemed like a squared-away dude, fifty-ish, high-and-tight haircut, not an ounce of fat and well-spoken. A well-seasoned agent, there didn't seem to be any nonsense about him which told me he was neither going to appreciate my jokes or **get** them in the first place. I thought he would probably be a good role model for young Jarvis and perhaps a mentor as well.

I did notice that the Land Cruiser had reinforced interior panels and tapping my finger on the door glass saw that it was bullet proof. If we Americans were going to be riding around looking all official like we were, we were going to need that protection. Tyler answered a few of my questions about the vehicle telling me it had "taken a few AK rounds about six months ago, scarcely denting the sheet metal." He added, "Also, on a trek down to Aden, Agent Farley and I…he's the other attache who is teamed with me…were ambushed shortly after leaving a PSO checkpoint. We took some automatic weapons fire, which didn't do much damage, but swerved, narrowly dodging an RPG round that was heading straight for our windshield. That we wouldn't have survived."

Lambreau asked, "Who did you suspect in the ambush…al-Qaeda?"

"Either them or Houthi rebels. You never know who's targeting you in this country. Actually, it could have been the PSO, the security police. I refused to pay to pass through the checkpoint and the asshole in charge could have radioed ahead and told somebody to let us know how they felt about it. Pays to carry a few million rials with you when you're on the highways."

Having noted that the doors on the Land Cruiser were heavy and shut with the thud of a bank vault door, I asked "How much does this vehicle weigh?"

It was Sa'ayd who answered me. "Approximately 10,000 pounds, Mr. McGowan. There's lead in the doors besides five inch carbon fiber panels. Of course the fiber doesn't weigh all that much. That's why no one should get hurt in this vehicle." I was surprised he spoke with only a slight hint of an accent.

"You seem to know quite a lot about the car."

"It is my business to know about a lot of things having to do with the security of not only the embassy but the people in it. And that is especially important when we are traveling," he said.

"How long have you been working for the embassy and specifically the Legat as an interpreter?"

"Almost three years."

Playing dumb, which is not always difficult for me, I asked "How did you go about getting this job?"

Tyler, who was riding in the front beside Sa'ayd, shot a quick glance at me in the back seat as though it was a question I shouldn't have asked. I had the impression he was very high on his interpreter.

"I was brought into the embassy by a friend who used to work here."

Tyler added, "Be assured, Mr. McGowan, Sa'ayd was fully vetted before he was selected for this position. I'm sure you'll find this out if you don't know already; the man he replaced did not leave here on the best of terms."

That was putting it mildly. I was sure we'd talk more about that later.

As we approached the embassy gate, one of the Marines decked out in battle dress and cradling his M-4 held up his hand for Sa'ayd to stop. Although I was sure the Marines knew the vehicle and had brought it to a halt a hundred times, the corporal still looked inside to assure he recognized the front seat occupants. The gate lifted and he waved us on.

Our vehicle then continued on to the parking lot outside the chancery building. Tyler told us, "Grab your bags and follow me. We have apartments for you. I'll show each of you where you'll bunk." He then looked at his watch face. "It's 1835. The dining hall is in that building." He pointed. "We'll have dinner at 1930. Fried chicken tonight, my boys. A taste of home."

CHAPTER 28

At the head of our table was the mission leader, Legat attache Special Agent Roy Tyler. Most of the rest of the team was there as well…Special Agent Lew Jarvis, CIA operative Jake Zant, State Department Counterterrorism Director Keith Lambreau and moi. Coming in a good ten minutes after we had begun our dinner were Yemen CIA Director Avery Gerard and Agency technician Mike Daniels.

Gerard was a huge man about six-five, who in a hot spot like Yemen also makes for a big target. I guessed he was in his upper forties, rugged looks, square jaw, large, meaty hands, looking much like a Rams linebacker. A man of presence to say the least. He had been on the job in Sana'a only two weeks but with the Agency more than fifteen years. I almost laughed when I heard him open his mouth. Expecting to hear a booming basso, what came out instead was the voice of a tenor.

As we ate our vittles, we got better acquainted, giving one another a two minute synopsis of who we were, what we did and what we did before that. When it was my turn, I only took twenty seconds or so, kind of like giving my name, rank and serial number. I've never been comfortable tooting my own horn. However, it was Lambreau who saw fit to brag on me, telling everyone I was "the archetypal model for the classic government operative." Whatever that meant. Mike Daniels added that as he watched me operate on my last visit under immense duress, he'd work with me anytime, any place. I showed my appreciation to him with a slight nod and smile. And so the people at the table who really didn't know me kept staring at me like I was some intergalactic guardian of the universe. I hoped I didn't disappoint them. May the force be with me.

When most had finished with the strawberry shortcake, Agent Tyler began a dialogue. "Gentlemen, we have an interesting task ahead of us. Our priority is to locate the nuclear weapon and accompanying chemical weapons that disappeared from a cave in the Jabal Kanin Mountains three weeks ago we believe at the hands of former Company field agent, Sam Galloway. Per our source right here at the embassy, we believe he has partnered with al-Qaeda, actually one of its local kingpins, Jarum Muhammad, to sell the bomb to the highest bidder. Muhammad had boasted that the current offer by the Syrians is five mil and another three for all of the chemical weapons. As the Iranians had been promised the weapon by another criminal mind if and when he got his hands on it, they may up the ante."

"Before you go any further, I have a question."

"Yes, Mr. McGowan."

"We had been told your source was the man we met today, your driver and translator for the embassy. Is Sa'ayd still in contact with this Muhammad?"

"No. He severed ties with him quite some time ago."

"I'm…not understanding this. If the ties were severed long ago, considering we only knew about these weapons a month or more ago, how does Sa'ayd know Muhammad is hooked up with Galloway and they're planning to unload the bomb and other weapons on the Iranians?"

"Insightful question, Mr. Gowan…or are you still **Agent** McGowan?"

"Bruce."

"I beg your pardon?"

"Call me Bruce, Roy."

"Okay, Bruce. Sa'ayd, after not having any contact with Muhammad for over two years, accidentally ran into him at a hookah bar. There was a lot of smoking and khat chewing and apparently Muhammad got a little too wired and thinking he could trust Sa'ayd, got a little loose-lipped."

"I know you're high on Sa'ayd, Roy, but can we trust that he's not al-Qaeda as well? After all, he and Muhammad were frat buddies at one time."

The question apparently didn't set well with Tyler as his mouth immediately formed a scowl. "You're wrong about him, Bruce. Of course, you seem like the kind of guy who doesn't like being wrong."

I grinned. "Yeah, I was wrong once…that's when I **thought** I was wrong."

Tyler continued. "Seriously, he's proven his worth here on a number of occasions. He's the one who brought us the information about Muhammad and Galloway. If they were in cahoots, we wouldn't know any of this."

I gave him a two-finger salute. "Okay. Just had to get that out of the way."

"Understood."

Zant asked, "Will Sa'ayd meet up again with Muhammad? That appears to be our best opportunity to find these weapons…and Galloway."

"Unfortunately, he doesn't know where Muhammad is camped out and has no way to get back in touch with him."

"Maybe Sa'ayd can continue frequenting the hookah joint and bump into him again some night," I said.

"We have been sending him back on a regular basis, but so far Muhammad hasn't materialized."

Jarvis asked, "What is the plan from here, Agent Tyler?"

"We're splitting up to begin canvassing the Humaydah villages as early as tomorrow. I have made up three maps for three teams of us. I have also laid on two of the embassy Land Cruisers and a Land Rover. Here's how we will partner…Agent Jarvis and Agent Gerard are Team A; Mr. McGowan and Mr. Lambreau, Team B; Mr. Zant and myself, Team C. A long-time embassy employee named Zayda, a former PSO policeman will drive Team A; Technician Mike Daniels, who speaks fluent Arabic, will pilot the Team B vehicle; and Sa'ayd will drive Agent Zant and me. As you see, we'll have three vehicles with one each Bureau and Company agent collaborating and two counterterrorist agents partnering. Each of our drivers will know the landscape and each will be able to communicate with tribal leaders. You should find the village chieftains friendly since the tribes are supported by America's ally, the Saudi government. They despise both the Houthi rebels and al-Qaeda and have battled both. In other words, the enemy of my enemy is my friend, or something like that. There are over fifty villages within the corridor between the northern mountains and where the sweeping dunes of the Empty Quarter begin. Somebody in any one of these villages had to have seen a large flatbed truck and other vehicles in movement whether they were traveling at night or not. Any questions so far?"

I was going to make the comment that I'm used to being on the A Team and not a B player, but didn't raise my hand.

Tyler continued. "I imagine it'll take at least a week to cover these villages. We should be welcomed for lodging at night. As some of the tribes will live in tent city, your sleeping bags will come in handy. If you're sleeping on the ground, watch out for scorpions."

I glanced at Jarvis. Told you.

"Do not drink their water. Cholera and Yemeni water are closely connected. You will have a week's worth of water and canned food in your vehicles. In addition to your personal side arms, you'll be issued assault rifles…M-4 carbines. If you get into serious trouble, we will have on call two drones which are equipped with Hellfire missiles. They can be on station within ten minutes. Mike Daniels will be the drone field controller. You will each have radios set on a freak I will give you when we start out tomorrow. One agent per vehicle will maintain contact with the other vehicles. Everyone else, don't use it unless you personally get into trouble. We need to keep the traffic down. Use your sunscreen liberally and watch out for the biting flies with all of the goats and camels around.

"You can pretty much trust the people in these Bedouin villages. The PSO you can't, even if you lay rials on them. Neither can you always count on the Yemen Army to tell you the truth as they play both sides of the fence. After all, this is the land of lies and flies."

I liked this guy. Organized, quippy and super knowledgeable. But so am I. I hoped our egos wouldn't clash. But, for a week or so, we'd be going our separate ways.

"We'll meet in the parking lot outside your apartment building tomorrow at 0700.

Bruce and Tom, we'll need to get our heads together after we break up here to go over your routes and list of villages. I have marked your maps accordingly. I'll also provide you your final coordinating instructions."

Very comprehensive briefing. Tyler was obviously some kind of Army or Marine commander in his previous life. I'd have to get to know the guy a little better.

Gerard, Tyler and I stayed in the mess hall after the others had departed for their apartments. Apparently the three of us were not only our vehicles' RTOs, but in command of our own mini operations as well. Tyler placed our maps out on the table in front of us.

"Bruce, you will be working the upper villages in the Al-Jawf region that bleeds from the mountains into the Rub' al-Khali. You have to watch out for the tribal opposition going on at this time against the aggressive Republican Guard. And you, Tom, in addition to your search for Galloway and the weapons, you will be doing a casualty assessment of two villages that were pretty much wiped out by the Guard. As you know, there are reports of more than 1,500 villagers being slaughtered. And Bruce, after you cover the Al-Jawf villages, move west into the Hadramaut Region where you'll find the Hadrami Tribal Confederation, as many as eight villages there. Guys, as there are pockets of al-Qaeda all along that upper tribal region, I don't doubt you may be accosted. They've been targeting U.N. vehicles that look like ours and there have been casualties."

"And you are sending a troop of Marines with us, right?" I said.

"You need help, Mike will bring the fire and brimstone."

In other words, this could be a suicide mission.

Tyler showed us our routes and the locations of each major village system. In each village may also be two or three separate hamlets. Deja vu for me from forty years ago. Thanks to Agency Intel, he had also pin-pointed probable locations of al-Qaeda.

Let's see…as I'd likely encounter Houthi rebels, pockets of ISIS, Popular Resistance Committees, unfriendly PSO, and AQAP (Al-Qaeda in the Arabian Peninsula), I could find myself at any time in some real ca ca.

We broke up at 2115 and I returned to my temporary quarters. My overnight stay in the American Embassy compound would be like living inside a small, walled city. Besides the main concentration of buildings, it had a chancery, a snack bar, the dining hall, a barber shop, an apartment complex and a parking garage. I figured I had better enjoy my bed and get some good sack time as the next week, and maybe longer, I'd be camping in the sand with the camels and goats.

CHAPTER 29

I had a hot breakfast of eggs, toast and coffee at 0630, made a run back to my bathroom and was then standing tall in the parking lot at 0700 sharp. Wearing my olive drab ammo vest over a short sleeve beige shirt and a pair of tactical pants, I looked as macho as the next guy. Most of us had donned ball caps while Jarvis and Zant looked ready for the Outback in their bush hats. When everyone was in position to move out, Tyler and Daniels issued us our M-4s, ammo and flak jackets. I threw the protective vest into the front floor of the SUV and popped one of the magazines into the carbine. I then asked Mike Daniels to join me at the vehicle's hood where I spread out our map.

"Mike, when you pull out of here onto Sa'awan Street, follow it all the way to Hadda and then head north toward the tribal areas of al-Hazm. We'll then be going more than 50 miles along that road. I'll give you plenty of notice where to turn off."

"Roger."

Just as I was getting ready to slide into the passenger seat, a small SUV pulled up a couple of spots away. When she swung her legs out of the driver's seat, exposing her shapely thighs, all conversations abruptly stopped in mid sentence. Shirley Compagno had arrived for work. As she walked by us, she took off her scarf and shook out her long chestnut hair.

"Hi, Mr. McGowan," she greeted. "It's good to see you back again." She then stepped off to the side and gave me a hug. "You all have a good day," she said, as though we were all off on a fishing trip. As she sashayed her way from the parking lot to the building, all eyes seemed to be stuck on that most perfect derrière of hers.

Lambreau looked at me and shook his head. "What the hell, McGowan?"

I merely shrugged.

Tyler then said, "Saddle up, everyone. RTO guys, radio check every hour on the hour with a sit-rep until 2200 each night. These are high-tech radios with a range of 200 miles. I'll have the base component with me. Remember, if you get into something you can't handle and need to put some big shit on bad guys, call Mike. Good hunting."

As our driver, Mike, turned out of the compound, Lambreau in the rear seat asked me, "What do you think of Tyler?"

"He's got his sierra together. Beyond that, we'll see."

"He reminds me of you when you used to be you."

"I'm no longer me? If I'm not, then who am I?"

He laughed. "You know what I mean. The guy is cool…and methodical."

"Right."

Mike Daniels then jumped into the conversation. "Yeah, I didn't have a chance to say anything to you last night, but great to see you again, Mr. McGowan. I thought when you left a few weeks ago that was it. But here you are again."

"Call me Bruce, Mike. You make me sound like an old fart with the mister stuff."

"Alright…Bruce."

I asked him, "Did Galloway say anything to you the day he left that would have given you any indication he was taking off?"

"Not a thing. When he didn't show up for work the next day **and** the day after, I contacted my highers. They immediately sent a couple guys here to investigate. At first, none of us were sure whether he had gotten whacked somewhere out there on the street and his body had just not materialized. But when I found the phone message to someone in Syria and it didn't match the number for our field operator there, I got suspicious. I flew the I.A. guys out to where the weapons were and found that the cave had been cleaned out. No one else except the young man named Sameer knew where they were."

"What happened from there?"

"We went to Sameer's village and interrogated him. I'm convinced it wasn't him that pulled the weapons out of there. He came across as a straight-up guy and everyone agreed he was telling the truth. The last he said he saw of those crates was when he went there with you."

"Yeah, that kid wouldn't have had the kind of contacts necessary to sell those weapons."

"What do you think about Tyler's trusted translator Sa'ayd?"

"I think he's alright. Like Agent Tyler said, if he wasn't a straight shooter, why would he have come forward with the information on Muhammad?"

"Yeah. What's your take, Keith?"

"I would liked to have interrogated Sa'ayd myself to see if anything Muhammad told him provided a clue as to where he's in hiding. Before I left Washington, I put Muhammad on the State Department's most wanted terrorist list. If we don't find him, I'm just another gun on this trip."

I said, "The Bureau wants the weapons, the CIA wants Galloway and we want Muhammad…not just because he's partnered with Galloway to sell the big bomb, but because with his terrorist agenda, he's a threat to the security of the United States. The Intel we have reflects he's the al-Qaeda big cheese in this country."

"Yes, what you just said puts our purpose here in perspective. But, I know you personally want closure on these weapons."

"I do have a bit of history invested."

We were only about ten miles outside of Sana'a on Highway 313 when we came upon
Dar al-Hajar, the magnificent palace built atop natural stone cliffs in the rugged part of Wadi Dhahr and where we ran into our first PSO checkpoint. It was where I learned the PSO was a POS. After allowing a number of crappy vans and Hilux pickups with a half dozen terrorist-looking males brandishing AK-47s to pass on through unaccosted, we were told to pull over.

One of the security officers approached Mike and shoved the muzzle of his AK toward the driver's side door, demanding "Pazz-ports!" Mike showed his first and then Keith and I passed ours through him to the officer. He took over two minutes to match our photos with our faces and then tossed them discourteously back into the SUV. He said something in his language and Mike interpreted it for us. "He wants to know our business in this country."

I said "Tell the asshole it's none of his business."

"You really want me to tell him that?"

"I don't know. Just tell him what you want, Mike."

Mike answered him in a few short words. The officer then said something back.

"He wants two million rials and we can go."

"Tell the fat little bastard there's nothing stopping us from passing through anyway."

Mike told him. That didn't set well with him. He began yelling.

"He says his last word is one and a half million."

"Tell him **my** last word is a half million."

He told him. The man turned and began talking with another officer who I thought may be his superior. He then brought the answer back to Mike.

"They will take no less than one million or we'll sit here all day. I suggest we pony up, Bruce."

"Whatever."

Mike took from a cloth bag some bills and handed it to the officer. He in turn jerked it from Mike's hand and said only two words. I don't think it was 'thank you.'

I then said in a loud voice, not mincing words, "Take the money and shove it up your ass, prick."

The officer shouted back at me, "I think **you're** the prick, American. Now get this vehicle out of here."

Mike and I exchanged looks. When the man walked away, the three of us broke out in laughter.

As we drove away, I noticed that the ranking officer immediately got on his phone. The man who stopped us then fed him a piece of paper which undoubtedly contained our tag information. Mike saw it as well in his rear view mirror and said, "We're soon going to be passing through an area with high ground on either side. Perfect spot for an ambush. Probably wasn't a good idea to piss these people off, Bruce."

Keith remarked, "I thought everybody in this country expected foreigners to bargain with them. It's supposed to be the business way."

"Bargain, yes…insult, not so much," Mike replied.

"My bad, I guess," I said.

"Some of the PSO are in cahoots with al-Qaeda in the northern sector of the country, " Mike added. "If we continue on 313, we'll be shaking hands with them."

"What do you suggest, Mike," Keith asked.

"There's an alternate route to get into the tribal area. I recommend we take it."

"I put us in this situation; I'll trust your judgement in getting us out of it," I said.

"It's more rugged and mountainous. Will take longer."
"I'm fine with it, Mike. Do it."

We took the road and found that in encountering 10 to 12 percent grades, the heavy Land Cruiser's transmission groaned and whined in defiance. As parts of the road became rutted and slippery, that added to the struggling vehicle's misery. But as we approached the Al-Jawf village of Ya'dan, the terrain though over 4,000 feet above sea level began to flatten out.

The village itself was nothing but a conglomeration of mud huts with thatched roofs. When we pulled to the village gate, several men dressed in thobes and heads wrapped in keffiyehs came to greet us. Their faces, warm and friendly, wore deep furrows from many years tending the earth and flocks under the merciless sun. Mike greeted them first in Arabic and as we followed after him, they bowed respectfully, and grinned showing what teeth they had in their mouths were painted green from the khat leaves.

Mike knew what to ask them. In the past month, had any of them seen a large truck with a covered flatbed along with perhaps two to three other vehicles moving along any of the roads? They shook their heads. And the guerrillas known as al-Qaeda, did they usually see them? Do they come to their village? One of the men did the talking. Mike told us later he said, al-Qaeda is not welcome in their village. They are thieves and murderers. Some of the villagers had been assaulted by al-Qaeda and two of their woman raped. The people no longer see them traveling about. Because the villagers are a poor people, al-Qaeda has little interest in them.

We were welcomed to have a meal with them that consisted of sheep loin which was the best part of the animal. We smiled and respectfully declined. Mike told us we were not insulting or disrespecting them in declining their offer, but we did have food of our own. We were also on a mission and could not spare the time. We thanked them and left back down the trail. I imagined we would be repeating that scenario dozens of times over the next few days. It was another deja vu experience considering I had visited a series of similar villages on my last trip searching for young Sameer.

After I had reported my third sit-rep to Roy Tyler at mission command, we broke for lunch. Mike prepared a couple containers of Sterno to heat up our cans of stew, beans, soup and whatever else was thrown in our bag of goodies. I could see how the canned food was soon to get old, making me pine for an occasional MRE or LRRP ration. I couldn't believe I was actually wishing for something I swore I'd never eat again. We then set up a hasty camp, ate our meal and moved on to the next village.

CHAPTER 30

As we had moved from the more craggy terrain to the fringe of the desert, we began to see parts of the Rub or Empty Quarter. The road was now largely sand and although we had a four wheel drive, if we went any deeper into the desert, we'd be stalled out. Mike knew to keep the Land Cruiser on firm soil. On our way to the village of Kiamen, which Agent Tyler had circled on my map, we came across a Bedouin encampment. What looked to be a nomadic caravan, we observed around thirty men and women taking refuge from the afternoon sun under four large tents. Their camels sat perched on their knees under the few palms that were providing them shade.

"Do you want to approach them, Bruce?" Mike asked.

"Do you think they speak Arabic or some tribal language?"

"Most everyone in both the established tribal villages and among these nomads will speak Arabic. Many of these nomadic groups have been displaced through the years when their villages were destroyed by either government troops or the rebels. As such, they won't be friendly to anyone wearing a uniform or riding around in the beds of these small pickups looking to cause trouble."

"Like al-Qaeda."

"And the Houthi rebels."

"Go ahead. Let's approach. We don't necessarily look military."

He nodded. "And they have been accepting of Amrikans, as we're called."

Mike wheeled us toward the camp, careful not to get too far off solid ground. When we stopped to exit the vehicle, he said, "We should leave our carbines in the Land Cruiser, otherwise, they may see us as a threat."

Our trek from the vehicle to the tents covered about a hundred meters and as we walked in their direction slowly, but assuredly, two of the men rose from their folding chairs to meet us. Mike threw up his hand in greeting fashion and I was reminded of a scene out of the 19th Century American west where White men might have been walking into an Indian village not knowing whether they were a peaceful tribe. Maybe they'd invite us to sit around in a circle for a khat chew.

Mike then greeted them in Arabic and one of them said something back. They were smiling, which was good. One of the men then gestured with an outstretched arm to join them in one of the tents. Get out of the blazing sun, White dudes. We did. Under the tent they had laid blankets over the sand which we sat on at their beckon. One of the Bedouins asked, in other words, just what the hell we were doing way out there in no man's land. Mike apparently told him we were on a search for some people and then began asking the same questions he had posed to the Ya'dan villagers earlier. The man answered him at the same time gesturing toward the east. He was talking about somebody.

Mike relayed to us that they had seen a convoy of Yemen Army troops only hours before moving in the direction in which he was pointing, but no civilians driving a flatbed truck of any type. Not today, not ever.

They offered us tea, but I respectfully declined as I didn't want anything hot. Neither did Mike nor Keith want anything to drink as well. The longer I sat there, however, I was coveting a bottle of our water in the SUV. To be neighborly, we sat with them for another twenty minutes and then told them we appreciated their hospitality, but had to run. I don't think we said or did anything that would cause them to remember us as ugly Amrikans.

Further east on the map was one of the larger villages in the tribal confederation, Moriba, which we found to be erected upon the last rocky terrain before reaching the towering dunes. A Mesa Verde looking settlement, the homes and buildings were actually amalgamated into the natural landscape, the people taking advantage of every cavern, cave and cavity of the rocky environment. Before entering the village, I performed a radio check with Tyler, giving him a 'negative' report of our activity thus far.

Lambreau suggested this might also be the place to retire the day and find some comfortable lodging. I agreed. It had been a full day and I wasn't anxious to break out my bedroll or crash in the SUV. On the road into Moriba, we came upon a roadside souq where I asked Mike to stop. I thought some fresh vegetables and fruit might complement our dinner, whatever that was going to be. Snatching up some mild peppers, a couple ears of baked corn and a half dozen plums, I asked our banker, Mike, to shell out a few rials. He and Keith selected a few items which included a shank of lamb. I thought about the lamb as well, but the flies changed my mind. I could wash off the veggies and fruit.

At the market stand, scores of men and women dressed in the traditional dishdashas and burkas, respectively, the women's faces completely covered save for the eyes, milled about, some buying, some fondling the fruit, most all looking curiously at the three caucasian men so out of place in their village…and all carrying M-4 carbines. But when the afternoon salat commenced, all quickly departed, found a place on the ground to throw down their prayer rug and began the ritual. We stood respectfully until the call to prayer was over and then Mike asked one of the men wearing a kufi where the village chieftain was located. The man pointed to a cliff dwelling high up on a rock that looked as though it should belong to the tribe's leader. But he said the sheik was not there. He had been ill and was down the valley at some type of medical climic. Mike then asked the man if he himself spent much time on the road away from the village. He said he did as he made deliveries of the produce. That's when Mike bombarded him with the battery of questions about the flatbed truck and an American. The man shook his head. The only large truck he had seen was in an Army convoy and that was only one hour before.

As expected, we were still hitting walls; however, this was only our first day and we had spent much of it on the road.

We had to pay just shy of a million rials for a fifteen by fourteen room that bunked the three of us on as many cots. On the cots were nasty mattresses about three inches thick. The urine stains I understood were free. The sheets and pillow cases did little to cover up the stench. I was going to sleep on my bedroll anyway. With my carbine beside me.

In a small courtyard outside our inn, we broke out our dinners and bottled water. I opened up a can of tuna to go with my cold but baked ears of corn and two of the plums. Lambreau devoured the leg of lamb while Mike Daniels took a second look at

his piece of sheep and changed his mind.

Before turning in, I took my radio out on the village perimeter where I could get better reception and made my final call in. Tyler acknowledged and added, "May have something going already on my end, Bruce. Will keep you guys apprised. Have a good night. Out."

The village was now quiet, my having just heard Isha or the final call to prayer of the day. Off the perimeter wall, the moon, hanging low over the desert, bright and full, cast an eerie glow onto the endless sand giving me the impression I was on another planet or even in a post-apocalyptic Mad Max movie and I was the last human in existence. I wondered what Adriana was doing right about that time. It would be something like four in the afternoon. I pulled out my cell and saw that the planet had no signal. I'd probably need to be closer in to Sana'a or one of the other larger cities. But, then I realized that might be a matter of days as there were no large cities up near the Empty Quarter.

I made my first radio transmission at seven the next morning just before we moved out. Tyler and Zant were headed toward the tribal village of Sanshu about sixty miles to the southeast of us. I relayed to Keith and Mike parts of Tyler's message. "Sa'ayd received a call from a mutual friend living in Ma'rib who said he had spoken the day before with Muhammad. The friend believed Muhammad and a small group of his alQaeda friends were in Sanshu, a suburb of Ma'rib. Tyler said he and his team should be at their target location by early afternoon."

"Appears that's a good start for them," Keith remarked. "Hopefully something will come out of it."

I noticed on our way out of Moriba, a small pickup pulled away after us. There were two occupants in the cab and two in the bed. I could see that the two men in the truck's bed were brandishing AKs. Of course eighty percent of the people in the country were carrying. That in itself was not what was alarming. The fact they stayed with us a dozen car lengths back for several miles **was.**

"Mike, when you get a wide space in the road, pull over."
"You see them, too?"

"Yeah, could be village thugs or even al-Qaeda."

When Mike pulled off, the pickup driver slowed to a stop behind us and sat.

"Grab your AR, Keith; we're getting out. You too, Mike."

When we stepped out of the vehicle, we turned and stood by our doors. The two men in the bed then climbed out and stood by the sides of their truck.

"Ask them why they stopped back there."

Mike yelled the words, but there was no response. The driver and passenger then exited the pickup as well and all four began a slow and calculated walk toward us.

"Keith, on full automatic, fire about a ten round burst over their heads. I'll throw some lead at their feet. On the count of three. One, two, **three.**"

When we opened up on them, all four apparently didn't want any part of us and turned to run. One of them dropped his AK in the process. Once inside the pickup, the driver spun it around one-eighty and sped back toward Moriba.

"Not al-Qaeda," Mike said. "They would've found cover and fired back. These were likely punk kids who thought they could roll some rich Americans."

And so we forged on, this time a bit further west into the Hashid tribal area near Amran. The tribes there had been in recent conflict with Yemen's official government and army, and considering they had been colluding with both the Russians and Iranians, we might just find they were not so friendly to Americans. Most of the tribes were supported by the Saudis; these weren't. The Hashid town of Ishtai was next on the map.

We had covered a lot of ground that morning, the second day of our search, finding that we were actually within forty miles or so of the Red Sea coastline. The terrain looked somewhat different with more trees and foliage, but still not that far from the beginning of the Empty Quarter. So far, no one had seen a large truck almost surely having a covered flatbed, although if one had, it was likely thought to be a military vehicle. I was beginning to wonder if we had good information. The only sighting was via satellite and the image was reportedly not all that clear. The truck disappeared moments after traveling north toward the tribal villages. However, if all the traveling was done at night, no one would likely have seen the truck anyway. I suddenly began fearing we might be chasing a ghost. Nonetheless, the WMDs were real, Galloway was real and Muhammad was real. We all needed for something to break and wasn't sure traipsing around Northern Yemen looking for a needle in a haystack was going to do it.

Ishtai was a moderate size community with better built houses than the mud huts we had seen in a couple of the villages. Some were made of stone with tile roofs and it was obvious this tribe was a good deal better off economically than the people in the mountains and desert rim areas. Crops were in the field as were cattle, goats and sheep. Grass was greener in spite of the arid climate and more of the populace owned autos, vans and pickups. The village mosque appeared to be historic, perhaps dating back two to three hundred years and was well kept. We arrived just in time to hear the third call to prayer or 'asr.

In a village such as that, I was wondering who would be the best people to answer our questions…and who could we trust. Just before we entered the village gate, we were immediately stopped by the Political Security people (PSO) for the second day in a row. I wondered if **these** guys would be less anal when they approached us. I'm sure Lambreau and Daniels wondered the same thing about **me**. This time I'd behave myself. After all, it wasn't me who was handing out the rials.

Recognizing we were Anglo, the security officer spoke to us in English. No pretending this time. "Please provide passports."

He looked them over quickly and handed them back. But then he told us to "Step out of your vehicle."

Mike asked, "Why? Is there something wrong?"

"We need to check inside."

"There is no contraband in here, officer," Mike said.

"Yeah, no soap, no deodorant, no mouthwash," I added.

"Be nice, Bruce," Keith reminded. "We want to get through this and into the village."

However, we complied with the PSO demand and stepped from the SUV. Immediately, four other security goons descended on the Land Cruiser and began opening our bags.

"Why do you have machine guns?" the first officer asked.

Mike replied, "For our personal protection."

"What are you doing where you need protection?"

I answered that one. "Because this is a shit hole country full of criminals, terrorists and dishonest bastards wearing uniforms."

"Bruce, man you're going to get us tossed in a Yemeni jail," Keith chided.

The officer smiled. "Yes, that is exactly what I can do. I do not need a reason."

Mike then interceded. "Officer, we are from the American Embassy and have diplomatic immunity in your country. We cannot be held. If you have questions about that, I can give you a number to call."

That exchange apparently prompted him to rethink his harassment. He merely stood for a few seconds stroking his beard with his fingertips.

"Then you will get back into your vehicle and go about your business."

When we re-entered the Land Cruiser, we found our bags had been dumped out and personal items strewn about. No doubt we'd find things missing. Before we proceeded, the officer looked past Mike at me and said, "You need to change your attitude, Amrikan, if you want to survive in Yemen. Go now."

Lambreau laid his hand on my shoulder and said, "No retort, Bruce. We're good here."

Actually, I wasn't going to say anything back to the A-hole. He had already gotten my message."

Having gotten through the checkpoint, and without paying one rial, we continued on into Ishtai. It might have looked like a lot of other civilized towns in Yemen, but it was still a tribal village. The males were darker skinned with long, thick beards, and most wearing Bedouin shemaghs. The women were clad in black burkas from head to toe. I wondered if some of them might actually be male perverts inside the burkas dressed to where they could go unnoticed into the women's restrooms. Oh, wait, the restrooms were the little sheds out back of the houses that only seated one at a time.

There was a kind of community house similar to a couple I had seen on my last trip into the mountain villages. As people were going in and out, we didn't find it necessary to knock or ask permission to enter. But when we stepped inside, there sat more than a dozen men smoking hookah pipes. Those that weren't, had a mouthful of khat. This was where the people who had no jobs spent their days getting stoned. But three White guys walking into a room full of tribesmen that looked like they might at any time cut our hearts out with their jambiyahs, made the hairs stand up on the back of my neck. I could just as well have been a city dude in the 1800s walking into a saloon ordering a sarsaparilla and being accosted by the Dalton and Clanton gangs. But, although there were only three of us, we had guns and they had knives. Bullets out-rank blades every day of the week.

However, all they did was just stare at us. Nobody approached and nobody said a word. Friendly? Not so much.

Finally, Mike said something to one of the men who looked like he could be the chieftain. For a moment the man merely sat and puffed on his pipe. But then he replied in two or three sentences at the same time shaking his head. Mike dropped his head into a slight bow and turned to leave. We all backed out at the same time.

"That was the village sheik," Daniels said. "Same answers here as in the other villages. No one strange except us came into the village and no one has reported seeing a flatbed truck. I'm thinking we might as well go on back to Sana'a. We'll not find anything canvassing these villages. I think Galloway is long gone and probably out of country. If he's aligned with al-Qaeda and has an out of country contact, the weapons are in Syria and Galloway is sitting on the Waikiki with millions in his bank account."

"You're ready to give up this soon, Mike?" I asked.

"Just being a realist, Bruce."

Lambreau put in his two cents. "Well, I for one am not ready to give it up. And hopefully, Agents Tyler and Zant will make something out of this lead they have on Muhammad. Is there anything from Jarvis and Gerard?"

"Their report is negative as well. But I think you're right, Keith; our best opportunity as a team appears to be with what Tyler uncovers in the Ma'rib area." I checked the time. "It's 1405. I need to call in, anyway."

Mike said, "While you're doing the radio check, I need to pull off the road, Bruce. I have a call to make of my own…a call of nature."

I chuckled and as he walked down a path into a ravine, I climbed up on the side of a hill to assure I had both range and signal. "Charlie One, this is Bravo One, radio check." There was no immediate response. I then moved further up the hillside. I called Tyler again. I waited about thirty seconds, moved to another rock and waited.

Finally, "This is Charlie. Bruce, meet me on a different frequency. Switch to Channel
4. Out."

I did so and reestablished contact. "Charlie One, this is Bravo One, over."

His voice came in. "Roger, Bruce, are the other two in proximity?"

"No, why?"

"Something our driver Sa'yad said that raised my antenna."

"What was that?"

"It was about Muhammad and who he thought he was allied with. I've got a new name for you."

"I'm all ears."

"Muhammad is…wait, got something happening here. What the hell is that? **Good God!**"

Tyler's phone then apparently cut off. I checked and my signal was strong. I called back.

"Charlie, this is Bravo, over."

No response.

"Charlie, do you read me?"

Again, silence.

I went higher onto some rocks. "Charlie, this is Bravo."

Nothing.

I then switched back to Channel 1. "Charlie, this is Bravo, over."

Nothing there. "Alpha, this is Bravo. How do you hear me?"

"Loud and clear, Bravo."

"Have you been able to reach Charlie?"

"I did a commo check with him a few minutes ago. Then I listened a few minutes later as you made contact. The last thing I heard was when he asked you to go to an alternate freak."

"Roger. We were talking and then he cut out in the middle of a sentence. I'm switching back over to try again. Unless his radio petered out, he should be reachable. He's actually in between you and me."

"Understood, Bravo. I'll wait."

Again I went back to Channel 4 and tried to raise Tyler to no avail. I have this sixth sense about me that rarely lets me down. Something was wrong. I could smell it.

CHAPTER 31

When Mike came back up the hill, I pulled him and Lambreau together to fill them in. "May have a problem, gents. I can't reach Tyler. I was talking to him one second and he was gone the next."

"Maybe he was suddenly out of range or his battery failed," Keith said.

"Could be, but what bothers me is something he said."

"Which was?"

"He said, 'Wait, got something happening here; what the hell is that?…followed by him shouting 'Good God.' He sounded frantic."

"Probably nothing, Bruce," Keith said. "Try again in a few minutes."

I nodded. I then looked at our map. After studying it for a few moments and noting the next village Tyler had circled, I tossed the map aside. Mike asked, "Where to now, Bruce?"

"I'm thinking. Give me a few minutes. We didn't eat lunch, so let's sit here a while, eat something and talk about this."

"What's there to talk about?" Mike asked. "We have our itinerary."

I took out my P-38 and began opening a can of peaches. "We're not hitting any more villages today, Mike."

"Why not?"

"Two reasons: this is useless and as we were supposed to rendezvous with the Alpha and Charlie teams tomorrow at the designated coordinates, we're doing it early…this afternoon."

"But Tyler will be pissed. I know enough about this guy to tell you he doesn't like it when people put a kink in his plans. You go to the rallying point today and he won't be there."

"Then we'll camp out there tonight and wait for him. No, better yet…he was headed for the village of Sanshu near Ma'rib. That's where we're going now."

It was Keith who was now questioning my decision. "Bruce, I think we need to follow the plan. I have to agree with Mike."

"I don't want to pull rank, Keith, but Agent Tyler put me in charge of this team and that means I will use my discretion where necessary. We're going southeast toward Sanshu." I set my can of peaches down on the hood and unfolded the map again. "If we stay on this road, we'll take the right fork about two klicks down. That road is Highway 290 and will take us to Ma'rib. My best calculations, looks like about 30 miles south. We ought to reach the area by 1800."

"I've been through there, Bruce," Mike said. "Houthi rebels have taken over that entire area around Ma'rib. Might run into some trouble."

"This whole country's trouble, Mike. You know that better than most anyone."

"I just say we follow our plan. But, whatever. You're in charge."

Several times during our trek south along 290 I tried reaching Tyler. Dead silence on the other end. I then had another thought. I had his cell number…somewhere.

I just couldn't remember where I had seen it. After picking my brain for more than ten minutes, I had a **eureka** moment. Tyler had written it in the right upper corner of the map. I pulled my cell and dialed the number. The call went immediately to his voice mail. "This is Special Agent Roy Tyler. Leave a message and I'll get back to you."

"Roy, Bruce McGowan. I couldn't reach you on the radio, so I'm trying your cell. Call me back."

A few miles further, Mike pulled the vehicle into a gas station. I was noticing the needle had been plunging toward the E. "What kind of gas mileage does this Land Yacht get, Mike?"

"Considering the weight and the mountainous areas we've covered, maybe 8 to 10. It has a 25 gallon tank and we were full up yesterday morning."

"Next time we bring the Prius."

"Bruce, can you pump?" Daniels asked. "I need to hit the latrine again. Stomach's been bothering me all morning. Here's my embassy credit card. You can give it to the clerk inside when you're done."

"Sure, Mike."

The tank seemed like it would never quit drinking, but when it was full up and I heard the clunk, I returned the nozzle to the pump. After giving the clerk the credit card, I saw that Mike had still not left the rest room. When I walked to the door preparing to knock and check on him, I heard his voice inside. He was either on his cell or the hand radio assigned to him. Maybe a call to the embassy or to his Agency boss, Gerard. But, in listening closely through the door, I noticed he was speaking Arabic. Maybe he was conversing with Sa'yad. But if so, why in Arabic? Sa'yad spoke better English than Mike did Arabic. But then I heard the commode flush and I began walking back toward the SUV.

By 1730, we had crossed over into the Ma'rib region. So far, there have been no ambushes, no rebel activity, and no trouble of any kind. My GPS told me we had four miles until we reached Sanshu. However, a half mile further along the road, I saw that vehicles in front of us had come to a stop. When Mike pulled up to the rear of a van, we noticed that people had gotten out of their hot vehicles and were gawking at something simmering further up the road.

"I don't like this, guys. Grab your ARs and let's take a walk."

We then locked the SUV and set out for whatever trouble was up ahead. The voice in my head was at it again. I wasn't liking what I was thinking. The more I thought and imagined, the quicker my step. Finally, what I saw, stopped me in my tracks. Before we were able to go any further, a PSO officer held up his hand. He spoke broken English, "Must not go there."

Mike began communicating with him in Arabic, but I stopped him. "No. I want to hear what this is first hand. No translation." I then turned to the officer. "Tell me in your best English what happened up there."

"People say they saw vehicle come. Then from sky there was white smoke…come across like this and hit vehicle. There was big explosion and vehicle is gone. There are many pieces."

"The people inside?"

"Three. All dead. Bodies very burned. That is all I can say. You must now return to your vehicle."

"Sir, I have to know who was in that vehicle."

"We do not know. Maybe people like you." He pointed to our carbines. "Same kind of weapons."

The nausea in the pit of my stomach just got more intense.

I tried to form my words as articulately as I could so he would understand me. "My name is McGowan. We believe these were Americans from the embassy in Sana'a. We are from there as well. We must look at what's left of the vehicle and see the bodies. Do you understand what I'm saying to you?"

"Yes, but this is official scene and I cannot…"

"You can and you will," I insisted. "Go talk to your supervisor…your leader."

The officer turned and went to where his captain stood near the carnage. A moment later he returned. "You may come with me."

In anticipation of what we'd see, my stomach was almost in my throat. "Let's go."

The SUV was nearly unrecognizable. There were major sheet metal pieces strewn for thirty yards. The interior compartment was still burning even hours after it probably occurred. Off to the side of the road were three yellow tarps under which lay what remained of three bodies. Their badly damaged M-4s lay beside them. Nothing recognizable was left inside the vehicle. The vehicle itself appeared to be of the same type as ours…a white SUV. I confirmed that by finding the rear panel that still bore the name Toyota Land Cruiser. And then we came to the difficult part…identifying the bodies. I knew it was them. All evidence pointed to it.

I looked at Lambreau and Daniels. "You ready?"

They nodded.

Standing by the yellow tarps, I took my time and then finally a deep breath. One by one I lifted all three. Their faces were undistinguishable, but I recognized shreds of what was left of their clothing. I thought Keith was going to be sick as he heaved twice. I felt like it myself. Mike stood expressionless. When I covered them back up and began walking away, my boot kicked something black in the sand. When I picked it up, I saw it was a passport. The face inside belonged to Tom Zant.

As we walked from the scene, I stopped to talk with the PSO captain. "Do you speak any English, sir?"

"A little. Sergeant Lanjwani will help me."

"Thank you. At any point you do not understand, this man, Mr. Daniels will help interpret."

He nodded.

"Captain, the men in this vehicle were our friends, employees of the American Embassy. Who will investigate this?"

"I have official person coming soon who will tell how this happened. We do not think it was a bomb. Maybe rocket launcher. We will find out."

"I know what it was," I said.

"If these were friends, then you know what they were doing here. What was it? I think you are also here on a mission? Was it the same?"

"I can't go into that with you, Captain. But can you do something for us?"

"What is that?"

"Have the ambulance people take these bodies directly to the American Embassy."

"But our rules are to take people killed to the uh…mushriha."

"The word is morgue in English, sir," the sergeant corrected.

"Understood, Captain. Please, no autopsy. Our people in the United States will do that. So, as soon as they're received by the mushriha, can you promise their bodies will go immediately to the embassy?"

"I will promise."

"And for our records, you are Captain who."

"Naroom. Captain Naroom at your service, sir." He then clicked his heels.

"Thank you, Captain. You are most professional and I will tell our people at the embassy of your professionalism."

"Pro…profess…I do not know the word."

"It means you do good work," I said..

He clicked his heels again and popped a quick salute. These PSO officers I liked and they were professionals indeed.

"Captain, one other thing. Can you have one of your men go to these dead men and take the identifications from their clothing? There will be wallets and passports like this one." I showed him Zant's.

"We must keep them with the bodies, McGowan."
"No. We have to have them for return to the embassy and ultimately the families. Please do as I ask."

He nodded and then told one of his officers to carry out my wishes. While the man was securing the IDs, I pulled Keith and Mike off to the side. "We'll need to regroup. Although this mission is being officially run by the Bureau, I'm taking the bull by the horn. I'm sending Jarvis and Gerard back to the compound. Eventually we'll go back there as well, but I've got something in mind while we're in this area."

"What, Bruce?" Lambreau asked.

"Muhammad is somewhere close by and we are going to find him."

"He's gonna have a good number of al-Qaeda types around him. If we do find him, we can't take them **all** on."

"We'll see about that."

CHAPTER 32

Before we left the fatal scene, I jotted down the names of the dead on a sheet of paper torn from my pocket notebook and gave them to the Captain. I also gave him the official embassy contact card that Tyler had provided all of us as well as my cell number. Then with Team Charlie's wallets and passports in my hand, the three of us walked solemnly back to our Land Cruiser.

After we loaded ourselves back in the SUV, I told Mike to "Pull the vehicle off to the side of the road out of the traffic lane. I've got a message to send."

Daniels backed us up, turned around, drove a hundred meters further along the road, finally pulling off into a vacant lot out of view of all the vehicles which were still piling up.

I first took the radio off my belt and keyed the mike. "Alpha One, this is Bravo One, over."

Gerard answered. "Alpha One…go ahead."

"Avery, Bruce McGowan. Bad news. After not reaching Charlie Team by radio or cell, we changed course to go meet them to see if there was a concern. They were attacked outside of Sanshu. Their vehicle was destroyed and there no survivors."

"**My God!** What happened…IED, RPG, what?"

"To be determined. PSO will investigate, but I have my suspicions."

"A freaking nightmare. We need to stop the mission and return to base."

"My thoughts as well. I'd like you to notify the embassy and Jarvis needs to report the incident to his highers." "Are you on your way back?"

"No. You all go ahead. I have something I need to take care of. You'll see us whenever. Bravo out."

I then turned to Lambreau. "Keith, suggest you go ahead and report this to the Secretary. Do you have the capability on your cell."

"I do. I will in a few minutes. What I'm wondering is what you have up your sleeve. What more can we do here?"

"We are going to complete Tyler's investigation here in Sanshu. It's where Jarum alMuhammad is supposedly holed up. And Mike, you're going to help us find him."

He turned in his seat toward me, his forehead deeply furrowed. "How the hell can I do that?"

That's when I pulled my Glock and placed the muzzle within inches of his temple. "How? You know how. You know where he is."

Lambreau placed his hand on my left shoulder. "Bruce, what the hell are you doing?"

"Sewing up my suspicions, Keith. What we have here is the proverbial red herring. I didn't see it until I looked at that death scene and then heard what the captain said. That was no RPG round or IED that hit their vehicle. The captain said people saw a white streak from the sky before the explosion. That would have been a Hellfire missile sent from an unmanned aircraft. Did you see the impact site? Not only was the vehicle totally destroyed, there was a crater left that could only be the result of a 100 pound HEAT warhead. Al-Qaeda doesn't have any drones. Neither do the Yemen Army or the insurgents. They wouldn't have any reason to target us, anyway. And how would they know that we were out canvassing the countryside. No, only one man had the drones on call and we're looking at him."

"McGowan, you're crazy!" Daniels exclaimed. "I always said you were a nut case. What have you been doing…chewing khat, snorting coke?"

"I thought you told everyone you'd work with me anytime and anyplace."
"Maybe I was delusional when I said it."

"Here's what happened: when you disappeared down over the embankment to supposedly take a crap, you were actually calling your controller back in Washington or Timbuktu or wherever the guy is and telling him to put a missile on an enemy Toyota Land Cruiser on the road to Sanshu. How did the drone pinpoint the right vehicle with all the other SUVs on the road? Knowing that Tyler was getting too close to Muhammad, did you in advance have the vehicle shadowed?"

Daniels sat somberly without an expression and without a reply. I tightened my grip on the pistol and nodded. "Everything I just said is true, isn't it, Mike?"

Lambreau interjected, "Bruce, you'd better be right about this."

"Oh, I **am** right, Keith. Also, Company man, you fabricated the entire story about Galloway. Did he disappear because you killed him?"

He turned his head toward me, his eyes cold. "He's alive, McGowan. Stored away in safe keeping. Don't worry, I plan to let him go after I effect this deal with Iran."

"Iran and not Syria." I laughed. "Of course. Everything was a lie, including the message between Galloway and a Syrian contact. My guess is that when I went after Chalmers and he went down, you saw the opportunity to take over his deal. You're a real piece of crap, Daniels."

"I gotta hand it to you, McGowan, I never counted on you putting it all together." He then began clapping.

"Save it, maggot. Get out of the vehicle and lay down on your belly, hands behind your back."

But what he suddenly did instead was throw the gearshift into drive and stomp on the accelerator. The G force of the thrust threw me off balance and at the moment I regained my equilibrium, we slammed into a tree. When I went sprawling into the dash, my gun went off, the bullet passing through Daniels's left forearm. That's when he bolted from the vehicle, drew his gun and began sending rounds through the open door. Fortunately, I had landed on the front floorboard and his shots were errant. By the time I was positioned to exit the Land Cruiser, he had disappeared into the brush.

Both Lambreau and I, guns in hand, charged into the thick foliage as well. I motioned for him to branch off to the left while I pushed forward through some fairly tall khat. After about ten minutes of searching, it was apparent we had lost him. Upon our return to the SUV, I took an assessment of the front end damage. Considering it was reinforced with the heavy metal and thick fiber, only the bumper suffered injury.

"What now, Bruce?"

"Go ahead and make your call to the State Department to give them a sit-rep while I get back hold of Gerard."

I split off from Keith so that we wouldn't be talking over one another and keyed my mike. "Alpha, this is Bravo. Do you copy?"

"Go ahead, Bravo."

"To make a long story short, your cohort, Mike Daniels, is the one who called in a drone strike on Charlie. Galloway is not the bad guy. He is supposedly alive but being held somewhere. I confronted Daniels, but he managed to escape. I wanted you to know this in case he contacts you. We will be looking for both him and Muhammad who is supposedly in the Sanshu vicinity. Do you copy?"

"Copy, Bruce. You are sure about Daniels."

"Dead sure. Alert the embassy and your highers."

"Roger. Agent Jarvis has notified his highers of the situation. On my end, I'll have all drone activity cancelled. He might just send missiles **our** way."

"No doubt. Lambreau and I will continue our efforts here. Will advise further. Out." Knowing Mike Daniels, a Company man, was well-trained and slick as an eel, he wasn't going to be easy to find. However, if he managed to rally with Muhammad and realizing we were still out there looking for the both of them, I figured they would turn the tables and begin looking for us. But, as he would no longer have the drones at his beck and call, we had an even chance of putting the hurt on him. To our disadvantage, however, was the fact that Muhammad likely had at least a platoon of al-Qaeda warriors who might start looking for the two of us. I thought about asking the PSO captain if his people could do a house to house search in Sanshu, but knew they had their hands full what with the rampant crime, traffic issues and Houthi rebel activity. Moreover, the word on the street was they were too scared to go after alQaeda and usually left them alone.

I was now driving the Land Cruiser just as I had placed myself in position to drive what was left of our mission. The mission itself was no longer a village search for anyone who may have seen the flatbed we were looking for. I didn't know what to believe now that we learned Mike Daniels was a rat. He is the one who made up the story about the direction the truck was traveling which sent us on a wild goose chase. He must have been laughing his ass off inside. He had concocted the story to send us looking for Galloway, all the while buying time to make his deal with the Iranians. I felt like an idiot. The worst part of the equation, however, was that three good men had lost their lives.

As we were now allowed to go past the death scene, I saw that a wrecker-hauler had started picking up the pieces of the SUV. What was left was a huge hole in the asphalt that extended well onto either side of the road. We actually had to drive off the road into the grass to go around it.

The sign up ahead read Sanshu, ten kilometers. I wondered if Daniels had caught a ride with someone into the town or knowing we'd likely be heading there, if he went instead to Ma'rib, the larger city. He had a hole in his arm that needed medical attention. It was my guess that he'd be headed for Muhammad's location and our best information was that his terrorist partner was hiding out in Sanshu.

"I'm wondering about something, Keith. Agent Tyler was going to tell me something about his driver and faithful companion, Sa'ayd. And then he was about to mention someone else. My guess is that someone else was Mike Daniels. I'm thinking Sa'ayd knew about Daniels. Maybe the mutual friend Sa'ayd was in touch with had learned it was Daniels rather than Galloway who was actually partnered with Muhammad. Daniels couldn't take any chances on us finding out, so he sent the missile. It would be so easy to blame the attack on either the rebels or al-Qaeda. The only thing is, his partner in the Iran deal is al-Qaeda. Does any of this make sense?"

"Like you said, Bruce, there's much that we don't know about nor ever will. What happens when we get to Sanshu?"

"We'll find out. Looks like Sanshu is only a blip on the map. If an al-Qaeda element is there, chances are they'll be expecting us and two Americans in a Toyota Land Cruiser won't be hard to spot."

"Then I assume we're not driving straight into the town."

"It's almost dark. We'll be parking somewhere off the road, putting on some camo stick and doing a little night recon. Ready for some action, Keith old man? I'll bet it's been a while since you got your ass dirty hunting down terrorist pricks."

"Could be fun."

CHAPTER 33

Neither of us had eaten anything, but we decided after viewing our compadres' burned and shattered bodies, our stomachs would probably come up into our throats. I did have a bite of a melting Snickers for some energy. Just outside of the town limits I found a grove of buckthorns where I could hide the SUV. When I pulled us in, I exited the vehicle and stepped back toward the road to assure the SUV couldn't be spotted.

After we applied my camo stick liberally to our faces and hands, I threw my black jacket over my bush shirt and put my black ball cap back on my head. Lambreau's jacket was a dark brown like his cargo pants, but they would look black in the dark. However, as we weren't wearing the traditional thobes and keffiyehs, we Americans in our western wear wouldn't be fooling anyone if spotted. But I didn't intend for us to be spotted.

We performed a weapon check and threw fresh clips into our M-4s. I remembered we had expended a few rounds the day before in chasing off the banditos. From what we could see through our night vision goggles, at the edge of the tree line, Sanshu was about the size of my hometown in West Virginia. Some of the houses were built into the rocks like we saw in Moriba while others were less substantial mud huts. On the main street which was nothing but a dirt road, was a vegetable stand. All of the goods had been taken away for the night. On down the street I saw a kind of community house which we found was common to nearly all the villages. There appeared to be some activity as two or three men wearing dishdashas were standing outside conversing. But then on the hillside behind a series of irregularly-placed mud huts was a larger structure that was either a mosque or an ancient temple of sorts built of stone but crumbling in places.

As we zig-zagged in between buildings as stealthily as we could, careful that no one could detect our movement, we got a closer look at the structure. There were only a couple of windows that I could see, and I did think I saw a faint light inside for only a couple seconds. It may not have meant anything, but as the place looked otherwise uninhabited, the brief light drew my curiosity.

"What do you think?" I whispered.

"Looks like it could be a good place for someone to hide," Keith whispered back.

"Let's move on up the hill."

Although there was a road that wound its way up to the structure, we stayed off of it and chose a rugged slope instead that provided us stepping stones. When we were about halfway up, the sound of a small truck engine broke the silence. Looking back down on the main road, I saw them. In the bed of a mini pickup were four men in skull caps bearing rifles which from that distance looked like AKs. As they passed the community center, the three men we had seen talking quickly went inside and closed the door. The truck then took a right turn onto the driveway that led to the ancient structure. Its engine and transmission whined as it struggled to make it up the trail. When the truck stopped at the base of some broken steps, the four men jumped out.

The driver and front passenger followed. We stayed hidden behind a natural wall of rocks.

"Has to be al-Qaeda," I said. "The residents disappeared as quickly as these guys arrived."

Moments after they entered the structure, lights began to flicker inside from either candles or lanterns.

"What's your plan, Bruce?"

"Come on. Let's see if we can find a way in."

"Really?"

"I want to get a better look."

"Fine. You're in charge."

When we were nearly at the top, with Keith close behind, I flanked the structure and found a ground level window. But before we could get close in to the opening, we suddenly heard footsteps coming from a stone pathway above us. After flipping off our night goggles, we dove off into some plants and took the prone position. And that's where the man stopped. He wasn't armed. He had stopped to take a leak. Fortunately for us, when he pulled out his manliness, he was facing the opposite side of the path where the ground fell off into a ditch. Our faces hidden by the weeds were only a couple of yards from his feet. The piss took longer than I anticipated. In my head I said to myself, "what is he, a race horse?"

As soon as he was finished and he began shaking himself off, I grabbed his ankles and jerked him toward me. He went down in a flash making a splat sound, landing squarely onto his face and exposed penis. Had to hurt. Before he could gather himself up, I pulled out my Ranger knife and placed the blade under his neck at the Adam's apple.

"Do you speak English?"

He didn't respond.

I asked him again. "Sprechen sie English?" Yeah, I know it was German, but I was trying anything.

He shook his head as though he wasn't understanding anything.

I flipped him over and again laid the knife onto his neck. Placing my finger to my lips, I said "Shhh," which in any language is "Shhh." I then pointed inside the building. "Al-Qaeda?"

He shook his head again, but his eyes said he was lying. I flipped the knife around and cracked him on the head with the end of the handle. I pointed again. "Al-Qaeda?"

For a short moment he froze. His eyes were as large as fifty cent pieces. And then he did the right thing. He nodded.

"Thank you," I said, after which I drew my Glock and clocked him a good one this time. He would be out for hours. I then rolled him off the stone path down into the weeds.

"Okay, we wait," I said.

"I get it. Someone comes looking for this guy and we take him down as well. One by one we should get 'em all, huh?"

"Something like that. Does all this bring back memories of the days you were chasing bad guys?"

"The adrenaline's surging through my arteries like electricity."

I bumped fists with him. "That's what I want to hear. You're taking down the next guy."

We waited something over ten minutes and then we heard the next set of footsteps. This time we made ourselves thin against the building. The man called a name, something like "Barak." When there was no response, he called again and drew closer to us. This one was cradling an AK. When he rounded the corner of the building, his large honker met the muzzle of Keith's Beretta. Keith then gingerly took the AK out of the man's hands.

"Do you speak English?" he asked the man. "And keep your voice low."

"I speak small English." Which I think meant a little.

"Step over here against the wall." He led the man by his shirt down the path into a darker area and slammed his back into the stone wall. Placing the muzzle against the man's forehead, he asked another question. "How many more are inside. And don't lie to me. I know there are at least four more."

"Six."

As we knew of four, I wondered who the other two were. Keith asked him. "Is there an American in there?"

He nodded.

"A man named Daniels?"
Again he nodded.

"Who else?"

"A medical man."

"And the American has a bullet wound in his arm."

He nodded yes.

"Where are they in the building?"

That's when he figured he had given us too much information and suddenly became brave, clamming up.

But Keith then asked one more question. "Is Jarum Muhammad in there?"

Again he didn't answer.

"I'll ask you once more…is your leader Muhammad in there?"

The man remained stoic.I didn't know whether his silence was a yes or no.

"Put our friend to sleep, Mr. Lambreau."

Without hesitation, Lambreau then slammed the butt of his pistol hard against the right side of the man's head. He went down like a sack of cement. I grabbed his shirt and pulled him into the weeds to spend the night with his friend. The blow was hard enough to kill him. But if so, who the hell cared.

Lambreau gave me a thumbs up. "That felt like days of old. I need to get my ass back out in the field when I get home. What now, boss?"

"Back to the window. That's where we're going in."

As we hadn't had much opportunity to look the structure over, I noticed an image chiseled on the outer wall of a carving that looked to be wearing a crown. But as it was stone dark on that hillside, I couldn't tell much about it. Maybe the image of a king? Perhaps this was actually a castle that dated back during the reign of some monarchy. My curiosity getting the best of me, I took out my pen light and looked the carving over. The image wearing a robe and standing with out-stretched arms was a king all right. The crown was one of thorns. This was at one time a Christian church going back even to the 5th Century A.D. before Islam came and destroyed many of the churches. Before I left the states, I read a bit of information on the internet about religious history in Yemen and found there were still ruins of several churches dating back that far that one could visit. Except these religious ruins were being occupied by heathen terrorists. I flicked off the tiny beam and worked my way around to the open window, Lambreau close on my heels.

Peering through the naked frame, I saw nothing but black. Where the men were holed up was obviously in another part of the church. After we climbed through the opening I had to actually feel my way around the room considering it was as dark as the inside of a cave. Could I risk turning the pen light back on? Knowing that a lantern had been lit when the al-Qaeda squad went inside and none of that light was filtering in, the men were nowhere close to us. I went ahead and flicked it on. As I had the light on its lowest beam, I couldn't pick up everything in the room at once, but did see there was nothing to stumble over. The only thing in the room besides us was a scurrying rat. I hate rats.

Finding a large wooden door that would lead us deeper inside, I was reluctant to open it. Knowing the church was centuries old, I figured in opening it, there would be a loud creaking…if I could get it open at all. Maybe it would have just been better to waltz on in the front door and surprise the bastards. They would be expecting the sleeping men back anyway. I've always depended on the element of surprise.

Throwing it open and spraying the room with lead would have been surprise enough.

But being the envelope pusher that I was, I decided to go ahead and try the heavy door anyway. Step one was getting the ancient handle to engage which would release the tumbler. When I dropped the handle down, I heard the click. Step two was getting the door to budge. It wouldn't. It was either stuck or locked. I then placed my shoulder against it. Still no give.

"Keith, be ready to cover me."

"Gotcha."

After one last gargantuan heave with my shoulder, the door suddenly sprang open, the momentum of my push causing me to sprawl onto the floor inside. There wasn't much of a creaking, but I made enough noise going through the door to make up for it. When I picked myself up, I saw that I was in a kind of corridor. Light filtering in from a room at the end of the hallway provided a minimal degree of illumination, enough for us to see where we were. As we moved with a careful degree of stealth along the wall and edged closer to where the light was coming in, we heard voices. It appeared they hadn't heard my clumsiness as their conversation wasn't frenzied. Neither did we hear anyone coming our way.

Off to our right only a few feet from where we heard the voices, I spotted another room. Shining my pen light through the opening, I saw that was where they stored their food and supplies. So, we went inside.

"Check it out, Keith," I whispered. "There, beside that box of Ramen noodles, a dozen Russian F1 grenades. Take a few. They may come in handy." I also pointed out two crates of 7.62 ammo, also Russian, commingled with boxes of other food stuffs. Further back in the room a long table with eight chairs sat against a wall. The room's light would come from a kerosene lantern which sat on a smaller side table.

Suddenly the door to the lighted room opened and one of the al-Qaeda troops made the turn toward the room. When he saw us, as he was unarmed, all he could do was yell out. I responded with a butt stroke with my M-4 that caught him on the chin. He was down and out instantaneously. When I heard the others scurrying about, shouting and clutching weapons, I pulled the pin on one of the grenades and tossed it into the room. Before the four second fuse ran out of time, there was more shouting and the sound of footfalls running away ensued. Seconds after the deafening explosion, Lambreau and I stuck the muzzles of our carbines through the door and on full automatic sent a dozen rounds apiece into the room. When the smoke from the grenade and our M-4s cleared, we tried taking an account of the carnage.

Unfortunately, either the grenade or our rounds killed the lanterns and we could see nothing. I didn't want to flick my pen light to **on**, or anyone who may have survived our attack would make me a target.

Still standing in the corridor outside the room, we waited and listened for any sounds coming from the room such as groaning or the movement of shoes. It was quiet…deadly quiet.

Keith then pulled his Maglite out and asked, "Do you think it's safe?"

"You've got the light."

"That's not what I asked you."

"Just turn on your light and roll it through the doorway."

"Good idea."

As soon as he did, green tracer rounds answered. Luckily we had remained against the stone wall on either side. I then tossed my second grenade in. After the flash and simultaneous whump, it appeared the problem was remedied.

However, the grenade had also destroyed the flashlight and I now had to rely on my pen light again. Now fairly assured it was safe, I took a quick look inside the room with the pen light on its brightest mode. There were three bodies. One was lying partially against the front door, his hand still on the handle where he had tried to get out. The first grenade had ripped out his back. A second man lay well inside the room who looked to have fallen victim to our M-4 rounds. The last man was still clutching his AK-47, likely the gunman who had fired at us. As we found the room to be rectangular and larger than the others, I thought maybe ten or fifteen centuries ago it might have been a sanctuary.

It appeared the six men from the pickup had been accounted for…two lying in the weeds, one in the hallway with a busted head and the three lying dead in what we thought was the sanctuary. But something was wrong with the picture.

CHAPTER 34

One of the unconscious men lying in the weeds had told us the wounded American and his medical provider were also in the church. If so, where were they? They sure as hell weren't in the same room with the dead guys.

"Keith, let's split up. If there are other rooms in this skeleton of a church, we need to find them."

It didn't take us long. I didn't see any other rooms, but Keith found a vestry of sorts through an opening at the rear of the sanctuary. As I was the only one of us who had a light on me, he called me to come take a look. When I scanned the 10 by 10 room, we saw a cot, a chair and a slew of bloodied bandages. A door at the rear of the room had been flung open. When we stepped out onto the ground and walked to the opposite side of the church, we heard the engine to the small pickup start up. By the time we got to the front, we caught a final glimpse of the truck's taillights disappearing down the driveway and out onto the main road. We didn't have a shot.

It would have dome no good to hustle down off the hill and back through the woods to our Land Cruiser in an attempt to pursue the pickup. Daniels would be long gone.

"So, what do you think, Keith? Was any one of these yahoos Jarum Muhammad?"

"Do you still have his photo?"

I pulled it from my cargo pants. We then went back inside and began comparing faces of the dead with the photo. Muhammad had a distinguishing feature the others didn't.

The photo revealed a scar that began at the edge of his right eyebrow and continued down onto his cheek made perhaps by the blade of a knife. Jambiyah fight? None of the dead had such a scar. Neither did the guy in the hall with the smashed face. We then went back outside to pull the sleeping guys out of the weeds. Shining the pen light onto their faces, we found no scar as well.

It appeared all we had accomplished was reducing the al-Qaeda population in the Ma'rib area by three. When the other three came to their senses, one might hope they'd confess their sins and see the errors of their ways. Al-Qaeda was not a favorable lifestyle.

After sneaking back down the hill and past the mud huts, I took a look back at the community center. Now a half dozen villagers were standing out in front of the building looking up at the old church, wondering what the hell happened with all the gunfire and explosions. Whatever the case, no one would be venturing up there. I had the impression the less they had to do with al-Qaeda the better. They knew nothing and would tell nothing.

When we returned to the Land Cruiser, we decided it was as good a place as any to bunk for the night. We dropped the back seat and Keith took the cargo bed. I was just as comfortable with reclining the front passenger seat and stretching out. However, before I did so, I had the remainder of my Snickers, emptied my bladder in the trees and tried once again to call Adriana. Still no signal. I had promised to call her every couple of days. She was soon going to be worried. Before I allowed my lights to go out, I dry-brushed the peanuts out of my teeth, then swished my mouth out with the bottled water.

And so, Daniels had taken flight. But where was Jarum Muhammad?

It appeared we were back to square one with locating Daniels and Muhammad. Had they connected? Other questions…where was Galloway being held and where were the WMDs. It almost seemed finding the weapons had taken a back seat. We hadn't been on the mission but three days, but it felt to me like it had been a week.

I figured Daniels might have escaped to Ma'rib, one of the larger communities in Yemen. There he'd probably dump his hack of a medical man and get treated at an actual hospital. I didn't get a good look at his arm before he took off, but I knew my bullet passed completely through his arm. Whether it snapped the ulna or radius, I had no clue. The longer he went without professional care, the greater the danger of actually losing his arm. My Glock spit big-ass .45 caliber bullets.

Before we left Sanshu, I broke out a tin of Vienna sausages, some crackers, and a can of fruit cocktail. A wholesome breakfast. Lambreau tore open a packet of dehydrated sausage and eggs and poured in boiling water heated up by a can of Sterno. I then used the Sterno to heat up some instant coffee. I love camping out in places like rural Yemen, the land of biting flies, dried-up streams, and all the khat one can chew first thing in the morning. It don't get no worse than that.

Ma'rib was on the same road that would take us to Sana'a and I thought a good place to stop was the police station. We could relate our story and hopefully the police could follow up with the hospital to see who within the past twelve hours was treated for a gunshot wound. Of course, a lot of people got shot on a daily basis in Yemen. However, how many Americans get shot?

There are two Ma'ribs…the ancient, crumbling city that had seen its share of strife and the Ma'rib Governorate where more than a quarter million people live. After passing the historic part of the city where it was believed the Queen of Sheba was from, we entered the contemporary district. Almost immediately, we spotted a police unit parked at a curb. I pulled in behind it and got out to ask directions from the officer to his station. He spoke no English. I then pointed to his badge and at a building and he finally got the message. He motioned for me to follow him.

The station was deeper into town about six blocks from where we found the officer. I wheeled up to the curb in front of the building and then saluted the officer as he pulled away. Keith and I exited our vehicle and leaving our carbines covered up inside, I locked the Land Cruiser. Once inside the building, I asked the first officer we saw if he spoke English. He said he did a little, but would send us to someone who spoke it very well. The man's name was Sergeant Zarak.

We sat with Zarak for over ten minutes telling him we were from the American Embassy in Sana'a and that we were tracking an American who was responsible for the deaths of three of our friends on the road to Sanshu. We also told him about the al-Qaeda terrorist named Jarum Muhammad who had colluded with the American to commit crimes of international terrorism.

He said, "We know of this Muhammad and that he is the leader of al-Qaeda. He has for many months been making attacks on units of military loyal to the Hadi government, but since the Houthis have taken power, Muhammad and his al-Qaeda people have now made attacks on them. Our own officers have been ambushed on the roads; so, yes, we are at war with Muhammad. We would like to capture him."

"This American named Michael Daniels needed to have his wound treated," I said, "and if he went to your hospital, he may still be there. He will then know where Muhammad is."

"Then we will go there now."

Ma'rib General, a 120 bed hospital, one of the more modern buildings in the city, served the populace in all 14 districts of the governorate halfway to Yemen's capital in Sana'a. With all of the cholera, TB and dengue fever cases, not to mention the gunshot and knife wounds associated with the civil strife occurring in the country, it was little wonder why there was standing room only in the emergency room. The wards were full and from what Sergeant Zarak told us, many non-life threatening cases were turned away daily. As to the people themselves, none of the women we saw was without the burka, so I was wondering, halfway in jest, if the surgeons removed the women's garment before they operated. And if they did, would their husbands then beat them when they got home for exposing themselves. But I tend to wonder about the most imbecilic things.

When we stopped at the ER desk, Zarak asked the nurse, also covered from head to toe with the exception of her face, if an American male had processed through the emergency room for a gunshot wound. I saw her nod and then say something back to the sergeant in Arabic. Zarak then drew his sidearm and said, "He is still here. He had surgery and is through this door in recovery." Both Lambreau and I still had our pistols on our belts and at the same time placed our hands on the grips.

As we walked by the rooms, the nurse saw two men wearing keffiyehs outside a room at the end of the hallway and said something to Zarak. He then relayed to us what she said, "Those men are not supposed to be there."

I looked down the corridor, but no one was there.

"I don't see anyone, Sergeant," I said.

"Then they have quickly gone. They went into the room. The nurse said it was the American's room." He then began running and we stayed close on his heels.

When we reached the door, Zarak took a position along the wall and then slowly turned the doorknob, fearing he would be met by a hail of bullets.

I removed my Glock and said "I'll cover you, Zarak."

When he kicked the door open, I took a crouch position and swept the muzzle of my gun around the room. The room was empty and the window open. When I ran to it, I saw that the three men had already disappeared into a crowd of people walking along the street. Daniels's I.V. was lying on the bed where he had hastily torn it from his arm. A small drop of blood from the needle had trickled onto the sheet. I quickly climbed out the open window and ran toward the road to see if I could catch sight of the fleeing Daniels. People on the street froze in their tracks at the sight of the crazy American with the gun in his hand. Several of the women screamed and began breaking away, so I holstered my Glock. Again, Daniels had disappeared. Three times in the last twenty or so hours. And I was betting that one of the Arab men who helped spring him from the hospital was Jarum Muhammad.

I had no idea of the direction they had run and was pretty damn sure Daniels's accomplices had a vehicle waiting somewhere close. I returned to the inside, this time through the front entrance. Zarak had already contacted his superiors to put the equivalent of an All Points Bulletin out. He had also called a cohort with the PSO to look out for a vehicle with an American White man inside. Unfortunately, he couldn't give them a vehicle description, but as they'd likely be fleeing on one of the roads out of the city, it was a sure bet they would encounter PSO checkpoints on every artery.

CHAPTER 35

The distance between Ma'rib and Sana'a was about 75 miles, but according to the GPS on my cell, it would take nearly three hours. If we would be running into checkpoints, it was going to be longer. My conjecture about that was correct. We weren't two miles outside Ma'rib when we hit the first one. We crawled for more than fifteen minutes behind a dozen or so vehicles ahead of us, all of which were being stopped and searched. As we didn't see anyone being held off to the side of the road, I took it we'd be fine as well.

Wrong again.

When it came our turn, two PSO officers shoved their weapons through both of our open windows and a third policeman, a lieutenant, yelled at us in English, "Get out of the vehicle!"

I wasn't going to sit there and argue, so we both slowly opened our doors and stood beside the SUV.

"Put your hands on your head and face your car."

We complied and both policemen then took our pistols from our holsters. Finally, I asked, "What is this about?"

"We are looking for an American criminal. You are Americans?"

"Yes, but we're not the people you're looking for. We are from the American Embassy."

"Show me your passports!"

"Okay, I am going to reach in my pocket and pull mine out. Don't get nervous with those AKs."

Keith said, "I'm reaching for mine, too."

Each of the officers handed our passports to the English speaking superior. He studied them and then asked, "Which one of you is the man called Daniels?"

"Neither of us," I said. "You might be able to speak English, but obviously you can't read it."

"Bruce? Easy," Keith said.

I continued. "If you will call a Sergeant Zarak at the Ma'rib Police, he will tell you who we are. Here is his card." I handed it to one of the policemen. "I realize you're looking for the man Daniels, but so are we."

"Who are you and why are you looking for him?"

"We are investigators out of the embassy. United States federal investigators."

The PSO supervisor called the two men with guns to come talk with him. He then got on his cell phone, and looking at the card, apparently got hold of Zarak. Taking two or three minutes to converse, he closed the conversation and said something to his men. They then turned around and brought our pistols and passports back to us."

"Okay, Amrikans, you are free to go. Do not cause trouble while you are in this country."

"We don't intend to, Lieutenant. But, you can do something for us. Radio all your checkpoint locations from here to Sana'a and tell them to pass us through."

"I will do this on one condition…you will pay money."

"Why would we have to do that? You're policemen…public servants. Or are you also crooks?"

"You must do what I ask."

And then I remembered. I didn't have any rials and neither did Keith. Mike Daniels had all the money in a zip-open bag and he took off with it, which wasn't very considerate of him.

"Uh, Lieutenant, I have no rials on me. You can search me if you don't believe me."

"You must have rials somewhere in your vehicle."

"I don't…I promise you." I did have about $200 in U.S. currency in my wallet, but I'd be damned if I would give that up.

He came closer to me and picked up my left wrist. "That is a nice watch. Gold, I believe. I will take it."

"The hell you will."

Keith said, "Bruce, go ahead, give it to him. When we get back to the States, the government will buy you another one."

"It's not that. Adriana gave it to me for our fifth anniversary."

"I'll give her the money to replace it. We have to get through all of these checkpoints and if you don't give him the watch, he won't call ahead."

"Listen to your friend," the lieutenant said.

"I am getting back in my vehicle and driving away…with my watch. And you will make the call. Get in the car, Keith."

Lambreau let out a long sigh and got back in. I know he was put out, but I didn't give a damn.

The lieutenant didn't say a word as I drove away. His venomous eyes did the talking for him. He'd call ahead all right, but he'd be telling the PSO units awaiting us to keep putting the Amrikans through the wringer.

It wasn't long until the road to Sana'a became twisted and plunged through fissured clefts on either side as we gradually began picking up higher terrain. The foliage around us began gradually disappearing and once again we may as well have been on Mars. As we negotiated the curves and turns, I fully anticipated there'd soon be another checkpoint, but in thirty miles we hadn't experienced one. I checked the gas gauge and saw that we now had a quarter of a tank. We still had some forty miles to go. I needed to nurse the vehicle as best I could so that we wouldn't find ourselves stranded in the 100 degree temperature. Even if we came upon a gas station, I didn't have the embassy credit card nor even one rial. But I did have a watch.

After passing through a small village which was nothing but a bump in the road, we again began climbing. I remembered that Sana'a was touted as having the highest elevation of any capital city in the Arabian peninsula. As we began rounding a fairly sharp curve compelling me to slow the vehicle even more, I caught a glint off something on a piece of rocky hillside to our left. It could have been nothing, but when I saw the white Toyota Hilux sitting back off the road beneath an overhanging boulder, I jammed on the brakes.

Lambreau turned his head quickly toward me and yelled, "What's happening, Bruce?!"

I looked back at him and slammed a round into the chamber of my M-4. "Prepare for war, Keith."

It was one of those split second deals where I threw the gearshift in reverse and stomped the accelerator just as the RPG gunner targeting our vehicle fired. The rocket propelled grenade missed our windshield by inches and exploded harmlessly into a ravine off to our right.

"Bull-shit!" Lambreau exclaimed.

Anticipating more rockets might be on the way, I knew we had to get out of the SUV. We were sitting ducks where we were. If there was one RPG, chances were there were others. I hit the gas again and fishtailed the truck into a small cove of rocks to our left out of sight from where the weapon had been fired.

"Grab your carbine, Keith, and jump out! Run to the right and drop down over the hill!"

We both jumped at the same time, ran like gazelles and slid down into the ravine just as a propelled rocket from a second location impacted with the Land Cruiser. As the grenade had this time gone into the windshield triggering a head-splitting boom, the fiery effusion peeled back the roof and set the entire vehicle on fire.

"Good God!" Keith yelled. "If we'd stayed in there ten seconds longer, we'd have been vaporized." He slapped me on the shoulder. "Good call, Bruce."

"We're not out of this **yet**. Come on."

"Where?"

"Just stay close behind me."

Running at a crouch, I kept low and out of sight behind a series of boulders and began working my way around to where we could cross the road again and start up the high ground to flank the attackers. I wasn't sure if they had seen us abandon the SUV, but I was going to assume they did. They'd either be looking for our corpses or for us to move in on them.

With as much stealth as I could muster, assuring I wasn't slipping on the rocks and kicking stones down to the road, I made every effort to stay sure-footed. Keith, I wasn't sure about. Long separated from field duty, I feared he had gotten soft and wasn't as tactically agile.

But then I saw the gunner up ahead scooting down a rock. You see, I was never the type of cop, even in my FBI days, to yell out, "Freeze! Drop your weapon!" Never give the bastard an opportunity to run or shoot at you first. Still in a crouch, from the hip I fired a three round burst that blew the man off the rock, his body falling down to the road.

But then suddenly I was shocked by explosive gunfire going off to my rear. When I wheeled around, I saw Keith standing, behind me, carbine smoking, and my would be assailant dead on the slope above me. His AK had slid down the boulder and was laying near my feet.

My question about Keith's sharpness had been answered.

"I owed you that from a couple minutes ago," he said.

I nodded my thanks.

But were there others? I motioned for Keith to follow me up to where I had spotted the gunner's nest. When we got close, that's when we began taking AK fire. Bullets ricocheting at our feet compelled us to dive off to our left behind a series of large rocks. I lifted my M-4 over my head and fired a half dozen rounds wildly on full automatic. There was no return fire and I wondered if I had struck him.

But then I heard a voice…not anyone yelling from where the attacker was perched. It was coming from my radio.

"Give it up, Bruce. You can't win this one."

Mike Daniels. He still had his radio. Keith gave me a bewildered look.

"Hello, Mike," I replied. "How's the arm?"

"I'll live. You won't. There are more of us up here than you think. Toss your guns down the slope along with your sidearms. I'll make it quick. You won't suffer."

"You know me better than that. I'm coming for you. I have to hand it to you, though; you got away from us on three different occasions. But not this time."

"Then come on, Bruce. Let's see how good you are." He fired a volley of rounds which pinged harmlessly off the rocks above me. From our left another weapon then opened up. Those rounds came dangerously close causing us to duck further down between some huge rocks. They had us penned in. If we tried a retrograde back down the slope, we'd be dead meat.

"Before one of us dies, Mike, I have to know something; where are the WMDs?"

He laughed. "I had you stupid shits looking all over hell and half of Georgia for them…from the Yemen tribal lands to the Empty Quarter. Those weapons never left the Jabal Kanin Mountains. All we did was move them to another cave not two hundred yards away."

"And Galloway? Where did you stuff him?"

"He's still in Sana'a, chained up in some warehouse. Not to worry, He'll be released when my friend Muhammad is satisfied the big bomb is safely in my contact's hands and I'm on my vacation the rest of my long, long life."

I took my fingers off the mic. "Keith, those hand grenades you stuck in your cargo pants last night, did you take them out?"

He smiled and passed one to me.

"Great. I knew I could count on you."

I had to make the toss true and accurate. The range had to be dead-on. I couldn't throw it too short to where it would roll back down and blow us off the hillside.

"Keith, fire a volley in the direction of the gunner on our left to keep his head down."

When he sent a burst of ten or so rounds up the slope, I pulled the pin and called once again on my old pitching arm which I hoped wouldn't let me down. The grenade made it to the top of the gunner's nest. When we heard the **whump** and saw the smoke, scores of rocks trickled down the slope along with the gunner's AK-47.

"Let's go," I said to Keith. "We're taking his position."

I was fairly certain where Daniels was perched, so I moved around the lower part of the rocks and crawled on my hands and knees up the side of the boulder until I reached the crest. Keith was right behind me, only not managing the crawling part all that well. When I reached the dead gunner, I saw he only had half of a head. So I wouldn't have to look at him, I shoved his body down the slope.

Even though I had reached the spot where I thought I could actually see where Daniels was set up, I found he had relocated. Unfortunately, he had placed himself in a better position to spot us. That's when he unloaded. His rounds caught us both. One of the bullets creased my left shoulder and another hit Keith in the thigh. Solid hit. After we dove further back into the rocks. Another gunner began peppering us from a different direction. I couldn't tell from where.

As blood was pouring from Keith's thigh, I yanked off my bandana and began creating a makeshift tourniquet. Finding a branch close by, I snapped off a limb and began twisting the knot I had made. The oozing subsequently stopped. And then so did the shooting.

Suddenly I heard the keyed squelch on my radio. "Bruce, you still there?"

"I'm here."

"You die hard, my man."

"Why don't you throw your weapon down and I'll do the same? I'll meet you on these rocks somewhere in between. Just you and me and knives. Whoever walks away gets to keep the WMDs."

"You'd like that wouldn't you, Bruce. My left arm's in a gel cast, but I think you know that. Ex-Ranger and Special Ops guy, expert with a knife, fighting a one-armed man. That's mighty big of you to offer. No, as long as I can sling bullets at you, I got the advantage. By the way, you wanted to meet my friend, Muhammad? Say hello, Jarum. Game over, McGowan."

That's when more AK fire began pouring in on us. The bullets' ricochets sent pieces of rock into my face. As we were now slightly higher up than Daniels and Muhammad and we had one more grenade, I thought I'd try another throw. Although I didn't exactly know where either of them was, I figured I could at least shake them up a bit and maybe one of them would briefly show himself.

"The game is over when I say it's over, Daniels."

I then pulled the pin and tossed the grenade down the slope to where I saw the last puff of smoke from Daniels's weapon. As it took about the same four seconds to roll down as the length of the fuse, when the explosion occurred, Daniels did as I hoped. He exposed his head while getting to his feet to run to a different position. That's when I was ready with my M-4. It was only a fifty meter shot, so the split second I saw him in my sights, I pulled the trigger. The last sight picture I had was when the top of his head came off.

CHAPTER 36

As Keith wasn't able to see the magic moment, he asked me, "Did you get him?"

"Just a piece of him is all."

But then a bit of trepidation must have happened with Muhammad, because I saw him roll out of his position and run. The last glimpse I caught of him, he was disappearing down the rocky slope toward the small pickup. I fired a shot, but I was too late to catch his head. I was going after him. I knew Keith couldn't move so I told him to "Stay put; I'll come back for you."

"I'll be fine," he said. "Nail his ass!"

As I hoofed it down the slope, I yelled back, "Keep that tourniquet tight."

While Muhammad was sliding down the slope, I decided to flank him by taking the steeper choice. I figured I could just about get to his truck before he did…that is if I didn't break my neck. But by the time he was at his door, I had just reached the edge of a small rock cliff a dozen feet above him. He then backed the truck away from the rocks to turn around with intent of going back toward Ma'rib, I tried to get off a shot. Unfortunately, all that was visible of the truck was its bed. In a matter of seconds, he would be gone. But then I realized I had committed the unpardonable sin. My magazine was now empty and in my haste to jump out of the doomed Land Cruiser, I failed to grab my extras. So, I made the crazy decision to toss the M-4 and do a Bruce Willis by jumping the ten feet down into the truck's bed. Yeah, I could have broken my neck as I was no stunt man; but, surprisingly, I had made a faultless landing. A perfect ten.

Muhammad, however, in feeling the thump and seeing me in his rear view mirror, gunned the truck, causing me to stumble and nearly tumble out of the bed. My body half hanging off the tailgate, I somehow managed to grab hold of it and pull myself back in.

Not to be outdone, Muhammad took his pistol, smashed out the rear glass and while driving with his left hand, began firing at me with his right. Knowing it was coming, I dove down flat onto the bed, the rounds passing harmlessly over me. I counted nine shots. As it appeared to be a Russian-made Parabellum, if the clip was full, he had another nine. When he could no longer see me, he stuck the gun through the bustedout glass with an intent to fire down into the bed. However, before he could get the first shot off, I wrested the gun away with both hands and tossed it off to the side of the road.

I then pulled out my Glock and placed it through the opening onto the back of his head. But Muhammad wasn't through. Suddenly, swerving the truck to the left and then right, I was knocked off balance. All I could do was hold on. The truck fishtailed violently to a point where I thought we'd turn over. At the very least, I thought I'd be thrown out. Finally, I regained enough of my equilibrium that I was able to take the butt of my Glock and whack him in the back of the head. It was enough of a blow to knock him out. Of course, that might not have been my best decision. Muhammad slumped into the steering wheel and the truck began drifting off the road.

As the truck was heading for the ravine off the left side of the road, I dove through the window opening and began steering the truck back to the center of the road. However, I still didn't have good control of the vehicle, mainly because Muhammad's foot was on the accelerator. In trying to steady the vehicle, I nearly ran a van coming from the opposite direction off the road. The driver let me know how he felt about that by laying on his horn. Finally, I grabbed Muhammad by his shirt and flung him onto the passenger's side. I then climbed fully inside the truck's cab, pulled the hand brake and coaxed the pickup off to the side of the road. About that time, Muhammad started coming around and I gave him a solid right to his bearded jaw to again rattle his brain. Reaching across him, I lifted the door handle and then with my foot, booted him out onto the ground.

After exiting and rounding the truck, I stood over him, waiting for him to come around. When he did, I bent down with my knee on his testicles and placed my knife against his throat. If I wasn't sure before, his tell-tale facial scar confirmed it was Muhammad. With my left hand, I slapped him in the face a couple of times. "You speak English, Muhammad?"
He nodded.

"I'm only going to ask you one question. Where's Galloway? I want to know where you stashed him."

"That is all? You don't want to know about the weapons?"

"Daniels already told me they're in another cave adjacent to where we first found them. I just want Galloway."

"I will tell you if you let me go."

I pressed my knee harder into his groin and he cried out in pain.

"You're in no position to bargain, goat man. The tip of this blade is less than a centimeter away from severing your carotid artery. I sweep it across your throat and you bleed to death in two minutes…if you're lucky, three. Of course, as many innocent throats as you've cut, you know that."

He grinned."I am not afraid to die. You will do me a service. I will have much reward awaiting me."

"If you don't tell me what I want to know, you will have much **pain** awaiting you."

He didn't respond. He only stared at me with his cold black eyes. I wasn't going to waste my time beating his brains out to get him to talk. Something else had to happen.

And then it did, unfortunately not what I expected. Suddenly, his hand came up and in it was a rock as big as his palm. It didn't knock me out, but the blow to the side of my head dazed me. Before I realized it, he was onto me. This time, the six inch jambiyah that I failed to take off him was in his right hand, cocked and ready to be driven into my neck. I grabbed his wrist just in time. His right arm was equally as strong as my left and gradually the blade edged closer to my throat. His left hand was holding my right arm down. A bigger man than I expected, he was as strong as an ox…and smelled like one as well.

He grinned. "You will die, McGowan."

"Yeah, I know I will, Muhammad…just not today." My knife, still in my right hand, somewhere I found the strength to out-muscle him. I then thrust it upward, slicing a hunk of meat from his forearm which caused him to release his grip. My next thrust was into his upper chest. He immediately began gagging, grabbing his throat as he rolled off me onto the ground. I wasn't sure if I had hit an artery, but the blood began pouring profusely.

From my cargo pants I then pulled my handkerchief and pressed on the wound to try slowing down the blood flow. "This is your opportunity, Muhammad, I will stay here all day if necessary to stop you from bleeding to death. All you have to do is tell me where Galloway is being held."

But his eyes began rolling back. "Stay with me, Muhammad!" I bellowed. "You can make it! I'll help you."

He then whispered something I couldn't make out. I placed my ear close to his mouth. "What are you saying?"

His words now clearer but still a whisper, he said, "I don't want to die. Help me live."

"I'm trying. Believe that." But the pressure I was applying wasn't working. The blood was now gushing and had completely soaked the handkerchief. I had likely severed his aorta.

His words were now barely discernible. "I will tell you."

"What will you tell me, Muhammad?"

"Gal…Galloway is…in a warehouse in…Sana'a. The Halaal…" He then began gasping for air to no avail. Blood now drained from his mouth and he closed his eyes. His last breath was a gurgle.

Several vehicles had passed by going in both directions, but anyone who may have seen Muhammad's body lying beside the pickup still continued on without stopping. Had death become so commonplace that people were rendered apathetic and uncaring? Not that I **wanted** anyone to stop.

After placing Muhammad's body in the truck's bed and closing the tailgate, I turned the vehicle around and drove back to the ambush site. Our Land Cruiser which I had parked on the side of the road was still smoking because the interior was smoldering. I guessed people went by it as well, a bit curious, but disinterested nonetheless.

After parking the truck back in the same place it was before, I went up the hillside to get Lambreau. Passing by Daniels, I was glad to see he was still dead. I had gotten two very valuable pieces of information from two dead men within the past fifteen minutes. However, I wasn't sure if we had enough from Muhammad's last words to find the warehouse. Halaal was either a word or part of a word and I could only suppose it was the name of a warehouse. If we did find him, somebody had to be keeping him under guard. That meant at least one more al-Qaeda bastard to take down.

"By damn, you did make it back," Keith said.

"You had your doubts?"

"Actually, no. I've seen you in action enough to know you'd get this guy. You did, didn't you?"

"He's waiting for us in the pickup down on the road."

"He **what**?"

"He's dead, Keith. How's the wound?"

"The bleeding's stopped, but it hurts like a bitch."

"Let's get you out of here and to a hospital in Sana'a."

As he leaned into me, I helped him ambulate down the slope to a point where he could slide on his butt the last few feet to the road.
"This is our new ride," I said as I helped him into the passenger side. "I'm going back to get Daniels's body. The other goat humpers I'm leaving up there for the buzzards."

After I loaded Daniels in, I pulled back onto the highway. Sana'a was an hour away.

"Just wondering about something, Keith. Did Daniels and Muhammad expect that we'd be going back to Sana'a, that we'd be hot on his tail on this very road? Or were he and Muhammad in cahoots with the PSO, especially the pricks at that checkpoint we went through?"

"While I was lying back there on that hill, the same thought crossed my mind. Too coincidental. I say the PSO alerted them."

"Yeah."

Speaking of the PSO, less than ten miles up the road, we hit another checkpoint. Although we had done our best to cover the bodies in the bed with a half-burnt blanket from the Land Cruiser, the security cops found them. As our story about being U.S. federal agents chasing these bad guys for the last couple of days was dismissed as bovine scatology, we were cuffed and carted off to a PSO detention center in Sana'a. Not only did they confiscate all our weapons, to include my bloodied Ranger knife, but they took our phones and radios as well. Apparently, there was no such thing in Yemen as the one phone call.

I told the precinct commander, COL Zukarai, that if he did not notify the American Embassy immediately, there would be hell to pay. The U.S. Marines would level the place. So that he would be saving face, which was important to the PSOs, especially the uppity-ups, he delayed his contact with the embassy for nearly five hours. Keith Lambreau got the better part of the deal as he spent those five hours at Sana'a General. Me? I got to share a filthy cell with not only a cop murderer who reportedly went berserk from an overdose of khat, but a wild-eyed donkey humper wearing only a loincloth and a turban. Oh, and there were also two rats as big as cats and a thousand cockroaches.

But, thankfully, five minutes after the jailer turned out all the lights, two familiar faces showed up to rescue me…the two men who had made it back safely to the embassy compound, Jarvis and Gerard.

"Bruce, is all that your blood?" Jarvis asked. He of course was referring to my bloodsoaked shirt where Muhammad had sprung a nasty leak.

"Not all of it." Some of it also belonged to Lambreau. And then I had all but forgotten about the bullet that had creased my shoulder. I wondered why my shirt felt like it had been glued to my upper arm. I supposed I needed to have it looked at.

"Let's get you back to the compound. I understand Keith Lambreau was taken to the hospital with a wound. Is it serious?"

"It is to him. It appears to be a clean-through thigh wound. But, as far as I could tell, the bullet didn't hit his femur."

"I hear you took out Daniels and Muhammad. You're the man, Bruce."

Gerard added, "Yeah, great work, but I guess we still know nothing about the WMDs and where Galloway might be?"

"I think we do. Before he bit the bullet, Daniels was kind enough to tell me he and his towel head friends merely moved the crates to another cave in the same area of the Jabal Mountains. We just need to go on the hunt to locate them. And then Muhammad made a deathbed confession about Galloway being chained up in a warehouse somewhere. He gave me a name, Halaal. I don't know if that's a business name or a person."

Gerard replied, "I hope that's good enough information. I want to get our man out of there as soon as we can. He's been there too freaking long as it is."

"I agree," I said. "Why don't you go ahead and research the name I gave you while I out-process with my innkeepers? If you find something, I'm going with you guys."

While Gerard was checking his iPad for the business name or an individual with the name of Halaal, I retrieved my possessions from the jailer. I secured both Lambreau's and my weapons, wallets, passports, cell phones and radios. But my gold watch was not among the items.

I then began a conversation with the two jailers, using the kindest words I could think of. "Alright, which one of you simple-minded sand rats stole my watch?"

I'm not sure if the two men understood English, but they sure as hell understood my tone of voice. And when I tapped my wrist, I'm sure they knew what I was bellowing about. But they only looked at me with startled eyes without word. So did Jarvis and Gerard.

However, it was when I slapped a magazine in my Glock and chambered a round that the smaller of the two men went to their desk drawer and produced the watch. I don't know if they really thought the crazy American would unload on them, but the jailer wasn't taking any chances. In hindsight, I shouldn't have been wearing the damn watch anyway as expensive as it was, attracting so many larcenous eyes. And with all of the shooting, fighting, stabbing and other roughhousing I was doing, it's a wonder it didn't get busted. I told myself, the next time I went on vacation to Yemen, I'd be again wearing my $25.00 Timex.

When I was through with the out-processing and scaring the crap out of the jailers, I left with my two jail busters. Gerard had already come up with two possibilities on the name: one was Halaal Imports and Exports and the other Halaal Crating and Storage. Either sounded like good possibilities.

"Are you sure you wouldn't rather remain at the embassy tomorrow while we canvass the locations?" Gerard asked me. "Agent Jarvis and I can handle this."

"You two might need some back-up. Wherever Galloway is found, chances are he won't be alone. Daniels had to have someone at least checking on him, providing food and drink, whether he had him under full-time guard or not. That being the case, there could be some resistance."

"Suit yourself, man. But, in my book, you've earned some big time R and R."

CHAPTER 37

After we were checked in by the Marine guards at the embassy gate, we went immediately to the dining hall for some real food. Gerard and Jarvis had arrived at the compound earlier in the day and relaxed for a few hours. A few of the embassy employees having a nine-thirty drink at the canteen gave my bloodied clothing a curious eye, probably wondering if I had just escaped from a Zombie village. I washed my face, hands and arms anyway in the rest room and returned to our table to order myself a thick, juicy steak and a cold beer. Jarvis and Gerard had waited for us. They had been in no mood for food to this point.

We sat somberly for a few minutes while awaiting our grub, each of us sad and disconsolate at the loss of our compadres. We did exchange occasional glances, but words seemed inadequate.

Finally, Jarvis said to me, "Bruce, you said everything you had was destroyed when the RPG hit. I have an extra pair of cargo pants and a couple of shirts you can have. I'm not giving up my boxers, though. You can wash yours out tonight."

I chuckled at that and said "Thanks. I can't wait to hit the shower. I assume I can have my apartment room back."

I had to hand it to young Jarvis. His continuing dialogue at our table began changing the mood."I don't know how you managed it, Bruce, but somehow you figured it out. Somehow, you determined it was Daniels who was the bad guy and that he had sent the missile that took out Agent Tyler and Mr. Zant. Then you tracked these perps and brought both of them down. I want to be you when I grow up."

I had to laugh at that, but then said, "Don't forget, Keith Lambreau partnered with me to make that happen. He paid for it with a bullet through his leg."

"Still, I am quite impressed and can one day say I worked with the great Bruce McGowan. I am sure somewhere in the Bureau's training modules will be examples of your cases that you worked."

I laughed again. "Yeah, the **lessons learned** files. But stop it; you're embarrassing me."

I was becoming more impressed with young Lew Jarvis. In a scant four days, he seemed to have metamorphosed from a green, razor-straight desk jockey to a desert seasoned field agent having experienced the harsh elements of a third world hell hole while also facing the reality of death. I was now seeing a different look in the rookie's eyes along with his four day stubble, sun-splotched face and new-found comportment. Although his village itinerary had not placed him in a position to engage with any combatives, the short week had done much to change that virginagent deportment of his.

"Gentlemen," he continued, "with Mr. Lambreau sidelined, it's just us three now. I talked earlier with the assistant director, apprising him where we are at this point. Just to let you know, I have now been given the green light to oversee the remainder of the mission, given it's still Bureau-driven. We're almost there with the operation. Avery, we'll first go find Sam Galloway and then if you can get us an aviator in the next day or so, we'll go looking for the WMDs. I might have been handed the lead on this mission, but one thing for sure, I'll be listening to the both of you. You've been in combat, you've made life and death decisions and you have been involved in the kind of covert missions that I will never experience. If you will just provide me your thoughts and recommendations here on out and we'll finish this deal up."

Yeah, the kid was going to be all right. I smiled and shook his hand. "Let's go make this deal happen, boss…right after you buy me that juicy steak."

When I got to my room, Jarvis brought me by the clothes he promised and I again thanked him. After a twenty minute long hot shower, I began washing out my boxer shorts in the sink. When that was done, I opened my window and hung them on the outside handle for Shirley Compagno to see when she arrived for work the next day. No, that was not an invitation for her to come up and party. It was just a joke, alright? My undies should be dry by first light. As to mañana, I had arranged to meet Jarvis and Gerard in the parking lot at eight.

After throwing a sheet over my naked body, I grabbed my cell phone and dialed home. Adriana answered on the third ring.

"Hey, sweetheart, did you think I would ever call?"

"I was wondering. Are you getting things accomplished there."

"Just about sewed up. We have a few more days and I'll be home."

"Thank God. I miss you like crazy. Are you doing well otherwise?"

"Yep. Deepening my suntan. I just had a nice, thick steak. And for our enjoyment, we might go out later and party with some of these camel-faced women."

"Ha ha. I've seen some of those Arabian women."

"Well, I haven't. All of them are covered up with burkas. So, is all well there with you, Madam Mayor?"

"Still reigning over the kingdom. I just got my scepter out of the repair shop where I banged it too hard at my last council meeting."

I laughed. I was convinced she had inherited my sense of humor. "Well, hey, I guess I gotta go. I wanted to hear your voice tonight before I went to sleep."

"I'll still be saying prayers for your safe travel. Come home, soon."

"Love ya, Babe."

"And I love you as well, Skip. Goodnight."

For the first time in days, I was starting to feel a sense of closure. We made some big time progress, mission-wise, although we had a ways to go, and I got to spend a little time on the phone with the woman I loved. But, before the sandman came, I would be saying prayers for the souls and families of our friends.

When we left the compound the next morning, I asked Avery Gerard to swing by the hospital to check on Lambreau. But after we arrived, we were told Keith had just just been released. He was currently in the business office talking with a clerk. As his paperwork was being processed with the embassy which was paying the bill, as soon as he signed it, he could go. Because the medical technicians had to cut his pants off him, we found him still in a gown. Thank God someone had made sure the back of the gown was tightly tied.

After a nurse carted him out to the front entrance in a wheelchair, I helped him ambulate to the SUV. I was surprised at how well he was walking on the leg and that he was in good spirits.

He would go with us to the Halaal locations, but stay in the vehicle as we began our search for Galloway. A large-frame White man walking around in a gown may have been of concern to a few people. Especially parents. From

Sana'a General we took Janora Street over to Kashi which was on the way to the first location, Halaal Imports and Exports. When we pulled off the street, we found the building to be a two story, modern brick structure. From the number of cars, vans and pickups in the parking lot, I thought perhaps the business employed somewhere around fifty people.

After exiting the Land Rover we first circled the building on foot to determine if it was a business with nothing but office space or was there also a warehouse operation. At the rear of the structure, we observed loading activity involving two cargo vans. We tried not to appear too nosy, but a couple of workers had already started wondering what three Anglo dudes were doing lurking about. One of them was shouting something we couldn't understand, so we casually walked around to the other side of the building. With all of the activity of people going in and out of the complex, I doubted Galloway was some place inside being held prisoner. Jarvis was the one who pulled the plug on any further look at the place. We would, however, keep it in mind if the other site didn't pan out.

Before pulling away, Gerard then checked his GPS for the directions to Halaal Crating and Storage. The name sounded as though a warehouse could be included within the operation, but again, if there were a lot of employees on site, chances are some curious person would already have found the room where Galloway was being chained up. After all, he would have been held there for over a month.

When we arrived at the address on the GPS, we found a building that had seen better days. At the front of the structure was an empty parking lot with grass growing up through the asphalt. The windows on the sprawling building were also boarded up. The business was gone. Half of the building's sign was missing and all we could see was the faded name, Halaal. Although there were no vehicles in the lot, I thought that the absence of same might be intentional. If the kidnappers were on station guarding a prisoner inside or even stopping by occasionally to bring food and water, they would be parking elsewhere so as not to arouse suspicion.

Gerard pulled the Land Rover in between some trees off to the side of the building and the three of us got out. After we did a gun and magazine check on our M-4s, Jarvis began hustling at a crouch across the grass to the front door with Gerard and I at his heels. As expected, we found the door locked. Keeping our bodies close to the wall, we rounded the right side of the building and Jarvis put his hand up as we approached a side door. Trying the knob, he found it locked as well.

As we moved quickly around the corner to the back, we encountered a paved drive that led to a loading dock. Before we moved further, I whispered to my compadres, "Over there." Pointing to a side street, I said, "Two pickups. No other buildings or houses around them. That tells me at least two baddies inside."

Jarvis nodded. "We don't want to try the large door at the dock, but see the smaller door on the left side? One way or another, that's where we go in."

Now, more slowly, we advanced toward the door. Unfortunately, we found it locked as well. "No problem," Jarvis said. From his cargo pocket he then took out a series of bump keys on a ring. I was again impressed; the junior G man came prepared. Choosing a key that looked to fit, as gingerly as he could, he punched it into the lock and turned the knob. As Gerard and I stood to either side of the door with guns ready, Jarvis slowly opened it, at the last moment moving away from the door in case he was met with a spray of bullets.

For several seconds the three of us stood aside the door waiting for any movement, noise or bullets from the inside. Hearing or seeing nothing, we quickly moved through the door and pulled it quietly to a close behind us. Following the agent's lead, we continued our movement through the large bay until we were all the way to the far wall where there were three doors. Wondering what was behind door number one, Jarvis stepped and turned the knob. We stood at the ready with fingers on triggers in case we walked in on one of the kidnappers. All we saw was darkness. Gerard then shined the beam of his flashlight through the opening, finding a room measuring about 15 by 15 and containing nothing but stacked boxes.

And so we went to door number two. Was there a valuable prize awaiting us or a booby trap in the form of an AK-47? My turn with the door knob. When I pushed open the door, I was greeted by a hallway with daylight radiating in from somewhere, perhaps from the rooms on the left and right having windows. The three of us moved without sound, slowly and methodically, stopping and then sticking our heads quickly around the door faces.

As I found myself leading the two, I suddenly stopped my progress and listened. Voices. Two male voices coming from one of the rooms. I laid my index finger over my lips and they both nodded. Again, we began moving, this time within inches of the wall until I reached the room with the voices. Here's the thing. As we expected these were the kidnappers holding Galloway, they could as well have been watchmen or security guards protecting the premises. Therefore, I didn't want to go into the room with guns blazing. I'm sure Gerard and Jarvis understood that. So, I pointed to Gerard and motioned for him to remain in place. Then I pointed to Jarvis and placed him to the right side of the doorway. Finally, I gave them fingers one, two and three at which time I bounded to the left side of the door and shoved the muzzle of my M-4 through the doorway.

Whether they knew English or not, I said to the two men who were sitting in chairs at a desk, "Don't move!"

One man apparently didn't understand English, but he should have understood the business end of a carbine. When he reached for his AK sitting against the wall, before I had an opportunity to fire, from the right side of the door came the sharp report that sent a single bullet into the man's chest. He was dead before he hit the floor. The second man stood with his hands in the air. I quickly put him down on the floor and tossed his AR out into the hallway.

However, we didn't know it, but a third dude in a skull cap ran from a room behind us, brandishing a pistol and aiming it at Jarvis. Fortunately, the gun misfired and that's when Gerard came down on the man's head with one of his meaty fists, laying him out cold.

I didn't know whether it was because he had killed his first man or the realization that he was one misfire away from death, Jarvis stood motionless as though he were in a catatonic state, eyes wide and transfixed. Carefully, I took the carbine from his hands and placed my hand on the back of his neck.

"You all right?"

He nodded three or four times. "Yeah."

"You did good, Lew."

He continued to stare at the dead man. Maybe that's how I reacted the first time I ended a man's life. He'd be okay, but he'd remember this one.

CHAPTER 38

As big man Avery Gerard had put Jarvis's would be killer out for hours, we only had one man to which we could talk…that is if he knew even one word of English. And that word was "Galloway." He had to know the name of the man they were holding. The three of us then pushed the man down in a chair and stood around him in hopes our imposing presence would intimidate him.

It was Jarvis who finally regained his composure and pointed inwardly at his own chest. "Jarvis," he said. He then pointed at our prisoner in the chair.

"Farouk," the man replied.

"Farouk, where is Galloway?"

The man looked bewildered as though he didn't recognize the name.

"Galloway!" Jarvis repeated with a little more oomph in his voice.

The prisoner shook his head.

"No English?"

Again, he shook his head.

Finally, I pointed to Jarvis's handcuffs. He then took them off his belt and held them up in front of the man's face. "Galloway," he said again, hoping that the bozo would equate the cuffs with the name of his captive.

Slowly, the man began to point out the door. Jarvis stood him up and began walking him out to the hall. He then pointed down the corridor and began walking in the direction. We followed. At the end of the hallway, he turned right and continued. Jarvis's hand was on the kidnapper's shoulder in case he saw an opportunity to run.

Finally, the man stopped at an open doorway which appeared to be a storage room. As Gerard held him, Jarvis and I walked in. There sitting on a cot, his hands cuffed with a heavy chain to a large ring on the stone wall was a hollow-eyed Sam Galloway.

We moved quickly to him. The skin on his wrists was red and rubbed raw in places where I assumed he had tried many times to break loose. He looked malnourished as well and was barefooted, his feet dirty. A completely full piss pot lay beside the cot which his captors apparently did not readily attend.

"Sam, are you all right?" I asked.

At first, I thought he had lost his comprehension as he didn't respond. But then he said, "What the hell took you guys so long?"

Gerard then grabbed hold of Farouk and took him to where Galloway sat. He pointed to the cuffs. "Open them!"

From his pocket Farouk took a key and popped them open. Galloway then stood and rubbed his wrists. Pausing a moment to get his balance, he suddenly threw a roundhouse punch which caught Farouk between the eyes, sending him hard to the concrete floor.

"Okay, I feel better, now. Anybody got a beer on them?"

Pulling out his cell phone, Gerard then called the number he had for the Sana'a police, gave them the address in Arabic and told them to come pick up the three kidnappers, one of which they needed to plant by sundown in the ground, him being Muslim and all. Gerard said he would be available to give them all the particulars if they wanted to meet him at the embassy.

Not having done more than stand on his feet for a month, Galloway wasn't walking all that well. However, the three of us took turns helping him down the hallway and out the door to the Land Rover. We'd wait to get his entire story when we returned to the embassy. Once there, we'd have a lot to talk about.

Galloway lived in an apartment only three blocks from the embassy. As he had been snatched at night from his bed and his captors hadn't given him an opportunity to lock up, he wasn't sure what possessions he had left. Maybe there were even squatters living there. After we helped him from the Land Rover, we all went inside. Someone had been there alright as his television was gone, a couple pairs of his pants and some shirts, food from his fridge and cupboard, all of his firearms, and even his mattress. However, they left his box springs. Even though he planned to report the robbery to the police, he figured it was futile. They'd never even look for the perps. But, as he had recorded the serial numbers to his weapons, it was possible one of them might be found on someone involved in a murder. As pissed as he was about his loss, at least he was home.

We sat and conversed while he took his long shower and then found a set of clothes and boots to put on. He looked like he had lost more than twenty pounds since I saw him last. He said his captors had not fed him much that he could eat and only one meal a day at that. So, as he was understandably famished, we took him to the embassy canteen for a full course lunch. However, since Lambreau's leg was starting to seize up on him, we first dropped him off at his room for a few hours' rest.

Sam Galloway didn't say much as he sat gorging his chopped steak, a couple of times becoming choked. Gerard advised him to slow down and take smaller bites. He had all day to eat and no one was going to take his food away from him. When he was at the point where his shrunken stomach couldn't take in any more, he then pushed aside the remainder of his meal.

Although the three of us had made some small talk while Galloway was eating, it was Gerard who brought him into our conversation. "Sam, before today, as you know, I hadn't ever met you. They brought me in a couple weeks ago to replace you, believing you had betrayed your country by conspiring to sell off the WMDs. I don't know if you actually knew that."

"Not right away. I thought I'd been kidnapped for ransom. That would have been a joke…nobody I know has any money. All I knew was that three Arabs broke in on me, took me to that warehouse and threw me in chains. But, a couple days after they nabbed me, out of the goodness of his heart, Daniels came by and told me about his scheme. He said he wouldn't kill me, unless of course I tried to escape. I thought I knew that son-of-a-bitch. Hell, we had even become friends. Maybe that's why he didn't just kill me and bury me somewhere out in the desert. I guess he got the idea to put together a deal for himself when you brought down Chalmers. I never in a million years thought he'd turn traitor like that."

"Same goes for me, Sam," I commented. "But as much as I hate to tell you this, I had some damn harsh feelings about you when I heard you had gone bad. And I'm sorry about that. We were all duped."

"Yeah, that's what makes this so shitty. My reputation in the Agency is now tarnished. Even after my name is cleared, some people will still be wondering about me. There'll always be that stigma when my name comes up."

Gerard added, "Unfortunately, Sam, Langley had not only removed you from its employment files, but the feds put you on a most wanted list. But, it's fixed now. I notified the director as soon as I got Bruce's call about Daniels…that you not only needed to be reinstated, but that your file be purged of all deprecatory information. It's all in the works now."

Sam nodded his appreciation. "Hell, I even have to recoup my reputation in this very building."

"Except most people that work here have no idea you're even a spook and probably wouldn't have missed you anyway," Gerard added.

"Just wondering, though…do I still have a job here now that you've replaced me?"

"I haven't been told one way or the other."

Jarvis changed the subject. "Well, the last order of business is to nail down the WMDs once and for all. Since I don't know exactly where these Jabal Kanin Mountains are and you and Sam do, Bruce, how do we secure them and bring them out?"

"I wasn't involved in the retrieval plan when I was here a few weeks ago. But, as I remember, Sam, you'd get a crew to take them from the cave, load them up on trucks and drive them to an LZ where a C-130 would take them out of country. The big bomb would go to Pantex and the chemicals to Colorado."

"There shouldn't be any change in that. Do you agree Avery?"

"Absolutely."

"Then when can we get this done?" Jarvis asked.

"As soon as we locate the weapons," Galloway replied. "Bruce, Daniels told you he replanted them in an adjacent cave. Of course, as he had been lying about shit all along, that might have been a lie as well."

"There's only one way to find out. Get someone to fly us back out there and comb those rocks for other caves. If he did move them to another cave, considering the number of crates and their size, it would have been too cumbersome to move them too far."

"Good point," said Galloway. "Mike Daniels was the Agency's only chopper pilot. However, I think we have a Marine aviator attached to the consulate. We should be able to get him approved to help us on this. As this remains a Bureau run operation, who makes all the plans and arrangements to go get these weapons, the Bureau or the Agency?"

Jarvis replied. "The Bureau's assistant director did tell me to see this through, Sam, but since you previously already had the removal plan in place, I'm going to use my best discretion and have you guys handle the logistics."

"Fine," Galloway said. "But which one of us drives the train…you, Avery, or me? Officially I'm not yet back on the payroll. You're the new station chief."

"You initiated the removal plan, Sam. You continue to do it."

"Fine, then. I'll talk to the Marines and see if we can get someone to fly us out there. When we locate the weapons, we'll hire a few laborers to bring them down from the mountains to either some cargo trucks or put them on a flatbed."

"Now for the sad task," Jarvis said. "We need to arrange for Tyler's and Zant's bodies to be flown back to the states. My Senior Special Agent in Charge told me Agent Tyler was from Texas. His wife was notified of his death yesterday and the bureau is making all the arrangements for his body to be flown out of Sana'a to Dallas. But I'm wondering about Zant. Do you have any information on him, Avery?"

"We know he was from New York. I have informed Langley, but haven't heard anything back on how and when his body leaves Yemen. My highers are supposed to let me know. As to his family, I'm sorry to say I know nothing about them."

The conversation compelled me to think about the many times I might have taken the fatal bullet and the thoughts that had gone through Adriana's head about the possibility of me not returning. Action guys tend to think they're invincible and either intentionally or unintentionally block out thoughts of what their loved ones are going through. On this venture, it could easily have been me coming home in a box. And of all my exploits, this was the first real time I thought of how Adriana could handle that. She thought on this trip there shouldn't be any danger and Keith and I probably did a lot to convey that. I was here to help the government locate weapons. Even in last night's phone call, as far as she knew, I was riding around on a treasure hunt, soaking up the sun, eating rich foods and yukking it up with my chums. An easy way to make a hundred grand. I was determined now that I would never again place myself in a position to deceive her. My part of the mission was basically over. It was time. I was now free to go home. Keith as well.

Interrupting my thoughts, Jarvis then asked me, "Bruce, you are sticking around to see this through, aren't you?"

"Of course. I wouldn't think of deserting you fellas now that we finally have a bead on these WMDs."

CHAPTER 39

We all decided to go off compound for dinner. His first week at the embassy, Gerard had found a good restaurant with a Mediterranean flair near the historic area of Sana'a. He wanted to go back. Keith Lambreau said he was now rested up and his leg felt good. He would join us.

We arrived at Olineas at seven and took seats at the bar while waiting on our table. One of the few restaurants in Sana'a allowed to have an alcohol permit, we took advantage of the opportunity right off by having a couple beers on draft. As nobody wanted to talk shop or recent history, we shared information about our education, families and careers to this point.

Keith and I already knew some things about Jarvis, his Harvard Business School education and the fact that he had been an accountant, but we listened to him again as he shared his golden boy history for Gerard to hear. He had married his high school sweetheart four years before which seemed to figure, given his storybook life to this point. It made me thankful that it was not he who lost his life on the road to Sanshu. Of course, it was bad enough that Ron Tyler and Jake Zant lost theirs.

Gerard himself started out as a middleweight boxer, which explained the knockout punch he gave the Arab dude at the Halaal warehouse. At twenty-four he went went into the Navy, ultimately becoming a SEAL, then took some distance learning college courses in International Studies and was recruited eight years before as a field agent with the CIA. He never married, which made me wonder about him…not necessarily his sexuality, by the way.

Sam Galloway was probably the crustiest of all of us, having served in the Army's 82nd Airborne and spending two years in Iraq during the Enduring Freedom campaign. He was with the team that swept through a dozen of Saddam's 26 palaces reducing four of them to rubble. After being recruited by the CIA, he served in Colombia, Honduras, Iraq, Ethiopia and finally Yemen where he became the station chief. He was married once, but his wife gave up on him after three years with the Agency.

Keith Lambreau, a native Californian, told us he had graduated college from UCLA in
1994 with a degree in Criminal Justice, then applied and was accepted into the Secret
Service. After five years in Clinton's administration, he went to work for the State Department, ending up

serving with me doing some things he couldn't really go into, even though he was in the presence of two Sneaky Pete guys and an FBI agent. But he was now directing the organization. Married twice, neither wife worked out. But he was always on the prowl.

I wasn't really looking forward to telling my story, but with considerable coaxing from the Company dudes, I reluctantly began. But no sooner had I gotten the first words out that "I was born at a very early age…", I said, "I can't believe it, guys. Of all the gin joints in all of the towns…" That's when I ended my Bogey impersonation.

"What?" said Keith.

"Look over at the door. I've only eaten in two restaurants in this town and both times, the lovely Shirley Compagno waltzes in." I was wondering if Ambassador Simmons could be that far behind.

She was ushered to a table not far from the bar which made it easier for Gerard and Lambreau especially to put eyes on her. Wearing a tight, white dress, which I knew didn't set well with the hard-shell sharia pricks, she had on a head scarf that somewhat made up for it. She definitely had that Vogue look. I thought in the dim light of the bar I saw Lambreau's tongue dripping.

We were all pretty much quiet after that as even we two married guys paused to enjoy what nature had done to her. But then she caught sight of the five of us lined up on the stools. That's when she left her table and came to the bar to say hello.

"Wow, fancy meeting you guys here. Of all of the restaurants in Sana'a to eat dinner, we end up at the same place." I think I already said that, Shirley, or something similar. She then smiled, flashing her healthy set of perfect, white teeth. For some reason I was reminded of the grille on a '56 Buick Roadmaster.

"Hello, Shirley," I greeted.

"Hi, Mr. McGowan," she replied in that brandy-smooth voice of hers. "Would you and your friends like to join me for dinner, since we're all here together?"

"Thanks," I said. "But I'm sure you're dining with someone already."

"I was but he cancelled. I love this place, so I decided to come on by myself. Join me."

So, Simmons cancelled, eh, I said to myself. Did his old lady find out about the date?

"We'd be delighted," Keith replied. "At least, I would."

I looked at the others and then told her, "Why don't you and my friend Keith have dinner. The rest of us have a bit of business to conduct, don't we, boys?"

They nodded. Two's company, six is a mob. On the way to her table, Keith gave me a covert fist bump to thank me.

"Shall we wait for you, Lambreau?" I said.

Shirley answered for him, "If you all finish dinner before us, I can bring this handsome fellow back to the compound."

I smiled. "You all enjoy the evening then; I think our table is ready."

When I arose that next morning, I showered and put on still another set of clothes Jarvis had in his suitcase that I'm sure his wife had packed. Just after 0730, I went down the hall and rapped on Lambreau's door to see if he wanted to have some breakfast. There was no answer. I thought maybe he was in the shower, so I went back to my room for a few minutes, returning twenty minutes later to his door. Still quiet inside. This time I thought he had gone on to the consulate dining room, so I went on down the stairs and out to the parking lot. To my surprise, there, getting out of Ms. Compagno's car, was Mr. Lambreau.

When she saw me, she looked a little sheepish. He didn't. I just couldn't wait to hear all about it. Not. She went on into the office building as Keith and I walked to the dining hall. He seemed to be walking a little straighter and prouder.

"Don't ask, don't tell," he said. "Unless you want to hear the play by play."

"Come on, Lambreau, you're not in high school anymore and this isn't a locker room. You think I care?"

I had cereal and toast for breakfast. Keith had a hearty meal of steak and eggs with a side of hash browns. He smiled. "For some odd reason, I'm hungry as hell like I've somehow worked up an appetite."

"Oh, stop it," I said. Even though I knew he was itching to tell me, I had no desire to hear the sordid details.

As the day before, Galloway had arranged with the Marine detachment commander for their trained aviator to fly us north to the Jabal Mountains where we'd perform a new search for the relocated WMDs, we were taking off from the helipad at 0930. When breakfast was done and we had tapped our kidneys in our rooms, the five of us met on the roof of the main building of the embassy.

Our aviator was an impressive young Marine CW3 with a 30 inch waist by the name of Jennings who greeted us on the rooftop helipad with a sharp salute and a respectful "Good morning, sirs."

Galloway replied, "Good morning, Chief. I understand you can fly this thing."

"Cut my teeth on a bird just like this one, yessir."

"There are five of us who'll be riding with you. Will be tight."

"We can make it work, gentlemen. One of you will have to sit on the floor. I'm good here, so hop aboard."

The old Huey cranked right away, its blades finally getting up to speed and making that familiar wop wop sound that brought back memories of recons and CAs over triple canopy jungles and rice paddies. Loose sediment on the rooftop, where the hot winds passing over the desert had carried the shifting sands of the north hundreds of miles, temporarily blinded us. Once the Huey's skids began jostling on the helipad, it lifted faithfully as I'm sure it had done hundreds, maybe thousands of times over the decades.

It may have been the first time young Jarvis had ridden in a chopper of this vintage, and even though strapped down onto the canvas seat in the middle, he seemed a bit apprehensive, especially with the doors open on either side and the old bird kicking around like it was. I was the guy on the floor and when I allowed my legs to hang off the side, that seemed to unnerve him even more.

Navigator Sam Galloway, talking with our aviator on the headset, occasionally pointed and the Huey would then make its course changes accordingly. When the Jabal Kanin Mountains finally loomed ahead, Galloway told the warrant officer where to set the bird down. It was the same spot we had dropped into when Daniels was piloting the chopper.

After we disembarked, we began trudging up the steep slope along the path that took us to the cave that had stored the WMDs for over a dozen years. I personally wanted to see if anything had been left inside. There had been a hell of a lot of crates in there and the chemical weapons certainly wouldn't be as valuable as the nuclear bomb. Stopping on the large, flat rock outside the cave's entrance for a couple of seconds, I saw that the Arab blood spilled there was completely gone. A rain or two and weeks of broiling sun had bleached it out.

Only Jarvis and I went into the cave this time. When we climbed over the fallen rocks and set foot on the other side, the beam of my flashlight shone on nothing but water bottles, food wrappers, a plank of wood from one of the crates that may have been dropped and the bones of the trapped men from 2002 I had seen before. Satisfied that all weapons had been removed, we rejoined the others.

Galloway then brought us all together on the rock to organize the search. "Chief Jennings, if you would be so kind, I'd like you to join in on the hunt. We're looking for other caves on this mountain where several large boxes of chemical weapons and one very long crate containing a nuclear bomb have been stored. Depending on how many helpers Daniels had in moving the WMDs, logistically speaking, I'd say the cave can't be too far from here. We'll split up in every direction in a Star of David pattern and sweep this entire mountain. Each of us has a radio and flashlight and whoever finds them, call everybody else to your location. I hope everyone remembered your water. Here are some protein bars. If no questions, let's do this."

Up and down and to the flanks we set out. My direction was eight o'clock. I figured the people who carried the crates out would rather go down with them than up. However, it depended on where the caves were. I took it that Daniels had done his homework in scouting the mountain for other places to temporarily store the weapons. The cave needed to be cool, dry and in good proximity to where they wouldn't have to be carted far to load onto a large truck. However, as I had been thinking over the last twenty four hours or so, he had lied to everyone several times before; what if he lied to me about moving the WMDs to another location and instead had them liveried to some warehouse in Sana'a where they could be retrieved by the Iranian he was dealing with; or maybe he trucked them down to Aden where he would meet an Iranian vessel? If we didn't find the WMDs nearby somewhere on the mountain, there was no one left alive, except the unknown crew who moved them, to tell us where they were.

Within about forty five minutes, Gerard had located a cave, so we all stood pat wherever we were until he had finished exploring. However, after he had gone less than fifty meters further inside, the cave ended. He found it empty. And so, we resumed our search.

About fifteen minutes later, Lambreau radioed he had found a cave opening that was only large enough to squeeze a body through. As I knew the crate containing the nuclear device was the size of an automobile, I told him to forget it.

Over two hours passed after that without hearing a peep from anyone. The merciless sun beat down on us like hell's furnace. I was sapped as I knew everyone else was as well. I then retreated behind some large rocks to get out of the sun and drink the last of my two bottles of water. For some reason, the old west tune of Cool Water was stuck in my head…"Keep a-movin', Dan, don't ya listen to him, Dan, he's a devil not a man and he spreads the burnin' sand with water…"

I then leaned my head back against one of the rocks and scanned the craggily landscape below me. "God-forsaken country," I said almost out loud. If I was for some reason banished to this land for the rest of my life, I saw a cliff a few yards on my right of which I would be jumping off. But then I saw below the rocks of that cliff a large shadow. Taking my telescoping spy glass from the cargo pants I borrowed from Jarvis, I zoomed in on it. It wasn't a shadow after all. It was the mouth of a cave.

Hustling further down the slope, I stopped at the entrance. It looked large enough and I wondered "could this be it?" I turned on my flashlight and started in. It was cool, it was dry and it was wide enough. Less than 75 feet inside the cave, I saw the first of the crates. All of them were stacked high against each side of the cavern's walls allowing me to walk on the uneven rocks in between them, a kind of manmade hallway. And then, there it was. The Holy Grail of bombs, lying directly in front of me like Cleopatra's tomb.

Quickly, I exited the cave and raised everyone on the radio. "You can stop looking, gentlemen. I found the cave. The WMDs are inside."

"Where are you, Bruce?" Galloway replied.

"I'll slowly fire three shots so that you can get a bead on me." I then did so about five seconds apart. "Okay, was everyone able to pinpoint my location?" Each one of them gave me an affirmative.

Mission complete. Now it was up to the FBI and CIA to arrange for the extraction and transport of the WMDs to their final resting place.

CHAPTER 40

Epilogue

Chief Jennings and the Huey unloaded us onto the helipad at 1610. We shook his hand, and he rendered a snappy, parting salute. Agent Jarvis reminded him, as he had done at the beginning of the day, that everything he witnessed regarding the recovery of the WMDs was classified.

We returned to our quarters at the embassy while Galloway returned to his apartment off the compound. We set 1900 as the hour to meet back at the dining hall for dinner and a debrief. After taking my shower, I applied some more Aquaphor ointment on my wound, where a bullet in the gunfight with Daniels grazed my shoulder. As you remember, he got the worst of that exchange. However, Adriana would see me naked and ask me about it. Of course, I wasn't supposed to be involved in any gunplay on the trip. Maybe I ripped my shoulder on some briers.

We all took our showers and then began preparing for the evening mess. Jarvis then told Lambreau and me he'd be asking the embassy to arrange flights for us back to the States as soon as seats became available. But Keith told him not so fast. He said he wanted to remain in Sana'a to help arrange both the retrieval and the transporting of the WMDs. He felt compelled to see the thing through to the end since The State Department had authorized him to facilitate the recovery in any way he could. I think that was the first time I ever knew Keith to out-and-out lie. Like the others on our team, I knew damn well why he was staying.

At the dinner table that evening, the debrief was actually short. The only topic of discussion was about what logistics would be involved in removing the weapons from the cave, how they'd be transported to a holding facility and just when the C-130 would be arriving at the Sana'a Riyadh Airport. I was out of the equation. Sam Galloway again thanked us heartily for his rescue and that his name and reputation would ultimately be cleared. But then when each one of them began throwing praise in my direction for my leadership and sound and timely decision-making, I threw up my hand to stop them. "Thanks, guys, but we were a team…a very damn good team that together got us to where we are tonight. Let's let it go at that."

We broke up just before 2030 and returned to our rooms. Keith walked back with me since our apartments were in the same building. "How about a nightcap?" he said. "You'll probably be out of here first thing in the morning if you're able to get a flight."

"Yeah, okay. Maybe a snort. What do you have and where did you get it?"

"Some Wild Turkey from the bar in the dining hall. I gave the Arab bartender a fifty for the entire bottle."

"Fifty rials or fifty dollars?"

"If I didn't learn anything else on this trip, I found out how much rials are really worth. Fifty rials would be about twelve cents…so, fifty dollars."

I laughed. "Alright, hit me with just a couple shots. I'm beat."

"You've gotten old, McGowan. It's not even nine o'clock yet."

"I don't mind telling you, I got pretty damn drained in that heat out there today. And that had nothing to do with age."

We landed in his room and he then broke out the whisky. I'm not much on bourbon, but I will be social with people. I could throw up later.

"Bruce, I owe you big, pal."

"The RPG incident? Well, I had a feeling if we didn't vacate the Land Cruiser when we did, we'd be dead meat."

"I'm not talking about that. I'm talking about Shirley. You set me up with her at the restaurant. And I don't mind tellin' ya, that worked out nice."

"Something tells me you plan to stay here more than a couple of days."

"I think we actually have something going. She likes me and I like her."

"You're not starting this soapy high school romance talk again are you? So you nailed her…whoop-tee-doo."

He grinned. "Yeah, whoop-tee-doo."

"Okay, enough. I'm glad you had a little fun over here. From all the pain you endured with getting shot up, it's good that you experienced a little pleasure as well."

"Well, back to that deal on the road you mentioned? Thanks, man. You saved my bacon. Kicked my ass out of that vehicle and then after I got shot, you stopped me from bleeding to death."

"You know after I took care of Muhammad, I had second thoughts about coming back for you."

He laughed.

"Seriously, Bruce, why don't you come out of retirement? Work for us. We can recommission Team Zulu and you can lead it."

"You know better than to ask me that, Keith. Put yourself in my place…I'm now fully retired and living the Life of Riley with Adriana McGowan, the girl of every man's dreams. Even **yours.** Oh, that's right…you now have your **own** dream girl."

"I guess I knew what your answer would be. Lionel Byrd was right, you know; you were and still are the best in the covert mission business. I just never got to experience something like we just went through with you first hand. If you ever change your mind and need the money…”

“And about that. I’ll be looking any time for that hundred grand.”

“Check’s in the mail, Scorpion.”
I was able to get a flight out of Sana’a at three-thirty on EgyptAir, but there would be a night’s layover in Cairo. My flight to New York would go out the next morning, then on to West Virginia.

I got a room for the night at a hotel near the airport, had a decent dinner of steak and scallops and took a bottle of Merlot that I bought downstairs in the gift shop to my room. As I sat on my 12th story balcony looking out over the Nile, sipping my glass of wine and watching the red sun set somewhere way out over the desert, it began getting a bit chilly. It was a nice respite from the oppressive heat I had experienced for just under a week. In less than a day, I would be back to my simple life…cool, morning runs, great country vittles, clean, potable mountain water, nobody hates anybody, church on Sunday and a “good morning” smile from my lovely wife at the crack of every dawn. Excuse my grammar, but it don’t get no better’n that.

As I took another sip of the Merlot and listened to the sing-song voice of a muezzin chant his salat al-'isha, or evening call to prayer, over a loudspeaker, many things I began to ponder. Cairo was a peaceful city in comparison to others in the Mideast, especially cities like Sana'a. And the Muslim faith was supposed to be all about peace. But some of the very people whose prayer was sounded and chanted five times a day, danced and reveled in the streets that hateful day of woe when the twin towers went down. That debauchery occurred in nearly every Arab city, in every village. And then we went to war. We pretty much fought that war over the theory that the mad despot in Iraq had weapons of mass destruction and planned to use them. Well, a decent young Arab man stepped forward and helped me prove that was no mere theory. Somehow, I knew he himself would never have danced in celebration of that tragic day. He was one of the good guys. I smiled and then held up my glass to capture through its translucency the red, setting sun, appearing to my eye as a kind of precious ruby.

"Here's to you, Sameer. May you always have love and peace in your heart."

AFTERWORD

A month before this fictional account was supposed to be taking place in 2014, the Houthi rebels, comprised mainly of Zaidi Shia Muslims, launched an all-out assault against the Yemeni government. As you might remember, our protagonist, Bruce McGowan, became caught up in an attack on the city of al-Hudaydah. In actuality, in September of that year, the Houthi rebels captured Sana'a and took control of much of Yemen's northern provinces, placing the government's president at the time, Abdrabbuh Hadi, under arrest, forcing him and his administration to resign.

On the 13th of February 2015, about 100 U.S. Marines stood off Houthi rebels while the American government closed the embassy's doors. Over 300 of its employees stood down in orderly fashion. As the rebels set about seizing the complex, embassy staffers burned their files and documents with incendiary grenades. Marines destroyed all the heavy weapons and equipment as well. After staffers and employees boarded commercial flights out of Sana'a, rebels took into possession more than 25 embassy vehicles. At their own personal risk, two CIA field agents remained behind.

Be on the lookout for the next book in The McGowan Collection Series, Book 9, "A Lure To A Kill".

Praises for the McGowan Collection Series

Published in this order:

Wolf Laurel

The main character in this novel, Bruce McGowan, is truly a "John Wayne meets Clint Eastwood" cowboy. I love this character! This is a great read for anyone who enjoys reading about patriotic heroes, intrigue, espionage and covert action. Lee Martin is a true master of fantastic story telling and "suspension of disbelief". In fact, I would not doubt that some of the features in this tale hold quite a bit of truth. I could not put this book down and I have read all of the sequels since.

J. C. Laurie

Provocation: Return of the Weatherman

This second of three books with Bruce McGowan as the central figure is simply a great read that will not allow you to put it down until you have finished it. Without a doubt, one of the best mystery series I have ever read! Thanks Lee!

Andy Black

A Hateful Wind

I love it! Always another twist coming up. Really excited to be meeting Lee Martin at a book signing in 11/5 in Eatonton, Ga.

Muftr

Killing the Viper

I have read many of Lee Martin's novels. All have been great reads that never disappoint. Having known Lee Martin personally, I think I can see how some people believe Bruce McGowan is his alter ego. Having read "The Justice Club" before I started the "Wolf Laurel" series was by pure luck but a real treat. This was another great adventure in the life of Bruce McGowan and it was masterful the way he brought in a character from a book he had written outside this series. I have already started the next book, "Saving Eagle One" and have the following book sitting here waiting. Thanks Lee for sharing your talent with me. I'm sure I am not the only one that feels this way. Looking forward to many more books from you. WELCOME HOME BROTHER

Ernie F.

Saving Eagle One

One of the better books I have read in a long time. Can't wait for Lee Martin's next installment of this trilogy.

Rex Davis

Blood Protocol

Excellent story writer! Strongly suggest starting from the first book in the series. Continuity is well maintained through each book. Because my wife and are from
West Virginia the reading of each book takes us back in many ways. now that we live in North Carolina. My Marine military experience and the nursing experience of my wife make the books even more enjoyable. We have detected numerous "Easter Egg" comments and characters throughout the series of books and I am sure others who have any familiarity with Lee Martin the individual will also find characters or situations that sound/feel familiar. Good Reads Bottom-line.

Eugene Hoover

Red Kings Rising

Col. Lee Martin does it again. This another great book in the Bruce McGowan series. Another book that's hard to put down. I have read all of the books in this series along with his other novels and have never been disappointed. Lee is a very good author with a vivid imagination. His military background and obvious research make his story lines believable. Looking forward to the next book.

E. Fox

A Note from the Author

Be sure to read each of these books on the preceding pages in the order listed. In between *A Hateful Wind* and *Killing the Viper*, you may also want to read my novel *The Justice Club* where I introduce you to Atticus Steed, a compelling character who appears in two of the McGowan novels. Enjoy.

NLM

www.ingramcontent.com/pod-product-compliance
Lightning Source LLC
Chambersburg PA
CBHW032101310726
48972CB00001B/57